THE QUIET WAR

THE QUIET WAR

PAUL McAULEY

an imprint of Prometheus Books
Amherst, NY

Published 2009 by Pyr®, an imprint of Prometheus Books

Inquiries should be addressed to
Pyr
59 John Glenn Drive
Amherst, New York 14228–2119
VOICE: 716–691–0133, ext. 210
FAX: 716–691–0137
WWW.PYRSF.COM

13 12 11 10 09   5 4 3 2

Library of Congress Cataloging-in-Publication Data

McAuley, Paul J.
    The quiet war / by Paul McAuley.
        p. cm.
    First published: London : Gollancz, an imprint of Orion Publishing Group, 2008.
    ISBN 978–1–59102–781–2 (pbk. : alk. paper)
    1. Imaginary wars and battles—Fiction. 2. Climatic changes—Fiction. I. Title.
PR6063.C29Q54 2009
823'.914—dc22

                                                                    2009020754

Printed in the United States on acid-free paper

For Russell Schechter,
and for Georgina, *naturellement*

The Herr Doctor does not know about peoples.
William Golding, *Free Fall*

PART ONE

THE QUICKENING

I

Every day the boys woke when the lights came on at 0600. They showered and dressed, made their beds and policed the dormitory, endured inspection by one of their lectors. Breakfast was a dollop of maize gruel and a thimble of green tea. They ate quickly, each boy facing one of his brothers across the long table, no sound but the scrape of plastic spoons on plastic bowls. There were fourteen of them, tall and pale and slender as skinned saplings. Blue-eyed. Their naked scalps shone in the cold light as they bent over their scant repast. At two thousand six hundred days old they were fully grown but with traces of adolescent awkwardness yet remaining. They wore grey paper shirts and trousers, plastic sandals. Red numbers were printed on their shirts, front and back. The numbers were not sequential because more than half their original complement had been culled during the early stages of the programme.

After breakfast, the boys stood to attention in front of the big screen, flanked by their lectors and the avatars of their instructors. A flag filled the screen edge to edge and top to bottom, a real flag videoed somewhere on Earth, gently rippling as if caught in a draught. Its green light washed over their faces and set sparks in their eyes as they stood straightbacked in two rows, right hands starfished on their chests as they recited the Pledge of Allegiance.

The same rituals every morning. The same video. The same flag rippling in exactly the same way. The same scrap of blue visible for half a second in the upper left-hand corner, the blue sky of Earth.

One of the boys, Dave #8, looked for that little flash of blue every day. Sometimes he wondered if his brothers looked for it as well, wondered if they too felt a yearning tug for the world they had been created to defend yet could never visit. He never talked about it, not even to his best friend, Dave #27. Things like that, feelings that made you think you might be different from your brothers, you kept to yourself. Difference was a weakness, and every kind of weakness must be suppressed. Even so, at the beginning of every day Dave #8 anticipated the fugitive glimpse of that scrap of Earth's sky, and every time he saw it he felt a flutter of longing in his heart.

Their lectors and instructors recited the Pledge of Allegiance, too.

Fathers Aldos, Clarke, Ramez and Solomon in their white, rope-girdled habits; the instructors' faces floating in the visors of the man-sized, man-shaped plastic shells of their avatars. On Mondays, Wednesdays and Fridays it was instructors for ecosystem management, engineering, and sociology; the rest of the week it was theory of war, psychology, economics, and Hindi, Japanese, Mandarin, and Russian—the boys were already fluent in English, the lingua franca of the enemy, but some enemy communities still used the languages of the homelands of their ancestors, and so the boys had to learn those, too.

The instructors taught theoretical classes in the morning and the lectors taught practical classes in the afternoon and evening. Maintenance and repair of pressure suits, construction and deployment of demons and data miners, vehicle and flight simulators, immersion scenarios that acquainted the boys with every aspect of everyday life in the cities of the enemy. They practised martial arts, bomb making, and sabotage, and trained with staffs, swords, knives, and every other kind of blunt and bladed weapon. The practise versions were weighted so that they would find the real thing easier to handle. They learned to strip down, repair, and use firearms in all kinds of conditions. In the dark; in a centrifuge that buffeted them in every direction; in extremes of heat and cold and combinations of rain, snow, and high winds in the weather chamber. Sealed in their pressure suits. Underwater.

Every tenth day they were led in single file down a long umbilical passage to the cargo bay of a shuttle that took them into orbit. Floating weightless in the padded, windowless tube, where each move had to spring from the body's centre of mass and every blow caused an equal and opposite reaction, they had to learn hand-to-hand combat and use of weapons all over again.

The lectors punished every mistake. Father Solomon, who supervised the classes in martial arts, was quickest with the shock stick. Dave #8 and his brothers exhausted themselves in bruising bouts of boxing, capoeira and karate to win his approval, but most of them suffered at least one shock in each and every session.

Sometimes the practical classes were visited by an avatar that wore a woman's face. The lectors treated her with a deference they showed no one else and were quick to answer her questions. Usually she said nothing at all, watching the boys work for a few minutes or an hour before her face vanished from the avatar's visor and it marched out of the gymnasium and returned to its rack. The woman's name was Sri Hong-Owen. The boys had long ago concluded that she must be their mother.

It didn't matter that she looked nothing like them. After all, they'd been cut to resemble the enemy, treated with the same gene therapies, given the same metabolic tweaks, the same so-called enhancements. But the enemy had been human before they had perverted themselves, so the boys must have started out as human beings, too. And because they were clones, which was why they had numbers and why they were all called Dave (a casual joke by one of the instructors which the boys had incorporated into their private mythology), they must all have the same mother . . .

Although they had no proof that the woman was their mother, they had faith that she was. And faith was stronger than any mere proof because it came from God rather than the minds of men. She did not visit them often. Once every fifty days or so. The boys felt blessed by her presence, and worked harder and were more cheerful for days afterward. Otherwise their routine was unvaried, dedicated to the serious business of learning how to kill and destroy. Learning how to make war.

In the evenings, after Mass, supper, and the struggle sessions in which the boys took turns to confess their sins and suffer the criticism of their brothers, it was politics. Videos crammed with motion and bright colours and swelling music told stories of courage and sacrifice from the history of Greater Brazil, showed how the enemy had betrayed humanity by sheltering on the Moon during the Overturn, how they had refused to return to Earth and help in its reconstruction but had instead run away to Mars and the moons of Jupiter and Saturn, how a group of Martians had later tried to attack Earth by nudging one of the Trojan asteroids, whose elliptical orbits around the sun crossed the orbit of Earth, into a collision course. The plot had failed, and a suicide mission of righteous heroes had exploded hydrogen bombs over the Martian settlements at Ares Valles and Hellas Planitia, and deflected the trajectory of a comet falling sunward. The comet had been broken up by more hydrogen bombs and its fragments had stitched a string of huge craters around Mars's equator and wiped every trace of human life from the face of the red planet. But the enemy were plotting still in their nests and lairs on the moons of Jupiter and Saturn; were actively engaged in elaborating the greatest crime in the history of mankind by the anti-evolutionary engineering of their genomes.

The boys always knew which type of video would be shown because of the meal before it. Their favourite foods, sweet and swimming with fats, before history and heroes; gruel and plain boiled vegetables before crimes against humanity.

In snatched moments, they discussed the heroes they most admired and the battles they would have most liked to have fought in, and speculated about where they might go and what they might do after they had finished their training. Although war had not yet been declared, it was obvious that they were being trained to fight the enemy. Dave #27, who took extra instruction from Father Aldos on aspects of faith and the nature of Gaia, believed that if they were especially heroic they would be remade into ordinary human beings. Dave #8 wasn't so sure. Lately he'd been troubled by a simple paradox: if he and his brothers had been created by technology that was evil, how then could they ever do good? He brooded on this for a long time, and at last confided his thoughts to Dave #27, who told him that every kind of goodness can spring from evil, just as the most beautiful flowers may be rooted in filth. Wasn't that the story of the human race? Everyone was Fallen. Everyone who had ever lived was tainted by original sin. Yet anyone could achieve Heaven if they atoned for their sins by cultivating their faith, praising God, and tending His creation. Even the enemy had the potential to be redeemed, but they refused God because they wanted to be little gods themselves, ruling little heavens of their own making. Heavens that were heaven in name only, and were doomed to become hells to spite their creators' mortal hubris because they lacked the grace that flowed only from God.

"We are sinful in origin and aspect, but not in deed," Dave #27 said. "We do not use our talents to rebel against God, but to serve Him. We might even be a little closer to angels than other men, because we are wholly dedicated to serving the Trinity. Because we are holy warriors who will gladly and eagerly lay down their lives for God, Gaia, and Greater Brazil."

Dave #8, alarmed by the shine in Dave #27's eyes, warned his brother that he was committing the mortal sin of pride. "Our lives may be dedicated to the defence of God and Gaia and Greater Brazil, but that doesn't mean we're in any way like the heroes of the great stories."

"What are we, then?"

"Soldiers," Dave #8 said. "No more, no less."

He did not want to be special. It helped that he did not excel or outshine his brothers in any aspect of training or instruction, that he lacked Dave #27's love of discourse and argument, Dave #11's limber athleticism, Dave #19's skill in electronic warfare. He wanted to believe that lack of any kind of singular talent was a virtue, for differing in any way from the ordinary might foster pride that would lead him astray and make him fail in his duty.

One day Father Solomon caught him trying to examine his reflection.

This was in the gymnasium. There were cases of weapons down one long wall—short spears and javelins, stabbing swords and long swords, fencing foils and bouquets of knives, staffs, maces, bludgeons, truncheons, halberds, and pikes, longbows and crossbows and their arrows and quarrels, as well as the grinding stones and bottles of mineral oil and diamond-dust polish and files used to keep edges sharp and metal clean. There were projectile and energy weapons, too. Machine pistols, target pistols, and sniper rifles; glasers whose beam could cook a man from the inside out; tasers that fired clouds of charged tags; pulse rifles that fired plasma needles hot as the surface of the sun. Ranged along the far wall of the cavernous room were racks of armour, pressure suits, and scuba suits with integral airpacks. That was where Dave #8 sat cross-legged with his brothers, the components of the pressure suits they had dismantled during a routine maintenance exercise laid out in front of them.

Dave #8 was holding the chest plate of his pressure suit at arm's length, turning it this way and that. Its polished black curve gave back only distorted fragments, but there were no mirrors anywhere in the warren of chambers the boys called home and this was the best he could do. He was trying to see if there was something different in his face. If there was, then he would know that his suspicion that he thought differently was true.

He did not notice Father Solomon creeping up behind him on rubber-soled sandals, thumbing back the snap that fastened his shock stick to his belt.

When Dave #8 came round, with an all-over cramp and blood in his mouth, Father Solomon was standing over him and lecturing the other boys about vanity. Dave #8 knew that he was in trouble so deep that the exercise Father Solomon gave them after his lecture, assembling their pressure suits in a howling snowstorm in the weather chamber, would not be enough to atone for it.

In the struggle session that evening, each of his brothers stood up in turn and denounced him ringingly, as he had denounced them in other sessions after they had committed sins of omission or commission. He could not explain that he had been trying to catch sight of hidden faults in the reflection of his face. It was forbidden to attempt to excuse or explain any sins, and he was conditioned to believe that every punishment was just. He was being punished because he deserved it.

The theme of Father Clarke's sermon at Mass took as its text Ecclesiastes, chapter one, verse two. Vanity of vanities, said the preacher; vanity of vanities and everything is vanity. It was a favourite of the lectors, but that evening Dave #8 knew that it was directed straight at him, a righteous X-ray laser shrivelling his soul.

Burning with misery and shame and self-loathing, he sat through a video that documented in gruesome detail the brute lawlessness and cannibalism that had swept over the great North American cities during the Overturn. He was certain that he had failed especially badly. That he was a candidate for disappearance. For although the last disappearance had occurred when the boys had been very much younger, over one and a half thousand days ago, it had been drilled into them that their survival was forever provisional and they must struggle to attain perfection every hour of every day.

The disappearances had always happened at night. The boys would wake to find one of their number gone, his bed stripped bare, his footlocker open and empty. No explanation had ever been given; none was needed. Their brother had disappeared because he had failed, and failure was not tolerated.

In bed after the lights had been switched off, Dave #8 struggled to stay awake, but his conditioning soon won out over his fear. He slept. And in the morning was surprised to discover himself still in his narrow bed, with the bustle of his brothers rising and dressing all around him. It was as if he had been reborn. Nothing had changed, yet everything was charged with significance.

Full of joy, he stood with his brothers in front of the rippling flag on the big screen and with his right hand over his heart recited the familiar words with renewed ardour.

I pledge allegiance to the flag of Greater Brazil and to the undertaking for which it stands, one Earth under Gaia, indivisible, restored, replenished, and purged of all human sin.

2

Cash Baker was just twenty-six, with eight years' service in the Greater Brazilian Air Defence Force, when he was selected for the J-2 single-ship test programme. From inauspiciously ordinary origins in a hardscrabble city in the badlands of East Texas he'd risen through the ranks with astonishing speed. Luckily, he'd received as good an education as anyone in his neck of the woods could reasonably expect, and one of his teachers had spotted his preternatural mathematical ability and given him extra tutoring and steered him toward the Air Defence Force. He scraped into the top percentile in the induction tests, was streamed straight into basic pilot training at the academy in Monterrey, and a year later, on a hot, thundery day in August, marched at the head of the graduation parade for the class of 2210. He started out flying fat-bellied Tapir-L4s on supply missions to remote camps of the Wreckers Corps east of the Great Lakes, was quickly promoted to the combat wing of the 114th Squadron, flying fast, deadly little Raptors, and distinguished himself in a string of air-support missions during the campaign fought by General Arvam Peixoto's Third Division, clearing bandit settlements in and around the ruins of Chicago. The bandits were organised and highly disciplined, but for the most part poorly armed, although one time someone fired a reconditioned smart missile at Cash's bird and he had a hairy couple of minutes flying all over the sky before his battle AI broke the encryption of the missile's fierce little mind and it incontinently exploded.

Then he was transferred to the big base outside Santiago and flew long-range intercept patrols out across the Pacific during the Cold War between Greater Brazil and the Pacific Community, when for a little while it looked as if war might break out over possession of Hawaii. After the Cold War cooled down, he was selected for test-pilot school, and worked on a new generation ground-to-orbit fighter, the Jaguar Ghost. A dream to handle in orbit, but a pig during reentry. After three of the eight prototypes crashed and burned when their engines flamed on erratically or not at all while planing back into the atmosphere, and two more burnt up because of flaws in their lightweight diamond-paint heat shields, the programme was cancelled. But Cash had a lot of fun in the six months he spent testing the craft, loved the way the horizon flexed beneath him and the sky darkened until the stars came out as he arrowed out of the atmosphere, loved the serene oceanic feeling of seeming to float above the Earth while travelling at several thousand klicks a second. Up there, the terrible wounds left by the industrial age and anthropogenic climate change and the Overturn were mostly invisible. The dead zones in the oceans, the flooding along the shorelines of every continent, the deforested deserts of the Amazonian basin and Africa, the vast and tumbled deserts of North America, the ruined cities . . . all was lost in the shining vastness of the beautiful blue planet. Cash wasn't especially religious, but in orbit he understood for the first time what the green saints meant when they said that the Earth was a living organism whole and entire.

After the Jaguar fiasco Cash was returned to combat status, but by now he had a bad jones for test flying, and for space. He was chasing down rumours of a new kind of space plane when General Arvam Peixoto's office reached out to him. The general remembered Cash from the Chicago campaign, and Cash volunteered for the test programme as soon as he was asked if he wanted to come aboard.

So he went to the Moon, and the Earth seemed lovelier than ever, a lonely blue-white pearl floating in the black sky above the lunar wastelands. A hundred and fifty years ago some of Earth's richest, brightest, and most powerful people had underwritten the construction costs of a tented city, Athena, east of Archimedes Crater on the edge of the Imbrium Basin, moving there to escape the devastation and disorder caused by climate change and dozens of brush-fire wars fought over dwindling resources. Strip mines had processed lunar regolith for helium-3, and there was a sprawling site where sunshade mirrors had been manufactured and slung into orbit at the L1 point between the Earth and Moon. The helium-3 had been used in fusion reactors; the swarm of mirrors had cut down insolation and helped to stabilise the Earth's climate during the wild years of the Overturn, when runaway global warming driven by vast surges of methane released from Antarctic clathrates had threatened to cause mass extinction on a global scale. The mirrors were in orbit still, maintained by international crews. It would be at least another century before the effects of the Overturn and global warming were entirely ameliorated.

When it had become clear that the new supranational states that had emerged after the Overturn were determined to take control of the strip mines and shut down everything else on the Moon, the construction workers and the science crews, along with their families and many of the private citizens and their families and employees, had lit out for Mars and the moons of Jupiter and Saturn. Greater Brazil had claimed the city they had abandoned in place, and it had been refurbished by members of the Peixoto family, its most enthusiastic proselytisers for an expansion of the space programme. They had built a small fleet of long-range ships, had recently established links and trade routes with cities and settlements in the Jupiter and Saturn systems, and their skunk works had developed all kind of technological miracles, including a new kind of combat space plane.

Directly after disembarking from the shuttle from Earth, Cash and the other volunteers for the test programme were taken to a briefing room where General Arvam Peixoto walked them through the specs of the prototype of the new plane, the J-2 singleship. It was a hot bird, all right. A self-guided missile equipped with a new kind of fusion motor that used antiprotons to drive a fission/fusion chain reaction in microdroplets of deuterium and tritium, and was far more powerful than any currently in operation. There was a pressure-suit-sized life system at the J-2's sharp end, it had cut-back wings for atmospheric sorties, and it was armed with a pumped-pulse X-ray laser, a drum of single-shot gamma-ray lasers, a rail minigun that fired depleted-uranium flechettes, a variety of conventional missiles, and manoeuvrable proxies that after being fired from a fat cannon could do all kinds of imaginative damage when they caught up with their targets. Its flight guidance system, using long-range and sideways radars, and GPS and contour maps accurate to within ten centimetres, could fly it completely around the Moon at an average altitude of a hundred metres, and then do it all over again, with exactly the same flight profile. And it was so agile and so fast, General Peixoto explained, that in combat situations it demanded superhuman qualities from its pilots.

The general was a powerfully built man with shoulder-length white hair brushed back from his craggy face. He talked with an easy informal style, as if to members of his own family, making eye contact with everyone in the room. When his glance fell on Cash for a moment, the young pilot felt his heart swell with pride and passion.

"You are already the most able pilots in Air Defence," General Peixoto said. "There are none better than you anywhere on Earth or the Moon. But it is possible to make you even better. I'm not familiar with all the techniques involved, and I think it only fair that you should understand completely what we are asking of you. So I'm going to hand you over for a few minutes to Professor Doctor Sri Hong-Owen, who will walk you through what the procedure entails."

Later, one of the pilots, Luiz Schwarcz, whose family had a background in medical science, told the others that Sri Hong-Owen was a stone-cold genius who had risen to the top of her field under the sponsorship of the Peixoto family's green saint, that she'd designed a radical new photosynthetic system, created all kinds of vacuum organisms, developed many of the techniques that family members used to extend their lives, and much else. But at the time, during the briefing, Cash Baker didn't think much of her. Severe and awkward, dressed in the same blue coveralls everyone wore around the base, she was a plain woman of indeterminate age with a shaved, gleaming scalp and the palest skin he'd ever seen. She talked too fast, addressed the checklists, diagrams, and videos she conjured in the memo space rather than her audience, and answered questions with a brisk, take-no-prisoners manner, as if she thought the pilots were goddamned fools who'd failed to grasp the simplest of facts about the procedure.

Which was, when all the jargon and doubletalk was boiled away, some kind of rewiring or augmentation of their nervous systems that would allow them not only to plug directly into the plane's control systems, but also to briefly boost their neural-processing speeds. When Sri Hong-Owen was done, General Peixoto addressed the pilots again, telling them that it was an extremely radical procedure, that there was no guarantee that it would work in every case, or that everyone would survive it. If any of them wished to walk away and return to normal duties, there would be no dishonour in doing so, no shame, and no mention of it on their service record, he said, and asked those who wished to volunteer to raise their hands.

Cash stuck his arm straight up. So did everyone else. Someone down at the front was waving both his hands above his head. Because, hell, who didn't want to be a better pilot?

The first operation was performed under general anaesthetic and laid an artificial neural network around Cash's spine. The process of bedding in, as the network interfaced with his peripheral nervous system, was tedious and sometimes agonising, and during the seemingly endless rounds of tests that followed he found it weirdly unsettling to watch his right or left arm move by itself and his hands dance through a memo space with robotic swiftness and precision, solving spatial and kinetic problems without any conscious intervention on his part.

There was worse to come. He had to stay awake throughout the second operation, when the interfaces of the network were laced into his motor and sensory cortices, because the surgical team had to check that not only were his new talents in place and functioning, but also that nothing else, from his spinal reflexes to his memory, was damaged during the procedure that inserted them. So although he was given a nerve block and felt no pain, Cash had to endure the vibration and smell of burnt blood and bone as the bone saw cut open his skull, felt the sucking lift as the cap of his skull was lifted away, heard the mosquito whine of the bush robot that worked on his brain with manipulators that divided and divided a thousand times into clouds of cutting and recording tips nanometres in length, not much bigger than the neurons on which they operated. And although the brain has no pain receptors, he felt waves of phantom pain burn through his limbs as the bush robot tested each and every connection, was overwhelmed by discordant symphonies of emotion and taste and sound and hallucinatory shapes of every colour. Afterward, he was knocked out for two days while final tests were made, and then he and the rest of the pilots on the wing began their long convalescence.

They had to learn to use their bodies all over again, but they were young and fit and determined. They made rapid progress and turned everything into a contest. Laying bets on who would be the first to walk from bed to jakes unaided, who threw up the most (at first they all suffered from balance and inner-ear problems), who could deliver the greatest volume of piss when the doctors asked for a sample. Later on, when they were allowed to use the gym, they competed to see who could do the most press-ups or sit-ups, who could cycle or run the furthest on the machines, who could bench-press the heaviest weights.

Aldo Ruiz started to get into arguments with an invisible presence, hectoring the air in front of his face with passionate anger. He was taken away after he started to punch and slap himself, and the rest of the wing never saw him again.

The next week the tests started in earnest.

Complete physicals to begin with, more intensive than any they'd endured during induction. Then psychological testing, answering all kinds of questions about hypothetical situations and having to complete puzzles while wearing caps that monitored their brain activity. They also wore the caps while carrying out basic exercises on simulations of the J-2. Two of them were weeded out at this stage, for reasons never explained. The rest went forward into the testing and training programme.

No one bothered to tell Cash what would happen the first time his new abilities were activated. He was lying on a couch, surrounded by the usual gaggle of doctors and medical technicians, and then everything around him slowed. His hearing faded, leaving only a faint rumble; it felt as if he was sinking deep in tar; his field of vision dopplered down to red and narrowed to a patch about the size of his thumbnail held at arm's length. He couldn't turn or raise his head but could slowly track his eyes, moving that tiny patch of acuity like a spotlight to study a tech's ponderous blink (one eye squashing shut just before the other), watch another make a laborious mark on a slate. And then, just as suddenly, the world came back to normal. He was hot and horribly breathless, as if he'd just run twenty kilometres in full gear. His chest heaved as he tried to suck down air and his heart was slamming against his ribs and then the taste of metal flooded his mouth and he briefly fainted.

The doctors and techs wouldn't tell Cash if he'd passed or failed, wouldn't explain exactly what had happened to him, wouldn't tell him that it had been okay to faint. So he didn't know if he'd scratched out until he was returned to the ward, and found that everyone else had fainted when they'd been accelerated into what the techs called hyper-reflexive mode for the first time. In the night, Eudóxia Vitória and Bris Lispector both threw full-blown epileptic fits and the doctors took them away and the rest of the wing never saw them again. After the second day of testing Chiquinho Brown didn't come back, and Luiz Schwarcz claimed that he'd overheard one tech telling another that Chiquinho had died of a heart attack.

Those were the last casualties. Five weeks later, the survivors were passed as fit and fully integrated. They had each logged over a hundred hours on simulations, both with normal HUD controls and with their neural systems wired directly into control and guidance systems. Because they might be zipped into their birds for weeks at a time in a war situation, they'd all had their teeth extracted and replaced by contoured plastic ridges. Their appendices had been removed, too. Now they were let loose on the J-2 prototypes, flying with only HUD controls at first, basic point-to-point flights and simple combat simulations. After two weeks of these bedding-in trials, Cash Baker was selected to be the first pilot to fly in fully-wired mode.

It was a live-round discriminatory target exercise. He flew west—the bird was basically flying itself, but Cash was extended into every corner of its airframe—out across the dark plain where more than three and a half billion years ago lava had flooded the raw impact crater of the Imbrium Basin. When the target area in the slumped rim mountains at the far edge of the basin came around the horizon, the transition from being merely wired in to flying by wire was fantastically smooth: the J-2's trim altered by less than point zero one arc of a minute. It wasn't like flying the plane. It was like *being* the plane. Like having sex with it, Luiz said later, although as far as Cash was concerned, that first time, he couldn't remember when he'd ever had sex that good.

He'd been taught to visualise the trigger for his hyperreflexes as a big red button in the centre of his head. He pressed that button now, and everything went dream slow. He felt each individual jolt as the rail minigun loosed a hail of depleted uranium flechettes that shredded a simulated pressure dome, located the two rolligons with friendly markings moving across the plain amongst six others tagged as enemy, and targeted those six and crisped their control systems with precise gamma-ray laser shots within a second, and used missiles to take out a series of pop-up targets. Then the target area was behind him, and he gave up command and control to the J-2's battle AI and pushed the imaginary red button again. He'd learned how to stay conscious during the switchover by now, and was able to acknowledge the range officer's confirmation of his kills.

That evening there was an official celebration of the programme's success. The pilots hung in a tight group and sipped water and fruit juice while senior officers and scientists and techs tossed down shots of pulque and rum and tequila and grew loud and animated. General Peixoto made a short speech, was videoed shaking the hands of the pilots, and disappeared. Officers and the science crew toasted the pilots and each other with grand and florid eloquence, shattered empty glasses on the floor. The pilots left when one of the suit techs was persuaded to take off her shirt and the party started to get serious—they had medical tests the next morning just like every other morning, 0530–0630, and then an hour in the gym before the daily briefing over breakfast before they started work.

Everyone in the Air Defence Force believed that there was going to be another war with the Outers. The so-called peace and reconciliation initiatives would never amount to anything other than a colossal waste of time; the Outers had to be brought under control before they threw another comet at Earth, or developed some weird posthuman tweak that made them invincible. There was going to be war, and Cash Baker, raised on stories of the heroic deeds of his forefathers, couldn't wait. Meanwhile, he and the other pilots continued to work on the J-2. They flew solo missions and flew in formation. They flew over every type of lunar landscape, practised intercept missions in orbit around the Moon and Earth, tested their birds at every level of Earth's atmosphere. When they weren't flying in real time, they honed specific skills in simulations, attended seminars on redesign and improvements of their craft, and updates in combat theory, endured endless suit fittings, medical tests, psychological evaluations . . .

One day, about six months after Cash's maiden flight, the intelligence officer delivering the usual briefing session after breakfast gave way to the colonel in charge of the J-2 programme, who said without preamble that Maximilian Peixoto, the husband of the President and Commander-in-Chief of the Greater Brazilian Air Defence Force, had died late last night. He told the pilots that there would be no test or training flights until after the funeral, which would take place in ten days' time, and said that he had been instructed to choose four pilots who would fly their J-2s over the cathedral in Brasília at the end of the funeral service to honour the man who had been their commander. He named Cash Baker and Luiz Schwarcz and two others, and announced that there would be a special Mass in one hour.

Afterward, Luiz told Cash that this changed everything.

"Maximilian Peixoto wasn't just our Commander-in-Chief. He was also chair of the Committee for Reconciliation, one of the champions of making peace with the Outers. He set up the first embassies out there thirty years ago. He'd been working steadily ever since to establish trade links. And he naturally had the ear of the President. Now he's dead, his friends will have much less influence."

"This means what?"

"You really are an ignorant son of a bitch," Luiz said.

"Maybe I am," Cash said. "Or maybe I don't much care for politics."

"Well, you should. There are many people in the government who think it is pointless and dangerous to try to make friendly overtures to the Outers. They are not yet in the majority, but now they will be able to argue openly against peace and reconciliation. And General Arvam Peixoto is one who has always opposed reconciliation very strongly. You watch out. Pretty soon I believe that he will get the green light to put the J-2 into production."

"So we're finally going head to head against the Outers."

"Not quite yet, but we're a step closer."

"Well it's about time," Cash said.

3

It was the most important funeral to have been held in Brasília for more than twenty years. The avenues around the Catedral Metropolitana Nossa Senhora Aparecida were clogged with limousines and flitters. Drivers and security details eyed each other with professional interest. Drones wove amongst treetops. Helicopters beat wide circles under the hot blue sky. Wolves prowled the long park, Eixo Monumental, and half the city was paralysed by interlocking rings of security.

Inside the cathedral the harmonies of the *Agnus Dei* laced the air, soaring above solemn strings and the earth-shaking reverberation of the organ whose ranked pipes rose like a pleated steel curtain behind choir and orchestra. In front of the pure white block of the limestone altar, a tulipwood coffin rested on a bank of sweetly odorous lilies and orchids. Here lay Maximilian Pietro Solomon Cristagau Flores Peixoto, husband of the President of Greater Brazil, Commander-in-Chief of the Greater Brazilian Air Defence Force,

Grand Wizard of the Order of the Knights of Viridis, Steward of the Northern Territories, Chair of the Committee for Reconciliation, Rector of the Universities of Montevideo, Caracas, Mexico City and Denver, and so on and so forth, a great power in the world who had died from systemic organ failure at the age of one hundred and seventy-two. The dead man's dark face peeped still and solemn above the linen sheet that wrapped his body. His famous moustache waxed to sharp points. His eyes closed by gold coins salvaged from the wreck of a Spanish galleon.

His coffin was elevated above the sleeve of water that cut across the equator of the cathedral's circular nave. The water was as black as oil, disturbed here and there by spreading ringlets as fish tasted the underside of its skin. On the far side, the congregation in funeral finery packed three broad tiers of seats like a parliament of rooks. Almost every member of the Peixoto family was present, occupying forty rows of the middle tier, ranked by consanguinity. The widowed President sat on a canopied chair at the centre of the first row, resplendent in fuliginous robes, now and then reaching under the veil that covered her face to capture a tear in a tiny vase of cultured diamond. Behind the family rose solemn phalanxes of senators, senior officers of the armed forces glittering in ceremonial uniform, ambassadors and politicians from every country on Earth, and the representative from Rainbow Bridge, Callisto. On the flanking tiers were members of the other great families, ministers, governors, senior civil servants, and the servants of the Great House: an audience of two thousand people, with millions more watching pictures relayed from static cameras.

Professor Doctor Sri Hong-Owen didn't have a single drop of Peixoto family blood in her veins, yet she and her fifteen-year-old son, Alder Topaz, were sitting with the family nonetheless, on the far left-hand side of the fortieth row of the central tier. They were attending the funeral in place of one of the senior members of the family, Sri's sponsor and mentor, the green saint Oscar Finnegan Ramos, who these days never stirred from his hermitage in Baja California, even for an occasion as grand and important as this.

The long service was crammed with intricate ritual. Mass, a sermon celebrating the dead man's life, the service for the commitment of the dead, and now the requiem. No doubt the music was glorious, but Sri was tone-deaf and quite unable to appreciate it. As was her habit when forced to endure some tedious ceremony or committee meeting to which she had nothing to contribute but her presence, she retreated into her head, meditating on the latest tests of a promising new refinement of the standard gerontological treatment. Alder, thoroughly engaged with the occasion, nudged her when choir and orchestra and organ achieved an ecstatic climax. The archbishop, dressed in green and gold mitre and robes, glided toward the bier and asperged the corpse with holy water and with his thumb printed its brow with oil. Then he stepped backward and made the sign of the cross and loop, and the coffin soundlessly tilted above its bed of flowers and the body shot out feet first, shedding its linen shroud and knifing into black water that boiled up in a fierce flurry as hungry fish began to feed, returning Maximilian Peixoto's store of carbon and other elements to Gaia.

A moment later, the whistling roar of a wing of J-2 singleships flying low above the city in "missing man" formation shook the entire cathedral, and the choir and organ launched into the *In Paradisum*.

Sri's honorary position meant that she was among the first to leave the cathedral at the end of the service, but her lowly rank meant that she had to wait a long time for her ride. People streamed past and climbed into limousines that pulled away as others nosed forward. Flitters descended and ascended like bees at a hive.

Rothco Yang, the representative from Rainbow Bridge, Callisto, stepped out of the crowd and greeted Sri and Alder and told them that he had been most impressed by the solemn and splendid occasion. "One thing puzzled me," he said. "The fish."

"The fish?"

"The fish in the pool or moat or whatever it is called." Rothco Yang, dressed in black silk pyjamas and a black broad-brimmed hat, was fastened inside the cage of the exoskeleton that supported him against the pull of Earth's gravity. "I was wondering what happens to them afterward. After they are . . . finished."

"I really don't know," Sri said, "but I could look it up."

Alder said, "Nothing happens to the fish. They are holy, I think."

"Holy?"

"Blessed by the archbishop," Alder said.

Rothco Yang's smile gleamed under the brim of his hat. His head was propped by a padded neck brace. "And is this how all people are, what is the phrase, returned to Gaia?"

"Only the most important," Alder said.

"And the rest?"

"People who can afford it are buried in green cemeteries. Woods, wildflower meadows. Everyone else is directly recycled."

"I see. Another example of the stratification caused by personal wealth. Are you waiting for someone, by the way?"

"Our limousine appears to be stuck in the queue," Sri said.

"If you are going to the reception I can give you a lift in my flitter."

"I have too much work to do," Sri said. She had not been invited to the reception at the Palácio da Alvorado, but she wasn't about to admit that to Rothco Yang.

"Of course. In three weeks you leave all this behind."

"Three weeks if all goes to plan."

"This changes nothing in the short term. As for the long term, we must work harder to convince the waverers and naysayers."

"Of course," Sri said, but she knew that Rothco Yang knew that it would not be so simple.

Maximilian Peixoto had been at the forefront of the movement to build and strengthen diplomatic and economic connections between Earth and the Outer communities. He'd overseen the establishment of missions in every major city of the moons of Jupiter and Saturn, sponsored academic and artistic exchange programmes, won a sizeable budget for the development and construction of a new generation of interplanetary ships. And when the legendary gene wizard Avernus and Sri's mentor, Oscar Finnegan Ramos, had conceived the plan to gift the city of Rainbow Bridge, Callisto with a biome as a symbol of the new spirit of reconciliation, it had been Maximilian Peixoto who had steered the bill authorising funding for construction of its ecosystem through the reefs and snags of Greater Brazil's Senate, whipping up a scant majority by calling upon every favour he was owed and shamelessly using his privileged position as consort of the President. He'd hosted a grand reception for the construction crew just ten weeks ago, on the eve of their departure for Callisto. And now he was dead. The biome project would go ahead—the construction crew would reach Callisto in a few days, and in any case it was too late to cancel it without massive loss of prestige—but Maximilian Peixoto's death had thrown the alliance for peace and reconciliation into disarray. Sri's advisers had gamed the consequences, and most of the outcomes were grim.

Tiny motors in the joints of Rothco Yang's exoskeleton hummed as he leaned closer to Sri and her son. "I'll tell you a little secret. Although I'm no believer, I offered up a prayer for the success of our venture. In the spirit of Pascal's wager. If there's no God, what harm can my little prayer do? And if there is, then what better place and time to ask for His intercession? This is a fine and wonderful thing you and I are involved in. We must do all we can to see it through, and build on its success. Are you looking forward to seeing Callisto, young Alder?"

"Very much, sir," Alder said. "And Europa, too."

Rothco Yang mentioned several people in Rainbow Bridge who Sri and Alder simply had to meet, and tick-tocked away toward his flitter. People continued to stream out of the cathedral. Few spared Sri and Alder so much as a glance. Sri called her secretary and he apologised and told her that it would be at least ten minutes before her limo could reach her. She was thirsty and tired and irritable. Tropical sunlight burned across the plaza, flared from the shells of limousines and flitters. A helicopter circled incessantly above the crown of the cathedral. Sri retreated into her thoughts until the limousine arrived and she could at last sink into its cool upholstery and sip a glass of chill water and use the encrypted uplink to deal with the messages that had piled up, while Alder recounted details of the funeral service to her secretary.

The limousine moved slowly down the avenue, passing through roadblock after roadblock. Stopping and starting and stopping again. Then someone was rapping on the tinted window beside Sri. She looked up, startled. The man, an Air Defence Force officer, rapped again, made a brisk, impatient gesture. Jackknifed on the jump seat, Sri's secretary, Yamil Cho, spoke the word that lowered the window and asked the officer what he wanted.

"The general wishes to speak with you," the officer said, looking straight at Sri.

He stepped back smartly as she climbed out into hot dry air, led her past armoured vehicles that squatted toadlike under a line of royal palms. Soldiers stood in small alert groups, pulse rifles slung across their chests. Faces masked with black visors. The officer opened the rear hatch of an armoured personnel carrier and Sri climbed into a kind of cockpit lined on either side with screens and panels of robust switches and pinlights and joystick controls.

General Arvam Peixoto sprawled in one of the low seats. Sri sat opposite him and said, "This is a ridiculously public place to meet."

"Not at all. As I'm in charge of security, I can assure you that there will be no record of this."

"Ah. That is why you weren't at the service."

"I thought it would be best if someone in the family supervised the *cordon sanitaire*. But I did allow myself a quiet moment of contemplation when the body was committed to the hungry little fishes."

The general was dressed in crisp green fatigues, combat boots laced high up his shins. His white hair, vivid against his dark brown skin, was pulled back in a ponytail that coiled over the five stars on his shoulder tab.

"By the by," he said, "what did your good friend Rothco Yang have to say to you?"

"He offered his condolences," Sri said.

"Is that all?"

"Didn't your security drones pick it up?"

"I prefer to get my information firsthand wherever possible. Indulge me."

Arvam Peixoto put his head to one side as Sri gave an account of the brief conversation. A habitual gesture that invariably reminded her of a praying mantis. A cold insectile calculation about where to take the first bite. Where to slide in the sting.

"Hard work," he said, when she had finished. "Does he really think that hard work will rescue the peace initiative? Do you?"

"The peace initiative hasn't failed yet," Sri said. "So unless you know something I don't, I'm still going to Callisto."

"Your business is the future," Arvam Peixoto said. "You dream up new technologies that you hope will give it shape and direction. What direction do you think it will take now? Will it be vertical or horizontal?"

"You *do* know something."

"You see the future as a rising curve. Always improving. Always something new. But other people, they see the future as a plane. Horizontal. Spreading out. A process of consolidation. That's what this is all about. The horizontal versus the vertical. True humans versus dangerous fanatics who are creating monsters out of their children."

"Or overheated propaganda versus clear, rational thinking."

"One day, if you are not careful, that flippancy of yours will get you into serious trouble with the wrong people. What do I know? Let me tell you what I know. Let's get down to why you're here. This isn't just about poor Maximilian's death, although it has of course changed everything. I thought you might like to know that in a few months, the Air Defence Force will begin joint manoeuvres in cislunar space with the air force of the European Union. Why? Because we will be leasing the new fusion motor to the Europeans, part of a new trade agreement." Arvam Peixoto studied Sri and said, "You didn't know this."

"I knew that negotiations were taking place. I was not of course privy to the details."

"The negotiations are more or less over. A few snags and wrinkles have to be dealt with, nothing serious. As soon as the President comes out of mourning there will be a signing ceremony in Munich. What does this have to do with you? It is quite simple. The Europeans withdrew from the biome project and the rest of the hearts-and-minds nonsense because hardliners won control of their government. And now, after the unfortunate death of the Consort, after supporters of reconciliation with the Outers lost their most powerful voice, our own hardliners will be pushing for an end to the biome project too. I know that you feel a sentimental loyalty to our green saint because he discovered you and nurtured you. But he's an old man, and he's isolated himself in that beach hut of his. He's out of touch. More or less out of the loop."

The general's tone was teasing, but his steady, slightly cross-eyed stare showed no spark of amusement. The screens behind him displayed different views of the cathedral and the lawns and treetops of the Eixo Monumental and the avenues on either side. People were still coming down the cathedral steps, climbing into limousines and people movers. Household servants, civil servants. People like Sri.

She said, "Is this why you took the enormous risk of talking to me here? Something we have already discussed exhaustively? Let me say this again. Whatever happens, I am loyal to the family. To the family, and to Greater Brazil."

"The family appreciates all you have done in its service," Arvam Peixoto said. "Unfortunately, the family is not in agreement about what to do about the Outers. There are two sides. At least two sides. Yes, we have talked about this many times. But this is no longer a theoretical matter. This is real, Professor Doctor. It is what it is. And you're in the middle of it, and you're going to have to choose which side you are on. Sooner rather than later. And should you make the wrong choice, then I'm afraid that the fruits of your work and your reputation will not exempt you from the consequences."

"I see. Is that all?"

There was a faint singing in Sri's ears and her palms, pressed together in her lap, were unpleasantly damp, but otherwise she felt lucidly calm.

"I have a gift for you," the general said, and lifted a flat wooden box from one of the panels behind his chair and handed it to Sri.

Inside, glasses with thick black plastic frames lay on a pair of meshback gloves.

"They are spex," Arvam Peixoto said. "What the Outers use instead of phones. The lenses use virtual light to project pictures and text and whatnot

28

directly onto your retinas. The gloves are tipset gloves, you can use them to type on a virtual keyboard, move virtual objects around . . . Well, I am sure you will soon master them. Before you thank me, there's a little more to it. One of my tech teams added a camera, and a memory chip with a very high capacity and quantum encryption. You can download a small AI onto it, all kinds of things. And should you see something interesting, or attend an especially useful meeting, perhaps you could record it for me. I'm sure you'll know the kind of thing I might be interested in."

Sri understood at once. The Peixoto family was sending a team of negotiators to Rainbow Bridge, but because Arvam Peixoto was not part of the faction promoting peace and reconciliation with the Outers, he was out of the loop. So he was asking her to be his spy, gathering information for his analysts and strategists. Firsthand information, the kind he liked.

Arvam Peixoto said, "You'll have plenty of time to think everything through on your voyage to Callisto. When you return, I hope to have an answer, one way or the other. Oh, and bon voyage, as the Europeans would say."

Back in the limousine, Alder asked if she was in trouble.

"Not yet," Sri said and told her secretary to tell the driver to get a move on. "I have work to do."

4

Much later, Macy Minnot would come to believe that Emmanuel Vargo had been the first casualty of the war. But when she first heard about the ecosystem engineer's death she thought that it was nothing more sinister than bad luck. A freak medical mishap. An accident.

Like Macy and the rest of the construction crew, Emmanuel Vargo spent the twelve-week voyage from Earth to Jupiter in the deep sleep of artificial hibernation, drugged and chilled and consuming a minimal amount of oxygen and water while the Brazilian cargo ship fell through eight hundred million kilometres of sunlit black vacuum. He was still asleep when the ship went into orbit around Callisto, the outermost of Jupiter's four large Galilean moons, and first-class passengers and hibernation coffins and cargo pods were offloaded onto a tug that descended to the port, a cluttered slab cantilevered above a dusty plain west of the city of Rainbow Bridge. The tug touched down on a scorched landing apron with the lumbering delicacy of a hippopotamus attempting ballet. A mobile crane unlatched from the tug's cargo frame the truck-sized pod that contained the hibernation coffins and transported it to a pressurised hangar where the coffins were extracted one by one and loaded onto flatbed carts that trundled through subsurface tunnels to the medical facility at the edge of the port. That was where Emmanuel Vargo began to wake, and that was where he died.

Usually, revival from hibernation was routine. Most people woke with nothing worse than a shrivelled stomach, concrete bowels, and an existential hangover. But like every medical procedure, revival had its risks—signature syndromes, systemic organ failures, metabolic storms. After his core temperature had been gently raised to 37.5° Celsius, his blood chemistry had been adjusted, and he'd been injected with a cocktail of GABA receptor stimulants, Emmanuel Vargo suffered an episode of chaotic neurological decoupling. Instead of quickly and spontaneously developing the usual pattern of dynamic multi-locus activity, as in waking from ordinary sleep, his neurons began to fire at high rates without any kind of synchrony, disrupting consciousness and coordination of respiration, heartbeat, and blood pressure.

Most victims of CND survived with varying degrees of memory loss and aphasia, but Emmanuel Vargo's episode was exceptionally severe. The electrochemical activity of his brain writhed like a bag of worms. A crash team tried and failed to induce synchrony with microtonic pulsed magnetic fields. His blood pressure collapsed and his heart stopped and did not respond to defibrillation, injection of norepinephrine, or direct massage. While he was being hooked up to a heart-lung bypass, he suffered a major clonic seizure. Two more seizures followed in quick succession. After the third, brain stem activity ceased. Thirty minutes later he was declared brain-dead, and life support was disconnected.

Emmanuel Vargo had been one of the prime movers of the project to construct a biome at the city of Rainbow Bridge, Callisto, a symbol of cooperation and reconciliation between Earth and the Outer System, and a major step in the long campaign to defuse tension between Earth's radical green conservatism and the smorgasbord of radical doctrines and utopian philosophies of the Outer System's city-states and settlements. Avernus, the Outer System's most notorious gene wizard, had drawn on her prodigious stores of karma to sponsor the biome's construction, and Maximilian Peixoto and the green saint Oscar Finnegan Ramos had persuaded the Brazilian government to underwrite the cost of designing and quickening of its ecosystem. Although the green saint's great-great-grandson, Euclides Peixoto, had been appointed titular head of the construction crew, Emmanuel Vargo had been responsible for every aspect of the planning and organisation of Greater Brazil's contribution. He'd collaborated with Oscar Finnegan Ramos's protégée, Sri Hong-Owen, in the design of the ecosystem, liaised with the Callistan crew during the construction of the biome's tent, and would have been responsible for supervising the elaboration and quickening of the ecosystem from start to finish.

Euclides Peixoto said all this and more two days after Emmanuel Vargo's death, in a short speech at the ceremony that marked the official beginning of the construction crew's work. This was on the broad lawn at the northern tip of the biome's main island. Euclides Peixoto stood at a podium with the empty lake bed stretching behind him under the gigantic tent of diamond and polymer panes and fullerene struts, and his audience seated in front of him on a crescent of folding chairs: the Brazilian ambassador and his retinue of aides, members of the Peixoto family's trade mission, a colourful medley of representatives from the Callistan congress and the city council of Rainbow Bridge, the men and women of the construction crew. A little shoal of drones hung at different levels in the air, transmitting the ceremony to citizens of Rainbow Bridge and other cities and settlements on Callisto, Ganymede, and Europa, and to the mining camps on tiny, distant Himalia and Elara.

Sitting amongst the rest of the construction crew, Macy Minnot had to admit that Euclides Peixoto definitely looked the part. Handsome in a two-piece suit whose chlorophyll hue matched the coveralls of the construction crew, a black armband fastened around his left sleeve, he spoke in a sonorous but engaging tone. Eulogising Emmanuel Vargo's contribution to the project, recounting a couple of well-judged anecdotes, winding up by saying that despite their grievous loss everyone in the crew was determined to work as well as they could to bring to life a beautiful and robust biome, and honour the memory of an extraordinarily talented ecosystem engineer, someone he was proud to have considered a friend.

Hard to believe this was the same man who just two days ago had badly botched the announcement of Emmanuel Vargo's death. The crew had assembled for what they'd believed would be an ordinary briefing, and without any preamble Euclides Peixoto had told them that Maximilian Peixoto, the husband of the President of Greater Brazil, had died while they'd been in hibernation during the voyage from Earth to Callisto. And before they'd had a chance to absorb that bombshell, he'd blurted out that Emmanuel Vargo had died too, during the revival process. Before he could say anything else, Ursula Freye had spoken up from the back of the room. Ursula and Emmanuel Vargo had become lovers soon after she'd been recruited to the construction crew. Trembling and grimly pale, she'd said that it was obvious that Manny had been murdered by enemies of the project, and demanded an immediate investigation. Speller Twain, the crew's security chief, had tried to hustle her away and there'd been an undignified struggle. Shouts, jeers, shrieks. The meeting had erupted into chaos, and Euclides Peixoto had fled without explaining how the project would proceed after the death of its engineer.

Now, as the applause at the end of his speech pattered into silence, Euclides Peixoto invited the young girl who had won the lottery to step forward. Eight years old, tall and slender in a simple white dress, the child took the remote control from him and without ceremony pressed its red button. At dozens of points along the eastern and western shores of the lake, gouts of water burst roaring from fat pipes and crashed down to the lake floor. Vast clouds of spray billowed up, softening the glare of the chandelier lights strung along the high ridge of the tent and filling the cool air with a fresh, steely odour. Above another wave of applause, Euclides Peixoto declared in ringing tones that the quickening of the biome had begun.

Macy Minnot had never had much time for Euclides Peixoto. The man was not only a political appointee who'd been given his job because of an accident of birth, he was also a strutting fool who couldn't draw a trophic web, resurrect dead mud or even plant out a flowerpot, much less a forest or marsh, to save his life. But she'd liked and respected Emmanuel Vargo, who'd risen from humble beginnings to become one of the best ecological engineers on Earth, and had shown her many small kindnesses and courtesies after he'd selected her to be part of his crew.

That had been a little over a year ago, when Macy, recently promoted to gang leader, had been working with Reclamation and Reconstruction Crew #553 at Lake Champlain, on the northern border of newly conquered territory gifted to the Fontaine family. Guerrillas, wildsiders and tribes of squatters had been pushed out of the region after a decade of fierce fighting, and R&R #553 had moved in to undo a couple of centuries of ecological damage. Before the crew began its work, nothing much had lived in the lake but blooms of blue-green algae, mitten crabs, snakefish, and a pernicious variety of tweaked water hyacinth, fast-growing and hardy, that had been introduced to many freshwater bodies in the middle of the twenty-first century during early but misguided attempts at remediation. And thanks to the oil-burning culture of the twentieth and twenty-first centuries, a characteristic layer of sediment, polluted with fossil-fuel residues and heavy metals, covered the bottom of the lake: anaerobic, stinking, tarry black, and completely lifeless. Macy Minnot was in charge of the gang that had the job of transforming this oleanthropocene sludge into honest-to-goodness mud. They used big pumps to suck up sediment and pump it through baffles impregnated with polymers and plastizymes that removed heavy metals and other highly toxic substances, into a series of fermentation tanks where cocktails of tweaked microbes digested organic material; at the end of the process, the pristine mud was mixed with a balanced microbial population and pumped back onto the lake bed. It had taken three months to work down from the northern end of the lake to Malletts Bay. The crew had been hit by a couple of big storms and harassed by wildsiders and bandits—in the middle of one raid Macy had seen a smart RPG miss a pumping platform by no more than a metre, the thing making a long, lazy turn in midair and beginning to shark back in when its motor ran out of gas and it plunged into the lake and blew about a gazillion litres of water all over the crew barge. Mostly, though, the work was gravy. Hard and dirty, for sure, but tremendously worthwhile.

After its sediment and water had been processed and cleansed, the lake would be stocked with phytoplankton and waterweed, invertebrates and fish: an entire trophic web built from scratch and set running. Macy gave only lip service to worship of Gaia, but as far as she was concerned the restoration of a ruined, near-dead lake to something close to its pristine state was pretty much a religious experience. She loved her work and woke up every morning happy and grateful, eager to get going.

R&R #553 was commanded by Roxy Parrish, an experienced, sharp-minded woman in her fifties who took no bullshit from anyone, asked from her people only competence, hard work and loyalty, and in return provided them with unstinting support and protection from the worst whims and fancies of family bureaucrats. Every week or so she stopped by Macy's floating complex of barges, pumping platforms and coffer dams to check progress, discuss snags, and exchange gossip about the other R&R crews working the region. One summer evening, Roxy and Macy were up on the flying bridge of the crew barge, drinking beer and watching the sunset burnish the wide sweep of calm water that stretched out to low hills clad in ragged patches of newly planted forest at the eastern shore. A skein of geese laboured northward across the dark blue sky, calling each to each. Macy, as happy as she had ever been, took a sip of beer and thought that next year those geese would find a good home here, if they wanted to stop awhile. She said something to that effect to her boss, and Roxy asked her what she thought she would be doing this time next year.

"When this project is finished? I guess it depends where we're sent," Macy said. She was tilted back in her canvas chair, auburn hair loose about the shoulders of her denim shirt, roughened hands cradling her beer bottle against the waist snap of her jeans, work boots cocked on the rail of the flying bridge.

"This is a pretty good crew, so I can understand why you'd want to stick with us. But you're young, you have some talent, and you need all the experience you can get. I think you ought to take a look at this," Roxy said, pulling her slate from her sling bag.

That was when Macy first learned that the green saint Oscar Finnegan Ramos and the infamous gene wizard Avernus were sponsoring construction of a biome in the city of Rainbow Bridge on Callisto, Jupiter's second-largest moon, and the Peixoto family were assembling a crew that would engineer its ecosystem from scratch.

"Why me?" Macy said. "This is landscaping. It's a big job and it's in a weird place, but that's all there is to it."

"Read the specs," Roxy said. "Most of the park will be a freshwater lake. They need people who'll be able to quicken it, and one of those people will be responsible for the microbial ecology. It's interesting work and it will stretch you in all kinds of interesting ways. The engineer slated to lead the crew, Emmanuel Vargo, is at the top of his game, and I bet you could learn all kinds of new wrinkles from the Outers. They'd been developing and maintaining closed-cycle ecosystems for more than a hundred years. And then there's the chance to meet and maybe work with Avernus, who's about as famous as Darwin or Einstein or any other scientist you care to mention."

"I appreciate the hard sell," Macy said. "But it's an awful long way to go, and there must be a hundred people more qualified to work on this thing than me. A thousand."

"I wouldn't be too sure. You're one of the best microbial jockeys I know. You have a frank manner that sometimes causes friction with other gang leaders, but you're a hard worker, and you're young and smart and ambitious. And this kind of opportunity comes but once in a lifetime, Macy. You might not see that now, but you will."

"I'm beginning to get the feeling that I don't have much choice about volunteering."

"There's that frank manner I mentioned," Roxy said. "I'll be just as frank. I was hoping you'd go for this straight away. Not just because it would make my job easier, but also because I really do believe that this is a great opportunity for you, and of all my people you're the best candidate. So if you don't volunteer, then yes, I'll have to put your name forward, and you won't get to have any say in the matter. We aren't the Army or the Air Defence Force, but we do have a chain of command. And you're somewhere near the bottom of it."

Macy thought about that for a little while. Staring off at the V of geese dwindling away toward the darkening rim of the world, saying at last, "Can I at least ask you who asked you to ask me?"

"As a matter of fact it was the governor of this region."

"Louis Fontaine?"

"The same. Apparently he's still paying attention to your career."

"The governor doesn't owe me anything any more," Macy said. "And even if he did, I'm not sure if I'd kindly thank him for this."

Four years ago Macy had been working as an R&R labourer in Chicago, helping to remove the last traces of buildings and roads from the lake shore. It was one of the biggest reclamation projects in the Fontaine family territory. The downtown skyscrapers had been cleared years ago, but work on the suburbs and exurbs seemed never-ending. A runaway without any qualifications or patronage, Macy would have been working as a labourer still if Fela Fontaine, high on three different tailored pyschotropic drugs, hadn't crashed her stolen flitter.

The little aircraft had skimmed low and flat above hectares of tree stumps and rubble, sending people running in every direction, and had made a wide turn and had come back for a second pass, which was when it had clipped the rusted skeleton of an electricity pylon and lost its tail rotor. Spinning like a sycamore seed, it had augered into the lake a couple of hundred metres off-shore, and Macy had jumped into a boat and raced to where it was sinking amidst a spreading pool of burning fuel, suffering third-degree burns to her hands and arms when she'd pulled the unconscious girl from the wreckage.

Fela Fontaine's father was the governor of the Northeast Region. He'd visited Macy in hospital, paid for her medical treatment, and arranged a scholarship that put her through college, but she'd had no further contact with him or the rest of the family. Six months later, she learned that Fela Fontaine had committed suicide. As far as she was concerned that was the end of the matter. Sure, she'd been given an opportunity to better herself, but four years down the line she felt that she had proven her own worth. She'd graduated at the top of her class and worked hard at her first posting, the city-sized treatment plant out on Lake Michigan, where she'd solved a knotty washout problem in the remediation reactors and had earned promotion to gang leader. She'd always be grateful for the push she'd been given, but she wanted to put that behind her, wanted to be defined by what she could do, wanted to make her own way in the world without any help or patronage.

So she felt a spark of anger and resentment at the way the governor had casually reached out and interfered with her life; when Roxy Parrish tried to convince her that it really was a good opportunity, she said, "What does this have to do with him anyway? The biome is the Peixoto family's thing, not the Fontaines.'"

"You really should start paying attention to politics. Otherwise your pristine ignorance will get you into serious trouble one of these days."

"I know about the Outers. We had a war with them a hundred years ago. Some people want to make up to them. Some other people want to go to war with them again, because they're barely human any more. Some might call that politics," Macy said. "I call it foolishness. We got enough to do right here without trying to stamp on a bunch of people who don't happen to live the way we want them to."

"That's exactly the position of the Fontaines," Roxy said. "That's why we've been supporting the Peixoto family's attempts to reach some kind of reconciliation with the Outers, and that's why we support this biome project. Most of the other families opposed it, but the Fontaines and a few others stood shoulder to shoulder with the Peixotos when the bill went through the Senate. And because the Peixotos needed our votes, there'll be a couple of places for our people when they get to picking the crew. As for that, you're not the only microbial jockey being put forward. There are people from every region, but I think you have a good shot at this. I think you might just make it. You're young, but you're good. There's that work you did at Lake Michigan, and the way you make dead mud come back to life is a sweet thing to behold. Your reversion rate is so low it barely registers."

"Like you always say, it's easier to get it right the first time than do it over."

"It's easier, but it also takes a lot of skill."

"If I do get picked, it better be because of what I can do," Macy said.

"I don't think that Emmanuel Vargo is going to pay any attention to anything else."

"Well all right then. I guess you can tell them I volunteered."

Roxy took a sip from her bottle of beer. "Just this morning, a couple of my labourers stumbled on the remains of a wildsider shrine in the basement of some big old ruin—automobile parts, bones, a pyramid of more than a hundred human skulls. Some of them are small, children's skulls . . . The world is badly fouled up, kid. It's going to take a long time and a lot of work to fix it. If you do go up and out, I can promise you that there'll be plenty to do when you get back."

Macy tried not to think much more about it. She told herself that she had little chance of getting a place on the crew, that if it did happen she'd deal with it then, and meanwhile she had plenty of work to do. So she was surprised that she felt a keen pang of disappointment when, two weeks later, she heard that she hadn't made the first cut. She threw herself back into her work. The Lake Champlain project was winding down when Roxy called and told her that Emmanuel Vargo wanted to talk to her.

The engineer arrived in a tilt-rotor plane that stooped low over the treetops and touched down neatly in a meadow at the edge of the lake. He was a tall, square-shouldered man, dark-skinned and bald as a bullet, dressed in blue jeans and an expensive but rumpled yellow silk jacket with a coffee stain on one lapel. He shook Macy's hand with a hard-barked grip, studied her with a keen, searching gaze.

"Let's go for a walk in the woods," he said.

It was a beautiful crisp day in the middle of October. They rambled under trees laden with glorious reds and golds. Soldiers armed with pulse rifles moved ahead of them and behind them. Emmanuel Vargo asked perceptive questions about Macy's work before coming to the point and telling her that the person originally appointed to construct the microbial ecology of the Rainbow Bridge biome had resigned from the project.

"He's from the European Union, the Couperin family. Ten days ago the head of the Couperins died, and his successor cleaves to the hard line against the Outers. One of the first things he did was withdraw the three people his family had put up for the crew. Bad luck for them, good luck for us, because now we can appoint three Brazilians as replacements. That is why I am here, Ms. Minnot. To ask you to consider joining the crew."

They were standing in a little clearing. The leaves of a clump of maple saplings glowed red as fresh blood in the low afternoon sunlight. There was a chill edge to the clean air.

Macy said, "Can I ask you a question, Mr. Vargo?"

Emmanuel Vargo's smile showed crooked brown teeth and his eyes shone with fine good humour. "Anything you like."

"Are you here because someone high up in the Fontaine family recommended me?"

"I'm here because you're the best of all the microbial ecologists who were put forward. Unfortunately, political nonsense meant that I had to select someone else in the first instance. Fortunately, that same political nonsense gives me a chance to remedy the situation. You don't have much experience, but neither do most of the other candidates—the other families have been reluctant to volunteer senior personnel. It doesn't matter. In this case, where we are working in a new and unknown arena, ability counts for more than experience. And I believe that you are more than capable of doing the work. That's why I came out here to personally ask you to do me the honour of joining my crew."

Macy wasn't the kind of woman most men would look at twice, but when she smiled, her face lost its habitually guarded expression and was as utterly transformed as a shuttered room suddenly flooded with sunlight. She smiled now, saying, "Haven't I already volunteered? When do you need me?"

"How quickly can you pack?"

Macy flew out with Manny Vargo an hour later. The next day she started training with the rest of his crew. And now she was on Callisto. Now she had to prove her worth all over again.

It was going to be difficult. Not just because of Emmanuel Vargo's death, although that was bad enough, but also because Euclides Peixoto had taken over the day-to-day running of the construction crew. And although he was good at making speeches and flattering diplomats and representatives of Callisto's government, Euclides Peixoto knew nothing about ecosystem engineering and had never shown any interest in the design of the biome or in the training of the crew. That hadn't prevented him from telling Emmanuel Vargo how to do his job on more than one occasion. His ignorance about ecosystem engineering was perfectly matched by his lack of talent in people management, and like many men born into privilege and protected by that same privilege from the consequences of failure, he had no time for the advice of people he believed to be his inferiors.

Professor Doctor Sri Hong-Owen, who had helped Manny Vargo design the biome's ecosystem, would arrive at Rainbow Bridge in four weeks' time, riding a freighter fitted with the new fusion motor. In the interim, the project would have a better chance of success if the Peixoto family agreed to allow one of the local engineers to take over. Someone who knew what they were doing. Someone who could work alongside the crew and listen to their opinions. But that was not only politically unpalatable, it also involved a point of pride. And so the crew was stuck with Euclides Peixoto and his unpredictable whim of iron. Although he could draw on the advice of Sri Hong-Owen and a team of experts, it was entirely possible that he might take it into his head that he knew better than they did because he was on the spot and they were almost billion kilometres away. Or if he was confronted with some problem that needed solving right away, no time to consult with anyone back on Earth, he might either freeze up or make a bad decision and out of pride refuse to back down. And of course, most of the crew couldn't gainsay him. The Peixoto family was far more conservative than the Fontaines, and even under the Fontaines it wasn't prudent to talk back to anyone with the smallest degree of consanguinity, although you could at least bitch about the bosses behind their backs. Even that was too much of a risk under the Peixotos. Anyone caught criticising the people who owned their hides could be accused of treason, there were spies and snitches everywhere, and the punishments for disloyalty were severe, so everyone owned by the Peixotos kept their opinions to themselves. Macy was pretty sure that not even Ernest Galpa, now the most senior member of the crew, a decent old fellow who had worked with Emmanuel Vargo for twenty years, who had openly wept at the news of Manny's death, would dare challenge Euclides Peixoto if he decided on some course of action that threatened the success of the project.

Theoretically, crew members from other families could stand up to him with a degree of impunity. But Cristine Quarrick and Patrick Alan Allard came from the Nabuco family, which was even more old-school than the Peixotos, everyone knew that César Puntareñas was no more than a spy who reported directly to the Fonseca family council, and although Ursula Freye had a thirty-second degree of consanguinity within the Fontaine family, being the daughter of a second cousin of their only green saint, she was consumed by paranoid fantasies of a conspiracy that had murdered her lover. Macy could only hope that when Euclides Peixoto screwed the pooch—and she reckoned that *when* was much more likely than *if*—it wouldn't have anything to do with her sphere of responsibility. Because if he ordered her to do something idiotic, she'd probably be stupid enough to refuse, and then he'd cut her off at the knees, blacken her name, and send her back to Earth with a reputation as a wrecker. After that, she'd be lucky if she could get a job breaking rocks.

Fortunately, she didn't have much time to worry about the different ways the man could crash the project. She had plenty of work to do, and she had to do it quickly.

To begin with, the biome's microbial ecosystem—the combined metabolic repertoire of trillions of microscopic workers that underpinned the cycles of carbon fixation, nutrient recycling, and organic decomposition—had to be up and running before the lake could be planted out and stocked with fish and invertebrates. Macy needed to grow up starter cultures to seed the reed beds and stromatolite reefs that would filter the lake water and recycle nutrients, and she also had to liaise with the plankton team to produce a mixed culture of bacteria, blue-green algae and diatoms that would clarify the lake water by attaching to suspended fines and elaborating mucopolysaccharide threads to form fluffy accretions heavy enough to sink out of the water column. This process of flocculation, which would not only allow photosynthesis to take place at all depths of the lake, but would also produce an organic-rich layer of mud, would be initiated by injection of large volumes of the mixed culture into every sector of the lake during the formal opening ceremony. That was due to take place in thirty-two days, after Sri Hong-Owen had arrived and the lake had reached its final level. It was an inflexible deadline. But as soon as they started work, Macy and the plankton team ran into a serious problem: the diatom they planned to use, a tweaked strain of *Skeletonema costatum*, wasn't growing as fast as it should when cultured in the melt water that was filling the lake. If they couldn't get the doubling rate up to where it should be, they'd not only be short several hundred kilograms of diatom biomass, they'd also have to adjust the growth rates of all the other microorganisms.

It was the kind of problem that Macy enjoyed solving. Biome engineering was more of an art than a science, an intricate game or puzzle in which everything affected everything else, its complexity increasing exponentially with the addition of each new species. Plants competed for the nutrients and light; animals grazed on plants or preyed on other animals; microorganisms broke down dead organic material and recycled nitrogen and phosphorus and sulphur into forms that other organisms could use. If a single species was removed from or added to this web, the relationships between every other species were changed in large and small ways that could not always be predicted. Macy had the useful knack of being able to hold models of nutrient and energy flow in her head and examine them from every angle, visualising their interlocking checks and balances, predicting how changes in one parameter would propagate through the system. She wasn't as good at it as Manny Vargo, who'd been able to conduct the equivalent of two or three symphonies at once, with choirs and bells and thundering organs. But she was competent, she was used to hard work and impossible deadlines, and the city had given her two good assistants and sole use of a well-equipped facility on the west bank of the lake. She had every confidence that she would succeed.

The facility was set in and around the footing of one of the big arched struts that, elaborated from spun threads of fullerene, supported the biome's tent. At its base, the strut flared into a gourd-shaped structure ten storeys high, hollowed out with terraced apartments and rising above a plaza beside the empty black bowl of what would be a shallow bay when the lake was filled. Macy's laboratory was on the ground floor of the hollow strut, and the bioreactors where she and her two assistants were growing pure and mixed cultures of microorganisms had been set up in the plaza. That was where she was working when the crew's security chief, Speller Twain, and the youngest and newest member of the Brazilian diplomatic team, Loc Ifrahim, came for her.

It was eleven days after the lake had started to fill. Macy and her two assistants, Argyll Hall and Loris Sher Yanagita, were in the middle of a discussion about the problematical diatom culture when the two men walked in.

"We need to talk to Ms. Minnot," Speller Twain told Macy's assistants. He was a burly man with a blond crew cut and a pinched, sour glare. The sleeves of his coveralls had been ripped off, displaying muscular arms covered with military tattoos. "It's crew business, so take off, why don't you?"

"They have work to do," Macy said. Although she'd been expecting something like this, she was suddenly dry-mouthed and her heart was beating quickly and lightly. "Plus, you might want to get out of range of the cameras in here—believe it or not, there are citizens who have nothing better to do than watch me work. If you want to talk privately, we'd best do it outside."

The two men looked at each other and the diplomat shrugged and said, "Why not?"

Macy led them past the bioreactors to the jetty that stretched out into bay's dry bowl. She headed straight for the end, ankling along in the heel-and-toe shuffle that was the best way of walking in Callisto's light gravity, putting some distance between herself and the two men. She needed a little time to compose herself and to let go of the anger and dismay kicked up by their presumption.

When she turned, she saw that Speller Twain had stopped halfway along the jetty, leaning against the rail like a casual sightseer as Loc Ifrahim shuffled toward Macy. "Why don't you tell me exactly what's troubling you?" she said to the diplomat. "Then I can tell you why I can't do anything about it and get back to my work."

Loc Ifrahim smiled. "They told me you spoke plainly."

He was only a few years older than Macy, his narrow, clever face framed by black hair twisted into dozens of tight braids that brushed the shoulders of his white silk suit. Officially, he was part of the trade delegation, but everyone knew that he was a government spy.

"I won't apologise for my way of speaking, Mr. Ifrahim," Macy said. "I wasn't raised with your advantages."

"Actually, my childhood had precious few of what you might call advantages," Loc Ifrahim said. "But I was lucky enough not be raised in the bosom of some strange sect that believes universal truth can be found by playing mathematical games with pi. I'm curious—do you still believe in that, Ms. Minnot?"

Macy was used to taunts about her odd upbringing. She'd had to put up with them ever since she'd signed up to become an R&R labourer. "I've outgrown my childhood, Mr. Ifrahim. How about you?"

"I acquired all kinds of old-fashioned virtues which I still try to apply to the way I conduct my life," Loc Ifrahim said. "Loyalty to one's family and friends, for instance. How about *you*, Ms. Minnot? I know you have no loyalty to your family because you ran away from them. But are you loyal to your friends? Do you feel any loyalty to Ursula Freye, for instance?"

There it was, just as she'd thought.

"I'm not sure that she'd want me to call her a friend," she said. "We're from the same territory, but that's about all we have in common. Plus, Ursula has consanguinity, and she's a stickler for protocol. She made that pretty clear during training."

"She likes to pull rank on you. Even so, I'm sure you'd help her if she was in trouble."

"What kind of trouble?"

"How does Ms. Freye seem to you?" Loc Ifrahim said.

"I don't know. Tired and a trifle manic, I suppose. Like all of us."

"Manic, mmm," Loc Ifrahim said, seeming to like the taste of the word on his tongue. "Has she told you what she's been up to?"

"You seem to have a problem with coming to the point, Mr. Ifrahim. Since it isn't exactly a secret, let me speak plainly and get it out of the way. Ursula thinks that Emmanuel Vargo's death was no accident. She thinks he was murdered. She's been running around looking for clues, and now I would guess that it has caused you some kind of trouble. How am I doing?"

Loc Ifrahim's glossy black braids were strung with beads, different sizes, different colours. They rattled and clicked as he turned from Macy and gripped the rail at the end of the jetty with both hands and looked out, or pretended to look out, across the little bay. His cinnamon skin was flawless. He wore rings on every one of his fingers, and he had the neatest fingernails Macy had ever seen (her own, even though she kept them trimmed short, were ragged and broken, and the nail of her right thumb was bruised black from where she had jammed it in the sampling lock of one of the bioreactors). His perfume hung in the cold air between them, a sharp odour like orange peel and burnt sugar.

At last he turned back to look at Macy, and said, "Do you think that Mr. Vargo was murdered?"

"If you're working your way around to asking me to help you find out what Ursula's been doing, you should know that I'm no snitch, Mr. Ifrahim."

"I don't want you to help me. I want you to help her," Loc Ifrahim said.

"Do you have consanguinity, Mr. Ifrahim?"

Loc Ifrahim's smile didn't alter, but something changed behind his eyes. "No one in the diplomatic service has any degree of consanguinity. It ensures that we are entirely impartial."

"I don't have any either. But Ursula Freye, she has a thirty-second degree of consanguinity in the Fontaine family. And the Fontaine family own my ass. So if you want someone to persuade her to stop looking into the circumstances of Manny Vargo's death, I'm not the person to do it. If for whatever reason you don't want to talk to her, maybe you should ask Mr. Peixoto to deal with this. He's full-blood family, and he's supposed to be in charge of this crew."

"Oh, this isn't the kind of thing I want to concern him with."

"I don't think it concerns me, either."

"You're wrong, Ms. Minnot. There are many people in Rainbow Bridge who are not at all sympathetic to this project, or to Greater Brazil. By pursuing her inquiries, Ms. Freye may play into their hands and damage us all."

"So keep her in the biome. Have Mr. Twain put her under house arrest."

Loc Ifrahim said, "We *could* try to silence her, but Mr. Twain thinks it would cause more trouble than it's worth. And I have to say that I agree with him. We would have to explain to Ms. Freye's immediate family why we had to do it. And we can't stop Outers coming into the biome, of course, and we can't tell them why they shouldn't talk to Ms. Freye. No, it really would be best for all concerned if you had a quiet word with your compatriot. If you told her that we know what's she doing, that we understand her grief, and that we want to help her in any way we can."

Macy said, "Is that an order, or are you asking me a favour?"

"I could ask Mr. Twain to persuade you to do it," Loc Ifrahim said. "But I would prefer you to volunteer out of friendship and loyalty. Friendship to your compatriot, and loyalty to the crew and their mission. Because if Ursula Freye doesn't stop her silly little crusade, she'll cause trouble for the rest of the crew, she could well damage a lot more than this little project, and she'll most certainly damage the reputation of the Fontaine family. And even though you have no consanguinity, that will also damage *your* reputation, Ms. Minnot. People will say that you should have done something about it. They will say that you were implicated in Ms. Freye's crazy and completely unfounded imaginings. And I very much doubt that the Fontaine family will be pleased to hear that you stood by and did nothing to help."

"Dress it up any way you like, you want me to do your dirty work."

"Talk to Ms. Freye. I have persuaded Mr. Twain to allow you two days' grace. After that, he will want a report on your progress. For your sake, I suggest you have something positive to tell him," Loc Ifrahim said, and sketched a quick bow and shuffled away down the jetty toward Speller Twain, who pushed from the rail and touched the corner of one eye with his forefinger and then aimed it at Macy like a gun. Telling her, *I'll be watching you.*

After she'd run away from the sect, Macy had spent a couple of years on the streets of Pittsburgh. She knew all about good-cop/bad-cop routines. It would be funny, really, if she hadn't seen how Speller Twain operated. Like at the progress meeting two days ago, when Delmy March, the man in charge of the fish and mammal crew, had corrected Euclides Peixoto on some point about the timetable of the quickening. Euclides Peixoto had taken offence and told Delmy he wouldn't tolerate that kind of mealy-mouthed wrecking talk, and Speller Twain had detached himself from the wall where he'd been leaning and crossed the room in two lithe bounds and grabbed Delmy in an armlock and stuck the black spike of a jammer behind Delmy's ear, putting him into convulsions so bad he'd pretty near bitten off his tongue.

So instead of walking past the two men, who no doubt wanted to give her the benefit of some parting advice, Macy vaulted the jetty's rail and floated down four metres and strode away across the floor of the bay. Her thoughts were snarled up and some kind of physical activity was usually a good way of freeing them, but most of all, right there and then, she wanted to get away from everything, and as she came out of the bay's wide mouth she broke into a run, long fluid strides that quickly ate up distance, passing a low sandy promontory planted with young cabbage palms and yuccas, running on under the clear white light of the chandeliers and the irregular quilting of the tent toward the long oval of water that occupied the deepest part of the lake. A little to the south was the low black wall of the coffer dam that circled the site where an archipelago of tiny islands was being constructed, a last-minute change in the landscaping specifications, and beyond that was the terraced shape of the main island. The lake floor was constructed from the same material as the coffer dam, a thin skin of light and incredibly strong fullerene composite, black and finely striated like muscle, laid over an insulating substructure several metres deep that anchored it to the adamantine ice, shaped and contoured with shallows and slopes, trenches and raised table reefs. It was like running in an enormous, half-full bathtub.

Macy was beginning to sweat now. She pulled off her cap and ran on with her hair streaming behind her like the tail of a rusty comet. Running was much easier than walking in Callisto's low gravity, but changing direction was difficult because you still had the same mass but far less traction; you had to think ahead, make wide arcs around obstacles, and slow down gradually, because attempting a sudden stop was liable to make you tumble head over heels. Bill Highbridge had bruised a couple of ribs when he'd slammed into one of the boulders planted on the ridge of the main island, and Pilgrim Greeley had broken a wrist in a bad fall, but Macy had been running out on the lake bed every morning before breakfast, letting her thoughts settle out, getting ready to tackle whatever problems the day would throw at her, and she swung south easily and smoothly, moving parallel to the edge of the water that each day rose a little higher.

The water filling the lake bed from the centre outward was now about half a kilometre across at its widest point. In another week it would be lapping at either shore, and Macy would have to take her morning constitutional along the rim road. It was already an impressive sight: a broad channel of tawny water agitated by dozens of fast streams feeding it from the infall pipes along either shore, waves running back and forth, clashing in white riffles. There was no shortage of water on Callisto of course—the moon was entirely covered in water ice, a frozen world ocean wrapped around a core of silicate rock—but at around −170° Celsius the ice was hard as granite. To create the lake, it had to be mined and melted, processed to remove sulphur compounds and drive off excess carbon dioxide and add oxygen, and then pumped through kilometres of heated pipes into the biome's chamber. The outfall of one of those pipes jutted from the embankment a few hundred metres away, water steaming as it spewed out in a flurry of foam, the wild smell of it electrifying Macy's blood. The ice had been frozen for billions of years, but all it needed was a little free energy to weaken hydrogen-to-hydrogen bonding and effect a phase change from solid to liquid. Like bringing a fossil back to life.

The three huge machines that mined, processed, and melted the ice, the huge tent that housed the biome, and the biome itself, represented a enormous outlay of engineering, energy, and human work and imagination. Macy was determined to honour the Outers' grandiose plans with her own contribution, but although her skills hummed in her brain and trembled in her fingertips, although she'd spent several hundred hours planning every last detail with the plankton crew and poor Manny Vargo back in Greater Brazil, back on Earth, she'd been having sleepless nights ever since she'd arrived. The dreaminess of the low gravity and the strange taste of the air, the odd noises echoing in the high-ceilinged space in the hollow base of the strut (she had taken to sleeping in the lab), all contributed to her insomnia, but it was mostly due to nagging anxieties about everything and anything that could go wrong. She was ready and willing and able to do the work she had to do, but felt as if she was surfing a standing wave of exultation and apprehension. She was here. She had made it. Yet a single misstep might wipe her out.

And now, on top of everything else, she had to deal with this little job gifted her by Speller Twain and Loc Ifrahim, that smooth-talking smiler. The problem was, Manny Vargo's death might have broken Ursula Freye's heart and made her desperate and more than a little crazy, but the woman was also a crashing snob, stubborn and aloof. No matter how distressed and lonely she might be, she wasn't about to take advice from someone as low-born as Macy, and Macy couldn't think of anyone else in the crew who might help out. Most of them belonged to the Peixoto family, and despite all the exercises designed to unify them during training they'd quickly split into like-minded factions, little groups of three or four that crossed sexes and specialities and excluded outsiders. As for the rest, Cristine Quarrick and Patrick Alan Allard, from the Nabucu family, were married and inhabited a cosy little world of their own making with no time for anyone except themselves, and César Puntareñas was an unsympathetic character who enjoyed playing up to his reputation as a rogue agent.

Macy ran alongside the edge of the lapping water until she reached one of the streams that frothed down a moulded channel a couple of metres wide.

She jumped the channel with ease but landed awkwardly and tumbled head-long, a long sprawling slide that knocked the wind from her lungs. Sitting up, flexing her arms and legs, discovering nothing worse than a scraped palm and what was going to be a spectacular bruise on her behind, she saw one of the little camera drones that infested the biome hanging above the edge of the lake, a fat blimp about a metre long, its underslung camera pointing in her direction. She laughed and gave it the finger, wondering just how many citizens had watched her little pratfall, and then was struck with a notion of how best to reach out to Ursula Freye.

When she got back to the lab, she told her two assistants that she believed that they might be able to help her deal with a little personal business. She put a finger to her lips when they began to question her, led them out of the lab and along the jetty, and said that what she was about to tell them was confidential, they had to swear they wouldn't tell anyone else about it.

The assistants exchanged glances. They were both in their forties but looked about Macy's age, slim and fine-boned, looming over her like a pair of friendly giraffes. Argyll Hall with his paper-white complexion and cockatoo's crest of bright red hair; Loris Sher Yanagita with her bright green eyes, pupils slitted like a cat's. Macy liked both of them. She didn't doubt that they were reporting on her every move, but they were hard-working, competent, and, in their different ways, enthusiastic. Loris was quiet, someone who liked to listen rather than talk, and talked only when she felt that she had something worth saying, but she had an intense, slow-burning ardour for her work; she reminded Macy of the way wildsiders carried fire from camp to camp, smouldering punk caught inside a fold of clay. Argyll was a more vivid character, quick-minded and impulsive, brimming with half-formed ideas, talkative and endlessly curious about how things were done on Earth, and Macy's reactions to the way things were done here. Although Macy tried to appear unshockable, she was shocked, more than a little, by the tweaks Outers made to their bodies. Argyll had spotted this at once, and made a point of letting Macy know all about his little differences from the human norm. Physiological adaptations to microgravity, cellular mechanisms that enhanced repair to radiation damage, speedier reflexes and a ballet dancer's sense of balance, changes in his corpus callosum that enabled him to survive on catnaps for months at a time or enter a sleep as profound as hibernation, and a dozen lesser tweaks, from the reflective membrane at the back of his eyes that increased his night vision to perfect pitch. When Macy had given it back to him, asking why Outers didn't go all the way and grow hands at the ends of their legs instead of feet, Argyll had shrugged and smiled and said that maybe one day they would, and Loris had said, "Have you ever tried walking on your hands all the time? Even in our gravity, it's hard. They just aren't built for it."

"How about tails?" Macy had said, trying to be provocative.

Loris had thought about this for a moment, calm and serious and imperturbable. "I think they tried that in Camelot, Mimas. Of course, the gravity is lower there . . ."

Which had made Macy laugh. She liked Loris. Loris was a lot like her.

Now, before Macy started to explain why she was about to ask them for a very big favour, Argyll jumped right in and said, "I bet this is about Mr. Vargo's murder."

Macy felt a twinge of unease. "Were you eavesdropping, just now? Can people listen to us out here?"

Loris shook her head.

"We guessed," Argyll said. "I mean, it's pretty obvious. What else would that diplomat and the security chief want to talk to you about? So, do they think they know who did it?"

"They don't think it was murder, and neither do I." Macy paused, struck by an uncomfortable thought, then added, "Do people in the city think he was murdered?"

"I think the latest poll has it that around sixty percent believe Mr. Vargo was killed," Argyll said.

"There are polls on this?"

"Anyone can run a poll on anything," Argyll said. "How else can you find out what people are thinking?"

Loris said, "*I* don't think he was murdered, but Argyll does. You should ask him what they're saying on the thread about Mr. Vargo. The conspiracy nuts are having a great time."

Macy said, "I shouldn't tell you what I'm about to tell you, but I need your help. So promise you won't mention this to anyone, on this conspiracy-theory thread or anywhere else. Okay?"

Argyll drew an infinity sign on his chest with his forefinger and said, "Hope to die before I do."

"It means he won't," Loris said. "And neither will I."

"We want to help," Argyll said.

"Let's see if you can," Macy said. "It seems that one of my colleagues has been going out and about in the city. I need to know where she goes, if she's meeting anyone. Don't tell me you can't do it. I know that there are cameras all over the city. And they all feed into the city's net."

She'd decided that the first thing she needed to do was find out if Loc Ifrahim had been telling the truth, find out if Ursula really had gotten herself involved in some kind of clandestine chicanery. If the woman's visits to the city were innocent, if there was nothing to Loc Ifrahim's story but devilment, then Macy could tell him to leave her the hell alone and let her get on with her work. But if she had hard evidence that Ursula was involved with malcontents or hardliners, she could use it as leverage when she confronted the poor woman and tried her damnedest to convince her that they didn't have her best interests at heart.

Argyll looked disappointed, saying, "Is that all?"

Loris said, "Who is she?"

"Ursula Freye," Macy said. "And before you start asking me questions I can't possibly answer, this isn't anything to do with Mr. Vargo's death. It's all about helping a colleague of mine who's gone a little crazy with grief."

5

Two days later Macy rode a tram to the free zone at the northern edge of Rainbow Bridge. She'd visited the city twice before, but each time it had been to attend official functions—a kind of reception where she and the rest of the crew had been exhibited like exotic animals, and a theatre piece involving musicians, dancers, tableaux and projections in what had been billed as an interpretation of universal creation myths. Macy had recognised a couple of fragments from Genesis, but the symbolism of most of the performance had been impenetrable, the music had sounded like a train-wreck, and she'd had a hard time staying awake. So despite her forebodings about the enterprise, she felt an exhilarating mix of anticipation and liberation as she rode through the city on her own.

Rainbow Bridge occupied a froth of pressurised tents and geodesic domes, different sizes. Inside them, low-rise apartment blocks much like those Macy had helped to demolish in the ruins of Chicago were strung along streets radiating out from a central park, scattered at random across parkland, or, in the oldest parts of the city, crammed side by side, their roof gardens connected to each other by slender bridges. There were a few blocks of work-shops for small-scale industries and crafts, but most of the city's factories were located in smaller domes outside the city's cluster, amongst vacuum organism farms and refineries. The tram carried Macy through woods and meadows, down the centres of wide tree-lined streets. She got off at the last stop and put on the spex that the city had given her after she'd been woken from hiber-nation. Argyll had shown her how to use the navigation function, and its vir-tual display set a series of fat red arrows floating in the air that winked out one by one as, trailed by two drones, she followed them along a white gravel path between two- and three-storey apartment blocks with narrow gardens on set-back terraces and balconies hung with flowering vines or shaggy waterfalls of mosses and ferns. It was late in the evening. The panes of the dome polarised black, paths lit by tiny biolamps like green stars and a few dim street lights, and not many people about, for which Macy was thankful. She was dressed in a costume borrowed from Loris, baggy shorts and a pale blue T-shirt that hung to her knees, but most passersby seemed to recognise her as she ankled along, and several stopped her to ask her how she liked their city, or simply to say hello.

The last of the red arrows winked out as she stepped onto the escalator that carried her down into the city's free zone. One of the drones that had fol-lowed her across the city angled away; the other, no doubt run by Speller Twain, parked itself in the air at the head of the escalator, vanishing from sight as Macy descended.

Everyone knew everyone else's business in the city. It was a small, crowded place, and as in all the city-states and settlements of the Outer System, which preserved democratic traditions long vanished on Earth, there was a custom of public candour and open access to surveillance systems and every kind of stored information. At least half the population posted unflinching details of their everyday lives on the net; everyone expressed opinions about anything and everything; anyone could attempt to gain any public position by participating in popularity contests, and the winners of those contests had to facilitate decisions arrived at through a combination of public debate and expert advice, and took part in regular question-and-answer sessions about their work. This tradition of open exchange of informa-tion was giving the construction crew all kinds of problems. Hundreds of people visited the biome every day. They picnicked on the main island, flew kites, watched the water level in the lake rise centimetre by centimetre, wandered in and out of labs and worksuites and pestered the crew with pointless questions about Earth and their work. Yesterday, while taking a short stroll along the rim road before supper, Macy had been accosted by an earnest young man who'd had plenty of ideas about what she was doing wrong. She'd only just been able to keep her temper while she countered his points one by one. Others were having a harder time dealing with the inexhaustible curiosity of the Outers; Cristine Quarrick had lashed out with considerable verbal inventiveness at a little girl who'd come up to her and asked her why she was so ugly, the girl had burst into tears, and everything had been caught by a passing drone and had nearly caused a diplomatic incident.

The city's free zone was the only place where its citizens had any privacy. There were no cameras in the free zone; nothing that accessed or fed into the net. All the city's ordinances, apart from those covering basic human rights, were suspended. After putting a data miner to work in the records of the city's camera system, Argyll had discovered that Ursula Freye visited the zone each and every day. Usually she spent an hour or two there before returning to the biome, although sometimes she came out only a few minutes after she'd gone in, and once she'd stayed the night. No wonder Loc Ifrahim had been so vague when Macy had asked him who Ursula had been talking to; no wonder he and Speller Twain were so anxious to put a stop to it. Ursula had found the one place where no one could spy on her. Where the citizens would respect her privacy. Where Macy would have to go if she wanted to find out what the woman was up to, who she met with, what she talked about.

Macy had escaped from the Church of the Divine Regression and survived the gangs and cops in the slums of Pittsburgh, as well as numerous encounters with wildsiders and bandits in the borderlands: she was pretty sure that she could play this situation and come out in front. Even so, she felt a flutter of apprehension as she rode the escalator down into the free zone. She really hoped that this didn't have anything to do with Ursula Freye's determination to root out the truth about Manny Vargos's death, that Ursula was visiting the zone because she was looking for something clean and simple like sex or drugs, some release from her unreasoning grief.

It was always night, down there in the zone. A broad avenue followed the curve of the tent's coping wall, intermittently illuminated by multicoloured holos and neon. There were people wearing body-enveloping cloaks and masks, people wearing nothing but morph paint, patterns and images drifting across their bare skins like clouds, but most were dressed in the colourful tatterdemalion clothing that passed for everyday wear in the city.

Short backless jackets like yokes, jackets with rubber spikes or armoured plates, jackets patched from feathers or fur, ruched and intricately pleated shirts and cut-off kimonos that shimmered like water or mercury, kilts, baggy shorts, tights with ridiculous codpieces, plain shifts . . .

Some of them, recognising Macy and surprised to see her there, broke protocol and stared openly. She stared right back. She didn't feel in the least bit intimidated. Compared to the brawling streets of Pittsburgh, the zone seemed as artificial and safe as a children's playground. She passed body-mod shops, wireshops, smokehouses, meat markets where citizens bought or sold or gave away all kinds of sex. Even on the main drag, at least half the places were no more than recessed doors that gave away nothing about what went on inside. Others stood under gaudy and elaborate signs. The Gilded Palace of Sin. Fight Club. Lies, Inc. There were vanilla bars and restaurants, too. Macy hit those first, found Ursula Freye in the third place she checked out, a bar that called itself Jack Frost.

The name glowed red inside a holo of a melting block of ice hung above a narrow doorway. Macy followed two men into a passage hung with fur coats. They had to be artificial, cultured or machine-made, but the sight of them hanging in dense rows gave Macy a little shock. She had to swallow her queasiness before she could emulate the men she'd followed and pull on one of the soft, heavy furs and push through the rest into a dimly-lit cave.

It was freezing cold, covered in ice. A floor of rough black ice, booths and tables carved from ice dyed different shades of red, ribbed ice walls and a low ceiling supported by columns of fused giant icicles in which scattered lights shone like dim, frozen stars. Tinkling music hung in the air, delicate as smoke. Robots shaped like squashed crabs crawled over the ceiling and around and about the icicles, taking orders, scurrying off, returning to lower with whiplike tentacles drinks and tiny plates of food to table tops. The decor and dim lighting confused the transition between the interior and video windows displaying views of the moonscape outside the city.

It was only the second time that Macy had seen the surface of Callisto. She stepped toward one of the windows and its view of a cratered plain stretched to a horizon curved sharp and clean against a black sky where Jupiter's banded disc hung like a marvellously detailed brooch, didn't notice Ursula Freye until the woman walked toward her through the cone of light cast by the old-fashioned lamp post (exactly like one Macy had once seen in the preserved section of Pittsburgh) that stood in a continuous flurry of snow at the centre of the bar.

"It was Mr. Twain, wasn't it?" Ursula Freye said.

Macy nodded. She had decided to be as candid as possible, hoping that Ursula would be candid in return. "Him and Loc Ifrahim."

"The diplomat?"

"Yup. He did the talking and Speller Twain hung around in the background, flexing his muscles."

Ursula Freye thought about this for a moment. She and Macy were sitting on the fur-covered bench of a booth now. Two of Ursula's companions had left without speaking a word. The third sat next to Ursula, robed in a hooded floor-length white fur coat and, like the two who'd left, wearing a mask, this one in the form of a fox's sharp-snouted features.

At last Ursula said, "When he asked you to talk to me . . . did you get the impression that it was government business, or something else?"

"That's what I've been wondering," Macy said. "He seemed to imply that it wasn't exactly official. That he wanted to do you a favour. To talk to you, tell you—"

"I know what he wants to tell me. What did he tell you?"

"Only that you were meeting with people who could cause trouble." Macy looked across the table at the robed, fox-faced person who sat beside Ursula. "No offence. He said that, not me."

Fox-face didn't reply, but for a chilling moment the mask's amber gaze seemed to swallow Macy whole. It was uncannily realistic, every hair on the muzzle (white on the underjaw, auburn above) in place, every whisker. Its black lips were slightly parted, revealing a hint of sharp white teeth.

Ursula said, "Mr. Ifrahim told you that I was meeting with people. Did he tell you anything else?"

"He said that it could compromise the project."

"Do you believe him?"

"I don't trust him."

"You realise that you can be arrested for intruding on my privacy," Ursula said. "That's one of the few things that *is* against the law down here. I could cause all kinds of trouble for you, Ms. Minnot. And if I did, I expect Mr. Ifrahim and Mr. Twain would let you take the fall."

"That would only be fair," Macy said, feeling a warmth growing on her forehead and cheeks despite the chilly air, "because it was my idea to come here, not theirs. I thought we could talk freely here. But if all you want to do is threaten me, then fine, I'll go."

"And what will you tell your friends?"

"They're not my friends. I'll tell them that you didn't want to talk to me about whatever it is you're doing down here. That if they want to find out they'll have to come talk to you themselves."

"Do you think they will be satisfied with that?"

"I doubt it. But if they ask me to do anything else, I'll tell them that maybe I need to talk to Mr. Peixoto about it first. Get it all out in the open."

"And is *that* a threat?"

Sitting straightbacked in a black fur coat, shining blonde hair combed and neatly parted into wings that slanted either side of her face, Ursula Freye didn't looked in any way touched by grief or craziness. She looked cool, utterly self-possessed. She was more than twice Macy's age, but her skin was unlined and porcelain-perfect apart from tender pouches under her eyes, and her sharp blue gaze was lively and acute. Back on Earth, she could have had Macy flogged or jailed for insubordination. Or flogged *and* jailed, for that matter. But this wasn't Earth, they were sitting at the heart of a zone where ordinary rules had been suspended, and Macy felt emboldened.

"Whatever you're doing here is your business," she said. "And as long as it stays here I'd have no reason to tell Mr. Peixoto or anyone else about it. But if it affects the project, then it affects all of us."

"Have you ever been in love, Ms. Minnot?"

Macy hesitated for only a moment. She had decided to be candid, and as long as she could keep Ursula talking she might learn something. "There was a boy once. We thought we were in love for a little while."

"What happened?"

"I wanted to do better than scuffling a living in the streets, looked into joining the R&R Corps. Jax said no way he was going to leave Pittsburgh. It was where he grew up. It was all he knew. So . . ."

"You went your way, and left him behind."

Macy shrugged. "Something like that."

She remembered how she and Jax had argued about it for most of that summer. Finally, Jax had told her to do what she wanted, just as long as they didn't have to talk about it any more. She'd signed up the next day. By the time she shipped out for basic training, two weeks later, she and Jax had broken up. And then she'd been so busy, learning Corps discipline, how to use a gun and a pickaxe, that she hadn't had time to think of him that much, although she had wondered now and then, in the brief quiet time between lights-out and sleep, if he ever thought of her.

Ursula Freye said, "If you loved him, you would have stayed with him."

"We were both pretty young."

Ursula looked somewhere else for a few seconds, then pressed the button set in the centre of the table and told the robot that responded to the call that she wanted two brandies. Looking at her silent, fox-faced companion, saying, "Unless you want one too."

The figure shook its head once, right to left.

"One thing I know," Ursula said to Macy. "You don't choose to fall in love. It's something that happens to you, like a wonderful accident. I didn't plan to fall in love with Manny or anyone else on the crew. But it happened the first time we saw each other, right at the beginning of talks between our family and the Peixotos. It caused a political problem and it caused me all kinds of personal problems too. But it happened. People I thought were close to me, my friends, tried to get me to resign from the project or promise to stop seeing Manny. But I wasn't going to give him up, there was no one else of my rank remotely qualified to join the crew, and I was able to persuade the people who mattered that I was still loyal to the family, and that my relationship with Manny would help forge a closer alliance with the Peixotos. It caused Manny a fair amount of grief, too. Although he had already done most of the design work on the biome there were people in the Peixoto family who wanted to throw him off the project. But Oscar Finnegan Ramos had the final word on that, and he said let it be. So it worked out. We stayed together, and we came here. But if Manny had been forced to quit, I would have quit too. It wouldn't have been easy, because I would have had to go against the wishes of my family, but I would have done it. And now I wish that he *had* been forced to quit . . ."

There was a scratching noise overhead as the robot returned. It lowered two balloon glasses with swift precision, retracted its tentacles, scuttled away. Ursula Freye cupped her glass in both hands and raised it to her face and breathed in the fumes of the little puddle of amber liquid before drinking. After a moment, Macy took the smallest possible sip from her own glass. It was good stuff, a whole universe away from the jackleg liquor that R&R crews brewed from sugar and wild apples or cherries. Smoothly coating her tongue with a biting sweetness, burning a hot wire to her stomach.

"I'm going to tell you something that you can pass on to Mr. Twain and Mr. Ifrahim," Ursula said, sounding like a boss for the first time since she'd surprised Macy, decisive and definite. "They already know about it, but they didn't trouble to tell you. So if you tell them about it, they'll know that you really did talk to me. You understand?"

"Before we go any further, maybe you can tell me who your friend is."

"I can't do that. And really, you should know better than to ask. It's not just horribly rude down here; it's also illegal. What I want you to do now is listen carefully. Because I'm going to tell you why I know that Manny was killed."

"Okay."

"After I was told that Manny had died, I asked to see his body. And that's when I found out that something was wrong. I found out," Ursula said, looking straight at Macy, "that his slate had gone missing. And I knew right away that someone had killed him. They killed him, and they took his slate."

Macy waited, hunched in her heavy fur coat, cradling her balloon glass of brandy, feeling the cold of the ice table on the backs of her hands, the heat of her own blood on her face. Feeling that she had stepped over the edge of something.

"There are at least three different ways he could have been killed," Ursula said. "Someone could have sabotaged his hibernation coffin, or spiked him with drugs, or with a failed form of neuronal therapy that causes damage very similar to CND . . . Well, the details don't matter right now. All that matters is that Manny was murdered, and his slate was stolen."

"Do Mr. Ifrahim and Mr. Twain know that it's missing?"

Ursula nodded. "And if you tell them that I told you about it, they'll know that you talked to me. That you did what they asked you to do."

"I guess I should ask you what you're planning to do about it."

"Would you tell your two friends about it if I did?"

"If you tell me, sure. Why not? You're telling me what you want them to hear, aren't you?"

Ursula studied Macy for a moment, a smile touching her lips, gone. "I believe they may have underestimated you."

"I'm counting on it."

"Perhaps you think that I am crazy. That I have constructed a paranoid fantasy because I can't accept that Manny's death was a tragic accident. Oh, I wouldn't blame you if you did. I admit that I wasn't especially rational back then, and I can't have made a good impression when I burst into that meeting and vented my frustration. But I am rational now. I am utterly calm. And I know what I know. Part of what I do, a large part of it, is to locate and define places where emergent phenomena might arise from the interaction of two or more ecological parameters. In other words, I'm very good at spotting patterns before they have fully formed. So if you think that I'm seeing a conspiracy where none exists, let me assure you that it's as real as this glass," Ursula said, finishing off her brandy in a quick swallow and setting the glass down on the slab of black ice and sitting back, fixing Macy with a bright, starry gaze. "Maximilian Peixoto did so much to make sure that this project would be a success, and he died a few days before we arrived here. Our chief supporter in the European Union, Val-Jean Couperin, also died. And now Manny . . . They could have killed all of us, of course. Blown up the ship that brought us here, say, or the shuttle that took us up to the ship. But that would have been too obvious. Mass murder. There would have been a massive investigation, and it might have uncovered their identity. And at the moment, the enemies of the alliance between Greater Brazil and the Outer Colonies very much want to work under cover. They are not ready to reveal themselves because it would be a declaration of war. And they do not yet have the means to go to war."

A deep, purring voice said, "There will be no war."

Macy started. It was the fur-robed, fox-faced figure who had spoken. She realised that the person wearing the mask must be subvocalising through a throat patch that disguised his or her voice, but the effect was uncanny nonetheless.

"There will be no war if we can help it," Ursula said.

A silence stretched, and when it became clear that fox-face was not going to say anything else Ursula took up the thread of her argument again.

"When I was told that Manny had died during revival, I thought at once that it could have been murder. Because if they hoped to damage the project by killing one of us, Manny was the obvious target. He was the ecosystem engineer. He oversaw the design of every detail of the biome's ecosystem. He was responsible for recruiting and training the crew. And it was his will and personality that welded us into a single unit. But I couldn't be *sure* that he had been murdered until I found out that his slate was missing. Then I knew. I knew that they had killed him, not just because of who he was but because his slate contained something that his killers wished to keep hidden. Not the plans of the ecosystem. There are plenty of copies of those. I have a full set, fully annotated. So does Euclides. And people here in the city also have copies. No, they killed him because, even though he didn't know it, he was close to finding something they wanted to remain hidden."

"You don't know what it could be," Macy said. "This hidden thing."

"I have several ideas, of course. But no evidence pointing toward one or another."

"And you don't know who . . ."

"There are plenty of candidates. It could be someone in the Peixoto family who wants to diminish the considerable power of Oscar Finnegan Ramos. It could be a pro-war anti-Outer faction in one of the other Brazilian families, or the families of the Pacific Community or the European Union. Not to mention the numerous factions in the city states of the Outer Colonies that want nothing at all to do with Earth . . . At this point, it doesn't matter who did it. It only matters *why* they did it. And that's where you can help me, Ms. Minnot. I won't ask if you are loyal to our family. I know very well that most of the people in our territory aren't. But are you loyal to this crew, to what Manny was trying to build? Do you want it to succeed?"

"That's why I'm here. For the crew. The project." Macy was having a hard time meeting Ursula Freye's starry gaze. She knew what was coming and she dreaded it and she didn't know how to stop it.

"I have made friends here," Ursula said. "You and I want this project and all it stands for to succeed. So do they. I want to help them. And you can help them too."

"I'm here because I was told that you might be putting the project at risk," Macy said.

"And you can see that it's quite otherwise."

"I see no such thing. I'm sorry, but I don't. All I see is someone chasing after something that might not exist—"

"It exists. You will help me prove that it exists."

"You know something?" Macy said. "You're just like them. Like Loc Ifrahim and Speller Twain. They want to use me to get at you. You want to use me to get at them."

"I understand that I am putting you in a delicate position—"

"I don't think you understand it at all," Macy said, so loudly that the group of Outers at the next table, bulked like seals in their fur coats, turned to look at her. She hardly noticed, transported by a sudden rush of anger. "People like you, you don't see how it is for people like me. You float above it all. As far as you're concerned, life is effortless. But people like me, we're down in the muck. When things go wrong, we're the ones who suffer. We're the ones who get hurt. You have a whim: we pay for it."

She felt her pulse beat in her head, felt a giddiness that was nothing to do with the exiguous gravity. She didn't care, at that moment, what Ursula Freye did to her. This was the free zone, wasn't it? Well, she'd spoken freely.

Ursula surprised her. She laughed, a delicate, girlish chime, and said,

"You really don't have any idea, do you? You think that I'm free to do what I want? My whole life has been shaped by service to the family. The same family that protects you, makes sure that you have a job, food, shelter . . . All my life, I've done what I was told; what was best for the family. All my life, until I met Manny, and fell in love. We fell in love. We weren't supposed to, but we did," Ursula said, looking down at Macy from the remote height of her desolation.

After a moment, the fox-faced person spoke. "We will get to the bottom of it, Ursula."

"And that's another thing," Macy said. "Why should I consider for even a second helping out someone who won't even show their face?"

"This isn't about you and it isn't about me," Ursula told her. "It's about the project. It's about Manny. I know you respected him. I know you know that he was the heart and soul of this project. If there's even a remote chance that he was murdered, don't you think it's worth following through?"

"Believe me, we would prefer not to ask you to do this," Fox-face said. "But it is the only way forward. It may be the only way to save the project."

Macy's first impulse was to get up and walk away. But she was in enemy territory, she didn't know how many people in the bar, the free zone, the whole strange, low-rise city, were involved in this. She had been given privileged information and there was no telling what might happen if she didn't agree to help. So she took a deep breath, and said, "All right. I guess I'm fucked if I do and fucked if I don't, so tell me what you want and I'll see what I can do. For the sake of the project. Nothing else."

"It isn't anything," Ursula said. "Really it isn't. All I need are copies of the records and logs of everything that has been done since the crew started work on the biome. I can use them to run a dynamic reconstruction and integrate it. Look for emergent patterns, conjunctions—anything that might hint at potential sabotage."

"I thought you already had all that stuff. I mean, you're the economist. Don't you need it to do your work?"

"I have been locked out of the crew's database by Mr. Twain. If I need anything, I have to go through him. He's watching me, Macy. He downloaded a spy into my slate—for my own protection, he said. And he follows me everywhere. Everywhere but here. But you can do it, and besides, it really isn't anything. All you have to do is access the database and make a copy of the work logs and pass them to me. That won't be so hard, will it?"

6

It was all nonsense, Macy thought as she rode the tram through the night-time city back to the biome. She was angry and anxious and scared, and now that the ordeal was over, anger was winning out. It was all nonsense. All of it. There was no conspiracy. Manny Vargo had died because of some awful but unambiguous medical accident. There were a thousand reasons why his slate could have gone missing, from bureaucratic error to simple theft. And Ursula Freye had taken those two completely unrelated facts, her lover's death and the missing slate, and had forced a connection, and had kept adding other connections, selecting what suited her and rejecting anything contradictory until she'd caged herself in a paranoid fantasy.

And she wants to put me in that cage, Macy thought. She and her fox-faced friend. Speller Twain and that devious little creep Loc Ifrahim. They all want to use me in this joint fantasy of theirs.

She had agreed to make a copy of the work logs because at the time it had seemed to be the only way she'd get out of the free zone in one piece. Ursula Freye's craziness was catching. But now the implications of that promise were sinking through her, and she felt that she'd been caught in a trap. Making a copy didn't present any practical problems; apart from Ursula Freye, everyone on the crew had access to them, and they weren't copy-protected. But if Macy ripped a copy of the logs to a data needle, Speller Twain would most definitely want to know why, so she'd have to go to him first, explain what Ursula wanted, ask his permission to do it . . .

Well, Speller Twain and Loc Ifrahim would no doubt want to talk to her anyway, find out what Ursula had said to her. There was nothing she could do about it until then, and she hoped they'd veto the idea at once, tell her there was absolutely no way they were going to let her feed Ursula's fantasies by giving her a copy of the logs. Because then she could go back to Ursula and explain that she'd been denied access too, and that would be that.

Meanwhile, she still had her own work to do.

After a restless night, Macy got up early and ate a bowl of microwaved porridge and sipped lukewarm coffee (atmospheric pressure in the tent was just six hundred millibars, significantly reducing the boiling point of water) while studying the results of growth experiments using the problematical

Skeletonema cultures that Argyll Hall and Loris Sher Yanagita had finished up last night, while she'd been off wasting her time playing silly spy games. The data pointed to a clear and simple conclusion: the lag in growth rates of the *Skeletonema* diatom could be overcome by adding supplemental phosphate to the melt water. The simplest explanation was that natural levels of the macronutrient were somehow limiting growth of the diatom, although cultures of the other microorganisms were growing well and showed no deficiencies. Or it could be that there was a problem with the *Skeletonema* culture— it had mutated and acquired a kink in a key metabolic pathway. Still, Macy decided that it wouldn't hurt to investigate if something in the melt water, most likely the suspended clay fines, was binding phosphate and making it unavailable, and she was working up the experimental protocol when Speller Twain glided in, moving smoothly and quickly for such a big man, telling her that he wanted a word.

"Speak your mind," Macy said, trying to sound as cool as possible.

As usual, the security chief was wearing green coveralls with the sleeves torn off, a black rubber bag hitched high on his broad shoulders. He looked around at the cluttered benches, looked up at the cameras strung amongst the lights hanging from the high ceiling.

"Not here," he said, and steered Macy to the smallest of the store cubicles and told her to close her eyes tight.

She squeezed them shut and something bright went off, a flash that printed the blood vessels of her eyelids on her retina.

"There are cameras you know about," Speller Twain said, "and there are cameras you don't know about, the ones their so-called peace officers planted. That little flash will have taken care of anything, sound and vision."

He sat on a drum of powdered growth medium, told Macy to sit on another, and said, "You know why I'm here."

"I did what you and Mr. Ifrahim asked. I met her. I told her—"

"Let's get you wired up first," Speller Twain said, and pulled a stiff black handkerchief from his bag and asked Macy if she knew what it was.

It was a magnetic resonance imaging cap. Macy had worn one once before, back when she'd been a labourer, at an inquiry into the deaths of five of her workmates after bandits had tried to overrun their site. It measured activity in Broca's area and Wernicke's area, the regions in the left hemisphere of the brain that controlled linguistic ability. There was heightened activity in the two regions when you answered a question, synchronised if you told the truth, showing millisecond differences if you lied or dissembled.

"There's no need for this," Macy said. "I want to tell you what happened."

"Let's hope you do. Hold still."

The cap adjusted to the contours of Macy's skull, applying an unpleasant grip across her forehead and ears to the nape of her neck. Speller Twain took out a slate, shook it into stiffness with a practised flick of the wrist, and studied the images transmitted by the cap while showing Macy a series of simple geometric patterns on flash cards and asking her anodyne questions to establish baseline brain activity.

"We're good to go," he said at last. "Tell your story, and don't leave anything out. I'll know if you do."

Macy gave a brief account of her meeting with Ursula Freye, and the security chief questioned her closely, digging up all kinds of things she didn't know she remembered. He was especially interested in Ursula Freye's companions.

"They wore these big fur coats like everyone else in the bar, and they were masked," Macy said. Sitting knee to knee with this big man who seemed to take up most of the cramped space, cramming her into a corner, she felt a crushing claustrophobia. His square, solemn face unreadable. His gaze dark and cold and unblinking. "I didn't see their faces and I didn't see their hands, either, so I can't tell you what their skin colour was, or make a guess at how old they were. I don't even know what *sex* they were."

"But you said that they were Outers."

"I guess they were. The one who stayed behind was pretty tall. Taller than you, I think. The two who left weren't much bigger than me, but that doesn't mean they weren't Outers. They could have been first-generation, or even pioneers. I mean, there are still plenty of pioneers alive, aren't there?"

"'I guess' isn't good enough. I need hard facts," Speller Twain said, and stuck two fingers in the breast pocket of his coveralls and lifted out a bright red drug patch and peeled off the backing with a fingernail.

Macy said, "Now wait just a minute, you can't—"

"Yes I can."

Speller Twain caught her when she tried to stand, pushed her down with one hand and slapped the patch onto her temple with the other, effortlessly fending off her attempts to pluck it off as a slack numbness spread through her body.

"All right," he said, after a little while. "Why don't you tell me the name of the first person who fucked you?"

Macy didn't want to answer, but the words bubbled up like marsh gas and she couldn't help blurting them out. "Jax. Jax Spano. And fuck you for doing this."

"Fuck you right back," Speller Twain said evenly, studying his slate. "You Fontaines, you think your shit doesn't stink like everyone else's. Let me tell you that it does. We'll go through it again. From the beginning."

They went through it again, from the moment Macy had stepped onto the escalator and descended into the free zone, to the ride on the tram back to the park's dome. Speller Twain and the room seemed to recede to a great distance and she heard herself talking about things she had no memory of seeing or hearing. It seemed that the two people who'd left when she'd met with Ursula Freye had moved in the gliding way characteristic of people born and raised in Callisto's low gravity, and had been wearing Outer-style slippers. One pair patched together with differently coloured felts, the other woven from strips of plastic. Maybe these were false memories, or nothing more than a drug fantasy, Macy didn't really care, and at Speller Twain's prompting babbled on, giving word-for-word accounts of the conversation with Ursula and her fox-faced companion.

At last, the big man leaned back and said, "Just one more thing I need to know. Why did you follow her to that bar? Why go to all that trouble when you could talk to her right here?"

"I wanted to catch her out. And I thought she would talk more freely if there weren't any cameras around."

"What else?"

"I didn't want you to spy on me."

"Didn't work, did it?" Speller Twain said. "Don't worry. I'm not mad at you. You gave me what I needed to know. What you can do now is sit tight. I need to figure out the next move, so don't do anything else until you hear from me."

He stripped the cap from Macy's head and rolled up his slate, then speared another patch from his breast pocket, a white one this time, and with surprising delicacy stuck it on Macy's left temple.

"The antidote," he said, and stood up, slung the bag over his shoulder, and opened the door of the little storeroom.

"Wait," Macy said. "Ursula wants me to make her a copy of the work logs. What should I do?"

"I already told you," Speller Twain said. "I don't want you to do anything unless I tell you to. And don't talk to anyone about this. I don't need to tell you what will happen if you do, do I?"

Then he was gone. When Macy stood up, a ripe wave of nausea flushed through her. She made the bathroom just in time. Afterward, she stripped off her sweat-soaked coveralls and underwear, showered, put on fresh clothes and pulled the tab from a fresh cup of coffee. It took a while to drink it: she couldn't stop her hands from trembling.

Macy was working on another cup of coffee, her third, when her assistants came in. She told them that she'd gotten drunk with Ursula Freye in a bar in the free zone and had sorted out some family business, she was grateful for their help but everything was fine now, they needed to get down to some serious work. Argyll and Loris seemed to accept these lies with equanimity and Macy found that she was envious of their innocence, the simplicity of their lives in a city where everything was out in the open and nothing was hidden. Where people were more or less equal, where there were no bosses, no secret policemen who trapped you in a closet and mind-raped you. Where sin was an option on a menu displayed in a theme-park red-light district, and never followed you home.

She explained her thoughts about the *Skeletonema* problem, and they had a conference with the leader of the plankton team, Cristine Quarrick, who agreed to run a complete DNA and proteome profile of the diatom, paying special attention to half a hundred key enzymes and the genes that coded for them. Meanwhile, Macy and her assistants would try to find some time to run some simple experiments to check the diatom's phosphate uptake system and investigate nutrient binding in the melt water, but first there were the usual housekeeping tasks to be done.

Late that afternoon, they were working amongst the giant tubes and open vats of the bioreactors, taking samples to measure the viability and composition of the various cultures, when Loc Ifrahim called Macy. She ankled away from Loris and Argyll and put on her spex, and the young diplomat smiled at her from a virtual window that seemed to hang a metre from her face.

"I won't take up much of your time. I know that you are very busy."

"I'm also all out of favours."

"I'm not asking for a favour, Macy. I am asking for cooperation."

"And if I don't show willing, Speller Twain will pay me another visit. I know the drill, Mr. Ifrahim. Why don't you just tell me what you want me to do?"

Loc Ifrahim's smile was a work of art, solicitous, sympathetic, and about a millimetre deep. "You have much to do before the opening ceremony, and you're worried that this will take up valuable time. But don't worry. What we'd like you to do is very simple, and won't interfere with your work in any way. You told Mr. Twain that Ursula Freye wants to examine the work logs. She cannot access the database because Mr. Twain has suspended her privileges for the duration. Quite legitimately, of course, because she could be tempted to hack into it and alter the data to suit her fantasy. So she asked you to make a copy for her. That's all I want you to do."

"You're giving me permission to do this."

"I can hardly do that; I have no authority over anyone in the construction crew. No, all I can do is ask you to do this out of goodwill, for the best interests of the project. After you give Ms. Freye the logs, you see, she will analyse them and find nothing in them to confirm her fantasies of conspiracy and sabotage. And that, hopefully, will bring this unfortunate matter to a close."

"What if she's right? What if she does find something?"

"You are worried about blowback. There's no need. Three biome economists back on Earth have checked this data set independently, and none of them found anything untoward. All you have to do, Macy, is give her the logs and walk away."

"Give her the logs and walk away. That's it?"

"That's it."

"Does Mr. Twain know about this?"

"We have discussed it extensively. He agrees with me that this is the best course of action. In fact, he believes that it is essential. He was most insistent on that point. And I know that he is an impatient man who doesn't like to be kept waiting. So, Macy, I think that you had better do it sooner rather than later, yes? And don't forget to tell him when it's done," Loc Ifrahim said, and cut the connection.

Macy walked out along the jetty, thinking things through. The first lesson she'd learned after signing up to the R&R Corps was that keeping a low profile was an essential survival strategy. Obey orders, don't ask questions, never make a smart remark. Do your work, mind your own business, and most of all, never, ever get involved in disputes between your superiors, because if you do you'll most likely end up as collateral damage. Well, she thought, she'd been shoved straight over that line now. She was in bandit country, walking a narrow path toward an unclear destination with all kinds of unknown dangers lurking in the bushes on either side and no possibility of retreat. If she refused to do this little favour, Speller Twain would come after her, and at best she'd be looking at charges of insubordination, wrecking, and anything else he could throw at her. But if she went through with it, she couldn't be sure where it would lead; Loc Ifrahim's assurance that she wouldn't have to do anything else after she gave Ursula a copy of the work logs was about as much use as a bucket of warm spit . . .

She wished that she could talk about this with someone. She wished that she could let Argyll and Loris know what was going down, maybe ask for their help again, but she couldn't risk letting them know that there was something rotten at the heart of the crew. They were bound to ask all kinds of impossible questions, and if word got back to Loc Ifrahim or Speller Twain she'd be in even more trouble.

Well, maybe she didn't have any choice about giving Ursula a copy of the work logs, Macy thought, but she was damned if she was going to skulk around any more. So while Argyll and Loris finished their work on the cultures in the bioreactors, she downloaded a full copy of the work logs to a data needle and set off for the main island, where most of the crew were based.

The gentle contours of the island had already been landscaped, with broad green lawns spread either side of a central ridge planted with a nascent forest of stone pine, Monterey cypress, maiten, and boldo. Big chunks of dark green and black pyroxene rock, veined with crystals of shock-activated glass, stood amongst the young trees along the top of the ridge like scales on a dragon's back. All the plants had been force-grown in farm tubes from seeds and seedlings imported from Earth, tweaked to grow in the biome's relatively low light levels, and transplanted according to the designs of Artemis Lampathakis and Aurelio Ochoa, who had based the ecoarchitecture of the biome on the dry and temperate climate of Cordillera de la Costa on the Pacific coast of Greater Brazil. Evergreen trees and flowering scrub along the shores of the lake; a desert apron beyond the southern end, yet to be planted out with cacti and agaves and clumps of Washington palms.

The crew's living quarters and main worksuite were housed in a flat-roofed building at the northern end of the island, near the entrance to the railway that linked the biome with the city. The worksuite was open-plan, with islands of couches and chairs and memo spaces, a long table where the crew gathered every few days to talk about progress and snags. Tall picture-windows along one side looked out across a channel, almost completely flooded now, to a promenade along the western shore and apartment buildings tucked under the hem of the tent. Macy stalked down the length of the worksuite until she saw Ursula Freye, curled catlike in a sling chair with a slate in her lap and papers spread out on the half-life grass floor around her. Ursula looking up as Macy came over, starting to say something.

"Here's what you asked me to get," Macy said loudly, and threw the data needle at Ursula.

It struck Ursula above her small breasts and fell onto the lighted screen of her slate. Ursula picked it up and called after Macy, who was already striding away, feeling her face heat up as everyone in the worksuite turned to look at her.

But at least it was done, and she'd done it right out in the open in front of plenty of witnesses—no skulking around, no secrets, nothing to conceal.

7

Macy immersed herself in her work, staying in her lab as much as possible so that she wouldn't run into either Ursula Freye or Speller Twain, and tried to forget about what had happened. Tried to forget that Speller Twain could come back at any time and do whatever he wanted to her. Ursula Freye was protected by her consanguinity, but the security chief had demonstrated that Macy was just a grunt whose life and career were at the mercy of the whims of her superiors.

One piece of good news: Cristine Quarrick discovered that the *Skeletonema* cells weren't producing enough copies of the transport protein that bound phosphate ions externally and then pumped them across the cell membrane, which seriously reduced the diatom's ability to take up the nutrient at ambient levels in the melt water and was almost certainly the explanation for the low growth rates. Cristine used a transcriber to manufacture loops of DNA containing the genes that coded for transport protein production and added them to a small sample of *Skeletonema* cells via an off-the-shelf retrovirus, and this treatment ramped up doubling time and photosynthetic efficiency close to optimal levels. Producing enough retrovirus to infect the mass cultures of the diatom would cause a slight delay in production, but it wasn't serious. A matter of days, not weeks. They could easily get it done before the opening ceremony was scheduled to take place, and that was all that mattered.

When Macy asked Cristine if she had gotten around to doing a complete genomic analysis of the diatom, Cristine said, "The genes for phosphate transport proteins are there, if that's what you mean. They just aren't expressing properly for some reason."

"I was wondering if it was something that could be fixed more easily than adding extra copies of the genes."

"The problem *is* fixed," Cristine said, a sharp edge entering her voice. She was a brisk, brittle woman who didn't take kindly to any hint of criticism. "And I have plenty of work to do without making more work."

So Macy could put that problem to one side, and get on with growing up her own cultures of microorganisms. She discussed tweaks and snags in the quickening of the marsh ecosystem with Tito Puntarenas and Delmy March. She supervised the draining of a bioreactor where blood-warm temperature and the activity of more than three hundred species of bacteria and microalgae and protists had quickened a slurry of smectite clay fines and carbonaceous material into rich black living mud. Argyll and his father, a languid, nut-brown centenarian, one of the Outer System's best soil chemists, had helped Macy modify methods routinely used on Earth for the base materials available on Callisto, mostly minerals derived from palagonitised basalts mined from impact craters. Macy had learned a lot, and had been very impressed by the tour that Argyll's father, Jael Laudrisen Hall, had given her of the facility where topsoil was manufactured. It was far more difficult than making mud. Soil was not a random mixture of inorganic, organic and living material; it was highly structured at every level, fractally so. Stratified and textured and dynamic, it supported a myriad complex chemical reactions that were still not completely understood, mediated by soil water and air moving through pore spaces that occupied up to fifty percent of soil by volume. Soil water also transported material through processes such as leaching, eluviation, illuviation and capillary action, and supported a rich and highly diverse biota—hundreds of varieties of soil bacteria of course, and cyanobacteria, microalgae, fungi, and protists, as well as nematodes and worms, and insects and other small arthropods—that recycled macro- and micro-nutrients, decomposed organic material, and mixed and transported and aerated mineral and organic components. In natural conditions on Earth, it took about four hundred years to produce a centimetre of topsoil; a thousand years to produce enough to support agriculture. A significant proportion of the work of the Reclamation and Reconstruction Corps had been concerned with replacement of topsoil lost by erosion caused by overfarming, or poisoned by industry during the twentieth and twenty-first centuries, or stripped away by floods and hyperstorms during the Overturn. So Macy was fascinated by the huge reactors, vats, tanks, and table pedons where topsoil similar to the rich black chernozens of temperate grasslands of Earth was manufactured. AIs monitored and micromanaged every stage of the process, but really it was more like alchemy than chemistry, and a major expenditure of energy and effort.

"We don't need soil for the hydroponic farms, of course," Jael Laudrisen Hall told Macy. "And we could use humus and sand ground from basaltic glass as a substrate for the plantings in our parks and gardens, grow them like so many pot plants. But most plants grow better in soil, and it serves as a valuable buffer that helps to stabilise our enclosed ecosystems. And besides all that, it feels better between the toes."

Making mud was somewhat easier than making soil, but as far as Macy was concerned it was an equally honourable profession. As important as anything the construction crew did and maybe more so, for mud was at the base of most flows of nutrients and organic material in the biome's enclosed aquatic ecosystem. And there was an immense satisfaction in using carefully calibrated cultures of microorganisms to transform material left over from the creation of the Solar System into living mud, a self-organising bioreactor that structured itself into microdomains within upper aerobic layers and lower anoxic layers and could consume just about every kind of organic material and reprocess inorganic nutrients and return it all to the cycle of life. To the amusement of her two assistants, Macy drew off a small measure as it was pumped out of the bioreactor, tasted the gritty gruel and pronounced it good, nice and lively. Just right for the hectares of reed beds that the gardening team were growing in one of the farm tunnels under the city, ready to be transplanted onto shallow banks along the eastern edge of the lake once it was filled to the brim.

Macy's work was important, and there was so much to do. Five days after she had delivered the copy of the work logs to Ursula Freye, she and her assistants went out to check the reef in the channel to the west of the little archipelago that was being built beyond the main island. It was a broad table several hundred metres long, dissected by a maze of ridges and channels designed to maximise mixing of water driven through them by wave machines at the southern end of the lake. When the lake reached its final level, the ridges would be just a metre below the surface, and Tito Puntarenas and Delmy March would seed them with sponges, soft corals, and species of red algae and kelp tweaked to grow in fresh water, providing a habitat for fish and crabs and shrimp. In the channels between the ridges, sandy sediments rich in microorganisms and stabilised by a matrix of blue-green algae and the mucus-lined burrows of several species of tube worm and shrimp would filter huge volumes of water and provide a major contribution to recycling suspended organic material and essential nutrients.

The lake had begun to flood the reef a couple of days ago. The water listlessly sucking to and fro at the bottom of most of the channels was a lifeless yellow-brown soup thick with fines, but Macy and her assistants had sealed off a couple of dozen of the channels and laid down various mixes of quickened sediment and filled them with filtered melt water. Now, before the rising level of the lake overtopped the little dams that stoppered the channels, they motored out to the reef in a skiff and took samples. On-the-spot DNA sampling suggested that most species of bacteria and microalgae in most of the mixes had flourished, and Macy was in a good mood as Loris steered the skiff past the flank of the coffer dam that encircled the construction site of the new archipelago, heading back to the lab.

The tops of islands rose like small hills above the dam's low black wall. One was crowned with a grove of cypresses and the white pillars of a shrine in the style of ancient Greece; others were turfed with flawless green grass or planted with clumps of palms; the last and largest island was still being constructed by a balletic flock of robots perched on a pile of elaborately cross-braced scaffolding that looked like a truncated version of the Eiffel Tower. Their triangular heads, equipped with hundreds of tiny spinnerets that extruded fullerene composite strands as strong as diamond, bobbed and gyred as they patiently lengthened the spars and struts of the island's skeleton. One stood with its swollen abdomen pointing into the air and its head bowed while a technician raked clogged spinnerets with a wand spraying needle jets of water.

Argyll, who'd been watching the robots too, said, "It's going to look wonderful when it's finished."

"As long as no one decides to put some other last-minute change to the vote," Macy said.

"You have to shake off your linear thinking," Argyll said. "This isn't a top-down hierarchical society like Greater Brazil. This is the Outer System. We do things differently here."

"I know," Macy said. "Everything is provisional, and everyone has the right to an opinion on anything, even if they don't know the first thing about it. I'm amazed you get anything done."

"Well, we're not afraid of hard work," Argyll said.

"Nor are we. But it makes things a lot easier if you know what you are going to do before you start to do it."

"Easier doesn't mean better."

"Easier, and less wasteful," Macy said. "I don't know why anyone ever thought democracy was a good idea."

"The city has a surplus of robot labour," Argyll said. "And the islands really aren't much of an expense compared to the total cost of the biome. The only raw materials are graphite slurry to make the framework, a few boulders, and a couple of hundred tons of topsoil. And it really is going to look beautiful when it is finished. A shoal of little green islands with sailboats and water skis threading through them, people picnicking on them . . ."

"One thing we can agree on," Macy said. "We've taken your crazy ideas and made something good from them."

As they rounded the southern end of the coffer dam, another skiff scudded out across the lake, heading straight toward them. Macy had a bad feeling when she saw that Ursula Freye was at the tiller, but told Loris to slow down. If Ursula wanted something from her there would be no escape—she might as well get it over with now, in front of witnesses.

Ursula slowed too, drew alongside. Her blonde hair was tangled about her face and her gaze was bright and eager as she leaned forward and shouted to Macy across the narrow gap of water. "I found something! Something important! Meet me tonight! Eight o'clock! The place where we talked before!"

Before Macy could reply, Ursula gunned her skiff's reaction motor and the little boat raised its nose and drew a wide curve of white wake as it turned through one hundred and eighty degrees and skimmed past Macy's skiff again. "Eight o'clock! It will change everything!" Ursula shouted as she went past, and then her skiff heeled hard and shot away.

Loris said, "Do you want me to go after her?"

"Hell no," Macy said. She was badly shaken by the encounter, by the wild look Ursula had given her, her wild words. The woman was obviously convinced that she had uncovered something that proved or supported her crazy idea that Emmanuel Vargo had been murdered, and although Macy definitely didn't want to have anything more to do with this fantasy she had a bad feeling, as physical as seasickness, that she was going to be dragged back into it anyway.

"You Brazilians sure like your alcohol. I bet someone's going to have a hangover tomorrow," Argyll said, with a grin that reminded Macy that although he was twice her age, he was in many ways naive and oddly childlike.

They returned to the facility at the foot of the hollow strut and were eating supper and working up a full analysis of the reef sediment samples when Speller Twain walked in and told Argyll and Loris to get lost. Loris asked Macy if everything was all right; Speller Twain aimed his blank gaze at her and said that if it was all right with her he wanted to have a private conversation with Ms. Minnot.

"Everything's fine," Macy said. "I'll see you tomorrow."

After the two assistants had left, Loris giving Macy a troubled backward glance, Speller Twain said, "You know what this about."

The big man was leaning against the corner of a bench, flicking a magnifying screen on and off, on and off.

Macy said, "I know you could ask Ursula what she's so excited about."

"I could. But she is what she is, and you are what you are."

"It must make you mad, not being able to touch her because she's consanguineous."

"She thinks you're her friend," Speller Twain said, moving his hand back and forth across the lighted screen, making shadows flutter across the struts high above. "She'll tell you things she won't ever tell me. And you know that if you don't help me, I can have you pulled off the job right now and put in a hibernation coffin. And when they wake you back on Earth, that's where your real trouble will begin. But if you choose to help me find out where this leads, your exemplary work on behalf of the crew and the project won't go unrecognised."

"If it leads anywhere."

"That's for you to find out," Speller Twain said. "Eight o'clock, wasn't it? And at the usual place. Unless you two have been having meetings I don't know about, that's the bar down in the free zone. If you're going to do this, I think you'd better get a move on. You don't want to be late, do you?"

Macy rode a tram into Rainbow Bridge, got on another tram and rode across the city, and took the escalator down into the free zone, floating on a mixture of anger and anxiety. As she moved through shadows and neon glow toward the bar, Jack Frost, passing people dressed for every kind of carnival, a tall figure wrapped in a red cloak and wearing a fox mask stepped out of a passageway and caught her arm and said, "She isn't there."

Macy shook off the figure's grip. "This isn't any business of yours, so how about you back right off?"

The fox-faced figure regarded her for a moment, amber eyes gleaming above the auburn and white muzzle and the crooked sharp-toothed grin, then reached up and swept off the mask. "I don't want to see you hurt," Loris said.

Macy's anger surged over her spark of surprise. "You've been spying on me."

"Ursula Freye isn't waiting for you in Jack Frost," Loris said. "She's still in the biome. Speller Twain intercepted her before she could leave. I can't be sure, but I think he's interrogating her."

"Bullshit. He sent me here to try to talk some sense to her."

"No," Loris said. "He told you that he wanted you to find out what Ursula claims to have discovered. But it's clear that he and Loc Ifrahim have other plans. They've sent you here because they want to use you in some way, Macy. They want to set you up. To make sure that you take the blame for whatever it is they are planning to do."

"Bullshit," Macy said again, but with much less force this time, her anxiety fed by Loris's calm green gaze.

"Many people want the biome project to fail," Loris said. "People in my city and elsewhere in the Outer System. People in Greater Brazil; people working for the construction crew. Mr. Twain. Mr. Ifrahim."

"So you believe Ursula's fantasy."

"It may not be a fantasy."

"She's hurt. All torn up by Manny's death. Grieving. It's driven her a little crazy, and she's trying to justify an accident with some fantasy about murder and conspiracy. You encouraged that, for whatever twisted reason, and now you're trying to drag me into it too. No way," Macy said, and pushed past Loris, heading toward Jack Frost's little sign, glimmering silver and red amongst the shoal of holos and old-fashioned neon signage that swam in the artificial twilight of the free zone's broad avenue.

Loris matched her bounding stride, saying, "Is the problem with the *Skeletonema* cultures a fantasy?"

"We found what was wrong with them and we fixed it. And it wasn't sabotage."

"No, you didn't," Loris said. "The phosphate problem was a side effect.

Listen to me, Macy. Listen carefully. We checked every species your crew brought here, a simple and obvious precautionary measure. And we found two novel sequences in the *Skeletonema*'s genome. One is at the tip of chromosome four, a repetitive pattern of base pairs substituted for the telomeric sequence that usually caps the chromosome. A clock sequence. The other codes for six genes on the same chromosome, and is inserted next to a gene that produces one of the proteins that controls phosphate uptake. The clock sequence shortens by a single base pair at every round of cell division. And when it has shortened to half its original length it activates transcription of the second sequence. And that will produce a pathogenic RNA viroid, some six to eight weeks after the lake is seeded with *Skeletonema* culture at the opening ceremony. The *Skeletonema* population will crash, and bacteria feeding on all that dead biomass will use up all the free oxygen in the lake and wreck its ecosystem. Put on your spex. I'll show you the genomic analysis—"

"I'm sure you can show me just about anything you want," Macy said, and went through Jack Frost's narrow doorway and barged through the heavy fur coats hung in the corridor, out onto the ice floor of the dimly lit bar.

"You can see that I was telling the truth about Ursula," Loris said, after Macy had stalked around the bar and checked every booth.

"How do I know you didn't kidnap her?"

"Have I kidnapped you?" Loris said. "Listen to me, just for a minute. We think that we were supposed to find the sabotage to the *Skeletonema* cultures. We made no secret about checking the species sent from Earth. And if the deleterious effect of the inserted sequence on phosphate transport was a mistake, it was a very clumsy mistake. Someone wants to show that they could reach out and hurt the project. Perhaps they want to cause a scandal. Or perhaps they want to divert attention from something else."

Macy said, "Did Ursula find something?"

"I don't know."

"Was Manny Vargo murdered?"

"You and Ursula may be in grave danger, Macy," Loris said. "It may be too late to help Ursula, but I know that I can help you. Stay here. Don't go back to the biome."

"Or what? You'll arrest me?"

"Of course not. But it really would be a good idea if you stayed here until we found out what Mr. Twain is planning."

"I don't aim to be a part of anyone's plans," Macy said.

She left the bar and broke into a run. Down the long curve of the free zone, up the escalator, along grass-floored streets. She jumped onto a tram and stood at the back, catching her breath, watching apartment buildings flow past on either side. No one seemed to be following her; not even a drone.

She was more frightened than angry now, trying to stay calm, trying to think things through. One thing she knew: Speller Twain couldn't touch Ursula Freye. He could question her and threaten her, but he couldn't hurt her, and Loc Ifrahim couldn't hurt her either. Ursula would survive this, she could protect Macy if she wanted to, and she'd definitely want to protect Macy if she had some evidence of sabotage. So the first thing Macy needed to do was check out the *Skeletonema* cultures and sequence the diatom's genome.

She wondered why Cristine Quarrick hadn't spotted the clock sequence and the viroid genes, and had the chilly thought that perhaps Cristine already knew about them. That she was in on the conspiracy, too. Yeah, or maybe Cristine was just lazy or too busy. Or maybe Loris had made up the whole story, so there was nothing to find. You could get lost in a hundred different ways if you started to speculate. Stick to facts. Sequence the diatom genome. Look for those inserted genes. Find Ursula. Take it from there.

No one stopped Macy when she changed trams and rode into the biome; no one stopped her when she came out of the station at the main island. Night. Every pane of the tent polarised to black and the chandeliers turned down to a faint glow like tarnished starlight. Lights along the edge of the island glimmered above their slurred reflections in the lake. A faint nimbus enveloped the skeleton of the half-constructed island inside the coffer dam, throwing the magnified shadows of the robots working inside it across a slanting portion of the tent's roof.

A drone began to follow Macy as she left the station. She gave it a hard stare to let whoever was driving it—Speller Twain, Loris, some innocent busybody—that she knew that she was being watched, and walked on, determined not to look at it again, a tingling itch between her shoulder blades.

She hurried along the path that cut through the wooded ridge down the centre of the island, began to cross the slender bridge that linked the island with the eastern rim road—and all the lights went out. The little lights marking the bridge's footway, the chandeliers' glow, the spiderweb of lights hitched across the island, the lights around the station entrance and the crew's living quarters. Only the construction site was still lit.

Macy flinched when something softly splashed into the water below the bridge. She found her spex and put them on and dialled up the light-enhancement function, saw the fat cigar of a drone, presumably the one that had been following her, floating on the black wash. Something had knocked out the lights, the drones . . . A bad feeling rose up in her, thick as nausea. She felt horribly exposed, up there at the apex of the bridge's high curve, and she ran down its far side and ran straight across the rim road into the strip of parkland beyond, bounding light as a bird through the luminous dark, twisting this way and that to avoid clumps of flowering bushes and outcrops of rock, almost laughing out loud when, trying to halt her headlong flight, she pitched head over heels into a patch of oleander, rolling to a breathless halt amongst a tangle of scratchy branches and leaves, a snowstorm of waxy petals drifting around her.

She lay there for a little while, staring up at the black roof and listening with fierce attention. The whines and thumps of the robots working inside the luminous cup of the coffer dam; the reaction motor of a boat fading away somewhere on the lake; voices drifting across from the island, people calling out, asking each other what was going on. When she was as certain as she could be that no one was following her, Macy got to her feet and went on through the park, moving parallel to the rim road, slowing as she approached the huge shadow of the support strut. She drifted to the first of the bioreactors in the plaza under the arch of the strut, laid a hand on its warm flank and felt the reassuring purr of its pumps. The backup supply had kicked in, so she didn't have to worry about a mass die-off of her precious cultures. She threaded her way between the tanks, stopped.

Something sprawled on the grassy space in front of the entrance to the lab. It was a body. It was Ursula Freye.

She lay on her back, one arm carelessly flung out as if reaching for something, head turned sideways. She didn't move as Macy crept toward her, softly calling her name. Her nostrils were wet with blood and blood had run in a thick line down her left cheek. Her eyes were open but rolled back. Macy pressed two fingers under the hinge of her jaw, failed to find a pulse, and with a flash of freezing fear realised that Loris had been right all along. She'd been set up. She sprang to her feet so quickly that she left the ground for a couple of breathless seconds; as she floated down the string of chandeliers hung above the lake lit up bright as noon.

Even though the light-enhancing function of Macy's spex immediately cut off, she was dazzled by the sudden flood of brightness. She tore off the spex and thumbed tears from her eyes, saw a shadow race at her from the right, someone running too fast, losing his footing and plunging headlong. It was Speller Twain, bouncing up and aiming a taser at her, the kind that shot fractally compressed loops of superconducting nanowire.

Macy jinked left as a miniature lightning bolt scorched across the turf in front of her. Speller Twain shouted, ordering her to stop, but she was already running, bounding across the lawn like a gazelle pursued by a lion. A chain of bright sparks spattered the side of a bioreactor as she flew past, and she jumped high and caught the rim and pulled herself up, moving easily and fluidly in the low gravity. She ran the length of the boxcar-sized tank, jumped the wide gap to the next, ran along that and jumped to the ground and ran on across the plaza. Sparks exploded from the railing at the edge of the plaza as she hurdled it, spattering her with stinging flecks of hot metal, and she dropped straight down and ran down the gentle slope of the dry lake bed toward the beached skiff.

She was dragging the skiff into the water when Speller Twain vaulted the railing. He landed awkwardly and went over on his back, and his taser spat a bolt that shot straight up through the bright air and burst like a firework on a pane of the tent high above. As the big man got to his feet, Macy saw something move out across the railing above and behind him, saw him whirl around as the drone stooped down at full speed and slammed into his face.

He fell down again, and dropped the taser. Macy rushed forward and scooped it up, dancing away when Speller Twain made a swipe at her. She stepped backward toward the skiff, keeping the taser on him. He pushed to his feet and spat a mouthful of blood and told her that she was making a big mistake.

Macy was knee deep in water. Her mouth was dry and she had to suck up some spit before she could say, "Stay right there, Mr. Twain. I don't want to shoot you."

"You aren't going to shoot me," Speller Twain said, and flew at her.

She shot him. The bolt struck his chest and he belly-flopped into the water, jerking and flailing. Macy scrambled into the skiff and pressed the button that started its motor and jammed the tiller hard around, spinning the little craft through a hundred and eighty degrees as it accelerated away. She'd drawn a long arc past the mouth of the bay before she'd calmed down enough to realise that there was only one place where she could go now. She turned west, heading for the far shore, and activated the phone function of her spex. But before she could place the call, a window scrolled down and Loc Ifrahim leaned into her face and said, "Now you've gone and done it."

Macy tore off the spex and threw them out across the water as hard as she could, ran the skiff onto the dry lake floor at the foot of a set of stairs, swarmed up them to a broad promenade that ran in front of a low block of terraced apartments. She paused then, breathing hard, looking back across the lake. Her heart was banging madly in her chest. It was only ten minutes since she'd discovered Ursula's body.

A star flared in the middle air: chandelier light glancing off a drone that was dropping toward her.

Macy dodged around stacks of construction materials, charged through the broad entrance of the apartment block, lost her footing and flew across an atrium. She slammed against a wall and sat down hard, breath knocked out of her, pain in her left ankle. The drone drifted down a slanting shaft of light that speared through a round unglazed window and a stentorian voice shivered the air, calling her name, telling her to stay where she was. Macy raised the taser and took careful aim, but her hand was trembling badly and her first shot missed, howling away through the window. The drone jerked sideways, and Macy's second shot struck it in a shower of sparks that ruptured its helium-filled bag.

As it tumbled out of the air, she jumped up and took off, limping on her wrenched ankle, out through the far side of the atrium into a courtyard. Bamboos and giant jade-green cushions of mosses, raked black sand, the dry bowl of a black stone fountain. Macy plunged through an archway beyond. Stairs to her right wound to the upper storeys; stairs to her left dropped to the basement.

She knew from briefings that every building in the city had a basement passageway leading to emergency shelters and airlocks, in case there was a catastrophic failure of the integrity of one or more of the tents and domes. The Outers, who for more than a century had been living in an environment that would kill them in an instant if they made a single misstep, were very big on safety and emergency planning. Macy was betting her life on that caution now, hoping that even though the apartment building hadn't been finished its airlock would be functional. If it wasn't, she probably wouldn't have enough time to find another way out of the tent before Loc Ifrahim caught up with her.

The door at the bottom of the stairs was shut and nothing happened when Macy punched the big red button that was supposed to unlock it. She spent a panicky minute spinning the wheel that worked the ponderous manual mechanism, opening the door just wide enough so that she could slip inside, and then she had to turn another wheel to close it.

A narrow corridor sloped away, lit by dim lights embedded in the floor. She cannoned off its walls as she ran down it. Her ankle was hurting badly now, but she couldn't slow down. Loc Ifrahim would soon work out where she was going, and if he could turn the chandeliers off and on at will he might well have the ability to lock down the tent's emergency exits too . . .

The corridor went down a long way. The air grew colder. Her breath puffed out in little clouds; frost sparkled on the walls. There was another door; again, she had to turn a wheel to open it. Lights came on beyond, revealing a low-ceilinged bunker. During an emergency, citizens who weren't certified for rescue and repair work were supposed to hunker down in places like this until it was safe to return to their homes. The memory-plastic floor could grow seats or beds; a medical pod stood in one corner like an old-fashioned cabinet freezer; there was a tiny kitchenette and a pair of shower/toilets, crates of freeze-dried food and clothing and blankets. And there was also a ladder leading up into a shaft signposted with a cartoon of a round door emitting a little cloud: the universal sign for an airlock.

Macy hauled herself hand over hand up the long shaft and emerged into a small brightly lit antechamber where two dressing frames stood either side of a steel door. In a jittery rush, she stripped off her coveralls, pulled on a one-piece thermal liner, and stepped into the smallest of the bright red pressure suits that hung in the dressing frames. She pulled up the big double zip, used the concertina joints above elbows and knees to adjust the fit, fingers stiff and clumsy inside the suit's heavy gloves, shrugged into the harness of the lifepack, lowered the fishbowl helmet and latched it tight. A HUD lit up inside the faceplate and Macy stepped away from the frame and clumped into the airlock and started its cycle. Mist condensed around her and was whisked away as the air was evacuated, the outer door swung open, and she stepped out onto the surface of Callisto.

It was late afternoon. The sun, much shrunken but still the brightest object in the black sky, burned low in the west. Jupiter's exotically banded disc, a little over half full, hung high overhead. The airlock was housed in a blister that stood at the edge of a broad dusty apron marked everywhere with bootprints. Behind it, the flank of the biome's tent rose at a steep angle, a gigantic jigsaw of black panes and tension bars set between struts as sturdy and tall as skyscrapers. In every other direction cratered terrain stretched to a curved horizon just three kilometres away.

The pressure suit's navigation system highlighted and tagged features scattered across the stark moonscape. A flat-topped hill at the horizon to the northwest was the rim of Wealtheow Crater, with a vacuum organism farm spread in front of it. A line of construction robots parked in the shadow of a long, low berm two klicks away. A couple of utility shacks. And a silvery roadway that cut past the edge of the apron and swung around the tent that housed the biome. According to the navigation system, the road led straight to the city. It was a hike of some ten klicks that even in Callisto's low gravity would take Macy more than an hour—assuming she could manage to travel that far in the bulky pressure suit, with a sprained ankle. But she couldn't stay here. Speller Twain and Loc Ifrahim would soon figure out where she'd gone, and they couldn't let her escape.

Stepping through three layers of increasingly graphic warnings, Macy turned off the pressure suit's beacon, then started toward the distant line of construction robots. She was possessed by the same airy mixture of excitement, dread, and determination she'd felt when she'd escaped from the Church of the Divine Regression. Back then, she'd spent a year planning her escape. She'd accumulated and hidden a cache of supplies and a change of clothes at the perimeter, memorised three different routes to the nearest highway, written a worm that would shut down the security AI, stolen tranquilizers from the pharmacy to drug the guard dogs, prepared and rehearsed every step of her escape. But this time she was making it up as she went along.

She was close to the long row of construction robots now, heading toward a small bulldozer with a moulded seat elevated behind its broad blade. All she had to do was figure out how to start it up, and she could ride into the city in style . . .

An icon started winking in the virtual display that ghosted her vision: an incoming call on one of the short-range channels. She turned, felt a panicky rush of adrenalin when she saw a figure in a red pressure suit just like hers walking away from the airlock on the far side of the swale of tracked dust, shuffling as cautiously as an old man crossing an ice rink. She dodged between two of the big machines and doubled back on her tracks and found cover in the stark black shadow cast by a mesh wheel three metres high.

The figure was coming on, small and vivid against the dark ground, heading straight toward her. She patted the pouches and clips of her suit's utility belt, and had a clear picture of the taser lying on the floor by the dressing frame. Dumb, Macy, real dumb. Almost as bad as forgetting to jam the airlock. The icon was still winking. Well, the son of a bitch already knew were she was: if she answered his call, she'd at least know who she was dealing with.

"There you are," Loc Ifrahim said when she opened the channel. "Listen, Macy, I'm here to help you. Stay calm and don't do anything stupid. We can clear this up, just you and me."

"How are we going to do that?"

Macy was certain that Loc Ifrahim and Speller Twain had been planning to frame her for the murder of poor Ursula Freye. She'd ruined their plan by managing to get away, so now they had to kill her. If they didn't, if she fell into the hands of the city's peace officers, she'd blow their little plot wide open. She began to move toward the biggest of the construction robots, a crane mounted between three pairs of wide caterpillar tracks. She'd seen plenty of big equipment during her service with the R&R Corps, but this was a true monster. Its platform was at least fifty metres long and its telescopic jib, woven from skinny struts of fullerene composite and canted at a thirty-degree angle, was at least twice as long.

"We need to sit down together and get our stories straight," Loc Ifrahim said. "To begin with, I need to know what happened between you and Ursula."

"She was dead when I found her. You should know that."

"All I know is that Mr. Twain found you by her body. You attacked him, and then you ran away. It doesn't look good, does it? But I'm willing to hear your side of the story. I'm willing to sit down with you and work out what you have to do."

"I know one thing. Ursula was right. Someone is trying to sabotage the biome," Macy said, and cut the link.

She thought about calling Loris, but she didn't know how long it would take help to arrive. Or she could make a run for it, climb the steep side of the berm, head out across country. She had enough air and power to survive out here for more than two days, but she wouldn't be able to travel fast on her damaged ankle, and if Loc Ifrahim knew how to drive one of the construction robots he could easily chase her down. No, she thought, she was going to have to tackle him herself, right here, right now.

Macy stepped back from the shadow cast by the crane, then ran forward, pain spearing her left leg from ankle to knee at every other step, and jumped to the top of one of its broad tracks. She landed awkwardly, had to grab at the link between two plates of the track to stop herself rebounding. She lay there for a few moments, dazed and out of breath, then crawled to the end of the track. She was five metres above the ground, could see Loc Ifrahim moving along the line of construction robots, flitting from shadow to shadow, turning this way and that, aiming the taser at likely hiding places. Even when he paused in the deep black shadows she could see him clearly in infrared; the insulation and the heat-recycling system of his pressure suit weren't entirely efficient and he burned white as a ghost, more than eighty degrees hotter than his frigid surroundings.

If he glanced up she'd be finished, but he was too busy looking under the frames of robots, looking behind wheels and tracks . . . Macy crawled backward, stayed absolutely still and let ten minutes pass before she risked taking another peek. At first she couldn't spot him, but then she turned and saw that he was creeping past the far end of the crane, stooping to examine the shadows underneath it like a man searching for a lost pet. She pushed up and bounded down the length of the track and launched herself in a long, floating parabola and smashed into him and knocked him to the ground. He tried to rear up, but she grabbed his helmet in both hands and thumped it into dust soft and gritty as sugar, then opened the line-of-sight channel and asked him if he wanted to live.

"If you kill me, you'll die too, and not in a nice way," he said. "They expose murderers to vacuum."

"That's what I'll do to you if you don't keep still," Macy said and cut the channel. She was tired and in a lot of pain from her ankle. She didn't need to hear any more of his bullshit.

She couldn't find the taser—he must have dropped it when she'd knocked him down—but there was a plasticuff loop strung on his utility belt. She used it to fasten his arms behind his back, then pulled down the city's directory and made a phone call.

Loris answered at once, and asked Macy if she was all right.

"I want to thank you for knocking Mr. Twain down with that drone. That *was* you, right?"

"You didn't have to run, Macy. I know how you were set up. I was coming to help you."

"Do you know that Mr. Ifrahim came after me too? Luckily, I got the jump on him. In fact, I'm sitting on him right now. You can question him—"

"No, we can't. He has diplomatic immunity. What we can do is bring you in. Where are you?"

"If you let him go, he'll no doubt claim that Ursula and me were plotting all kinds of sabotage. Including the *Skeletonema* cultures, which are my responsibility after all. We had a falling-out, and I killed her. And I bet Twain and Ifrahim could make a good case that I murdered Manny Vargo too. Because he discovered that the wrong culture had been loaded."

"Or simply because his death would also damage the project," Loris said. "We don't know everything, Macy. Perhaps we never will. But we do know that you are an innocent party caught in the middle of it all. That's why we are willing to offer you protection."

Macy realised that she had been used to flush out Speller Twain and Loc Ifrahim. Set up. Staked out like a wildsider sacrifice. She said, "I really have been played by both sides, haven't I?"

"We are grateful for your help," Loris said. "I want you to know that you're not in as much trouble as you think you are."

"I know I can't go back to the crew, that's for sure. There's a bunch of construction robots parked outside the western flank of the dome. You can find me there."

"I'll be there right away," Loris said. "Don't worry, Macy, you've made the right choice."

Macy spotted the taser lying in the dust and pushed away from Loc Ifrahim and snatched it up. Loc Ifrahim rolled over and tried to sit up, subsided when she waved the taser at him. The icon of the line-of-sight channel started blinking again, but she ignored it. She had nothing more to say to the diplomat.

A few minutes later, the pressure suit's navigation system alerted her to the approach of a vehicle and bracketed a bright dot that slid low across the black sky. It quickly resolved into a single figure in a pressure suit riding a platform on top of a compass rose of thrusters. Loc Ifrahim sat up. Macy ignored him, watching as the platform came in, thrusters blinking as they made minute adjustments to its pitch, drifting low toward her, kicking up dust, settling on spidery legs.

Macy waved to it, remembering her breathless anticipation years ago on the dark road that cut through Nebraska's night, when she'd swung into the cab of the road train she'd flagged down and the driver had turned to her. A chunky woman with a blonde crew cut and a pitted complexion, asking her where she wanted to go. And she'd said, with the bold naivety forgiven only in the young, "Anywhere else."

On the platform, the figure in the pressure suit raised one hand, then touched its helmet.

Macy had already walked away from one life; now she was about to do it again. She switched on the short-range channel and said to Loc Ifrahim, "You can tell Mr. Peixoto that I quit."

And that was it: she was a refugee.

9

Sri Hong-Owen and her eldest son, Alder, travelled to Callisto in a small freighter, the *Luís Inácio da Silva*, that had been fitted with a prototype of the new fusion motor. It cut the record for transit between Earth and Jupiter by two-thirds, a fine demonstration of the Peixoto family's technological prowess, and an important contribution to their elaborate and extensive sales pitch to the Callistans. Sri had a packed schedule: touring farms and factories and laboratories, meeting with the Callistan Senate and leading citizens of Rainbow Bridge, taking part in a ceremony to mark the first stage of the quickening of the biome's lake, and so on and so forth. And she wanted to meet the gene wizard Avernus, too. First of all, though, she needed to straighten out the tangled business of the failed attempt at sabotage, the murder of Ursula Freye, and the defection of Macy Minnot, so she made room in her schedule for a meeting with the junior diplomat who seemed to be in the middle of it all.

Loc Ifrahim was summoned to Sri Hong-Owen's suite the day after she arrived. It was the penthouse of an apartment complex built into one of the huge struts of the biome's tent. He arrived precisely on time, was scanned and sniffed by Sri Hong-Owen's secretary, and left to cool his heels in the foyer. He supposed that the wait was meant to put him in his place and heighten any anxieties he might be harbouring, but he didn't let it touch him. It gave him time to go over his story again, and he could watch people come and go. He liked watching people, trying to work out their motives, trying to figure out what they might be thinking, whether or not they might be useful to him.

Presently, the pair of peace officers who had interviewed him about Ursula Freye's death came out of Sri Hong-Owen's suite. One, a tall, severe woman with a square of white hair sitting on top of her head like a cap of snow, smiled coldly at Loc and asked if he was going to be more cooperative with his boss than he had been with her.

Loc returned her smile. "Professor Doctor Hong-Owen isn't my 'boss.' I work for the Brazilian government, not the Peixoto family."

"I have the impression that you're more interested in yourself."

"And I can't help thinking that if your city was as interested in this project as it claims to be, it would not be harbouring Macy Minnot," Loc said.

"We both know that she had nothing to do with Ursula Freye's murder," the white-haired peace officer said.

"I know no such thing. In fact, I have given you evidence to the contrary. Evidence you have chosen to ignore."

"Waive your diplomatic immunity," the peace officer said. "Then I'll be glad to discuss your so-called evidence."

Her gaze burned with frustration and anger. Loc had agreed to a brief interview with the city's peace officers after Ursula Freye's death and Macy Minnot's defection, but they hadn't been allowed to interrogate him formally, let alone test him with an MRI cap; all they'd been able to do was listen to his statement, ask a few polite questions, and let him go. There'd been some loose talk in the Callistan Senate about expelling him, but it hadn't amounted to anything because there was nothing that directly linked him to Ursula Freye's death, and no one wanted to risk precipitating a diplomatic incident that could wreck the trade talks and the opening of the biome.

"Leave him, Dee," the peace officer's partner said. "He's just a bit player."

"I'll be right behind you if there's any more trouble," the white-haired peace officer told Loc, and turned away.

"Why would there be any more trouble now that Macy Minnot is in your tender care?" Loc said loudly as the peace officers walked toward the belt of rising and falling platforms that passed for an elevator here. Sri Hong-Owen's secretary glanced up from the slate he was nursing, but the peace officers didn't even look back.

Well, screw them. They'd made threatening noises during their investigation of Ursula Freye's murder, but they hadn't be able to touch him. They hadn't even been able to touch that oafish blunderer Speller Twain. No doubt they'd been doing their best to poison Sri Hong-Owen with their suspicions, but Loc had already anticipated that. He had everything covered.

At last, he was ushered into the suite. It was mildly impressive, a cavernous space with a halflife lawn that blended seamlessly into the virtual backdrop of the walls, depicting herds of extinct and fantasy animals grazing on a plain that stretched to distant mountains. Sri Hong-Owen was waiting for him at the far end, standing in the shade of a grove of bamboos and ferns that grew amongst a litter of big rocks. A slight, slender woman dressed in a tailored version of the green coveralls of the construction crew, her eyes masked by spex with silvered lenses and chunky black frames, her naked scalp as translucently pale as a porcelain bowl. Loc shuffled toward her in his grippy slippers, bowed as low as he dared, and said that he was at her service.

"We'll sit," Sri Hong-Owen said, and two flat-topped hummocks pushed up from the emerald-green turf.

They sat facing each other, knees almost touching.

"I've read the report about the circumstances of Ms. Freye's death," Sri Hong-Owen said. "Now I want to hear your version of events. Your point of view, your insights. Every little detail."

Loc had heard that the gene wizard had a reputation for impatience and frank speaking; even so, he was taken aback by this shocking directness. She appeared to believe that he was some kind of indentured servant answerable directly to her, but he ignored the insult to his status because he needed to charm her, and laid out his version of events with calm, fluent authority. Explaining that Emmanuel Vargo's lover, Ursula Freye, had insisted that his death hadn't been accidental, that he'd been murdered by a person or persons trying to sabotage the construction project. There were no grounds for her accusation beyond the fact that Emmanuel Vargo's slate had gone missing, but because she was consanguineous with the Fontaine family Euclides Peixoto hadn't been able to dismiss her case outright. He'd instructed Speller Twain, the construction crew's security chief, to deal with the problem as he saw fit, and Speller Twain had approached the embassy for help.

"Like Mr. Twain, the ambassador was wary of becoming entangled in political complications. And so the task fell to the most junior staff member, namely me," Loc Ifrahim said, with a small, self-deprecating smile. "Mr. Twain and I decided to enlist the help of the other member of the Fontaine family in the construction crew, Macy Minnot. At our urging, she attempted to reason with Ursula Freye, but Ms. Freye not only refused to give up her crusade, she also asked Ms. Minnot to help her by obtaining a copy of the construction crew's work logs. She wanted to examine it for evidence of sabotage, you understand, and she could not obtain it herself. As a precaution, Mr. Twain had taken away her access privileges."

"Why did he do that?"

"Actually, I advised him to do it. I was worried that Ursula Freye might be tempted to alter the records to support her contention that Emmanuel Vargo had been murdered. She seemed quite irrational, you see. Capable of anything."

"Ah. Then she was not locked out because you were worried that she might find some inconvenient truth."

"Not at all. We gave Ms. Minnot permission to make a copy of the work logs and hand it to Ursula Freye. A few days later, Ms. Freye claimed to have discovered something important. She arranged a meeting with Ms. Minnot, but we intervened and tried to talk to her."

Sri Hong-Owen said, "And did Ms. Freye tell you what she had found?"

Loc knew that the woman had uncovered the data Speller Twain had added to the work logs just before Macy Minnot had copied them, subtle clues hinting at a conspiracy involving Cristine Quarrick and Patrick Alan Allard and tied to the very real sabotage of one of the microalgal cultures, but he was able to say truthfully that Ursula Freye had been most uncooperative.

"After we let her go, she must have gone to talk with Macy Minnot. The surveillance system in the biome crashed, and Ms. Freye was killed. Mr. Twain gave chase, but Macy Minnot managed to escape."

"She shot him with his own taser, I believe."

"Yes, ma'am. After someone used a drone to knock him down."

"Where were you while this was happening?"

Sri Hong-Owen was leaning forward, hands planted on her knees. Loc could see himself doubly reflected in the silvery lenses of her spex. He was certain that she was studying the dilation of his pupils and the blood flow in the skin capillaries of his face, looking for cues that might indicate that he was lying, but he was confident that his training would foil any attempt to catch him out. Besides, apart from the omission of a few inconvenient facts, his story was more or less truthful.

He said, "I was nearby, using a drone to keep watch on Macy Minnot. Until the system fell over, that is."

"So you didn't see who killed Ursula Freye."

"Not until the drone came back online. As soon as it did, I had it follow Macy Minnot. Unfortunately, she shot it down with the taser she'd taken from Mr. Twain. I attempted to follow her myself, but she managed to get away."

"She overpowered Mr. Twain, and then she got the better of you."

"She served in the Reclamation and Reconstruction Corps before she was recruited for the construction crew. She had military training. And I regret that, unlike Mr. Twain, I am not a man of action."

"Mr. Twain claims that he saw her shoot Ursula Freye in the head with a nail gun," Sri Hong-Owen said.

"He gave a statement to that effect, ma'am. I believe that the murder weapon was part of the equipment issued to Ms. Minnot's laboratory, and was later retrieved from the lake."

Where Speller Twain, the damn fool, had thrown it.

"Mr. Twain also claims that Ursula Freye murdered Emmanuel Vargo," Sri Hong-Owen said. "Do you believe that?"

"It's certainly true that Ms. Freye was one of the last people to see Mr. Vargo before the crew was put to sleep," Loc said. "And after her death, Mr. Twain discovered Mr. Vargo's slate in her quarters. He thinks that she could have infected Mr. Vargo with an agent that caused his death from pseudo-CND when he was revived. But I have to admit that I can't quite square that with Ms. Freye's very loud and persistent claims that he was murdered, especially as everyone else was ready to accept that it was an accident. It's a very troubling inconsistency."

"Does Mr. Twain have any hard evidence for these suppositions?" Sri Hong-Owen said. "Apart from the discovery of Mr. Vargo's slate, which could easily have been planted."

"Mr. Twain claims that Ms. Freye and Ms. Minnot were working together to sabotage the project, and had a falling-out. Unfortunately, Ms. Minnot left Rainbow Bridge the day after she defected," Loc said. "Aboard a tug named *The Long March* that took her to the city of East of Eden, Ganymede. The tug is owned by a man named Galileo Wu. Mr. Wu is the granduncle of Loris Sher Yanagita, and Ms. Yanagita not only worked as Ms. Minnot's assistant; she is also the daughter of one of the members of Callisto's Senate."

He was beginning to enjoy himself. After Macy Minnot's escape, his quick thinking had pulled everything back from the brink of disaster, and he was confident that he could pin the deaths of Emmanuel Vargo and Ursula Freye on a new scapegoat. All he had to do was sow some seeds of doubt in the minds of Euclides Peixoto and this so-called gene wizard, and then his new friends would tie up the loose ends.

"So Ms. Minnot has serious protection," Sri Hong-Owen said.

"Indeed. We asked to speak with her immediately after she defected, but our request was refused. We tried again after she was moved to East of Eden, and again our request was refused. And without access to Ms. Minnot it has not been possible to take the investigation any further."

"What about the Fontaine family?"

"They would have to pay a great deal to reach that far, but since she is suspected of murdering a family member with one-thirty-second consanguinity, I would not rule it out."

"Even though the Fontaines have disowned Ursula Freye."

Loc smiled. "Well, they would, wouldn't they? The affair has caused them considerable trouble. And even if Ms. Minnot was carrying out their orders, they are hardly likely to welcome her back."

Sri Hong-Owen studied him for a moment, then said, "Let me show you something."

He followed her around the bamboos and rocks to a glass blister that clung like a raindrop to the slanting side of the great strut. Sri Hong-Owen walked straight across it but Loc halted in the doorway: the blister's floor was as transparent as its curved wall. Far below, water lapped the rocky shoreline of the lake.

"We can talk safely here," Sri Hong-Owen said, turning to Loc. She seemed to be floating in midair. "My people found several bugs planted in the suite, but they can't be certain that they found everything. This, though, is quite sterile. The glass is one-way, and a little engine vibrates it to prevent anyone eavesdropping. Come in, and shut the door."

Loc did as he was told, taking a single step onto the glass floor. He was certain that the gene wizard wanted something from him. Information, a favour, something he could give her now and draw on later.

"I had an interesting conversation with the peace officers investigating Ms. Freye's murder," Sri Hong-Owen said.

"I couldn't help noticing them leave," Loc said. He didn't want to antagonise the gene wizard, not now, when she was about to put her trust in him, so he didn't add that he knew that the confrontation had been staged in a clumsy attempt to unnerve him.

"They told me that Ms. Freye was killed by a nail fired into her medulla oblongata," Sri Hong-Owen said. "It killed her instantly. Either the person who murdered her was very lucky, or they knew exactly what they were doing. Also, the wound track indicates that the nail gun was angled downward when it was fired, and bruising of the skin of Ms. Freye's hands and neck suggest that she was seized from behind before she was shot, and her wrists were pinioned. That isn't consistent with Mr. Twain's claim that he saw Ms. Minnot and Ms. Freye struggle. And although Ms. Freye was shot at close range, the peace officers found no trace of blowback on the clothes Ms. Minnot left behind in the airlock when she escaped from the biome. No blood, no bone or brain fragments consistent with a close-range shot. There were traces of blood on Ms. Minnot's fingers, yes, but she told the peace officers that she had checked Ms. Freye's pulse. Then there is the question of the lack of fingerprints and DNA on the murder weapon. Perhaps Ms. Minnot was wearing gloves, but none were found. She certainly was not wearing them when she got Ms. Freye's blood on her fingers. In short, Mr. Ifrahim, the peace officers do not believe that Ms. Minnot killed Ms. Freye. And they do not believe Mr. Twain's witness statement, either. So let me ask you directly: do you think that she did it?"

Here it was. Loc let a little concern show on his face and said, "I have given you the official story. But now that we can speak freely? No. No, I don't think that Macy Minnot killed Ursula Freye."

"Who did?"

"I think we both know the answer, ma'am."

"Mr. Twain killed Ursula Freye, and he would have killed Macy Minnot too. But she escaped."

"I imagine he planned to claim that Ms. Minnot died while trying to evade arrest. The murder weapon came from a tool kit in her laboratory, and the viral program that took down the surveillance system appeared to originate from her slate. I confess, I would have believed him."

"And did he also kill Emmanuel Vargo?"

"I suppose it's possible," Loc said, as if the thought had only just occurred to him.

"You are also under suspicion, I believe."

"If I am guilty of anything, it is naivety. I trusted Mr. Twain too readily, and I am thoroughly ashamed of my part in his machinations. Most especially as he is free to act again."

"What do you mean?"

A small slick of pleasure seeped into Loc's heart. He had her. He knew that he had her. "After the discovery of the corrupted diatom culture, the construction crew members have been checking everything they brought with them. No trace of any other attempt at sabotage has been found. And Outers working alongside our people have grown up a fresh culture of the diatom, so the quickening of the lake will not be delayed. But it isn't hard to imagine that Mr. Twain may be planning some form of direct action. Assassination, perhaps."

"And who might he be planning to assassinate?"

"I regret that it is quite possible that you may be his target, ma'am. You, or Avernus."

"If she comes here, and we don't yet know if she will. Have you told the ambassador or Euclides Peixoto about your suspicions?"

"Alas, no. I have no evidence, and the ambassador has made it clear that he believes that the affair is at an end. And Mr. Peixoto, with respect, is somewhat . . . disengaged."

Sri Hong-Owen nodded. "That's true enough. Mr. Peixoto was given his position by an uncle who is more fond of him than he deserves."

Loc knew that her indiscretion meant he was winning her trust. "If there is anything I can do for you, anything at all, you have only to ask."

"And what about your oath of loyalty to the government?"

"The government exists to serve the families, ma'am."

"How old are you, Mr. Ifrahim?"

"Twenty-five."

"Twenty-five. You were born in the slums of Caracas, I believe. You have come a long way, and very quickly. You must be very ambitious."

"I want to serve as best I can, ma'am."

"You really are quite a creature, Mr. Ifrahim." Sri Hong-Owen turned to the view beyond the glass wall of the blister and said, "Come here. Stand by me."

Loc shuffled across the transparent floor, his toes cramping in his slippers, a vast and airy unease yawning in his belly.

Sri Hong-Owen was staring past her faint reflection in the blister's glassy curve, looking out at the lake and its scattering of green islands mapped between the leaning and faceted walls of the biome's tent.

"It's magnificent," she said. "It's hard to believe that twenty thousand people huddled on an icy moon far from the sun could be capable of anything on this scale. And yet it was built and pressurised and landscaped in less than a year. Do you know how they did it?"

"They have many robots—"

"Knowledge," Sri Hong-Owen said. "They have preserved much that Earth lost in the aftermath of the Overturn. And they have been adding to it ever since, while we spend most of our resources on reclamation and reconstruction. Which is good work, of course. Necessary work. Noble work. But think of how much more we could do if we had full control of the technologies and scientific knowledge preserved and developed by the Outers. That's why the Peixoto family agreed to Avernus's offer, why they sent out the construction crew to quicken this biome. For many years now they have been attempting reconciliation between Earth and the Outer System. This is a major step in that campaign. A show of faith. The beginning of what may be a long and fruitful trade partnership with the Outers.

"Like you, Mr. Ifrahim, I'm an employee. You work for the government; I work for the Peixoto family. But I'm sure you're aware that the potential rewards of this enterprise are so great that even humble employees like myself can hope for some small share. As long as we always put the family's interests before those of ourselves. As long as we are unfailingly and unflinchingly loyal."

Loc pretended to take offence. "I would hope that my candour about this wretched affair is proof enough that I want to help."

"It's obvious that Mr. Twain murdered Ursula Freye. If you truly want to help me, you are going to have to do better than that."

Really, he could have kissed her. Not only had she swallowed his story whole; she also believed that he was truffling for titbits in return for favours. He said, "Mr. Twain has already damaged your project, and he is almost certainly in league with people who wish to cause it further damage. Let me find out all I can. Then, perhaps, I can help you find a way to overcome the threat he poses."

10

Later, Sri Hong-Owen said to her son, "Can I trust him?"

"Only if his interests coincide with yours. If they do not . . . well, he sold out Speller Twain to save himself, didn't he? And we can't be sure that he told you the entire truth."

Mother and son sat close together amongst a scatter of cushions and pillows in the glass blister. Night had fallen in the biome. Alder's elfin face was underlit by the glow of the slate in his lap, which was playing a recording of the interview with Loc Ifrahim. Watching him study changes in the dilation of the diplomat's pupils, Sri felt a tender, helpless maternal love thicken her blood. She had cut her son's fatal attraction herself, from the architecture of his cheekbones and the classical proportion of his limbs to his feverish warmth and honey-sweet pheromone-laden scent, but she wasn't immune to his charms. Her beautiful golden boy. She was so very glad that she had brought him. He would turn sixteen soon enough: it was time he learned how really important business was done, and there was no finer opportunity than this, the ground floor of a deal of historical magnitude. And he would be of great help to her, too; his charm and charisma were going to be invaluable during public appearances.

Alder said, "He certainly *appears* to be telling the truth. But he's a diplomat and they're trained to pass simple lie-detection tests."

"There's no need to work out how much of his story is true and how much is mere self-aggrandisement. Instead, we should think about which part of it would do us the most harm if we acted on it and then found it to be untrue."

A crease appeared above the bridge of Alder's nose as he thought about this. "That's why you turned down his offer to spy on Speller Twain. It would put you in his debt. He would have power over you."

"Also, it would help him more than it would help me."

"Because he isn't innocent in this," Alder said. "He was working with Mr. Twain. And after the failure of their plan to frame Macy Minnot for Ursula Freye's murder, he wants to silence Mr. Twain before Mr. Twain betrays him."

"And who would Mr. Twain betray him to?"

"The peace officers?"

"He has diplomatic immunity. The most they can do is request his expulsion from their city."

"Well then, to Euclides Peixoto, I suppose. Or to the ambassador. Mr. Ifrahim would be in a lot of trouble if they found out."

"The ambassador is of no account because Loc Ifrahim is working for someone with considerably more authority," Sri said.

"Do you mean the general?" Alder said.

"Or one of the general's many friends and allies. As for Euclides, he was given charge of this project by his great-uncle because something as important as this has to be helmed by one of the family. It was an offer he couldn't refuse, but he has always made it clear that he has no real allegiance or commitment to it. Even so, his inaction over Ursula Freye's murder is due to something deeper than mere indifference. He's definitely gone over to the other side. I always suspected it. Now I know."

When Sri had met with Euclides Peixoto yesterday, straight off the ship, he'd shrugged away her questions about Emmanuel Vargo's death, Ursula Freye's murder, and Macy Minnot's defection, telling her that he'd ridden himself of the two Fontaine bitches, and fixed the sabotage attempt by growing up clean cultures of the diatom; as far as he was concerned everything had worked out pretty well.

Alder said, "There's no hard evidence that Euclides has changed sides. And besides, even if he isn't the best man for the job, Oscar put his trust in him."

"And Oscar is never mistaken."

"Not about things like that."

Sri and Alder had spent many hours discussing the ways in which the relationships and affiliations between the Peixoto family's key players were growing ever more polarised. Like his mother, Alder believed that peace and reconciliation was a better option than war, but he also believed that the family's green saint still had significant power and influence, a view that in Sri's opinion was supported more by sentiment than reasoned judgment.

"Perhaps Oscar was right to trust Euclides when he put him in charge of this project," she said. "But things have changed since then. Since Maximilian's death."

"But you haven't changed your mind."

"You know that I haven't."

As always, Sri was tempted to add *not yet*, but she didn't want to start an argument about her divided loyalty, her work with Oscar Finnegan Ramos and her work on Project Oxbow, not when she wanted to concentrate on the matter at hand. And besides, she really did want the biome project and everything associated with it to succeed. Not only because it would be no light thing to betray Oscar Finnegan Ramos, but because she had put so much into it, and it truly was magnificent. And because its success would surely be a major boost to her ambition to collaborate with Avernus.

She said, "What I believe has nothing to do with what Euclides believes. And it's obvious that he believes that it's in his best interests to switch sides, go over to the pro-war faction. It's the only way to explain his indifference to this crisis."

"Or maybe it's just that you don't like him," Alder said, still nettled by her insinuation that Oscar's judgement might be less than perfect.

"What's to like? He's vain and arrogant, and he isn't especially intelligent, either. Like many of the scions, he's noblesse without the oblige. They inherited their positions, Alder, but we earned ours. That's why we are better than them, even though they own most of the world. That's why we will survive this. Whatever happens, we'll survive."

There was a brief silence. Then Alder said, "Whatever happens."

"Good. Now, how should we deal with Loc Ifrahim, and his insinuation that Speller Twain may be planning to assassinate me?"

"We can't make a direct move against Speller Twain because he is still working for Euclides Peixoto. And we can't expect Euclides Peixoto to help us. So I suppose we will have to pretend to trust Loc Ifrahim."

Sri hugged her darling clever boy, kissed him on the forehead. "As long as he thinks we trust him, we have him in the palm of our hand."

"Speller Twain may not be the one coming after us," Alder said. "It may be Mr. Ifrahim. And if he is working for the general . . ."

"No," Sri said. "Arvam needs me. That's why he gave me that blunt warning at the funeral. If Mr. Ifrahim was telling the truth, if I am the target of an assassination plot, someone other than Arvam will be behind it."

"Still, it may not be wise to allow Mr. Ifrahim to get too close to you in future."

"The assassin, if he exists, won't make his move yet. It will be in a public place, where it will make the greatest impact."

"The opening ceremony."

"Exactly. Meanwhile, we behave as if nothing has changed. Call up your files. You can brief me on who I'm meeting tomorrow."

Sri had already endured a tedious welcoming ceremony—bad speeches full of uninspired platitudes, a wearisome round of introductions, dull conversations with duller dignitaries. There was worse to come. The day after she met with Loc Ifrahim, the tours and meetings began in earnest.

The sessions where the Peixoto family's negotiators outlined the advantages of trade and details of possible deals took up hours of her valuable time, but at least they were amusing in a lowbrow, circusy kind of way. Unlike government committees and family conferences in Brasília, the presentations and discussions were attended not only by senators from the city and outlying settlements but also by any citizens who pitched up out of interest or curiosity. There seemed to be little in the way of protocol or rules of debate. Anyone could say anything to anyone else at any time. Seniority meant nothing. Arguments were won as much by a refusal to give way to others as by logic, and a great deal of time was wasted in arguing for special interests or airing old grievances that had nothing to do with the topic at hand. One day, some old coot representing a Russian community on the far side of Callisto spent two hours making a filibuster speech in attempt to shoehorn advantageous terms for his family into a discussion document. And when he finally gave way, another interloper started reading out a list of pointless questions that took up the rest of the session, which finally broke up in disarray.

Sri wore her spex throughout, recording everything without a qualm.

Nothing important would be decided at these meetings, so it wouldn't in any way damage the interests of the peace and reconciliation faction if Arvam Peixoto was privy to it. The family's hard-shelled negotiators would hammer out details of any deals later on, in private sessions. From what she'd seen so far, Sri was of the opinion that they were more than capable of talking rings around the hapless Outers, and in any case the Outers were quite open about their interest in the new fusion motor. So far, it looked like Oscar Finnegan Ramos's long-term plan to ramp up funding of applied science, vigorously contested by those members of the family who believed it to be a waste of resources, was going to be vindicated.

She recorded the endless round of tours, too. The Callistans were inordinately proud of Rainbow Bridge and seemed eager to show their distinguished visitors every nook and cranny. There was a tour of the biome, of course, and of the tunnel farms and the undergardens that processed the city's waste, typical small factories and model apartments, pocket parks and the cemetery forest . . .

Sri wasn't cut out for diplomacy, but she had to pretend to take an interest in everything she was shown and endure the impertinent questions of ordinary Outers, who seemed to believe that they had a right to know everything about anyone. It didn't help that many of her hosts were only a few years older than Alder, enthusiastic, animated, sincere, and fantastically optimistic. Sri thought they were far too idealistic and naive, and she didn't think much of the cosmetic cuts of which they were so proud, either. She had no problem with adaptations to low gravity—alterations to the mechanism of bone-calcium reabsorption, fine-tuning balance and proprioception, two-chambered microhearts in the femoral and subclavian arteries to stop blood pooling, and so on. But the plethora of smart tattoos, spurs and scales and a host of other silly fancies were good for nothing but advertising the shallow vanity of her hosts, who blithely assumed that they were the pinnacle of human evolution, and their city a utopia, and were increasingly puzzled and embarrassed by Sri's cool indifference to their clumsy propaganda.

The only tour that really interested her was the last in an interminable series that had taken up far too much of her time: a trip to one of the vacuum organism farms out on the cratered plain north of Rainbow Bridge. Sri, Alder and their hosts travelled in a rolligon with a mostly transparent cabin, like a goldfish bowl on six fat mesh wheels. It moved at a stately pace along a broad road that sliced through low ridges thrown up by the seismic energy of ancient impacts. It was night. Jupiter's fat disc dominated the black sky. Stars were flung with careless extravagance everywhere else, thousands of them, hard untwinkling points of every colour.

The farm was set in a shallow crater ten kilometres across and half buried in the plain. A gap in the slumped ridge of its rimwall opened out to reveal a patchwork of fields of vacuum organisms stretching away to the curved horizon. Other farms to the east and west were vast monocultures of vacuum organisms that synthesised plastics, or slowly accumulated biomass that, if the conventional crops grown in tunnels under the city failed, could feed the population for several months. And there were thousands of hectares of vacuum organisms that accumulated on their surfaces coatings of pure graphite used in the manufacture of construction diamond or fullerenes. The fields of this farm, though, were nurseries for varieties that after propagation would be transplanted at metal-rich sites scattered across Callisto. Some were chemoautrophic, obtaining their energy from oxidation of elemental sulphur and ferrous iron; others used sunlight and electrochemical energy generated by temperature gradients in the crust, which their holdfasts penetrated for dozens of metres; all grew dense, finely-branched webs deep into the ice, leaching out metals and sequestering them in harvestable nodules. Metals, mostly derived from meteoritic impacts, were in short supply on Callisto and the other moons of Jupiter. The bolides and fracture-bed remnants of large meteorites could be mined, but a myriad of smaller impacts had salted the ice with thin deposits that only vacuum organisms could extract efficiently.

Vacuum organisms inhabited the borderland between machines and life: hives or self-organising swarms of various kinds of microscopic machines that behaved like cells in living organisms, making copies of themselves, changing their shape and metabolic repertoire according to simple rules programmed into giant self-replicating molecules analogous to DNA. They grew and multiplied in temperatures as low as −220° Celsius, forming structures that harmoniously complemented the stark moonscapes. The most common morphological types echoed the structure of lichens, from rugose or ridged scabs to filamentous tangles. A few elaborated delicate fans and fretworks, or flat fins rising in long rows from the adamantine ice, always orientated north to south to maximise the amount of light they could gather. And because insolation was low around Jupiter—just four percent of the average amount of light striking Earth's surface—every type of vacuum organism was a deep, light-absorbing black. Travelling in the rolligon along the raised road that cut through the fields of tan dust was like passing over a vast page of some ancient manuscript printed in the hieroglyphic script of a forgotten language.

Alder was fascinated by the robots that stalked along the rows of vacuum organisms, and by the fact that most of the farm workers were convicts serving rehabilitation terms. As he and Sri were shown around the laboratories where Avernus had worked in the early days of the Outer System, when creating vacuum organisms and improving the yields and varieties of the limited number of conventional food plants had made the difference between survival and failure, he asked all kinds of questions, shamelessly deploying his knack of acting much younger than he was, eager and charming and innocent as a puppy.

The laboratories were housed in low-roofed chambers with internal walls built of blocks of tan brick manufactured from compressed dust, their mortar courses blackened by age. Many of the rooms in the living quarters were empty—the convict labour force was housed in a new facility to the south— and most of the laboratories were as dark and empty as the living quarters, while the equipment in the rest was antiquated and clearly not much used. And despite the crisp linen, sparkling crystal and china, and fresh flowers on the tables, the commons where Sri and Alder and their hosts ate lunch seemed forlorn and derelict. It seemed that little research was done here these days.

Sri, who had first made her reputation by developing an artificial photo-synthetic system that was almost five percent more efficient than any designed by Avernus, told her hosts about the vacuum organisms grown around the lunar city of Athena. "You could cultivate them here, if you rigged lights. Or use vacuum organisms that utilise electrochemical energy, as in the first strains. I have cut many variations on those. You can plug fields of them straight into an electricity supply and stand back and watch them grow. I'd have to splice adaptions to the much lower surface temperature, of course, but it isn't a problem. I bet I could increase productivity by an order of two magnitudes."

One of the scientists who worked at the laboratory said that it was all very interesting, but they really had no need to increase efficiency. The population of Rainbow Bridge was stable, and conventional farms were currently overproducing foodstuffs.

Sri got blank, evasive looks when she asked what would happen if the population began to increase suddenly. If, say, there was a sudden rise in the rate of immigration.

"I don't think you can dismiss it so easily," she said. "You have a lot of empty territory here. Millions of square kilometres. Many of the people on Earth who are squeezed into cities would jump at the chance to homestead."

Her hosts politely expressed doubt that people from Earth would really want to come here, and pointed out that in any case it wasn't economically feasible. Sri retorted that most people had been confined to cities as the regreening of Earth progressed, and despite extensive anti-birth programmes the global population was still increasing because people were living longer. Sooner or later emigration was inevitable, and not just to the Moon, which could not support many people anyway, because of the lack of water. The new fusion motor meant that travel to the Outer System would be much easier, and in any case it wasn't very expensive, right now, to pack people into hibernation coffins and send them off in ordinary freighters.

She was trying to get a reaction from the Outers, but it was like prodding sea anemones. After the first couple of jabs they closed right up. Only Devon Pike, an ancient gene wizard who had some kind of honorary position at the laboratory, stood up to her.

He was a rail-thin but vigorous old man with a shock of white hair, a first-generation Outer who had worked in this facility with Avernus more than eighty years ago. From her homework, Sri knew that he had a small talent for patching traits from one species to another but showed little imagination. An able technician rather than a true artist.

"The fact is, madam, Rainbow Bridge is the oldest and largest settlement in the Outer System," he said. "It was founded almost a century ago, and despite longevity treatments and the early period of forced population growth we are still a little under twenty thousand souls. We live within our means. We do not intend to repeat the mistakes of Earth, and considering that repairing the damage caused by overpopulation and the Overturn is now akin to a religion, I am surprised that you believe that we can survive what you, on Earth, very nearly did not."

"Like it or not, the new fusion motor will change everything," Sri said. "It will effectively shrink the distance between the systems of Jupiter and Saturn, and allow you to explore and exploit new territory. And it will also bring Earth and the Outer System together."

"Then perhaps we'd be better off without it," Devon Pike said.

"It exists, grandfather," one of the young Outers said. "We can't unmake it."

"It will put Neptune and Uranus in easy reach," another said. "The Kuiper Belt too."

"We have no need for expansion," the old man said, and turned back to Sri. "You took the Moon from us. Also Mars, although you've done nothing with it since you slaughtered the Martians. Now you want to come out here and cause more mischief."

"Mars was attacked by the Democratic Republic of China—a country that no longer exists," Sri said. "It's ancient history. Times have changed. We acknowledge that on Earth every day, as we strive to undo the ecological crimes committed by our great-great-grandparents. And if I may be candid, I am amazed to find that there are people here who want to maintain the status quo simply because it suits them. You are against expansion. I suppose you are against the biome, too."

"The biome is a mistake," the old man said. "I have the greatest respect for Avernus. I do not doubt her generosity. But we don't need to be reminded of what we left behind. We have made new lives here."

"New? When was the last time these laboratories produced a new strain of vacuum organism? Not some modification or minor improvement to an existing strain, but something entirely novel."

"Well, I suppose you would have to ask the director . . ."

"I don't need to," Sri said. "Your research programme is at best trivial. Hobbyist stuff. You had the advantage over us for a long time, sitting out here with your archives and genome libraries, but we are catching up now. We have the energy and spirit and vision that you have lost."

Devon Pike spluttered out some reply, but Sri paid no attention to it. She felt a bright singing in her head. This wasn't propaganda. She had no time for propaganda. She really and truly believed it. At the neighbouring table, Alder was chattering away with a posse of younger scientists, handsome and slim in his red suit-liner. What a team they made, she thought fondly. Her hosts, of course, pretended to be politely amused by her forthright bluntness, and tried to steer the course of the conversation away from the reefs of controversy, but she cut through their babble.

"You achieved much, once upon a time. I admit it. You did more than survive. You created new ways of living. You kept scientific research alive. But you have lost the frontier spirit that drove you to do all those wonderful things. Societies as well as people become afraid of change as they grow older. It's human nature. The young have adventures while the old sit at home and nurture their memories. But the plain fact is that it is time to let go of the past. It is time to look ahead. This is supposed to be a democracy. Everyone has an equal say; anyone can put an issue to the vote. But for too long, Mr. Pike, your generation has had a disproportionate voice. If you don't believe me, ask your great-grandchildren."

"They should not forget what was done to us by Earth," Devon Pike said stubbornly. "What happened on the Moon, and Mars. Why we came here."

Sri looked around, but apart from the old gene wizard none of the people—not even the young Outers—would meet her gaze.

"Perhaps Avernus has a better outlook on the future," she said. "I look forward to finding out."

Sri knew that she and Avernus had much to talk about. Her confidence was unassailable. She wasn't the most influential gene wizard on Earth, not yet, nor the most experienced, but she was certainly the best. It was only natural that Avernus would want to meet someone who might be her equal.

After the biome project had been finalised, Sri had done everything she could to reach out to Avernus. She had even sent to the gene wizard's only permanent home, in Paris, Dione, a signed hard copy, bound in her own vat-grown skin, of the research paper that had made her reputation. But so far there had been no response, no hint of contact. She'd been on Callisto for eight days now, and she still didn't know if Avernus would be present at the opening ceremony. Her hosts retreated into maddening vagueness whenever she asked them about it, which almost certainly meant that they didn't know either, but were too polite to admit it. Alder had made little progress either, and none of Sri's contacts in the Peixoto family and the Brazilian government back on Earth had any hard information about Avernus's plans or whereabouts. Even her sponsor, Oscar Finnegan Ramos, had drawn a blank.

"She has always been a shy and elusive creature," he'd told Sri, in his last message. "Perhaps you know that I met her only once. A hundred years ago, it would be. Yes, just before the Overturn. It was a conference about metabolic pathway design in the first vacuum organisms. She led the research in that field, of course. She was years ahead of the rest of us. She'd been invited to give the speech at the plenary session, and right up to the last moment no one knew if she would turn up. I was going to take her place. And then, suddenly, a few hours before the speech was due, there she was, standing at the back of one of the open discussions. You can imagine the fuss. She was mobbed. As for her speech, well, I think it gave at least three people ideas that made their careers, and then she was gone. So don't worry, my dear. She will be there or she won't be there. You won't know until the day."

Sri couldn't tell Oscar that there was a strong possibility that someone—Speller Twain, Loc Ifrahim, *someone*—might be planning to assassinate Avernus. That they might be planning to assassinate *her*. Not just because she didn't trust the encryption on the radio link and the Outers were almost certainly listening in, but because Euclides Peixoto was probably eavesdropping, too. Not to mention General Arvam Peixoto. She was surrounded by enemies. She could trust only Alder and her secretary, Yamil Cho.

Immediately after the visit to the vacuum organism farm she met with the construction crew for updates on their work, and then briefly talked with the young diplomat, Loc Ifrahim, who told her that he had learned something of great interest.

"Mr. Twain has been visiting the free zone in the city."

Sri pretended that she didn't know anything about the free zone and let Loc Ifrahim describe it and its customs to her.

"There's a saying that what happens in the free zone stays in the free zone. But I have heard a rumour," Loc Ifrahim said, "that he has been meeting with citizens who oppose the project and the whole idea of reconciliation. There are people, I am sure you know this, who would do anything to make sure that this project will fail."

"Do you know who these citizens might be?"

"Alas, I don't. Not yet. But I do know that Ursula Freye visited the free zone several times before she was murdered. There is a connection, ma'am. I am sure of it. I will continue my inquiries, and you can rest assured that if I discover anything I will tell you without delay."

"He wants me to think that Speller Twain is plotting against me," Sri told Alder a little later.

"How do you know he isn't telling the truth? After all, Speller Twain definitely killed Ursula Freye."

They were lying side by side in the blister. Alder was spooning up the curdy flesh of a custard apple.

"Do you remember the peace officers I talked to?"

"Of course."

"The city government told them to abandon their investigation into Ursula Freye's death because it was politically sensitive. They weren't happy about that, and were very interested when I told them that Loc Ifrahim had offered me Speller Twain's head on a plate. They think as we do. That Speller Twain and Loc Ifrahim were both involved in Ms. Freye's death, and that Loc Ifrahim is using Speller Twain to divert attention so that he will be free to make his own move."

"But how can they help us if they have been ordered to abandon the investigation?"

"Like every kind of police, they are prone to bending the law when it suits them. They have been keeping a discreet watch on both Speller Twain and Loc Ifrahim. That's why I knew that Speller Twain has been visiting the free zone before Mr. Ifrahim told me about it. I even know what he's doing there. It has nothing to do with any kind of plotting. He is visiting a club where people have old-fashioned straight sex while wearing masks and robes."

"Perhaps the sex is a cover."

"There is no doubt that Speller Twain killed Ursula Freye. Perhaps he was ordered to do it by Euclides Peixoto. Perhaps Loc Ifrahim persuaded him to do it. Perhaps it was his own idea. But the peace officers are convinced that it had nothing to do with any faction in the city."

Alder popped a spoonful of seeds and pulp into his mouth and said, "I think I know why you don't want to make a preemptive strike against Mr. Twain."

Sri smiled. "You do?"

"You want one or both of them to make an attempt on Avernus's life. You save her, and she is grateful . . ."

"And she teaches me everything she knows? It's a pretty fantasy. But I'm afraid that's all it is—a fantasy. Something from one of your sagas."

Alder put on a sulky look, half-lowering his eyelids, pouting. It made him seem even more delectable. "Why don't you stop teasing me and tell me what you *are* planning? I know you aren't simply going to wait and see what happens."

"As a matter of fact, that's just what I'm going to do."

"So I don't have to worry," Alder said. "You have made arrangements to deal with everything. You don't need my help."

"Don't be silly. Why would I have brought you all the way out here if I didn't need your help, your special talents? Making friends, for instance. I'm good at upsetting or intimidating people, but as for being friendly . . . for that, I need you."

"Well, you made me the way I am."

"Tell me what you were talking about at lunch today. You seem to have made some friends amongst the younger scientists at the farm."

"Oh, it wasn't much," Alder said. "Except for one thing, perhaps. Although, compared to your plans, it won't seem very exciting."

Sri knew that he was aching to tell her what he had discovered, but had to tickle him and kiss him before he gave in, telling her that several of the young scientists working at the research farm had invited him to visit a little grotto that had been the prototype for several of Avernus's later projects.

"What kind of grotto?"

"Just a little crevasse," Alder said. "With vacuum organisms growing in it. It's old, though. Avernus made it when she was working on that farm, eighty years ago or more."

"What kind of vacuum organisms?"

Alder shrugged.

"Why don't I know about this?"

"It was discovered by some of my new friends two years ago. They've kept it secret ever since." Alder explained that fourth-generation citizens of Rainbow Bridge liked to go hiking and camping in what they called the back country. "They stay out for up to a week, travelling on foot for several hundred kilometres. They say that you can't understand the land unless you walk it. It sounds like silly mysticism, I know, but they are very serious about it."

"They spend all this time out there in their pressure suits?"

"They hike between shelters and oases. It's something they have been doing for more than ten years now. There are different tribes with different totems, and they follow different paths. At least, I think that's how it works. Burton spent a very long time explaining it to me, but most of it sounded like gibberish."

"Burton is one of the people who wants to take you to this grotto."

Alder nodded. "It isn't far from the research farm. A hundred kilometres or so."

"And Burton and his friends—"

"*Her* friends."

"They want you to walk a hundred kilometres."

"I've hiked further on the Moon."

"With Yamil Cho, and with a caravan of rolligons following you. Perhaps Yamil should go with you."

"I don't think my friends would like that," Alder said. "This is one of their secret, special places. They want to share it with me now because I'm their new best friend. And really, it isn't as risky as it sounds. If they get into trouble they can call up a gig."

His look was one of mute appeal. He'd set a treasure at her feet and wanted to be praised and rewarded. After a moment's thought, Sri decided to give in. It was time that she gave him some of the responsibility he craved. It would show him that she trusted him, and then there was the grotto itself, almost certainly one of Avernus's creations, full of who knew what secrets . . .

So she hugged him, told him how well he had done, how proud she was of him, and said that if any sex was involved he was to be careful not to get too carried away.

"You're finding out who you are. You should have fun while you do it. But be careful not to do anything that might come back on you later on. And if any of those convicts are involved, make sure they are screened first. And of course," Sri added, "you'll bring back samples and a full video record, as well as a precise reading of its global coordinates."

"I'm not stupid," Alder said, but he was smiling now.

Sri kissed him, full on the mouth. Tasting the silky sweetness of custard apple, and Alder's live sweetness beneath. "You're very far from stupid. I don't know what I would do without you."

12

For a hundred years, the Outer System settlements had been turned in on themselves, concentrating first on surviving in hostile and Spartan environments, then on establishing robust, durable ecosystems and economic and social mechanisms. But now they were trembling on the brink of a profound social and cultural revolution. A Prignogenic phase change driven by the eagerness of many young Outers to cut loose from the old, reactionary regimes of the city states on the moons of Jupiter and Saturn. To light out for new territory. The moons of Uranus and Neptune. Pluto, Eris, hundreds of dwarf planets in the Kuiper Belt. A few wanted to terraform Mars, dismantling one of Jupiter's small outer moons to manufacture solar-sail mirrors and thousands of tons of halocarbon greenhouse gases that would significantly warm the planet and cause outgassing of carbon dioxide and water vapour from the frozen regolith, adding to the small but significant increase in atmospheric pressure caused by the comet dropped by the Chinese onto the original Martian colonists.

This burgeoning frontier spirit, combined with radical notions about posthuman utopianism, was beginning to cause serious social and political unrest. The Outer System's economy was built upon a barter and social ranking system based on the value of volunteer work and exchange of scientific, cultural and technological ideas and information. But now the brightest and the best of the new generation were devoting themselves to planning new kinds of social groupings that deliberately excluded themselves from the mainstream. Young people were quitting the cities for oases, shelters and other microhabitats constructed by tireless crews of robots. And they were engaged in fierce and frequently divisive debates within the collectives and family trusts that owned most of the ships in the Outer System.

The new generation of Outers wanted to use the ships for exploration and to transport volunteers eager to found new settlements in the far reaches of the Solar System, but they were outnumbered and outvoted by their parents, grandparents and great-grandparents. Because everyone in the Outer System had access to medical treatments that had increased the average life span to a little over a hundred and fifty years, the democracies of their cities and settlements, and their collectives and trusts, were really gerontocracies, cautious and reactionary, preferring discussion to decision, argument to action. The older generations had controlling interests in the ships as well as in most of the infrastructure of the Outer System settlements, asserted that they were essential for trade and commerce within and between the Jupiter and Saturn Systems, and refused to sanction construction of new ships because of the cost. Oases and shelters were built by robot labour—the robots were mostly left over from construction of the cities and it was cheaper to keep them working than to decommission them—but there were no robot factories for spaceships. Every ship was more or less hand built, and although their hulls and lifesystems could be spun from diamond and fullerene composites manufactured from carbonaceous deposits easily mined or extracted from the icy regoliths of most moons, fabrication of their fusion motors and control systems required expensive rare earths and metals.

The would-be explorers and colonists were attacking this problem with vigour. They had worked up plans to set up robot factories that could settle on suitable asteroids and mine and refine metals that would be flung toward Jupiter and Saturn using rail guns built on site, and had designed ships equipped with lightsails and propelled by fixed lasers, or with sophisticated chemical reaction motors built from ceramics and fullerene composites. These slowboats might take a decade or more to reach their destinations, but their passengers would sleep out the voyage in hibernation. The younger Outers were determined to overcome their lack of financial and political leverage with their energy, ingenuity, and determination. They had time on their side, of course. Despite gerontological treatments and sophisticated medical procedures and therapies, simple mortality meant that sooner or later the rising generation would gain control of their families' trusts and collectives. But by then they would be as old as their grandparents were now, and they were too eager and too impatient to wait. Almost every sociopolitical model predicated breakout within a decade. If Earth could not reinforce its ties with the city states of Jupiter and Saturn and help to strengthen their conservative regimes, the Outers would diverge so quickly and in so many unpredictable ways that it would become impossible to find common ground with them. And that would make war inevitable.

But the new generation had not broken completely with the past. They admired and revered with an almost holy passion the work Avernus and other gene wizards had done in the early years of the Outer System, the novel designs for vacuum organisms and closed ecosystems that had made it possible to build permanent settlements on the moons of Jupiter and Saturn. Avernus was their green saint, their Darwin, their Einstein, an enigmatic genius shrouded in legend and rumour, a major inspiration for their own radicalism, the ambitions and yearnings they had not yet fully formulated. Sri found it very interesting that Alder's new friends had kept their discovery of the grotto from their elders, and very encouraging that they trusted Alder with their secret. If she ever got the chance to meet Avernus, the encounter would no doubt be encumbered with diplomatic protocol and ceremonial niceties. There would be little or no chance for any kind of frank discussion, scientist to scientist. But if Alder could get as close to the members of Avernus's famous crew as he had to the young scientists of the vacuum organism farm, he might be able to open informal channels that could be used to keep communication flowing and to keep track of Avernus after she left Callisto.

But even now, with only a few days to go before the biome opening ceremony, no one in the Brazilian embassy or in the Peixoto family's crew had been able to get anyone in the city to confirm whether or not Avernus would be coming to Rainbow Bridge. The *Luís Inácio da Silva*, eavesdropping on the Jupiter system's traffic control, had turned up nothing useful. There was plenty of chatter about the gene wizard on the social boards, but nothing substantive. Alder came back from his trip to the grotto with pictures and samples of elaborate fluted and rippled growths of chemoautrophic vacuum organisms that had been growing in their secluded environment for more than eighty years, but he had no news of their creator.

At last, Sri stepped on her pride and her caution and invited Loc Ifrahim to her suite again. He fed her scrappy bits of evidence against Speller Twain and repeated his offer to "deal with the problem," but said that he had heard nothing about whether or not Avernus would be attending the opening ceremony. It seemed that no one knew, and the absence of any hard facts made Sri anxious and impatient and prone to sudden squalls of foul temper that kept Alder and Yamil Cho on tenterhooks. And then, at an official reception the day before the opening ceremony, Euclides Peixoto sidled up to Sri and said, "She's here."

"Who is here?"

"Avernus—who else? If I were you I'd get yourself some new inform- ants," Euclides Peixoto said, "because they definitely aren't as good as mine, and I'm not even trying to get close to the crazy old witch."

This was in the central courtyard of the Greater Brazilian embassy. It was tented with swathes of pastel silks, its walls were hung with huge explosions of flowers and ferns, and its floor was carpeted with dried rose petals that yielded a heady musk as they were trodden underfoot by the great and the good of Rainbow Bridge, Brazilian diplomats and trade delegates, and representatives from Minos, Europa and other cities and settlements of the Jupiter System. The biome construction crew was huddled in one corner, clearly ill at ease amongst the finery and ritual courtesy, and in their uniform coveralls drabber than anyone else in the crowd, including the people serving cocktails and canapes and the string quartet that was playing selections of Haydn and Mozart. The courtyard was so crowded that if someone moved, all the people around them had to move too, so everyone was slowly rotating around everyone else like gears inside an ancient and especially complex clock mechanism. Sri was standing toe-to-toe with Euclides Peixoto, enveloped in a little cloud of his cologne.

"I never doubted that Avernus would come," she said coolly. "The biome was her idea. She underwrote the cost of its construction. So of course she would want to be present at the start of its quickening."

Euclides Peixoto's smile widened to show most of his startlingly white, even teeth. He was wearing some kind of ridiculous uniform that Sri reck- oned was of his own invention: grey jacket and trousers with pink piping, a slab of medal ribbons on his chest, a grey cap with a polished black visor pulled low over small and close-set eyes that always reminded Sri of some kind of mustelid. A weasel or stoat; a sneaky little raptor sidling through undergrowth, searching out tender prey.

"There's no 'of course' about it," he said. "Oh, I know how you scientists have to assume something is true before you can work out whether or not it is. I know you're natural-born optimists. But this isn't science. It's politics. And as my daddy always told me, never assume anything in politics, 'cause it'll make an ass out of you and me both. Avernus is paying for the biome, sure, but she hasn't shown a jot of interest in the design, hasn't said a single word to anyone involved. To us, or to our hosts here in the city. We don't even know if she likes what's being done in her name. So if you'd asked me yesterday if she was going to turn up, I might have said, 'Don't bet serious money on it.' But I *definitely* wouldn't have said 'Of course.'"

"You must be disappointed to be proven wrong."

"Don't get your hopes up about meeting her. She's on Callisto all right, but she isn't in the city, and I don't know if she's coming to the opening ceremony. I don't even know where she's staying. But I'll tell you what I'll do," Euclides Peixoto said, his eyes glinting with malignant humour under the visor of his cap. "If she does turn up, I'll probably have to talk about the biome with her, even though she's isn't at all interested in what we're doing. It won't cost me anything to mention your name. In case she hasn't heard of you."

"Thank you. But it won't be necessary."

"It's a genuine offer. When I was a kid, I used to put different kinds of ants in a jar, see which would win. I admit to being kind of intrigued about what might happen if you two geniuses ever go head to head."

"It's not a question of winning or losing, or who has the bigger and better ideas. It's a matter of entering into a dialogue. For the good of the family."

"Well, you be sure to let me know how you get on with whatever arrangements you need to make with her," Euclides Peixoto said. "If you have trouble making contact, if your people can't do their job, I'm ready to put in a good word. Because even though you're not blood, I like to think you're loyal to my uncle. But right now I got to go press some flesh and talk some small talk. And get outside of a drink or two before I make my speech."

Sri checked the data miner that she'd posted to keep watch on the city's boards, but it had nothing to report beyond the usual megabytes of idle speculation. She called her secretary and instructed him to find out what he could. She called Alder, lost somewhere in the reception's dense throng; he said that he hadn't heard anything but would ask every one of his new friends. Finally, she called the city peace officer, Dee Fujita. She claimed not to have heard about Avernus's arrival on Callisto, and told Sri that arresting Speller Twain and Loc Ifrahim, holding them until after the opening ceremony, wasn't an option. Not only because of Loc Ifrahim's diplomatic immunity, but also because there was no hard evidence of a conspiracy.

"We can't pull him in on suspicion," Dee Fujita said. "We can't do that to one of our own citizens, much less one of yours."

"Suspicion? He's already murdered at least one person."

"Unless you have clear evidence that either Speller Twain or Loc Ifrahim are planning to harm Avernus, I don't have the authority to touch them. Your only option is to take it to the Senate and argue that it is a matter of the city's security. You could swear out a deposition."

"Can you guarantee a result?"

"The Senate would first have to agree to put it to the vote. And then it would have to win the vote."

"And then the whole city would know about it."

"I keep forgetting that you have funny ideas about how government works," Dee Fujita said.

"I keep forgetting that you have funny ideas about using popularity contests to make decisions vital to the security of your city." Sri was simmering with frustration, on the edge of a tantrum. She closed her eyes, visualised the cold white Antarctic sky above an ice-flecked ocean, and said, "If I made a deposition, it would be like declaring war against Mr. Peixoto. I would have to be sure that you would back me up."

"I'll back you up by continuing to keep watch on Speller Twain and Loc Ifrahim. Let me know if you find out anything," Dee Fujita said, and cut the connection.

Sri couldn't leave the reception until the speeches were over, had to make small talk to people she didn't know or care about while trying to think through the implications of Euclides Peixoto's news, trying to calculate how she could reach out to Avernus in the short time left before the quickening ceremony. At last the crowd's intricate mechanism brought her face to face with Loc Ifrahim.

He inclined his head in a minimal bow, and asked her if she had further considered the matter they had discussed when they had last met.

"You've failed me," Sri said. "Avernus is here. And I had to find it out from Euclides Peixoto."

Loc Ifrahim's surprise seemed genuine. "If it's true, if it isn't yet another rumour, then none of my contacts know. Did Mr. Peixoto happen to tell you how he found out?"

"I didn't ask him. I'm disappointed in you, Mr. Ifrahim. Gravely disappointed. Either you aren't talking to the right people, or they aren't telling you the truth. Avernus is here. Somewhere on Callisto. Perhaps in this city, perhaps somewhere else—the vacuum organism farm, for instance, where she used to work. I want to know where she is, where she came from, and who she brought with her. Most of all, I want to know how to contact her. If you can find out anything useful I'll forgive you for failing me, and make sure that you are handsomely rewarded."

If he knew something but was hiding it from her, Sri wanted to force his hand. Make him give it up by bribery or by threat. And if he didn't know anything, she could still make use of him, and by making use of him keep him under close watch.

The young diplomat thought for a moment, then said, "I have a contact at the port. As soon as this little party is over, I'll talk to her."

"You won't wait until this is over because I need to know as soon as possible. Will you help me or not? Yes or no?"

"It may take a little time."

"Come to my apartment in three hours," Sri said, and turned her back on him and let the slow circulation of the crowd carry her away.

The Brazilian ambassador and the mayor of Rainbow Bridge gave speeches; so did Euclides Peixoto. His speech was short and said nothing new, but he delivered it well, crisply emphasising key phrases, winning gusts of applause that he waited out with a sly smile tucked into the corner of his mouth, as if considering some private joke. At last, Sri was able to slip away without causing a major diplomatic incident. When she reached her suite, her secretary told her that Loc Ifrahim had already arrived. He was waiting for her in the dark observation blister, a shadowy figure looking out at the lake stretched below, all black and silver in the crepuscular glimmer of the chandeliers, turning to her as she entered, telling her that he had some news.

"I leaned on my contact at the port," he said. "She talked to the pilots of every ship that landed there in the past week. It seems that Avernus arrived six hours ago, on a tug hauling a cargo of pharmaceuticals and luxury food items from Europa. The tug is owned by the family of its pilot, Vlad Izumi. He's twenty-eight, unpartnered, no children, a citizen of Minos, Europa—"

"She came alone? Without her crew?"

"There was one other passenger. A young girl, most likely Avernus's daughter."

"Yuli. Her name is Yuli. Where are they now? In the city?"

"They boarded a rolligon, headed north. If you give me a little more time I may be able to find out where it went."

"I need to know as soon as possible. And why did Mr. Peixoto know about this before I did? How could she arrive here without anyone in the city knowing?"

"The embassy has been monitoring arrivals and departures at Rainbow Bridge's port, of course. Anyone can do it. The information is openly available on the net. But Vlad Izumi, the tug's pilot, is not a known associate of

Avernus's, and she and her daughter weren't registered as passengers. Most likely they hitched a lift. It happens all the time. There's no border control here, no customs. I must assume that no one recognised them when they disembarked, and they didn't make any use of the phone system or the rest of the net. They simply walked away. As for Mr. Izumi, he is already on his way back to Europa, but he was quite happy to chat about his passengers. It seems that my contact was not the only person to ask him about them. Speller Twain got there first."

"I thought you were a good friend of Mr. Twain."

"I never claimed that he was a friend," Loc Ifrahim said. "Is there anything else that you need to know? As you can see, I'm more than willing to help."

His smile, just visible in the faint light of the chandeliers, was a thing of beauty, winning and duplicitous.

"There is one more thing," Sri said.

It was the prearranged signal to her secretary, who had been listening in on the conversation. When Yamil Cho stepped into the blister, lithe and neat in his black jumper and leggings, Loc Ifrahim's smile didn't change, but he couldn't quite disguise the unease in his voice. "I came here to help you, ma'am. And I can still be of help. For instance, in the matter we spoke about before."

"You mean killing Speller Twain?"

"Kill?" Loc Ifrahim mimed shock. "I think you misunderstood me when I said that I could help you undo the damage he has caused to your project."

"And did I misunderstand you when you told me that he had murdered Ursula Freye?"

Yamil Cho stepped toward Loc Ifrahim and the diplomat shuffled backward until he was pressed against the transparent wall of the blister, saying, "Of course he did. He admitted as much to Mr. Peixoto."

"Yes, you forgot to tell me that. And because I wonder what else you forgot to tell me, I will have to keep you here for a little while. Until after the quickening ceremony, at any rate."

Loc Ifrahim's gaze couldn't settle, moving between Sri and Yamil Cho. "My diplomatic status—"

"We'll say that you agreed to help me with my inquiries. Or I'll show the recordings of our conversations to the ambassador, let him work things out for himself. Perhaps I can't prove that you offered to kill Mr. Twain, but the implication is there."

"Very well," Loc Ifrahim said. "I'll stay here and play along with your silly scheme. But I can tell you now that this won't do you any good."

"Is that a threat, Mr. Ifrahim?"

"I'm afraid it's a fact, madam," the young man said. He had regained control of himself; his face was a bland mask devoid of any emotion. For the first time Sri realised the depth of his ambition and determination. It was something to be admired and feared.

13

Loc Ifrahim stuck to his story: he suspected that Speller Twain was planning something, but had no idea what those plans might be. Sri was tempted to put him to the question, but it would cause all kinds of trouble if she did it without the authority of Euclides Peixoto or the ambassador, and she didn't trust either of them. After some thought, she dispatched her secretary to the embassy, where Euclides Peixoto and his security chief were quartered. If Speller Twain left the embassy for any reason, Yamil would follow him wherever he went, and make sure that he knew he was being followed. Meanwhile, Alder had discovered that Avernus had visited the vacuum organism farm where she'd once worked, and had taken a rolligon and driven north, accompanied by her daughter and several of the young scientists who had taken Alder to the hidden grotto. Alder offered to give chase, but Sri told him that it would be a waste of time, and far too dangerous besides. Callisto's battered, heavily cratered terrain could hide entire armies, and unlike Earth it was not scrutinised by the panoptic gaze of spy and weather satellites. By now, Avernus and her little entourage could be at the grotto, or anywhere else within two to three hundred kilometres of the vacuum organism farm.

Wherever they'd gone, Sri was certain that they would return to the city in time for the opening ceremony. She was determined to make direct contact with Avernus, tell the gene wizard about the possible threat to her life, offer to talk to her privately. But meanwhile she could do nothing but wait, and try to get some sleep.

Early the next morning she was woken by a call from Dee Fujita. It seemed that Speller Twain was missing. "He visited the free zone after the reception ended last night. He went into the club he favours, and didn't come out again. We're interviewing everyone who was there. It will take some time—there's no guarantee that people will tell the truth, and unfortunately we can't compel them. But hopefully someone will volunteer something useful."

Sri closed her eyes. Thought of ice floes bobbing under a cold clean sky. She said, "He's going to do something. Something that takes time to prepare. While you waste time interviewing unwilling or ignorant witnesses, he is hiding somewhere in the city, getting ready to make his move."

"That's one possibility," Dee Fujita said. "Another is that Mr. Ifrahim made good his threat to take care of the man."

"Did Mr. Ifrahim visit the free zone last night?"

Sri was making a calculation. There would have been just enough time for the diplomat to have followed Speller Twain to the free zone before coming to her suite.

"Not as far as we know," Dee Fujita said. "If I wasn't certain that he'd hide behind his diplomatic immunity, I'd request an interview with him."

"I will deal with him," Sri said. She wasn't about to confess that she was holding Loc Ifrahim prisoner, and she didn't want the peace officer to chase after him and discover that he had gone missing too.

"And I will finish my round of interviews," Dee Fujita said. "If they turn up something useful, I will let you know at once."

But although surveillance footage showed Speller Twain entering the free zone, none of the patrons of his favourite club remembered any disturbance, and a random canvass of other visitors to the free zone found no one who remembered seeing him either. All the investigation achieved was to make Speller Twain's disappearance public knowledge. A group of concerned citizens of Rainbow Bridge set up an instant referendum on whether or not the opening ceremony should be delayed because of the possibility of disruption by unknown and unspecified enemies of the biome project; within an hour, more than eighty percent of citizens had responded. Opinion was violently polarised between those who felt that any delay would compromise or betray the principles of friendship and cooperation that the biome represented, and those who blamed the Peixoto family and their crew for all the trouble, and believed that it had been a mistake to have allowed them to participate in the biome's construction. In the end, a scant majority voted against any changes to the timing or nature of the ceremony.

After the results came in, Euclides Peixoto called Sri, demanding that she tell him everything she knew about the disappearance of his security chief, ranting about going into the city himself and tearing the whole bunch of freaks brand-new assholes. His anger was impressive, and didn't appear synthetic.

"You better hope that the big lunk is sleeping off the effects of a private party somewhere. That his disappearance doesn't mean that someone is planning to fuck us up," he said. "Because the ceremony is going ahead and I want you to be there, Professor Doctor. You'll be standing right beside me. So if something bad does happen, it's going to happen to you and me both."

The biome's lake had reached its final level, and the wave machines had been turned on. Chandelier-light sparkled on crests of long slow swells that passed down the length of the lake, moving south to north. They broke in broad ruffles of foam on reefs and rip-rap tables and sent up tall flowers of white spray when they struck the rocky shoreline of the main island, where people had been arriving ever since the station had been opened at midday.

It was seven in the evening now, just an hour before the lake was due to be ceremonially quickened, and still they came, families, groups of friends, couples and singletons, surges of people riding up the escalators under the glass wing of the station and melting into the carnival crowds that thronged the lawns spread either side of the forested ridge. Stands were giving away candied fruit and spun sugar, falafel and vegetable curry, sushi and savoury cakes, lemonade and green tea. There were stilt-walkers and fire-eaters. Acrobats pirouetted and threw shapes on top of poles or ladders; one swung through an intricate routine on a trapeze suspended from a giant tethered balloon. Children bounded everywhere like gazelles. Drumming circles drummed. The string quartet was playing a version of Handel's *Water Music* as Sri boarded the flat-topped maintenance barge moored at the southern end of the island.

The barge was hung from stem to stern with bunting and a tall transparent barrier had been erected around the edge of its deck to protect those unused to Callisto's low gravity from an accidental dunking. Many of the people who had been at the reception last night were already on board, including members of the Callistan Senate, the mayor, Euclides Peixoto, and the construction crew. As Sri came down the gangplank Euclides Peixoto bustled over to her, moving clumsily and unsteadily, getting in her face and demanding to know if she had any more news.

"Not a thing."

"I see you are here alone. Where's your son?"

"He's unwell."

"And your secretary, he's also unwell?"

"Unfortunately."

Yamil Cho was in the penthouse suite, guarding Loc Ifrahim and watching multiple viewpoints of the biome's tent transmitted by several dozen drones, trying to spot anything suspicious.

"Just remember that we're both in the same boat in more ways than one," Euclides Peixoto said, with an unforgiving glare.

The barge's motor started up, its crew prepared to cast off, and a woman and a young girl strolled hand in hand up the gangway. The woman was short for an Outer, brown-skinned, white-haired and broad-hipped, wearing a plain grey shift dress; the young girl's solemn face was half hidden by a tumble of glossy black curls. They paused at the end of the gangway, taking in everything around them, and across the crowded barge people broke into applause.

It was Avernus and her daughter, Yuli. The two of them were overtopped by the eager gaggle of young people who'd followed them onto the barge, several of them scientists from the vacuum organism farm. Sri had yearned for this moment ever since she had first been told about the project, but now, watching the gene wizard move slowly across the deck of the barge at the centre of a crowd of dignitaries, with the barge's motor throbbing underfoot like a monstrous heartbeat, she was seized by a sudden claustrophobic dread. Something bad was going to happen and as in a nightmare she couldn't do anything about it.

Perhaps she had taken a step forward without thinking or noticing, because Euclides Peixoto put a hand on her arm and told her in a harsh whisper to stand fast.

At the same moment a murmur went up from the people around Avernus. They were turning, looking out across the lake, pointing. Sri shook off Euclides Peixoto's grasp and floated to the edge of the transparent barrier. Something was moving toward the barge. A man. At first Sri thought that he was walking on water. Then she saw that his body hung limply in a webbing harness, and three drones anchored to the harness by short cables were dragging him puppetwise, his head lolling, his arms limp at his side, his legs washed to the thighs by the slow, broad waves rolling across the surface of the lake.

Along the shore of the island, people began to clap and cheer, thinking that this was part of the ceremony. But the people on the barge were much nearer, and could see that the man's throat had been cut. Could see as he was dragged closer by the drones that it was Speller Twain.

116

The recriminations over Speller Twain's death were immediate, vicious, and highly damaging. Euclides Peixoto incontinently blamed the city and demanded a full-scale investigation. The Callistan Senate countered by ordering a complete review of every aspect of the construction crew's work, and an inquiry into the deaths of three of its members. And as soon the Senate's investigations were completed, the crew's presence in the city would be put to a referendum. Supporters and opponents of the link with Greater Brazil were already gearing up for the political contest, throwing accusations and counter-accusations at each other.

Sri had her own idea about who had murdered Speller Twain.

"You told me you had contacts in the city," she said to Loc Ifrahim, just before she let him walk out of her apartment. "I should have known that they were working against this project. As were you."

"I have made many friends in this city, ma'am."

"Including people like the three citizens of Paris, Dione who left the city just before the ceremony. One of whom was seen several times in conversation with you in a bar in the free zone. They killed Speller Twain, didn't they? They kidnapped him when he visited the free zone, and they killed him."

"I would not know, ma'am. After all, I was being held prisoner here."

"Yes, I was stupid enough to give you an alibi while your friends did your dirty work."

Loc Ifrahim didn't bother to hide his amusement. "If you have no further use for me, I have much to do at the embassy. The ambassador has to deliver a response to the Senate's request for the facts surrounding the recent events. Perhaps I will see you at the inquiry."

"I very much doubt it."

Avernus had already quit Rainbow Bridge and was on her way back to Europa. Sri was determined to follow her. Perhaps she could redeem something from this farrago.

Before they left Callisto, Sri and Alder flew north in a boxy little gig, to Avernus's secret garden. Callisto was too far from Jupiter to be significantly heated by tidal stresses like those that warmed Io, Europa, and Ganymede, and its lithosphere had cooled quickly after formation. So its shell of water ice had not been modified by upwelling from the mantle or tectonic deformation, showed relatively little relief, and had preserved a record of the early period of heavy bombardment. There were several large impact basins, most notably Valhalla and Asgard, with central bright zones surrounded by numerous concentric rings of ridges separated by bright-floored troughs or furrows. And everywhere else the terrain was like a vast and ancient battle-field, spattered with craters of all kinds and sizes, many exhibiting fluidised ejecta morphologies, including lobed ramparts and pancake or radial fluid ejecta, that had modified or overlain older craters around them.

Avernus's garden was hidden inside a central pit crater some forty kilo-metres in diameter. The weight of the crater's rim, pressing down on the icy crust, had caused up-bowing of its floor, creating a fractured terrain of ridges and mesas dissected by riverine crevasses. Alder guided the gig to a spot near the centre of this maze and led Sri down a long, shallow pitch of ice gravel between sheer cliffs that pinched a ribbon of black sky high overhead. Although the ice seemed rock-hard it retained a little plasticity; in the deepest parts of the crevasse, pressure of the overlying mass had squeezed out an interlocking series of smooth lobes some twenty or thirty metres high.

Eighty years ago, Avernus had sprayed these bellying contours with min-eral-rich dust quickened with the seeds of a carefully selected mix of vacuum organisms. They had grown and spread into a patchwork mosaic that glowed pink and orange and dusky red in the headlamps of Sri and Alder's pressure suits, each patch a different strain, each rimmed with black borderlines where neighbouring strains were attempting to overgrow each other. Some were as smooth as polished ice; others were crusted with scales, or ridged like brain tissue. A few extruded wiry tangles of crystalline ferrous sulphate, red as fresh blood.

It was a random act of weird alien beauty that Sri had to admit was imposing, despite its obvious lack of utility. She felt that she had been afforded a glimpse of the great gene wizard's mind, even though she didn't yet understand what it meant, and took photographs and added to the sam-ples that Alder had snatched when he had been brought here by the gang of young scientists. Then they tramped back up the long slope to the gig, flew back to the city, and took the shuttle up to the *Luís Inácio da Silva* and departed for Europa.

Avernus had a head start of about twenty-six hours, but the *Luís Inácio da Silva*, equipped with the powerful new fusion motor, was able to cut a straight course between lobes of Jupiter's radio belts rather than follow the usual looping, fuel-saving, gravity-assisted orbital path. Just six hours after departing from orbit around Callisto, Europa swelled ahead of the swift little ship.

Like Callisto, Europa was a ball of silicate rock wrapped in a shell of water ice, but tidal stresses caused by the competing pulls of Jupiter and Jupiter's largest moon, Ganymede, heated its interior, and beneath its icy crust was a world ocean some twenty kilometres deep, kept liquid by hydrothermal rifts and vents where water was subducted into the lithosphere. Impacts, internal stresses, and plumes of warm water lofted by especially active and long-lived vents cracked the sheet ice of Europa's surface and liquid water welled up through the cracks and froze in long ridges. The moon's fractured surface was a palimpsest history of floodings and freezings, and its yellow-tinged sheen and delicate craquelure reminded Sri of an ancient ivory billiard ball that she had once seen in a museum of environmental atrocities in Quito, or ancient maps of Mars that showed fanciful networks of canals.

The *Luís Inácio da Silva* entered orbit around Europa just three hours after Avernus's tug touched down, but there was a long delay before the flight plan of its shuttle was approved by Europa's traffic control. Sri was happy to give Avernus a head start. She didn't want to turn this into an all-out chase. She wanted to find out where the gene wizard was staying and then open a line of communication, an overture to what she hoped would be a series of fruitful discussions. She had obtained the blessing of Oscar Finnegan Ramos for the mission, and he had reached out to an old friend of his in Europa's only large settlement, Minos.

From humble beginnings as a small and remote science base, the city of Minos had expanded downward, burrowing deep into the ice to escape Jupiter's radio belts, which delivered enough radiation to Europa's surface to kill an unprotected person in just two or three days. The crust where Minos was sited was just thirty kilometres thick, eroded by plumes of warm water lofted by a complex of hydrothermal vents along a ridge fault, and the city had extended shafts that reached down to the bottom of the ice and the buried ocean beyond.

Oscar Finnegan Ramos's friend, Tymon Simonov, was a gene wizard more than a hundred and sixty years old, one of the pioneers who'd taken part in the great exodus from the Moon. It took Sri and Alder more than a day to reach him, travelling in stages down a series of elevator shafts, a vertical journey that on Earth would have taken them to the edge of the discontinuity where the continental plates rafted on molten lava. On Europa, it delivered them to a canyon cut into the underside of the ice and filled with air. Huge biome chambers had been excavated on either side of the canyon, and its walls were hung with tiers of platforms gardened with alpine meadows and dwarfed pines and firs, jutting out above a silvery halflife membrane that flexed and undulated with the heavy wash of currents beneath. Despite the elaborate seals along the edges of the membrane, a faint curdled-egg odour of hydrogen sulphide leaked in from the anoxic ocean, and although chains of sunlamps brightened the air and panels of ice were tinted with bright, cheerful colours, it was very cold. The older citizens wore long fake-fur coats and tall fake-fur hats, and many of the younger citizens had been cut to give them thick, lustrous coats of fine hair and insulating layers of fat—seal-people with human faces and human hands and feet, clad only in shorts and many-pocketed vests.

Tymon Simonov lived in a pressurised, triple-skinned can that hung in black water to the west of the canyon, beneath a solid ceiling of ice that stretched away in every direction. His laboratories occupied all five decks, and he and his small retinue of robots seemed to be the only occupants. He told Sri and Alder that he preferred his own company these days, and was contemplating a solo voyage around Europa that would take at least two years to complete. He was hospitable enough, though, a spritely gnome with a pale, waxy face and a fringe of shoulder-length white hair around a bald pate. He wore patched shorts and a toolbelt, nothing else, talking animatedly as he explained that there shouldn't be any problem contacting Avernus once she reached where she was going.

It seemed that she had taken a shielded capsule along the half-completed equatorial railway, riding several thousand kilometres around the circumference of the little moon to the junction with a spur line to the farms at Tyre Macula. There was a very active hot spot under the great plain there. The crust was just a kilometre thick, eroded by an upwelling plume that in a hundred years or so would melt through to the surface and create a temporary sea, a slurry of ice and water boiling furiously in vacuum as it flooded the surrounding terrain before freezing over again. Water from the plume, rich in dissolved minerals, was pumped through huge tanks where bacteria extracted metals, nitrates and phosphates, and yeasts fixed carbon using metabolic pathways copied from indigenous microbes that grew around hydrothermal vents in the crushing blackness at the bottom of the ocean. Although carbon was not in short supply on Europa, most of it was in the form of carbon dioxide dissolved in the ocean. Apart from patches of vacuum organisms grown on the sites of meteoritic impacts, for many years the tanks had been the main source of carbon for construction diamond and fullerenes needed for the expansion of the city and the smaller settlements on Europa. Avernus had designed the bacteria and yeasts used by the tank farms many years ago, and still maintained an apartment there. Sri wondered if she had created any secret gardens. Wondered if she was travelling across the radiation-drenched surface of Europa because she planned to visit them.

Tymon chattered on as he gave Sri and her son what he called the "ten-cent tour" of his laboratories. Sealed aquaria contained various kinds of autolithotrophic weed cut from species of red algae and native bacteria, tube worms like slimy flowers as long as Sri's arm, sluggish albino crabs that sulked under rocks, and specimens of an eel-like fish, pale blind fingerlings wrapped in ragged filmy cloaks—external gills rich in symbiotic bacteria—that undulated with dreamy slowness around and around a cylindrical tank of armoured glass several centimetres thick and blood-warm to the touch.

The ancient gene wizard explained that he was planning to clone up thousands of specimens of this pseudo-eel and release them into the deepest parts of the ocean. "They will carry chips that will transmit data to clouds of microscopic receiving stations. And their batteries of modified muscle cells will sustain them for many months while they explore the trenches and vents."

"It sounds like an amusing little project," Sri said. "But wouldn't robots be more efficient? And aren't you worried about contaminating Europa's native ecosystem?"

Europan vent microbes, the only known examples of exo-life forms in the Solar System, were closely related to life on Earth. They contained DNA and RNA which coded for amino acids in triplet base sequences identical to those of terrestrial organisms, and according to the reliable clock of point mutations in tRNAs, evolutionary divergence between Europan and terrestrial organisms had begun three and a half billion years ago, long after life had become established on Earth. So it was likely that Europa had been seeded by a chunk of terrestrial rock that had been kicked into orbit around the sun by a mega-impact and had spiralled outward before being captured by Jupiter's gravity field and striking Europa's surface, and bacterial spores that had survived the journey deep inside the rock had been released into the moon's internal ocean when an upwelling melted the impact point. On Earth, certain species of bacteria had combined and evolved into multicellular plants, fungi and animals, a major evolutionary step that had been possible only because of efficient energy-generating metabolic pathways that exploited free oxygen released into Earth's atmosphere by photosynthetic organisms. But in

Europa's anoxic ocean, evolution had stalled at the level of colonial microbes, which formed crusts and sheets, lacework baskets and vases, and vast beds of long filaments around the hot, black water rich in minerals and hydrogen sulphide that issued from the vents.

Tymon explained that this rare and delicate ecosystem could not be harmed by his eels because the symbiotic bacteria in their gills had been cut from strains of native bacteria. "In any case it's too late to worry about contamination," he said blithely. "I'll show you why, if you like."

He led Sri and Alder through a crawl space into a tiny room with a round window of monomolecular diamond. Outside, the water seemed at first to be pitch black, but as Sri peered into the cold dark, shoulder to shoulder with her son, she began to make out hazy, linear constellations at the limit of sight . . .

There was a sharp jolt. The dim constellations pitched sideways, righted themselves. Sri turned and saw that little clusters of pinlights had lit up across the ceiling and a hatch had closed behind Tymon Simonov, who was sitting cross-legged, skating his fingers across a slate in his lap. The little room was a mini-submarine, she realised, a self-propelled pod moving away from the can to which it had been docked.

"We're taking a trip out to the farms," Tymon said. "You really should see them since you've troubled to come all this way, and it won't take long."

The pod's running lights came on, illuminating an ice ceiling that slid past a hundred metres above, undulating in long smooth swales, eroded by the relatively warm upwelling current, decorated by swathes of ferny platelet ice, no end to it, a ceiling wrapped all the way around the world ocean. And below was a yawning plunge of freezing, oxygen-free water, black, salty and acidic: a fish would drown in it as quickly as a human. Sri suppressed a spasm of claustrophobia, told herself that this compact little pod, with its pinlights glittering between strips of padding, its ticking fans and whirring little motors and humming gyros, was quite safe.

Perhaps Alder sensed her queasy moment of alarm, because he squeezed her hand and said, "I think those lights must be some kind of farm."

Behind them, Tymon said, "You have sharp eyes. That's exactly what it is."

The lines of little lights spread apart as the pod approached, resolved into long rows of lamps suspended from cables bolted to the ice above, each lamp illuminating a cross-braced frame some thirty metres long from which trailed long streamers that rippled to and fro in a sluggish current.

"Weed," Alder said.

"You've broken the quarantine barrier," Sri said.

She felt a strong pang of misgiving, wondering why she hadn't known about this. How could have it been kept secret? What else could the Europans be hiding, in their vast basement? What else could all the Outers be hiding, in crevasses and tunnels in their myriad moons large and small, in orbit around the gas giants, on lonely asteroids?

"Quarantine was broken as soon as the first aquanaut came through the shaft," Tymon said. "And it doesn't mean as much as we once thought it might, given that the native life is more or less the same as Earth's. Besides, these weeds can only grow if supplied with light. And apart from a temporary glow here and there where lava breaks through at a flow ridge, this is the only place there is any light in the whole ocean."

The pod sank lower, passing beneath the racks. There were hundreds upon hundreds of them, stretching away as far as Sri could see. Weed dangled from cables attached to the stretchers of the racks, filmy ribbons that in the pod's harsh floodlights glistened violet or purplish red or the reddish brown of dried blood. Mature specimens were a hundred metres long. The long rows of racks and the dangling weed flexed sinuously in the current like the hide of a gently breathing beast. A haze of molecular sulphur, the waste product of carbon fixation, smoked off them.

Although the upwelling water was rich in nutrients, there was little energy that native life could use this high in the water column. The hydrogen sulphide that issued from the hydrothermal rifts and drove oxidising reactions in the bacterial colonies around them was quickly broken down into unusable sulphates by water chemistry. The rifts were rare and rich oases of life; everywhere else in the vast and lightless deserts of Europa's ocean only thrifty chemolithrophs survived by splitting hydrogen from scanty molecules of metal oxides. But just as green plants on Earth used light energy to drive reactions that transferred hydrogen ions and electrons from water to carbon dioxide, forming the simple sugar glucose with oxygen as a by-product, so Tymon's weeds used light to reduce inorganic compounds containing sulphur and iron. They soaked up carbon dioxide and nutrients from the water and grew at a tremendous rate, each frond extending two or three metres a day. And it was easy to generate the power for the lights by capturing the energy of perpetual currents, or by utilising temperature gradients.

Sleek robots with pairs of articulated arms and rear-mounted fan motors moved here and there, cutting and gathering up long strands of weed, towing the harvest toward a distant processing station. Tymon steered the pod to an outer edge of the vast array, where construction robots were extruding new racks like bees busy in a hive. The farm was almost eleven square kilometres in area, presently contained some eighteen thousand racks, and was growing at the rate of twenty new racks a day.

It was a phase change, Sri thought. Like dropping a seed crystal into a beaker of supersaturated solution. Liquid one moment; a solid lattice the next. She saw in her mind's eye thousands of square kilometres colonised by these self-perpetuating farms, huge rafts hung at different levels in the deep ocean, and communities growing up around them, floating towns of seal people . . .

Tymon talked on, answering Alder's questions about the robots and the weed. The pod circled one of the stations where tanks and bioreactors set inside a web of scaffolding processed the weed. At the moment, the fixed carbon was used only for construction materials, and most of that was used to make new racks to grow more weed. But Tymon and others were working on various strains of edible weed, and weed that produced medicines, plastics . . . there was no limit, really, to what they could grow here.

By the time the pod turned back to Tymon's laboratory, Sri had worked out how the family could cut itself into this new business. She told the gene wizard that cheap and compact sources of power based on the new fusion technology could provide enough light for farms a thousand times the size of this one. She spun a vision of an ocean as full of floating farms as the night sky was full of stars: each farm would be like a little sun with village communities orbiting it. It might even be possible, she said, to seed the ocean with self-replicating electrohydrolysis plants that could oxygenate the water from top to bottom, so that a fully aerobic ecosystem could be installed, from bacteria to whales. And it would be easy enough to work out how to cut people so that they could breathe the water.

When she had finished, Tymon laughed and said that Oscar had been right about her. "You think big."

"Life is an unbalanced equilibrium. Once it's given the right conditions, it will thrive and spread. And you've given it the right conditions here. Unless you think very hard about the direction you want to take it, it may well take you somewhere you do not want to go."

"The farm is an experiment," Tymon said. "A successful one, if I may say so, but still, no more than that. The city will have to decide what to do next. That's where we differ from Earth. We decide by discussion and majority vote, and then we act on that decision."

"Without dissent?"

"Why not?"

124

"Perhaps not for much longer. Your so-called consensus is really a polite fiction, sustained by an environment in which dissent is limited by lack of resources. Give dissenters the opportunity to grab resources of their own, and see how long your consensus lasts. All they need are a handful of robots, construction materials, and a few weed spores. In a year they could parlay that into a farm the size of this one. In a decade they would have a city of their own. Imagine that happening a thousand times. You've taken the first step in colonising your ocean. You can't turn back from it."

Sri felt exhilarated, fully engaged. Forget the setback at Rainbow Bridge. She could hone her arguments against this old man and put them to Minos's Citizens' Assembly. And she could talk with Avernus, too. Plant a few seeds now, and come back later for the harvest.

"We have enjoyed a hundred years of consensus. I see no reason to change it," Tymon said.

"Yes, yes. Clever, cooperative, compassionate people living in a true utopia. I heard enough of that at Rainbow Bridge. But as far as I can see, the old impulses are still there, barely disguised by a few cosmetic cuts and tweaks."

Tymon laughed again, and said that she was forgetting that environment shaped human nature at least as much as genes.

"I haven't forgotten that at all," Sri said. "This ocean is a very different place from the ice caves of Minos, or the tents and domes of Rainbow Bridge. And there must be more places where people can thrive, all radically different from each other, calling for radical adaptions. And people will colonise them. The new fusion motor my family has developed will shrink distances, and make many places more accessible. Outers claim that they are evolving away from people on Earth, when in fact they're evolving away from each other at a much faster rate. What will happen to your consensus when the human race splits into a hundred species?"

She would have gone on to use the same kind of threat she had used against the Callistans, that if the Europans didn't colonise their ocean someone else would, other Outers or people from Earth, that the process of adaptation and colonisation must be controlled and directed, but Tymon interrupted her and said that she had a call from her secretary, and ported it from his slate to her spex.

"There's been a development," Yamil Cho said. "The citizens of Rainbow Bridge have voted for the immediate deportation of the construction crew. You must return to the ship at once, madam. Its captain has orders to return to Callisto to pick up Euclides Peixoto and his people as soon as possible."

15

And so the attempt to forge a closer link between the Peixoto family and the Outer System broke up in disarray. The *Luís Inácio da Silva* returned to Earth with the construction crew nested in hibernation coffins and packed into the hold, and Sri spent the next three weeks trying her best to avoid Euclides Peixoto in the cramped lifesystem as the little ship fell toward Earth.

Sri, Alder and Yamil Cho rode a shuttle down from orbit to Brasília. Bone-aching gravity, hot thick air, brawling avenues glimpsed through the tinted glass of the limousine that drove them from the airport to the clinic. Although they had exercised regularly and assiduously in the ship's centrifuge, it took them two weeks to recover from the debilitating effects of microgravity. In all this time, Sri heard nothing from General Arvam Peixoto. At last, she had Yamil Cho deliver to the general's offices a copy of the hours of raw footage she'd shot with her spex. He returned without any message from the general, and the general did not call during the days following. Sri told herself that it didn't mean anything. She had done what she had been asked to do. If Arvam Peixoto's silence meant that he was displeased she couldn't do anything about it, and trying to contact him would only make things worse. It was time to move on.

Alder went south, to Antarctica, and Sri and Yamil Cho travelled north and west, to the coast of Baja California. They took a train from La Paz, crossing the sea-drowned coastal plain of Baja California Sur and turning east, through a mountain pass to the little town of Carrizalito, where they picked up a car and drove thirty kilometres along the sea road. Sri hiked the last kilometre on foot, across a fleet of dunes that stretched between dry brown hills and the sea, to Oscar Finnegan Ramos's hermitage.

It sat in a broad notch at the seaward edge of the dunes, a low hut built from sheets of plastic in the shape of a ship's prow, shaded by a clump of wind-bent Norfolk pines, lashed and guyed with cables. Beyond it was the wide curve of the beach and the Gulf of California twinkling away under the achingly pure blue sky. Oscar waved to Sri as she came down a sandy slope combed with dry grasses, past a paddock where three goats grazed on bundles of cut brush. He was small and stoop-shouldered, wearing only a pair of baggy, faded blue shorts. His skin deep brown, his head hairless. He had tea brewing in a blackened kettle on a driftwood fire, poured it strong and dark into two chipped mugs.

"You walked here," he said. "Does that mean you are fully recovered from your trip?"

"Absolutely," Sri said. And although her legs and back ached, she did feel good, fit and strong and alert. She was slathered with sunblock and wearing a close-fitting micropore jumpsuit and a broad-brimmed hat.

"And Alder?"

"He did very well. I'm proud of him." Sri told the old man how Alder had seduced the young scientists and found out about Avernus's secret garden. "I would have made contact with her if it hadn't been for the incident at the opening ceremony. If I hadn't been recalled from Europa. I was this close," she said, holding her thumb and forefinger about a centimetre apart.

"I read the report you made to the Senate Subcommittee for Extraterrestrial Affairs. But I would very much like to hear the story in your own words. Tell me everything, and don't hold back."

Sri talked for an hour. She gave a thorough account of the crude attempt to sabotage the construction project, the murders of Ursula Freye and Speller Twain, and the involvement of the diplomat Loc Ifrahim, and gave her reasons for believing that Euclides Peixoto could have gone over to the pro-war faction of the family. She described Avernus's hidden garden and the little habitats that Alder had seen scattered across the cratered face of Callisto, talked about the potential of the weed farms in the Europan ocean, and said that in her opinion the split between the older and younger generations of Outers was irreconcilable.

"I think it was a mistake to try to help the older and more conservative Outers to keep control," she said. "We should instead be making overtures to the rising generation. I glimpsed a few of their secrets. I think there's much more to be uncovered, a wealth of opportunity. But we must move swiftly, because they are definitely on the brink of a rapid and unpredictable phase of expansion. In only a few years, there will be dozens of new communities at the edge of the Solar System, each one evolving in a different direction. So we must forge a lasting relationship now, and make ourselves allies of the diaspora. It's our only chance to exert any influence over it."

Oscar thought about this. Sri, used to his silences, sipped tea grown cool and bitter and watched the sea wind flatten grasses along the crests of the dunes, move through the boughs of the pines.

At last, the green saint said, "You're the cleverest of my protégés. It doesn't do any harm telling you that because you already know. But I think you are also the most romantic. It's not a criticism. It's an essential part of your creative imagination. You wouldn't have come so far without it, or done such great things. But it can be a weakness, if you are not careful."

"You think I've been seduced by the mystery and exoticism of the frontier? Everything I've told you is entirely factual. I thought long and hard about it on the voyage home and it all points to one conclusion. That we have a small and narrowing window of opportunity. That if we don't make an alliance with the Outers now, it will soon be impossible. Our only alternative will be to take control by main force."

"I think you need to take some time to fully absorb the meaning of your experiences. To think carefully and deeply about the implications of everything you learned. You need some grounding. You need to develop a little perspective," Oscar said.

He was sitting cross-legged, the soles of his feet tucked in the angles of his knees. An ancient and potent homunculus, not quite human, his joints swollen under dark leathery skin, his head seeming too large for his slight, crooked body, his ears pendulous, his naked wrinkled scalp blotched with colonies of benign cancers. Sri's guru, her master. His body was studded with medichines that filtered his blood, manufactured powerful antibodies against any trace of infection, destroyed cancerous cells, and continuously updated a medical team in Carrizalito. He was plugged into feeds from satellites and weather stations, and the consensus worked up from data collected by thousands of tiny free-floating machines that monitored the sea. He had direct access to the president of Brazil and to leaders and green saints in every country on Earth. On a whim, he could call up a fleet of construction robots and plant a forest, or have a mountain reshaped into his own likeness. A permanent garrison of soldiers protected a wide perimeter around his hermitage, wolves patrolled the dunes, and he had direct control of a statite hung in stationary orbit two hundred kilometres above, capable of zapping anyone or anything inside the security perimeter with its X-ray laser.

Now, as Oscar studied her with a sad and troubled gaze, Sri felt a falling sensation. Felt the first real taste of failure. The collapse of the biome partnership hadn't much troubled her: at bottom, it had never been anything more than a political gesture, and it had usefully made plain the divisions among the Callistans and within the Peixoto family. And although she had been angry and humiliated because she had been recalled before she could make contact with Avernus, she was over that now, had renewed her determination to prove herself a match for the woman's powers, or even surpass her. But if she couldn't convince Oscar that the family must redouble its efforts to forge a peaceful partnership with the Outers, if she could not persuade him about the vast and untapped potential of their rising generation, she would have to renounce her guru and give herself to the cause of Arvam Peixoto and the other enemies of reconciliation. She would have to give herself to war. She wondered, as she bore Oscar's gaze, if he knew this; if he knew about the footage she'd sent to Arvam, and all the rest.

"Come with me," he said at last. "I want to show you something."

They walked through a flower garden decorated with wrack from villages and towns drowned by the rising sea level and cast up along the beach—calcined bottles and crockery, ancient tin signs, plastic bottles of every shape and size scoured white by years of immersion, pieces of driftwood rubbed into shapes smooth as muscle. Beyond this, in the pale dry sand at the top of the beach, was a pen fenced with wire mesh nailed to stakes. The green saint climbed nimbly over the mesh and knelt down and carefully scooped a narrow trench in the sand, exposing a few soft white spheres. Turtle eggs.

"I tried this last year," Oscar said. "The fence keeps lizards and crabs from eating the eggs—you have to secure it deep in the sand. When the eggs begin to hatch, I'll pull it up and let the hatchlings scamper down into the surf."

"Did any of last year's batch come back?"

"Not that I know of."

"I suppose the sea isn't ready for them."

"A few might be out there. It is possible that they went back to some other beach. But you're probably right. There's still so much to make good. These might not come back either," Oscar said, as he pushed the sand back over the eggs. "But we have to keep trying."

Sri said, "If this is some kind of parable, I'm not sure if I completely understand it."

Oscar stood up, brushing sand from his knees. "We are engaged with a great work of penance. It's hard work, and perhaps much of what we plan to do is impossible. We'll always fail at it. But we have to try, because it is what we do. Making amends—it is why we are here. Reconciliation with the Outers is part of that. It is not a thing in itself. It is not for anyone's benefit or profit."

"There's more that we can do. Much more. I'll go again. As soon as you like."

"I want to build a peaceful link with the Outers as much as you do, but it has to be on their terms. If they refuse our efforts, so be it. Do you understand, my dear?"

"Of course."

What else could she say? Oscar Finnegan Ramos was powerful and capricious and not quite human. He could take away her laboratory, her career. He could order the satellite to kill her as she walked back to where Yamil Cho waited by the car. An incandescent bolt flung from orbit would vaporise her, leave nothing but a vitreous crater smoking in the dunes.

"There have always been members of the family who have been against reconciliation," Oscar said. "And they have been speaking more loudly now that the biome project ended so suddenly and unsuccessfully. We will not encourage them with another failure, or the possibility of failure. So we will retrench. We keep channels open, we wait until the right moment, and then we try again."

The green saint was two hundred years old. He had long ago learned patience, how to take the long view. But Sri believed that this time he was wrong. She knew that things were changing with tremendous speed. There was not enough time to wait until the small scandal of the biome project died away, not enough time to prepare the ground for another approach. On the trip back to La Paz, the flight to Antarctica, and for many days afterward, she thought long and hard about what she should do next. About peace, and war.

PART TWO

SURVIVAL OF THE FITTEST

I

One day, just before the boys were due to board the shuttle that would take them into orbit for one of their regular sessions of zero-gravity combat practice, Father Solomon told them to put on their pressure suits. "Today you will attempt something new."

Carrying their globular helmets in the crooks of their arms, the boys followed Father Solomon and the other three lectors into the shuttle's padded cargo bay and sat in obedient silence for two hours, strapped into bench seats, as the shuttle flew in a low, suborbital lob halfway around the Moon. After it landed, the boys fastened their helmets over their heads and each checked his neighbour's lifepack. They were clumsy in their stiff pressure suits, bumping into each other in the crowded space, excited and apprehensive. The air in the cargo bay was pumped out, a ramp dropped, and the lectors herded the boys in single file down its short slope onto the surface.

Dave #8 was one of the last to leave, following the others out of the shadow of the shuttle. A few of the boys fell to their knees, arms wrapped around their big round helmets. The rest, like Dave #8, stood and stared rapt with wonder at a desolate plain stretching away toward a range of hills, softly rounded as pillows, that curved from horizon to horizon. Everything was in clear and distinct focus, and because the plain was spattered with craters and tailings of rock of every size, and the hills were sharply silhouetted against a blackness as absolute as the end of the world, it was hard to shake off the impression that this was the floor of a room lit by a solitary light glaring low under a sooty ceiling. A light stronger than any Dave #8 had ever seen before, too bright to look at even through the polarised faceplate. It was the sun, a brilliant white spotlight swimming in a vast and absolute blackness, its harsh light reflected by the naked landscape all around . . .

Someone shouted wildly and three boys bounded away, chasing each other across the bright ground. Father Solomon and Father Ramez went after them, calling to them, ordering them to stop, to come back; Father Aldos and Father Clarke moved amongst the rest of the boys, gently encouraging those who had fallen to their knees to get to their feet, telling the others to line up.

Dave #8 took his place in the two ranks that he and his brothers formed by unthinking habit. The three boys who had run off were led back and joined the others without being admonished, and Father Solomon told them that they would pair up and each pair would be given a different set of coordinates. They would hike out to a selected spot, find a flag dropped there by a drone, and bring it back. It was a simple training exercise, the first of many that would familiarise them with every kind of landscape on the lunar surface. Father Solomon said that he knew that they would find this strange and intimidating at first, but he also knew that they would do well, and would not disgrace themselves or fail to complete their task.

Dave #8 was paired with Dave #14, and they set off toward a point northwest of the shuttle and three kilometres away, bounding along in the steady, stiff-kneed lope they'd long ago mastered in exercises in the gymnasium. The floor out here—the surface—was covered everywhere with a velvety powder that looked as if it would blow away on the slightest breath but gave only a little under Dave #8's boots. Sprays of dust feathered from his boots with each footfall and dust clung to his overshoes, staining their white weave with smudges of charcoal black. His boots and the boots of his brother printed sharp impressions in the dusty surface; when he paused and looked back at the way they had come, he saw an intertwined double track of prints that shone glassily in the relentless glare, receding away toward the shuttle. Its boxy shape, squatting on splayed and skeletal legs, looked strange and small and lonely and fragile in the empty moonscape under the black sky and the dazzling glare of the sun, and Dave #8 felt a sudden dizziness as his sense of perspective swoopingly enlarged and he realised that some of the features of the moonscape that looked small and close were really large and far away. It was difficult to estimate distances because in the vacuum everything far was as sharply focused as everything close at hand, and there was nothing to give any sense of scale. But those softly rounded hills must be big and far away, Dave #8 thought, because they looked no closer nor any larger than before, yet according to the navigation display glowing in the lower right-hand corner of his faceplate he and Dave #14 had already slogged across a kilometre of open ground toward them . . .

Dave #14 told him to keep moving and he hurried to catch up. His breathing was harsh and intimate inside his helmet and his heart was beating quickly and strongly. He was noticing everything around him and everything was new and exciting and charged with significance and the high resolution of reality. The sun was at their backs and threw their shadows ahead of them, flickering across low undulations in the surface as they bounced along, and the surface was a warm golden-brown straight ahead but looked darker to either side and grey or black directly underfoot. It was littered with little rocks sunk to different levels in the dust, and every rock cast a sharp shadow and was peppered and pitted with tiny holes. Craters from micrometeorite impacts, Dave #8 thought, and the connection between what he had learned and what he saw struck a bright snap of pleasure.

The plain all around them was cratered too, craters of every size from pinholes to small cups of smashed rock to deep bowls that could have swallowed the shuttle whole. The interior slopes of some of the craters were themselves pockmarked with smaller craters, and the larger craters had aprons of ejecta extending beyond them, rocks excavated and flung out by the impacts that had punched holes into the surface. Some of the rocks were huge: Dave #8 tracked two of his brothers bounding past a distant clump of fractured blocks bigger than the shuttle, then realised that he had fallen behind Dave #14 again.

The red dot that marked Dave #8's position on his navigation display crept toward the yellow cross of the designated coordinates, until at last he and Dave #14 reached the edge of a crater at least a hundred metres across. Its rim was dazzling white and slightly raised, and its dished interior sloped steeply down to a flat floor covered everywhere with clumps and carpets of broken rock.

Dave #8 looked all around and said, "I can't see the stars. I suppose the glare of the sun hides them. But where is Earth? Surely it shines much more brightly than the stars? Do you think we are on the far side, the side that faces away from Earth?"

"You have too much imagination. It makes you think too much about things that aren't important," Dave #14 said.

He was a stolid fellow, practical and dogged and tireless. As Dave #27 once put it, he would bash away at an intractable problem until he cracked it open by sheer force of will.

"The only thing we have to think about right now is retrieving the flag," he said. "And if you had been studying the floor rather than the sky you would have already spotted it."

Dave #8 looked at where Dave #14 was pointing and saw a red triangle standing in front of a squarish block of rock at the far side of the crater's floor. He said doubtfully, "Is it safe to climb down?"

"We have been told to bring the flag back with us, so we will have to go down there," Dave #14 said.

They descended a shallow slope that quickly grew steeper, so that they had to crab down in a fast-settling welter of dust, dust clinging to the legs and arms and chest plates of their pressure suits, settling on their visors and leaving smears when they tried to wipe it off. Dave #8 kicked a fist-sized rock that rolled down the slope ahead of him, slowly gathering speed as it tumbled until it silently smashed into a large half-buried block and lay still. Dave #8 felt a brief stab of fear. His suit was a fragile bubble of air and warmth; one misstep could send him cartwheeling, shatter his faceplate against some hard and unforgiving edge.

Dave #14 trotted out across a bank of small debris and gripped the wire shaft of the flag in both gloved hands and plucked its arrowhead-shaped root from the ground. Its red triangle shone with hallucinatory brightness against the monochrome rocks scattered all around. When Dave #8 reached his brother, he realised that the shuttle was no longer visible. That the two of them were more alone than ever before in their lives. Only the slanting sides of the crater circled around them; only the black sky and the pitiless spotlight of the sun above.

"One of us should have stayed at the top in case the other got into trouble," he said.

"We'll do that next time," Dave #14 said. "Now, I want to be the first to get back."

They followed the trail of their bootprints across the soft contours of the moonscape toward the shuttle, but the way back was not like the way forward. The short walk had changed them forever.

There were many more exercises on the surface. Long hikes across every kind of terrain. Navigating from point to point. Searching out caches of supplies. Teams set against each other, armed with pistols that fired pellets of compressed red powder that splashed against unlucky or less skilful targets and marked them as casualties in war games. The exercises were always held on the Moon's far side, never under a sky that held the blue-and-white crescent of Earth.

Some sixty days after the first excursion, Dave #8 was tramping alone through a saddle-shaped valley between two rounded peaks of the Montes Cordillera, pulling a small sledge of supplies, when he came across a trail of bootprints. They were a little larger than his own boots, so they had not been made by one of his brothers, and the pattern of the cleats was different. They could have been made yesterday or a hundred years ago; in the lunar vacuum, bootprints lasted for millions of years, until at last they were erased by the slow but relentless degradation of micrometeorite impact. He followed the trail as it swung around a shallow crater, down a slope to where it ended in a mazy jumble around parallel wheel tracks left by some kind of small vehicle that had turned here and headed east, in the direction from which it had come.

Dave #8 stood still, struck by the thought that he could follow the tracks eastward past the great ring of the Montes Cordillera and on, through the knobby hills and peaks of the Montes Rook Formation, to the Orientale basin at the very edge of the Moon's nearside. And see at last Earth hanging blue and white and lovely in the black sky. He was in the middle of a hike that was scheduled to last forty-eight hours. By the time the lectors realised that he was missing, he would be unlocatable. For a moment the thought was as strong as a muscle clenching, but then it faded. What would he do when he reached the nearside? Where would he go? How would he live?

Dave #14 had been wrong, he reflected, as he tramped back to his sled. He didn't have too much imagination; he had too little.

2

Now that the J-2 test programme was up and running, the pilots were rotated back to Earth on a regular basis for personal leave, morale-boosting visits to the plant where their birds were being assembled, consultation sessions with the designers of the new carrier ship, the *Glory of Gaia*, and meet-and-greet promotional junkets amongst higher echelons of the armed forces and the interlocked worlds of politics and the arms industries. Luiz Schwarcz returned from one of the latter with news that more pilots were going to be cut to fly the J-2, and some of them would be from the European Union.

"It makes all sorts of political sense," he told Cash Baker and Colly Blanco a couple of days later. "The Europeans stood by us when it looked like we might have to go to war against the Pacific Community, we have deep and long-standing economic ties with them, and they like the Outers even less than we do. After all, they refused to participate in any of the nonsense about peace and reconciliation, despite strong incentives to do so. If we go to war against the Outers—"

"*When* we go to war," Cash said.

"When we go to war, then, we will greatly benefit from their help," Luiz said. "The Europeans are the oldest and richest power bloc. There's talk that they will help underwrite the costs of building the *Glory of Gaia* and the other long-range ships. In exchange, they get access to our technology—the new fusion motor, and the hyper-reflexive upgrades."

"As long as the brass remembers that we're the first and best when it comes to taking the fight to the Outers, I don't mind who comes along for the ride," Colly Blanco said.

"I hear that," Cash said.

"You and me, we'll kick their asses," Colly said.

He was the youngest pilot in the J-2 programme, just turned twenty-one, and a much better pilot than Cash had been at that age, although not as good as Cash was now, not quite. A fierce, fearless little tyke from a mining town in the foothills of the Andes, who claimed that he'd learned to ride a horse and rope a bull before he could walk, fly before he could read. He was leading the other two through the dark corridors and rooms of the old city's service levels: they were hunting rats, a favourite activity of the pilots when they were off-duty and confined to base. They wore night-vision goggles equipped with motion detectors, carried little pistols that shot taser darts.

At an intersection where two corridors crossed each other at oblique angles, Colly held up a hand, then pointed left. Thirty metres away, a fuzzy blotch pulsated like a slow and steady heart in the dim shadows. Twenty rats, easily. Maybe even thirty. Cash and Luiz flattened against the wall behind Colly, jumped out into the intersection when he did. The blotch split into a whirling flurry as rats scurried away in every direction. Cash picked a target and shot, saw bright sparks flare down the narrow perspective of the dark corridor as taser darts struck the floor and the walls.

A brief search turned up only one corpse. A lean brindled grandfather rat more than half a metre from its nose to the tip of its tail, fitted inside a hollow ball that had been shaped from a chunk of foamed wall insulation by careful nibbling. It had elaborate notchings in its ears that Luiz claimed were tribal or status markings. A piece of well-chewed plastic was slung around its neck by a loop of wire.

Cash and Luiz didn't argue when Colly said that it was his kill.

"Little fuckers're getting smarter," Colly said, and booted the dead rat inside its ball of foam-armour into the shadows at the far end of the corridor.

"They're learning," Luiz said. "Developing culture. One of the medics reckons those notches are some kind of graphic alphabet. She's trying to decode it."

"Is that the woman who's giving you some?" Cash said.

"A gentleman never tells," Luiz said. He was as dapper as ever, a red silk scarf knotted at the throat of his coveralls, black hair sleeked back from his narrow brown face.

They weren't bothering to keep quiet now. They knew that all around them rats were crouching watchfully in cavities inside walls, in ducts and cableways. That news of their presence was spreading on the rat bush telegraph. Still, they weren't quite ready to give up the hunt and return topside.

The corridor they were following made a bend through ninety degrees. A faint blue light flickered through an open doorway ahead. They crept toward it one after the other. Luiz held up his hand, counted down from three by folding his fingers and thumb. They swung into the doorway, pistols locked on the source of the light, an old photoframe which someone had left on a desk a century ago. It was playing a short clip of a man swinging a small child around and around on a beach. White sand and hot sunshine and the vivid blue ocean of a summer's day of the long ago, little sailboats out on the water. The old part of the base was full of mementos of abandoned lives like this. Clothes on hangars inside closets. Freezers stuffed with mummified food. A children's playground littered with toys.

Luiz picked up the photoframe, briefly studied it, then tossed it to Cash, saying, "Think they're still alive, on some moon or other?"

"The kid, you mean?"

"Maybe the man too. Some of those Outers live a long time. A lot more than a hundred-odd years."

"You know what you should be asking?" Colly said. "You should be asking what switched that thing on."

Luiz and Cash stared at him, and there was a sudden scratching and skittering overhead and ceiling tiles gave way and a blizzard of dried rat shit poured down. Colly swore vividly and fired his taser at the holes in the suspended ceiling, bolt after bolt lighting up the room with hot white sparks and sending shadows dancing wildly. Cash watched the shadows over the sight of his taser, looking for movement and finding none. Luiz was laughing.

"What's so fucking funny?" Colly said.

"They ambushed us," Luiz said, and started laughing again.

"It could be worse—they could have used rocks instead of turds," Cash said, barely getting the words out before he too was convulsed with laughter.

Colly glared at them in disgust, brushing commas of rat shit from his coveralls with abrupt motions, running his fingers through his cropped hair and violently shaking his head.

"These rats, they're getting very smart indeed," Luiz said, as they walked back down the dark corridor. "They set a trap, so they must be able to think ahead. To plan. And they worked out what would lure us into their trap, so they must be able to think like us, too."

Colly shook his head. "Smart rats, man. Who needs smart rats?"

"Sri Hong-Owen. The ancestors of those rats suffered so that we would not die in vain," Luiz said.

"Don't riddle me, stringbean."

"He means Sri Hong-Owen tested her stuff on the rats before she did us," Cash told Colly.

"So you might say that, in a way, the rats are our brothers," Luiz said.

"*Your* brothers, maybe," Colly said, with the hard look he used when he believed that he was somehow being insulted or set up as the fall guy in a joke.

"We're definitely going to have to work on our game," Luiz said. "If we can't get the better of a tribe of rats, we could get into some serious trouble when we go up against the Outers."

"No way," Cash said. "We're way better than any of those tweaks. They claim they're evolving into *Homo superior*, but we're already there. We're the real deal. When it comes to it, we'll kick their asses for sure."

3

East of Eden, Ganymede, occupied a narrow crevasse at the south-eastern edge of the dark and cratered terrain of Galileo Regio. The floor and sides of the crevasse were insulated and pressure-sealed with layers of fullerene composite and aerogel, and it was roofed with the same material, and the roof was covered in two metres of stony material, excavated from a nearby crater, to provide protection from the drench of radiation from the outer edges of Jupiter's radio belts. There was a small industrial zone at the southern end of the crevasse, and the rest was a pastoral landscape: meadows and groves of olive and citrus trees punctuated with narrow ponds and marshes along the floor; pine woods with an understorey of ceanothus, choisya, bearberries, myrtles, and other flowering shrubs climbing the terraced walls. Public buildings and small villages of apartment blocks sat amongst the steep woods under tents of transparent polymer stretched between fullerene struts, like giant models of the compound eyes of insects or exotic and jewel-like phytoplankton.

The settlement had been founded some fifty years ago by a group who believed that the other inhabitants of Jupiter's moons had grown too soft, too bourgeois. Although their home was pleasantly bucolic, East of Eden's citizens were austere and close-minded, keen on conformity, custom, and civic duty, and they prized the acquisition of scientific and philosophical knowledge and the virtues of artistic achievement above all else. They each spent several days a week helping to run the settlement's basic services and maintain its infrastructure, but as far as they were concerned their real work was scientific research without any clear aim or application beyond the gathering and cataloguing of esoteric knowledge for knowledge's sake, or the production of intricate sagas, operas, symphonies, plays, and other works of art. They had developed and refined new meditation techniques, revived the ancient black arts of psychoanalysis, tweaked decorative plants and animals, engaged in the study of abnormal mathematics and philosophy, worked in obscure corners of the sprawling tangle of theories left over from failed attempts to unify physics, and much else. And they spent at least as much time talking about their art and research as doing it, discussing strategies and plans with other members of art covens or research gangs, arguing with rivals in virtual workshops, even organising face-to-face conferences. Their government, a form of direct democracy similar to that of the city-states of Classical Greece or the early years of the Roman Republic, involved endless discussions, too. There were no elected representatives, no instant polls or referenda. Assemblies in which every citizen could debate and vote were held once a week in villages and once a month for matters concerning the whole city. Luxury was a crime; self-sacrifice a virtue. Everything that wasn't forbidden was compulsory.

As far as Macy Minnot was concerned, it was about as utopian as an anthill. She'd moved to East of Eden three months ago, immediately after her defection. The government of Rainbow Bridge, Callisto had insisted on it. Officially, it was for her protection. Unofficially, as she well knew, the Callistans were eager to be rid of an inconvenient reminder of an embarrassing incident.

East of Eden had volunteered to take her in not out of charity or sympathy, but because it discharged an obscure debt of honour it had long owed Rainbow Bridge. She'd been assigned a counsellor, a vinegary old man named Ivo Teagarden, and had been given work as a general labourer in East of

Eden's farms, but her access to its net was restricted, she was forbidden to travel outside its limits, and she couldn't shake the feeling that she was part prisoner, part zoological specimen. Nevertheless, she was determined to make the best of it. She'd poured her energy into making over the studio apartment she'd been assigned, in the village of Lot's Lot: laying and polishing a bamboo-wood floor, painting the walls different shades of green and pink and playing with the lighting, retiling the little wet room, growing herbs and chili plants in pots on the flagstone patio, training a fig vine around the door. She told herself that she was settling into the first real home she'd ever had, but in her low moments the apartment seemed more like a cell, and East of Eden's inward-looking pocket utopia habitat a prison.

So far, she'd made few friends. Ivo Teagarden. The proprietor of her favourite café in Lot's Lot's refectory, Jon Ho. Sada Selene and her little gang of refuseniks. A nodding acquaintance with a couple of people who worked in the farm tunnels. Most citizens were frostily polite or indifferent; only a few went out of their way to express outright hostility. Chief amongst the latter was Jibril, a member of the self-styled Elohim transhumanism crew. Everyone else called them cosmo angels, because they used plastic surgery and trivial cuts to give themselves a weird stylised beauty and dabbled in all kinds of so-called mind-enhancing treatments, from colour therapy to tailored psychotrophic viruses. They were also androgyne neuters, because they had the fantastically old-fashioned notion that higher consciousness could be achieved only in the complete absence of every form of base, animal sex. They took the names of angels, erased their former identities from public record, and spent their leisure time hanging around public places, preening and fluttering like minor aristocrats. Most had something to do with the performance arts. East of Eden's best fado singer was a cosmo angel; so were several of its leading microentertainers. Jibril was a virtuoso of psychoactive theatre, and Macy had been on the receiving end of yo's performances ever since she'd first arrived in East of Eden, from sarcastic remarks or mocking questions made in passing to confrontational diatribes about base human stock compromising East of Eden's aesthetic totality, or the pollution of its gestalt. And every encounter was on camera, and edited versions were dumped on East of Eden's net for the delectation and entertainment of anyone who wanted to watch.

Back in the training barracks of the R&R corps, Macy had once called out a woman who'd been bugging her and they'd fought to a standstill behind the mess block, honour even. But after she made the mistake of trying the same tactic with Jibril, standing up to the cosmo angel and telling yo that there were plenty of places where they could work out their differences, the confrontation, which had ended with Macy stalking away in disgust from Jibril's fluttering mime of outraged sensibility, had quickly became the most popular of all the cosmo angel's pieces. Ivo Teagarden explained that cosmo angels suffered from an advanced but harmless state of narcissism, and said that Macy should think of these encounters as a contribution toward Jibril's therapy and a way of enhancing her own standing in the community. Jon Ho told her it didn't much matter, because most people didn't follow psychoactive theatre these days. Only the gang of self-styled refusenik kids took Macy's side, albeit mainly for ideological reasons.

"Cosmo angels confuse evolution with a lifestyle choice," Sada Selene told Macy. She was the oldest of the refuseniks, a lanky and intense girl of fifteen. "What they do to themselves? It's about as radical as getting a tattoo. It's a mockery of all the wild and radical possibilities of true transhumanism. Something safe and codified, reinforced by constant self-policing. Which is just about typical of all that's wrong with this backwater, puritanical, head-in-the-sand place."

"They pretend they're devoted to a high ideal, but they're really running away from their own true nature," another refusenik said. "Like nuns. You ever heard of nuns?"

"She's from Earth. It's crawling with all kinds of religious weirdos," a third refusenik said. "Green saints. They're a kind of nun, right?"

"Kind of," Macy said.

"The point is," Sada Selene said, "the cosmo angels don't threaten the status quo. That's why the system tolerates them, and why it hates us. Because we want to take control of the course of human evolution. Because true transhumans are always in flux, evolving in a hundred different directions. No so-called utopia can deal with that because by their very nature utopias are static. They hate change because it's a direct challenge to their fantasy of perfection."

Macy liked the refuseniks because they were pretty much the only people in East of Eden with whom she could have a straightforward conversation. But although they claimed to be rebels without a pause, they were really just a bunch of alienated kids going through a difficult phase. Despite all their noise about living outside the law and their open contempt for the settlement's claustrophobic codes and customs, they hadn't ever attempted to change them, and it was unlikely that their boasts about leaving the settlement when they attained majority would come to anything. They refused to participate in civic life, but they camped out in empty apartments, lived on dole yeast and whatever they could cadge from passersby, breathed the settlement's air, drank its water, and used its net. Still, they were bright and challenging, and they supported Macy because she was their enemy's enemy. They posted favourable comments about her on Jibril's site, and told her that she could always count on them if she got into trouble.

Early one evening, Macy was sitting at the counter of Jon Ho's café when she saw Jibril and two of yo's acolytes coming toward her. The café was at one end of the refectory terrace that occupied the top of the biggest apartment block of Lot's Lot, with views through the hexagonal panes of the village's tent toward pine woods on the other side of the crevasse. A nice enough prospect, although the trees were dwarfed, no more than five or six metres high, and they were just a couple of hundred metres away, squatting under the grey-blue vault of the roof. It reminded Macy of the room she'd shared with Jax Spano during the brief spring of their love back in Pittsburgh: if you stood in the centre you could touch the walls on either side, not just with your fingertips but with the palms of your hands. The café was small, too. Nicely compact. A short counter topped with split bamboo polished to a mirror finish, a bench long enough for six customers, and a hissing steel coffee machine that Jon Ho had built from a design three centuries old.

The coffee wasn't exactly coffee—coffee bushes took up too much space in farm tunnels, so the Outers generally grew a species of moss tweaked to produce oily caffeine-rich nodules—but it was the best Macy had found since she'd left Earth, and Jon conjured up tasty snacks on a little hotplate and allowed customers to keep a bottle of their favourite liqueur or spirit behind the counter. He'd worked a spell as a ship's engineer, was more widely travelled and more tolerant than most of East of Eden's citizens. He liked to listen to Macy's stories about life on Earth, and she liked to talk to him about tweaking strains of moss to improve the quality of their coffee; the art of making minuscule metabolic changes to ensure an exact balance of dozens of different flavonoids, alcohols, aldehydes, and essential oils was very like adjusting the balance of microorganisms to produce the sweetest, liveliest mud.

Jon was telling Macy about his latest attempt to produce a strain that would mimic the mellow flavour of Sumatra Mandheling when she saw the three cosmo angels threading their way through benches and tables, tubs of mosses and ferns and flowers, and cafés and vending stalls. Past a man and a woman leaning toward each other over a chess board, a man staring at figures tumbling through the glow of a memo space, a group of children learning how make bread at a table outside the bake shop, squealing and chattering as they slapped and pummelled gobs of dough.

Jibril saying loudly, "Can you really find the face of God in an irrational number?"

Macy knew at once that the cosmo angel had somehow found out about the Church of the Divine Regression and she stood up as adrenalin surged into her blood. Fight or flight. Dismay and anger.

"Please, help me understand," the cosmo angel said. "I know that the string of digits after the decimal point in pi is infinite, with no set of consecutive digits repeating itself indefinitely. But even if there was a complete description of the universe hidden somewhere inside, surely you'd need an infinite amount of time to unravel it. And as for finding God—"

"I'm not going to waste my time saying anything at all to you," Macy said.

"But I'm *genuinely* interested," Jibril said, blocking Macy's way as she attempted to push past.

The cosmo angel was two and a half metres tall, slender as a reed, and as usual dressed in a minimum of clothing, short-shorts and sandals and a bandolier belt, so as to best display yo's poreless white skin, yo's gallery of tattoos, the iridescent scales splashed on yo's chest. Yo's green and gold eyes glittered above razor-ridged cheekbones. The two acolytes, equally tall and slender, loomed over Macy, hemmed her in. A drone hung above, its underslung camera aimed straight at her.

"What kind of god were you looking for?" Jibril said. "The white-bearded patriarch of old? Or someone in your image?"

"Heaven forbid," one of the acolytes said.

"No, we must try to be charitable," Jibril said. "Still, the idea of any kind of god in Macy Minnot's image *is* rather distasteful."

Jon Ho asked the cosmo angels if they were going to let her customer leave in a peaceable manner and Macy told him she didn't need his help and set her hands flat on the tops of the stools either side of her, pushed straight up in the light gravity, and sat on the counter and swivelled and stepped down on the other side.

"A wide-hipped, spraddle-legged chimpanzee," Jibril called out as Macy walked away. "It doesn't really satisfy any description of the creator of the universe, does it?"

The next morning, Jibril and yo's little coven were waiting for Macy at the entrance to the pedestrian subway that connected East of Eden to its cut-and-cover farm tunnels. The two acolytes recited numbers in sing-song unison while Jibril loudly asked Macy if she really thought that God would let Herself be uncovered by simple arithmetical tricks. Macy walked straight past with her fists balled in the pockets of her jerkin, ignoring the drone that kept pace with her. But the cosmo angels were there the next day, too. Asking her if she was plotting to spread the good word here and turn everyone into zombies searching for the secret of the universe in the entrails of an irrational number.

She refused to give them anything, not so much as a word or a cross-grained look. They put the footage up on their site anyway.

"You shouldn't take it personally," Ivo Teagarden told her. "As far as Jibril is concerned, you're raw material for yo's art."

"Dragging up a life I left long ago is pretty personal."

Macy had dreamed about the church the previous night. The cluster of trailers hunched around the old missile silo in the tawny light of one of the dust storms that blew out of the sere and empty desert of the ruined prairie circled all around. The stacked levels of servers and drives of the ancient and vast parallel computers in the silo, each level floored with steel mesh and crowded with cased racks of circuitry knitted together by neat runs of colour-coded cabling and fat grey arteries of optical cabling, shuddering in the thunderous vibration of the fans that kept the servers from overheating as they ground through endless calculations.

Macy's first job, after she and her mother had joined the church, had been to clean the server stacks; despite the seals, dust constantly infiltrated the silo and would quickly cause breakdowns and seizures if it wasn't vacuumed up. Later, Macy had graduated to the first level of prayerful exploration, flying across virtual landscapes created by simple arithmetical transformations of pi's infinite, divine regression. These regions had already been thoroughly explored, but they were useful for indoctrination and training, preparing the acolytes for higher levels such as the Fields of Forty, where Macy's mother flew down fractal branches spewed by transformation functions based on ratios between fundamental physical properties of light and mass and gravity that mirrored, so it was taught and so it was believed, the deep structure of the universe created by a mathematical God whose presence might yet lurk in His creation.

Day after day, year after year, the holy mathenauts flew down virtual renderings generated by complex transformations of pi's regression, searching for nonrandom spoor that might be the footprints or fingerprints of the Creator with a fanaticism that Macy had found ever more futile and claustrophobic as she grew older and her mother, by now a holy creature starveling thin and half crazed from spending eighteen hours a day searching the divine regression, drew away from her and the rest of the real world.

Macy had left that life behind when she had run away. Left behind her mother and the only people she had known. She wouldn't have it back.

"Perhaps you could sit down with Jibril," Ivo Teagarden suggested. "Settle your differences face to face."

"Jibril and its—sorry, *yo*'s crew would video it and put it up on the net with demeaning little comments."

"Then video them videoing you and post it. Make your own art that critiques Jibril's."

"I'll think about it," Macy said.

The old man meant well, but he thought that Macy could think like an Outer. She couldn't. She was a stranger in a strange land. Trying to imagine the long and possibly endless exile that stretched ahead gave her a strange, vertiginous feeling. A scary-bad rush in the pit of her stomach that made her realise just exactly what she'd gotten herself into: year after year of breathing canned air, the low-grade but ever-present fear of a blowout or some other sudden and comprehensive disaster, cramped horizons and closed spaces. Living with strangers who had nothing in common with her. Strangers who sometimes seemed barely human.

The next day, one of her rest days, she wandered over to the neighbouring apartment block, where a green market was being held. She was buying peppermint tea-moss from a woman who grew it in one of the little gardens terraced up the side of the crevasse when she saw a drone hanging above the neighbouring flower stall. And there was Jibril, stalking down the aisle with yo's two acolytes following close behind.

"I have a question," Jibril said loudly, and with a flourish raised a laser pen above yo's shaven and tattooed head and conjured in the air the polychrome fishscales of one of the simpler inscapes of pi. "Can you show me where God is in this picture?"

When Macy turned on her heel and set off in the other direction, Jibril made the mistake of chasing after her and trying to stop her by grabbing hold of one of her arms. Macy swung around, her anger sudden and bright and fierce, and struck the cosmo angel in the chest with the heel of her hand and said, "You want a show? How about having it out with me, right here and now?"

147

Jibril tried to twist away and Macy snatched at yo's bandolier belt and they both lost their footing and waltzed sideways into a bank of cut flowers. Flurries of petals settling around them as Macy pinned Jibril down and told yo at length and in great and passionate detail exactly what she thought of yo's stupid so-called art. The acolytes twittered and wrung their hands, torn between trying to rescue their leader and making a record of the performance. A small crowd gathered and a pair of peace officers appeared. They managed to separate Macy and Jibril, but Macy, recklessly elevated by her anger, broke free and flew three metres in one bound and managed to land a solid punch on the side of the cosmo angel's face. She felt Jibril's teeth click under her knuckles and the cosmo angel went backward and sat down, shockingly red blood spilling from yo's pale lips, and then the peace officers got hold of Macy and hauled her away.

The drone captured everything. The footage was on the net inside an hour, and shot straight to the top of the charts.

Macy stood before the citizens' court the same day. Jibril, yo's cheek swollen and bruised, pressed charges; Macy refused to apologise or show remorse and wouldn't let Ivo Teagarden make an apology on her behalf. In the gallery, a little group of refuseniks began to boo and heckle and a majority of the audience shouted them down. The senior of the two peace officers who had arrested Macy asked for a vote, the audience overwhelmingly found Macy guilty, and the peace officer made a short speech about the necessity for everyone, born citizens and incomers alike, to respect the civic codes that enabled people to go about their business without fear or hindrance and told Macy that she would serve forty days' community service, and the sentence would start immediately.

4

Global warming and the release of vast quantities of methane and the subsequent catastrophic destruction of a substantial portion of the biosphere during the Overturn had caused massive perturbations in the heat engines that drove Earth's weather systems. Radical measures, such as the cloud of sunshade mirrors that cut the amount of sunlight falling on the Earth's surface, and the forests of synthetic Lackner trees whose sails removed vast tonnages of carbon dioxide from the atmosphere, had significantly lowered Earth's average global temperature, but it would be many decades yet before the planet's climate returned to something approximating preindustrial conditions. In Antarctica, glaciers around the coast had retreated, ice-sheet extension in winter was much reduced, and during the brief summer ice and snow were entirely absent along most of the coast of the Antarctic Peninsula.

Sri Hong-Owen had built her home and a research complex on the coast of Graham Land, at the northern end of the peninsula. Her retreat, her fastness, her fortress of solitude, set above a fjord whose crooked mouth sheltered it from the cold currents, icebergs and fierce, salt-laden gales of the Weddell Sea. Sri had constructed a biome along the shore of the fjord, modelled on the ecosystem that had briefly flourished there during the warmest part of the Pliocene. Hummocky sedges thickened amongst the rocks of the tideline, and a heath vegetation of low, close-knit swales of Antarctic beech, *Nothofagus antarctica*, and dwarf willow, blueberry, Labrador tea and birch, grew up the steep sides, interrupted by small, lush meadows of grass and mosses that in the brief summer were bright with yellow buttercups and dandelions, bluebells, white asters, and pink and rust-red willowherbs. Hares and two species of vole grazed the heaths. Rookeries of Chinstrap and Gentoo penguins contested for space along the shore. There was a small colony of Weddell seals. Skuas and fish eagles rode the fierce, frigid winds. There was even a small wood in a sheltered valley beneath Sri's house, where Antarctic beech trees grew six or seven metres high amongst mossy rocks. Sri was walking there with the younger of her two sons, Berry, when her secretary called and told her about the problem on the Moon.

It was early March. Autumn. The beeches were draped in oranges and yellows. A scant snow fell from the grey sky, dry cold pellets pattering on moss and drifts of fallen leaves. Black squirrels made frantic guerrilla sorties to collect beech mast; they would soon go into hibernation and doze away the six months of darkness and subzero temperatures. Sri reprimanded Berry when he threw a stone at an unwary squirrel that came too close. He was a sturdy boy, shorter and heavier than his brother. Like Sri, he was wrapped in a quilted coat and quilted trousers, the coat's hood cinched tightly around his face as he kicked with aimless ferocity at the crumbling, moss-bearded trunk of a tree that years ago had fallen in one of the winter storms.

Sri had spent a lot of time thinking about Berry's future recently, trying to find something he could be good at, something he could enjoy. He was a sulky, obdurate child, not especially bright, showing little interest in anything he couldn't eat or break, but there must be a spark somewhere inside him, something she could kindle.

Now, she made him kneel beside her and showed him the invertebrate life wriggling in the thin loam under the mossy log. Dozens of tiny springtails (the only terrestrial invertebrate in Antarctica, before the Overturn), worms recoiling into their burrows, pill bugs, a large black beetle with curved pinchers. There were more than two hundred species of insects in the wood and the heaths and meadows—even a species of bumblebee that Sri had introduced to pollinate the summer flowers. Berry was searching for another beetle, down on his hands and knees in the leaves and moss, explaining how he could stage a fight between different insects, something that reminded Sri of Euclides Peixoto, when her phone rang.

"There's a problem at Oxbow," Yamil Cho said, without preamble. "A code ten."

Oxbow was the superbright facility. Code ten meant that there had been an attempted breakout, and fatalities.

"How bad?"

"Five down, plus collateral damage. Your attendance has been requested. I have taken the liberty of arranging transport—the *Uakti*."

It was the shuttle that had been used as a test bed for the first of the new fusion motors. Yamil Cho told Sri that it could make the trip point-to-point in less than six hours.

Berry had been kicking at the dirt and stamping on insects he'd uncovered. Now he started to make excited noises, trying to get his mother's attention. She turned her back on him and said to her secretary, "When is it due?"

"A little over an hour. A suborbital lob from Brasília."

"Come pick me up when it's here," Sri said, and called to Berry.

He trotted over, proudly displaying the treasure he'd unearthed. The brown arc of a human rib bone, no doubt from a casualty of one of the twenty-first-century wars fought over oil and methane clathrate fields in the Weddell Sea. When Sri had begun her work here, there had still been remnants of oil platforms out in the open water, and tankers and warships sunken or grounded along the coast. She'd pulled in every favour to have them broken up and removed, and had done much else to clean up the peninsula. Removing crashed planes and the carcasses of tanks and other vehicles. Uplifting a barracks and a graveyard. Using bacteria she'd cut herself to digest a vast sluggish spill of oil that had accumulated in a deep trench thirty kilometres offshore, the source of hard tarry cakes that had washed up along the shore after storms. But there'd been a lot of fighting here, and things had lasted a long time in the cold. It was still possible to turn up souvenirs of the wars almost anywhere along the peninsula. Weapons and ammunition, clothing, trash, and bones like the rib Berry clutched like a frail dagger.

Sri felt a shiver of presentiment and told her son to throw the grim little memento away, speaking so sharply that he did what he was told without arguing.

"There's more, under the log," he said.

"Someone will come and clear it away," Sri said. "You run to the house and get some hot chocolate from the housekeeper."

"I didn't do anything wrong."

Berry's face was set in a scowl that Sri knew could quickly turn to tears and a tantrum. She dropped to one knee and cuddled him and said, "I know you didn't. But I have to go away for a few days, and I need you to be my good little soldier while I'm gone."

"Are you going back to Brasília? Can't I come this time?"

"I'm going to the Moon, and much as I'd like you to come with me I'm afraid you can't. Don't pull a face. I'm not taking Alder either. Go on home now, quick as you can!"

As her son scampered away toward the house, Sri set off in the opposite direction. She needed a little time alone. She wanted to think about the implications of the breakout and the peremptory summons, work out her best response.

She climbed out of the wood, following a path that switchbacked up the side of the valley to a crest of sedgy heath. Tramped along the ridge as it rose eastward, climbing through fields of lichen-blotched boulders, at last reaching a wide shelf of bare rock that gave her a panoramic view down the crooked arm of the fjord to the open sea. Facing into the cold, clean wind and thin flurries of snow, she could survey the entirety of her little kingdom. The steep patchwork heath cut by the neat fold of the little wooded valley. The glass-and-steel boxes of her house cantilevered above the western side of the valley, and the little campus of the research complex spread along the shore toward a prospect of snow-capped mountains. The dark water of the fjord was littered with bergy bits. Beyond its narrow mouth, fleets of icebergs sailed the wide sea, and three vertical lines scratched the grey sky at the horizon, precise as brushstrokes in a Japanese print, feathering into tiny plumes that bent northward: smoke lofted by volcanoes that had become active after the lithostatic pressure of the Antarctic ice cap had diminished.

But the ice was returning. Winter came a little earlier every year to the fjord, left a little later. In fifty years or so its grip would be permanent. Everything Sri had quickened here, the little wood, the heaths and meadows, the scampering squirrels and the hares and voles: all of it would soon be gone, yielding to snow and ice.

A fine lesson in impermanence, Sri thought. Nothing remained the same forever. Every niche-clinging individual or species that stubbornly refused change invited extinction. Adaptability was the key to survival. The world was being revived, not remade or restored, and change was the engine of revival. Oscar Finnegan Ramos and the other green saints promoted a holy mission of returning the planet to a prelapsarian paradise, but with the exception of a few garden spots protected by vast expenditures of energy and effort it would not be possible to reverse entropy and replicate and maintain a historical state. Their vision was a mirage. The world must be free to find its own point of equilibrium. Reclamation and remediation were a beginning, not a means to an end. After the world was reclaimed and renewed, human beings must relinquish control, allow new states to emerge.

Sri believed that the biosphere was a vast space of possibilities. Billions of years of life on Earth had explored only a small part of that space. So much more could be unlocked with just a small toolkit and a little imagination, and nothing was unnatural because nature was not limited to the variations on a few themes that evolution had so far realised. She dreamed of a thousand Earths, all different. A thousand gardens of plenty, harmonious, burgeoning with wonders.

She knew that it would take her many more years than the century and a half granted her to realise those dreams, and knew that at least one other person not only shared her ambition but could give her the key to true longevity. Until now, she had served Oscar Finnegan Ramos dutifully. He had set her on the career that had consumed her life. He had underwritten her research and protected her from the scorn and political manoeuvring of her rivals, and the fanatics who believed that change was dangerous and stasis holy. But all the while, Avernus—or rather, the ideal that Sri had erected in her mind's eye—had been her secret mistress. Sri had begun to grow away from Oscar Finnegan Ramos's ideas long before she had travelled out to Callisto and Europa; the superbright facility on the Moon was part of her increasing independence. It had provided a number of wonders, including the improved fusion motor, but containment had always been a major problem. Keeping the truth from Oscar; keeping the superbrights safely penned.

And now containment had been breached again. Security precluded transmission of any details. Beyond the plain fact that five superbrights had died, Sri wouldn't know how bad the incident had been until she had talked with the staff and seen the damage for herself. But she was certain that things had reached a critical point this time. She'd just returned from a punishing month in Brasília. Committees, policy reviews, think tanks, long-range planning sessions with the Joint Chiefs of Staff. The enemies of reconciliation were in the ascendant, emboldened by the death of Maximilian Peixoto and the failure of the biome project. A senior senator who had championed trade with the Outers had been unseated by a sex scandal. An emergency bill authorising funding for the conversion of several freighters into warships had been rushed through. Everyone gossiped about power shifts within the legislature and amongst the families. There were rumours that the Pacific Community was about to embark on its own programme of shipbuilding.

Rothco Yang, the representative from Rainbow Bridge, was deeply pessimistic. "We are talking about conciliation instead of reconciliation now," he told Sri over dinner. "Appeasement. Minimising the political and economic damage in the event of war between Earth and the Outer System. Rainbow Bridge has never wanted war. We have always championed the mutual benefits of peace and cooperation, but that is becoming increasingly difficult."

Peace was still and would always be the best option, but support for peace was dwindling on both sides. Rothco Yang said that none of the Outer cities, not even Rainbow Bridge, could accept the terms that the most radical of Earth's radical greens were demanding—complete surrender of political and economic autonomy, and an end to so-called anti-evolutionary genetic engineering and exploration of the outermost reaches of the Solar System.

"Many in your government are in no mood to make concessions, or recognise our neutrality," he said. "And at the same time, several cities in the Saturn System are eager for confrontation. They believe that the long supply line between Earth and Saturn will fatally weaken any hostile forces. Yet they are even more vulnerable. Their cities and settlements are fragile bubbles of air in an unforgivingly hostile environment. It would take very little to bring them down."

Rothco Yang looked exhausted. His jaunty optimism was entirely gone. It was almost possible to believe the face-saving fiction that he must soon return to Rainbow Bridge because his health was badly compromised by Earth's gravity and raw unfiltered air. He and Sri parted on equable terms, wishing each other the best, promising to stay in touch, but they both knew that they were laying to rest a worthy but lost cause.

No, it was no longer the season for peace and reconciliation. Sri remembered another conversation in Brasília, much shorter, far more unpleasant. She'd been lunching with her aides and two fellow scientists during a break in a long and hostile session of a subcommittee on protocols and ethics of research into the human genome, and Euclides Peixoto had come over to their table. The smiler with the hidden knife. After a brief exchange about the aftermath of the biome project, he'd asked Sri what great project she would turn to next.

"That's not my decision. As always, I'm at the service of your family."

"Really? I know you've been happy to serve because our interests have always coincided with yours. But I wonder what you'll do now things are changing," Euclides Peixoto had said, adding that from now on he'd be following her career with great interest.

Sri wished that all her enemies could be so lazy and foolish. So obvious. And although Euclides's crude threat had been unsettling, it was also a useful reminder that she must soon make a choice. Now, on the ridge above her fortress of solitude, under a grey and lowering sky with Antarctic wind flensing her to the bone, she realised that she'd already chosen. She could have refused the summons to the Moon, and it was likely that Oscar could have protected her from the consequences, but although she could not be entirely sure that she'd survive it she was glad that she was going. For a little while, she could feel unburdened. She had thrown off the past and could face the future's garden of forking paths if not with hope then at least with equanimity.

At last her attention was caught by a bright scratch far across the ocean, moving fast, coming out of the north and making a sharp turn toward the shore, its thunder catching up with it now, rolling across the bleak hilltop where Sri stood. She watched as the sleek little shuttle slipped in above the fjord, slightly lower than where she stood, its twin ramjets rumbling in turbofan mode. It was painted black above white like the killer whales she'd reintroduced to the Antarctic biome. Red lights flashed at the tips of its stubby wings. Its tail fin was decorated with the green flag of Greater Brazil. As it eased toward the landing pad beyond the research complex, Sri called her secretary and told him to come and get her. A few minutes later, a small helicopter whirred up from behind the distant house.

The *Uakti* climbed in a steep curve above the Weddell Sea. Eighty kilometres up, at the edge of space, its fusion motor ignited and Sri, Yamil Cho, and the shuttle pilot were slammed back into their crash couches as it accelerated toward escape velocity.

The pilot was a young man by the name of Cash Baker, one of the wing of combat pilots Sri had gifted with neurological enhancements a year ago. She asked him how his modifications were bedding in, and he told her that everything was working just fine, he was on his way back to Athena after meetings with engineers who were supervising the final stages of the refit of a freighter converted to a carrier for J-2 singleships. Sri cut him off when he began to eulogise the carrier's properties, told him that she was going to sleep out the trip.

The ability to fall asleep at will was a trivial cut she'd given herself in her salad days. She'd given it to Yamil Cho as well. They slept together side by side in their crash couches while the *Uakti* powered across three hundred and eighty thousand kilometres, woke at almost the same moment. They were swinging close around the Moon's dark and ravaged far side toward a swift dawn and Earthrise, and the pilot was gossiping with traffic control, guiding the shuttle in to a perfect landing on one of the pads north of the low tents and domes of Athena.

A rolligon ferried Sri and Yamil Cho past fields of vacuum organisms to the old research station where Sri had spent her apprenticeship. A string of low buildings covered by berms of dust and rock, it was now the cover for the facility deep underground. The rolligon drove past a gig and several tracked vehicles into a brightly lit garage. After the outer door shut and the garage had been pressurised, two women, slender black-haired identical twins dressed in red skinsuits, escorted Sri and her secretary to an express elevator that descended to the first level of the facility. This was where the superbright chimpanzees lived. Just as the research station was cover for them, so they were cover for the second level, where Oxbow's real secret was hidden.

General Arvam Peixoto was waiting for Sri in the conference room, standing at the wide armoured-glass picture window that looked out across the green arbours of the superbright chimps' habitat. The director of the facility, the chief of security, and the head of the research and development team were there too, bracketed by two more slender women in red skinsuits. Sri wondered who had cut them.

"Five," Arvam said. He was dressed in a grey flight suit slashed with zippered pockets and his long white hair was done up in a ponytail. A pistol with a chequered steel grip rode his hip in a black leather holster. Saying, "Can you believe it? Five. And they reached the surface, too."

"Are any still alive?"

"The second layer of security got them all. But it was damned close. These monsters of yours are getting too damned smart."

"I think you should tell me everything," Sri said.

Arvam gestured to the director, Ernest Genlicht-Ho.

"They tunnelled out," Genlicht-Ho said. "Fortunately, the so-called deathstar satellite spotted them immediately, and took appropriate action."

He called up video in the room's memo space. A panoramic view of the lightly cratered surface to the west of the research station zoomed in on a sudden geyser of dust that fell away to reveal five naked figures climbing out of a pit, each inside an inflated bubble of gold-tinted plastic. Views from various angles and distances showed a shuttle dropping toward the figures out of the black sky, the five golden bubbles bursting, collapsing over the figures inside as they thrashed and quietened and lay still, the shuttle swinging past low overhead, its motor still burning as it smashed into the ground and ripped a long trench across the plain.

Ernest Genlicht-Ho explained that the superbrights had infiltrated the security system, established a communications link with traffic control at Athena, and taken control of one of the shuttles. "As for the escape itself, one of our subjects broke out during a routine medical check. The tranquilizer administered to him turned out to be distilled water. By the time we realised that the security system had been compromised, he'd killed two doctors and five wranglers, and had freed four of his siblings."

The superbrights seemed to have accessed the security system by use of a quantum tunnelling device. It had transmitted data at a very low bit rate— the security chief believed that it had taken them more than six months to assemble the viral subpersonality that had taken control of the system's AI during the escape attempt—but the superbrights had had nothing but time. After they'd finally subverted the security system, they'd used it to gain access to the medical robots, swapping tranquilizer capsules for distilled-water placebos used in medical studies. The five who had broken out had used shaped explosive charges to tunnel their way through the containment perimeter and thirty metres of lunar regolith; the bubbles that had protected them from vacuum had been part of an experiment that one of them had been conducting with a new kind of memory plastic. They had been within ten seconds of reaching the shuttle when the security satellite had fried them with microwave bursts and killed the shuttle's AI.

"You have to admire the little buggers," Arvam told Sri. "They don't give up. Their first attempt, two of them bite out each other's throats, and a third almost gets free when the wranglers go to clean it up. Then they compromised the security AI and used that ultrasound gadget to make everyone in the facility as sick as dogs. Two of them actually broke into the garage before the wolves caught them. And now this. They got into the security AI again, even though I was assured that new firewalls and personality mirroring had made it impossible. That virus of theirs took down the wolves, too, which means that two who almost got away on the second attempt must have been in contact with the ones who stayed behind. Am I correct, Doctor Genlicht-Ho?"

"It appears so." Ernest Genlicht-Ho's face was the colour of unsized paper. Beads of sweat stood out on his forehead. "The first two sorties may not have not been separate incidents, as we thought, but part of the preparations for this attempt."

"Tell her the rest," Arvam Peixoto said.

Genlicht-Ho looked at the floor. "There is a possibility that one or more of the wranglers gave them help."

"More than a 'possibility,'" Arvam said. "Someone called in that shuttle. They couldn't have known about such a thing, let alone accessed it."

"With respect, they manufactured a neutrino backscattering device three years ago," Genlicht-Ho said. "It turned out to be quite profitable, actually, a form of deep radar with far greater range and resolution than anything commercially available. It is possible that they could have mapped an area around the station some twenty kilometres in diameter during its development. The spaceport falls comfortably within that footprint."

"Perhaps they knew about shuttles. But they certainly did not know how to access one remotely. For that they would have needed help," Arvam said, looking straight at Sri.

"Put me to the question, and you'll see that I had nothing to do with this," Sri said, cold and angry and afraid. "Question my secretary, too."

"I don't doubt your loyalty," Arvam said. "As for these three, they are damn fools for allowing this to happen, but they are not traitors. That leaves the wranglers. None of them are ever allowed to leave level two, much less the facility, but it is possible that the superbrights turned one of them somehow, or made him into their puppet. Or perhaps one of them is a sleeper—an agent inserted when this facility was first set up. We're questioning everyone involved, of course."

Arvam was smiling and his voice was even and pleasant, but his gaze was ice cold. Sri's fear twisted a notch higher. She had seen him like this before, and was certain that he was planning to make an example of someone. If he tried to shoot her, or if he told his bodyguards to kill her, Yamil Cho would have to put them all down. And then, providing she could get out of the facility, she'd have to put into effect her plan to flee to the Outer System, no question about it . . .

Still smiling, Arvam asked Ernest Genlicht-Ho if he had any suggestions about moving forward from this.

"We should separate them from each other," the director said. "All of their escape attempts have required cooperation between several individuals. If they were isolated, it would greatly reduce their ability to formulate and execute a plan."

"It sounds expensive," Arvam said.

The chief of security agreed that it would indeed be very expensive. "Unfortunately, given their ability to use ordinary laboratory equipment to communicate over great distances, it would be necessary to build individual facilities. Either in different parts of the Moon, or in orbit."

"But the potential benefits are enormous," the head of research and development said. He'd thrust his hands into the pockets of his smock to conceal their trembling. "They have already produced the fusion motor, deep radar, the pulse rifle, a new type of polywater . . ."

"What do you think we should do?" Arvam said to Sri. "You cut these little buggers. Can we keep hold of them?"

"It will be very difficult. They have learned too much. They have a deep desire to escape. There will be more attempts, and each will be more sophisticated than the last."

The security chief quivered. "With respect, sir, Dr. Hong-Owen is quite right. On the one hand, we have to be one hundred percent vigilant one hundred percent of the time. On the other, all they have to do is wait until there is a lapse they can exploit."

Arvam said pleasantly, "So you're bound to fuck up again, is that it?"

"We are only human," Ernest Genlicht-Ho said. "And they are something more than human."

Arvam looked at Sri. "Tell me what to do."

Sri was ready for the question. She'd been ready for it ever since she had heard about the code ten.

"Destroy them."

"Right now?"

"They can't work in isolation. They are successful only when they work as a gestalt, but we can't contain that gestalt. So the experiment must end."

"That's what I thought," Arvam said, and drew his pistol and shot Ernest Genlicht-Ho twice in the chest. The security chief straightened his back and closed his eyes before Arvam shot him, but the head of research and development bolted toward the door and one of Arvam's bodyguards sprang on him like a cat and broke his neck. Sri stood as still as she could, Yamil Cho poised beside her, as Arvam holstered his pistol and said, "Well, that's that."

"Not quite," Sri said. "I must deal with the surviving superbrights."

"Of course. And my people will deal with the wranglers, once we have established which one of them helped the superbrights, and why. What about the chimps?" Arvam said, turning to look out of the window.

Sri stepped up to join him. Near the top of a tree some ten metres away one of the chimps sprawled on its back in a platform woven from bent and broken branches. Its dark brown eyes gazing at infinity as its fingers spidered across a slate resting on its chest, conjuring a dense flow of symbols. Sri had created it and others like it from genome templates of the western common chimpanzee, *Pan troglodytes verus*. Cuts had forced the growth of fast, dense neuronal connections that massively boosted intelligence beyond the level of ordinary human genius, but the chimps had turned out to be a dead end. Those few which had not gone insane or committed suicide hammered out intricate flights of weird and highly complex mathematical reasoning as instinctively as breathing, but most of their work consisted of esoteric proofs of well-known theorems, and was of little interest to anyone apart from the research team that sifted a few useful nuggets from the reams of calculations. And those nuggets were growing rarer. The chimps were evolving away from conventional mathematics, spinning baroque fantasies that even the best human mathematicians had trouble connecting with reality.

Sri would mourn their passing, but their usefulness was at an end, and she felt only a small pang of sorrow when she told Arvam Peixoto, "We don't need them any more, either."

"Good. Now let's deal with the real problem."

About forty people in the upper circles of the Peixoto family, including Oscar Finnegan Ramos, knew about the chimps, believing them to be the source of wondrous technological advances that in the last ten years had made the family the most powerful in Greater Brazil. But only the crew of Oxbow, Sri, her secretary, Arvam Peixoto, and six members of the family's inner council knew about level two, the real source of the near-magical technologies. That was where Sri and Arvam Peixoto went now, past robot sentries equipped with triple copies of hardened, hardwired and heavily shielded core processors, down a long moving-floor ramp, past more robot sentries and two of Arvam's red-clad bodyguards, into the secret within a secret.

The master surveillance room where shifts of wranglers usually worked around the clock was deserted except for a trio of robots balanced on their ball-drives. Memo spaces showed views of every room and corridor in the second level, views from every angle of the superbrights' cage. It was a big sphere with soft plastic walls, cluttered with shelves and equipment racks, workbenches and immersion tanks, exercise machines, two closed-cycle toilets and a single shower unit. Sleeping bags hung like shed cocoons. In the beginning, after a brief two-year force-grown transition from birth to adulthood, fourteen superbrights had lived and worked there. Sri had cut them from human embryos, using techniques that she had developed while experimenting on the chimps, adding to the mix a form of low-scale autism so that, using behavioural cues, the superbrights could be trained to absorb new techniques and blocks of knowledge, and work with intense concentration on problems set them by their wranglers. They had evolved their own language, a shorthand of expressions and finger-shapes that conveyed complex ideas with astonishing rapidity; when they were all working on the same problem, they moved and worked with harmonious synchrony, as if engaged in an elegant and endless free-form dance.

Now nine of her brilliant children were dead, killed during various escape attempts, and the survivors were penned in one of the medical cells, surgically anaesthetised, awaiting their fate. Sri felt a mix of pride and sorrow. Proud because they had achieved so much in so short a space of time. Even the fierce and ruthless determination with which they had worked to escape was to be admired. Sorrowful because they had reached the inevitable end that she had forecast when she had first drawn up plans to create them.

She pressed a palm against a screen that checked her DNA and metabolic signature. She uploaded the necessary key into the system, then told Arvam that she'd like to see the superbrights one last time.

"I never before believed that you were sentimental," he said. "All right. Two of my people will take you."

Sri couldn't enter the medical cell because its air was tainted with anaesthetic. All she could do was stand at the door and look through the judas. The five superbrights lay on pallets, memo spaces displaying trace readouts above their heads. They were androgyne neuters, naked, pale, hairless, and about a metre tall. Child-sized, but nothing like children, with broad chests, large heads and small, delicate limbs. Their faces were calm and still beneath asymmetrically swollen foreheads—Sri had discovered that the most stable personalities were obtained by selective stimulation of growth of the left cerebral hemisphere. Although they had a strong familial resemblance, with close-set eyes and flat noses and small, down-curved mouths, she recognised each one and said goodbye to each in turn before activating the key and opening a vent connected to the vacuum of the lunar surface.

A pale mist distilled from the air and was quickly shredded and whisked away. The mouths of the sleepers gaped wide as they gasped for air; their chests rose and fell with rapid irregular convulsions and abruptly stopped moving; bloated tongues parted blue lips and swelled further and ruptured, spattering blood; blood burst from their nostrils and leaked from the corners of their eyes, boiling in the vacuum even as it streaked their pale skin. Trace readings flatlined.

The sleepers were dead. This part of Sri's life was over. She turned away, sorrow and self-pity swelling her heart.

"That was well done," Arvam said. "It reminds me that I should also thank you for the many hours of amusing material you sent to me after your little trip to Callisto."

"I thought you had forgotten about it," Sri said.

"Oh, I never forget a favour. Now, I want to see how your other children are doing. I think we'll be needing them very soon. After all, the end of one chapter is always followed by the beginning of another, eh?"

5

Father Aldos banged through the gymnasium's double doors, hurried past boys paired on green mats and thrusting and parrying with knives, and mounted the low platform at the end of the long room. He talked briefly with Father Solomon, then clapped twice to get the boys' attention.

Dave #8 bowed to his partner, Dave #15, who bowed to him, and they both turned to face front as all around them their brothers did the same, like a single movement reflected in a hall of mirrors.

"We have visitors," Father Aldos said. His handsome *café con leite* face was darkly flushed, his gaze pinched and anxious. "Important visitors. You will all now stand ready for inspection."

The boys straightened their backs and raised their heavy practice knives in front of their faces. All of them bare-chested and barefoot, wearing only loose white trousers tied at waist and ankles. Plastic greaves strapped to their forearms. For several minutes nothing happened. Dave #8 stared past the blade of his knife at an imaginary point hung in the air a metre in front of him. Sweat cooled and dried on his chest and back, on his naked scalp. He was excited and apprehensive and was wondering if his brothers felt the same way. At last there was a bustle of activity at the edge of his vision. He cut his gaze to the left, saw that four strangers had appeared at the entrance to the gymnasium. Uniformed in black combat coveralls and visored helmets and combat boots, armed with short-barrelled carbines, they took up positions either side of the entrance as more people appeared. Two men and a woman, closely followed by Father Clarke and Father Ramez.

Dave #8's heart bumped inside his chest. The woman was the woman whose face sometimes appeared in one of the avatars: Sri Hong-Owen.

There was a faint stir in the boys' ranks as she moved past them to the low platform where Father Aldos and Father Solomon were waiting. She talked briefly with the two lectors and turned and studied the ranks of the boys. She was dressed in a long quilted coat that hung open over a knitted garment and quilted trousers and knee-length boots with ruffs of white fur around their tops. Her pale and naked scalp gleamed in the harsh light. Dave #8 felt his blood beat in his face as her sharp gaze moved over him.

The smaller of the two men who accompanied her was clearly the most dangerous. Slim and supple in a black shirt and black trousers, his posture relaxed but his gaze sharp and alert. The other man was much older, dressed in a grey flight suit with a big pistol holstered at his right hip. He had an air of confident authority, stepping to the edge of the platform, his voice ringing out across the room when he told the boys that he was General Arvam Peixoto.

"My family, the Peixoto family, owns the facility. Everything that happens in it is under my command. I am here today because your basic training is coming to an end. I know that will be hard for you to accept. You have been in training all your lives. In fact, it is the only life that you know. But training is not an end to itself. It is time now to put the skills you have learned here to the test." The general paused, looking past the boys at the racks of weapons and equipment along the walls, then said, "I see all manner of weapons here."

After a moment, Father Solomon volunteered, "We have trained them for every eventuality, General."

"I see bows and arrows."

"They are silent weapons and can carry a variety of payloads, from simple barbs to tethers or vials of nerve gas or explosive. Also, arrows will travel great distances in low gravity. And in the vacuum and zero gravity of true space, they will continue to fly without losing velocity until they strike their target. Also, practice increases hand-to-eye coordination—"

"And swords too," the general said. "Knives I can understand. Knives can be useful in close combat. Swords, though. In what kind of battle might swords be useful?"

"Again, hand-to-eye coordination—"

"It seems to me that you indulge these boys. You train them for everything, and as a result they are useful for nothing in particular. They are not focused." The general turned to Sri Hong-Owen and said, "How do you think we can help them focus?"

"Don't involve me in this," she said.

"But these are your boys," the general said. He was smiling, but it was only to show his teeth. "Your creations. The flesh of your flesh, transformed by your skill and hard work. Surely you must have an opinion."

Dave #8 was struck by a fierce and holy exultation. Dave #27, the wisest of his brothers, had been right all along. They were not Outers. No, they were weapons to be used against the Outers, and so they had been given the form of their enemy, but they were not doubly fallen. They were human. They could be redeemed. His joy surged up inside him. He had to bite the inside of his cheeks to stop himself shouting out and he was trembling from head to foot, and the brother standing in front of him, Dave #11, was trembling too.

"If you brought me here to prove something," Sri Hong-Owen told the general, "then do what you feel you must. Don't make it into a game."

There was a brief silence. Father Clarke said, "If this is a question of their prowess, if you would like a demonstration, I am sure that something can be arranged. They are skilled in all the weapons you see here. As well as several kinds of hand-to-hand combat, of course. It will take very little time to set up a demonstration of their prowess in any form of combat."

The general turned his chill smile to the lector. "How about knives?"

"Well, of course," Father Clarke said. "They were engaged in a training exercise in knife-fighting when you arrived. If you would like them to continue—"

"Who is the best?"

"At knife-fighting?"

"At everything. Your most apt pupil."

"They are trained in a wide variety of techniques . . . It is hard to say."

"I'll make it easier," the general said. "Who is the one you would save, if you could save only one?"

"I don't quite follow you," Father Clarke said. He was clutching his pectoral cross in his right hand, knuckles squeezed white.

"Number Eight," Father Solomon said. "If you must use one of them, use Number Eight."

"Is he the one you would save out of all of them?" the general said. "Or is he the first you would sacrifice, if you had to?"

"He is the best."

Father Solomon looked as though he wanted to use his shock stick on the general.

"Let's see. Bring him to me."

Father Solomon turned to face the boys and said, "Number Eight. Step forward."

Dave #8, his knife still raised in front of his face, took the regulation three paces off the edge of the green mat onto cold, polished concrete. He knew that Father Solomon had chosen him as a punishment, but he was determined to do whatever was asked of him to the best of his ability.

"There's no need for this," Sri Hong-Owen said. "Haven't I just now proved my loyalty?"

"That was no more than housekeeping," the general said.

"The boys are loyal," Father Clarke said. "Utterly so. As are we, general."

"Has their loyalty ever been put to the test?"

"They pledge allegiance every day," Father Clarke said. "Every moment of their lives is dedicated to service of God, Gaia, and Greater Brazil."

"And to service of the Peixoto family too, I hope."

"Well, of course," Father Clarke said quickly. "I mean no offence—"

"Then their lives are mine, yes?" The general stepped off the platform and glided up to Dave #8, saying, "Is your life mine, son?"

He was about thirty centimetres shorter than Dave #8, but his gaze had the force of heat beating from the heart of a forge.

Dave #8 did not know how to answer. He looked over the top of the general's head at Father Clarke, who nodded once, pinch-faced and miserable. Through what felt like a mouthful of hot sand, Dave #8 managed to say, "I am at your service, sir."

"You will do as I command."

"Sir, I am at—"

"My service. Are you a parrot, son, or a soldier? No, don't look at your teachers. Look at me. Answer my question."

"We are soldiers, sir." The blade of Dave #8's knife was trembling in front of his face. He willed his muscles to lock tight, but that only made the tremor worse.

"*You* are a soldier," the general said.

"Yes, sir."

"Have you ever killed?"

"Yes, sir. In simulations."

"But not in real life. You have not fought to the death."

"They're each worth as much as a singleship," Sri Hong-Owen said.

"They're worth nothing unless they can fight," the general said, his gaze locked on Dave #8.

"It isn't their primary purpose," Sri Hong-Owen said.

"Infiltration, espionage, deep cover, all the rest of that spooky shit, I don't deny it may some day be useful, but it isn't something I understand," the general said. "Fighting though, skill and courage, those I *do* understand. And they can be tested right here, right now."

"I can arrange a demonstration of any kind of combat that you wish to see," Father Solomon said.

The general ignored him, asked Dave #8 to hand him his knife. Dave #8 brought the knife down smartly, reversed it, and offered it to the general hilt-first. The general swiped it through the air, tested the edge of its blade with his thumb, and handed it back. "Are you ready to use this in my service, son?"

"Yes, sir."

Dave #8 saw that the slim man in black was poised on the balls of his feet. Ready to make a move because he thought that the general might be about to give the order to kill Sri Hong-Owen.

"Father Solomon thought I wanted the best of you killed as a lesson to the rest," the general said. "So he didn't pick out the best, as I requested, but the one he likes least. He disobeyed me. Kill him."

Dave #8 understood the general's order, but didn't understand why he'd given it; although he'd been trained to obey without thought, his loyalty to

165

the lectors was as strong and deeply rooted and unconditional as love. He might not have done anything at all if Father Solomon hadn't tried to escape, jumping from the platform in a billow of robes and bounding past the boys. Dave #8's training took over and he lunged after the man, caught up with him in three long, floating strides, and knocked him down. The man tried to pull his shock stick from his belt, screamed when Dave #8 slashed his wrist, and kicked out frantically, sliding crabwise across the polished concrete floor. Dave #8 dropped straight down, pinning the man's shoulders with his knees, and slammed his free hand against the point of the man's chin and made a single swift pass with his knife and flipped to his feet.

Father Solomon clapped his hands to his neck. Threads of blood pulsed through his fingers and spattered his white habit. He looked up at Dave #8, his mouth shaping words no one would ever hear; then his gaze lost focus and he shuddered all over and his grip on his neck slackened and his head slumped sideways. A puddle of blood crept out around it, rich and glossy, its smell sweet and heavy in the cold air.

Dave #8 was breathless and trembling violently. His bare chest was spotted with Father Solomon's blood. The light seemed brighter, somehow. Everything in the room stood out with sharp particularity. His brothers were still standing at attention, but had turned their heads to look at him. Off to one side, the general clapped slowly and loudly. He was smiling. On the platform, Sri Hong-Owen was leaning into the embrace of the slim man in black. Father Clarke was bent over a spatter of vomit, making small choking noises. Father Aldos's eyes were closed and he was praying. Father Ramez floated down from the platform, told Dave #8 to step back, and knelt by Father Solomon and put the flat of his palm on the dead man's forehead and began to recite the last rites.

"You did well," the general told Dave #8. "If only I had a thousand like you. What do you say, Professor Doctor? Is that possible?"

The woman looked at him with cold scorn. "You'd have to build a bigger creche. And then wait seven years."

"Mmm. I don't think we have that long, so we will have to make do with what we've got." The general smiled at Dave #8 again, turned to survey the other boys. "We will ride back to Earth on my shuttle, Professor Doctor. It isn't as fast as the ship that brought you here, but that's to our advantage. We have much to discuss."

6

Her first night in the women's dormitory wing of the rectification facility, Macy was cornered by three long-term inmates and beaten up. She fought back and lost a tooth and gained a black eye. After that initiation she was mostly left alone and quickly fell into the routine. Eight hours locked in her cell, an hour of free association with the other inmates, the rest of the day taken up by work and remedial activities—interactive tutorials with an expert AI, participation in group exercises supposed to make her understand herself and her failings, and one-on-one sessions listening to the achingly boring, self-centred monologues of a dull-eyed old woman, Sasaki Tabata, who was serving community service without remission because she had murdered her lover and cooked a portion of his buttocks and eaten it.

After that, work was a relief: three hours each day out on the surface, sealed in a pressure suit heavily encumbered with radiation shielding, picking fat graphite buds from vacuum organism pavements stretched across dusty ice under racks of lights. No doubt this stoop labour was supposed to be humiliating, but Macy didn't mind it: it was the first time she'd been outside East of Eden since she'd arrived on Ganymede and she was astonished and delighted by the alien panorama. Fields of vacuum organisms—highly organised colonies of bound nanomachines that catalysed complex reactions at very low temperatures—pieced across a plain of dark, dusty ice spattered with the pits of small craters and blocky clumps of ejecta, and a ragged scarp curved across the horizon to the north, the rim of a crater more than ninety kilometres in diameter. Jupiter's swollen disc hung high above, waxing from slender crescent to full glory and waning again in a cycle of a little over seven days, fixed in the same place in the black sky because Ganymede, like Earth's Moon, was tidally locked and always presented the same face to its primary. In the middle of Ganymede's night, the moon's shadow was cast small and sharp on the tawny ripple-edged band at Jupiter's equator; when Ganymede swung through Jupiter's shadow during the brief midday eclipse, the gas giant was a black hole in the starry sky, faintly limned by sunlight refracted through its atmosphere, lightning storms ten times bigger than Earth writhing and flickering at its poles.

Working in the vacuum organism fields, Macy learned to trust her pressure suit's bubble of warmth and air and to appreciate the silence of Ganymede's naked and unforgiving icescapes stretched cold and still under the infinite black sky, and there were blessed moments when her consciousness sank into her muscles and time melted into an eternal now and everything around her, the awkward casing of her pressure suit and its whines and hisses and whirrs, the fields of vacuum organisms and the stark plain beyond, flowed into a single pure experience.

So it went. She slept or tried to sleep in her cell, endured Sasaki Tabata's monologues and the stupid lectures and the tedious remedial exercises, lost herself in physical labour. One day out in the vacuum organism fields, three weeks into her sentence, she'd just been admonished for about the hundredth time for staring at the scenery rather than working when another voice cut in on the common band.

A man's voice, saying, "Have some heart. Anyone could get lost in that view."

"You can look all you want when you have finished here," the warden said. "Meanwhile you work."

Unlike prisons in Greater Brazil, the rectification facility allowed male and female inmates to freely mix at work, in the talkathon sessions, and in the canteen and gymnasium: only the dormitory wings were segregated. Later that day, Macy was eating her evening meal at one end of a mostly empty table when a man slid in next to her and said, "It's funny how a planet looks at its best when it's hung over a landscape. A lot of people claim Saturn is way more beautiful, but Jupiter has this untouchable grandeur, don't you think? I'm Newt, by the way. Newt Jones. Newt short for Newton, but don't hold that against me. You're Macy Minnot. I hear you're from Earth. Which makes us both strangers here, right?"

He held out his hand, a curious, old-fashioned gesture. Macy shook it. His grip was bony and cool.

She said, "How did you know who I was? I mean, from out in the fields."

"Suit ID." Newt Jones was studying her in a frank, friendly fashion. He was tall and pale, his long, angular face softened by a guileless grin. Macy had trouble guessing Outers' ages, but he didn't look much older than her. Maybe even a year or two younger. He said, "You don't know about suit ID?"

"I barely know which end of a suit is which. I guess I'm more of a stranger than you."

"Oh, I don't know. Where I originally come from, it's a lot further from here than Earth."

Newt told Macy that he'd been born in a short-lived commune on Titania, Uranus's largest moon, that although his family had moved back to the Saturn System and settled on Dione after the commune had split up, as far as he was concerned he would always be a Uranian, one of the few. He ran his mother's ship, towing any kind of load to every kind of destination. He'd come to Jupiter on what he called the Grand Tour because Jupiter and Saturn were presently in conjunction, had done some excellent business on Callisto and Europa, but had ended up in East of Eden's rectification facility after being caught trying to smuggle interdicted pharmaceuticals into the settlement.

"Nothing serious, but they're famously puritanical here. They talk a lot about elevating and improving their minds, how they think better than anyone else, yet they ban every kind of psychotropic stronger than caffeine or theobromine. How crazy is that? All I was trying to do was put a little sparkle in the lives of a few of their citizens, but they caught me and they gave me ten days. It's nothing. *Nada*. I can do it standing on my head. Despite the heavy gravity they have here—did you know that it's more than five times the pull on Dione? People can fly on Dione. Really. Before I started out on the Grand Tour I had to build up some muscle with doses of promoter and a fearsome exercise regime. But why are you here? You're famous, the hero who put a stop to some nasty business in Rainbow Bridge. Or so I heard. I guess you must have done something pretty serious to piss them off. Did you murder someone? Put plastic in the glass recycler? Hoard kudos? Pick a flower?"

"I wouldn't say sorry."

"That'll do it. What was it that you weren't sorry about?"

"I hit someone."

"I bet they had it coming."

Macy couldn't help smiling. "Let's put it this way: I felt a lot better after I did it."

"If you don't want to talk about it you don't have to talk about it."

"It's just that I have to talk about it every day in the group sessions."

"I had to stand up in one of those this morning and explain what I did," Newt Jones said. "Someone asked me if I was willing to learn from my errors and I said sure, if it meant not being caught the next time."

He asked Macy how she came to be living in East of Eden in the first place, asked her if she'd mind telling him how she'd been caught up in the murders and attempted sabotage that had famously brought an abrupt end to Greater Brazil's participation in the Rainbow Bridge biome project. She was halfway through the story when a bell rang. It was the end of free association time.

"We can talk tomorrow," Newt said, as he and Macy scraped the remnants of their suppers into the recycling bin. "It isn't as if we have anything else to do."

Macy found herself looking forward to it all the next day. At the end of the shift in the vacuum organism fields, they sat together in the canteen and she finished her story. Newt asked all kinds of questions about it, and about life on Earth, too. The usual run-of-the-mill stuff she'd learned to answer by rote, how people lived and why they couldn't move about freely, the reclamation projects and the vast ruined areas yet to be reclaimed, and questions that arrived sideways, unexpected and jolting. What did the air taste like? Were there places with no oxygen? Did rain hurt? Was it true that weather changed the way you thought? What was it like to sleep under the stars with no roof overhead?

"I tried that once," Newt said. "Inside a plastic bubble I inflated outside the ship. It bugged the hell out of me, frankly."

"I guess it helps to have a horizon," Macy said.

She remembered nights in the ruins during her early days in the Wreckers' corps. The smell of campfire smoke and the sound of wind walking through trees or whining about broken walls, night air cold on her face and bare arms and the stars slowly wheeling overhead, the bright points of satellites and ships moving amongst rigid constellations. Talking with Newt woke all kinds of memories in her and with those memories came feelings and emotions that she had almost forgotten. She felt homesick at times: not hopelessly so, as she had during her first days of exile, but definitely wistful.

They talked for an hour every evening for five days. Newt was amused by Macy's stories about life on Earth and tried his best to amaze her with tall tales about his life hauling cargo and passengers from moon to moon. She felt at ease with him, as if she had known him all her life. He wasn't especially handsome and was far too bony to be cute, but he was animated and funny and easygoing.

He couldn't understand why Macy was stuck in East of Eden, why she couldn't just pick up and go when her sentence was over. He said that there was plenty of work on any moon she cared to name for someone who knew microbial ecology. Maintenance work in city farms and in habitats, quickening new oases . . .

"You could write your own ticket," he said.

"I'd have to persuade East of Eden to let me go first."

"They don't really want you; you don't want to stay. What's the problem?"

"Politics. People in Rainbow Bridge still want to try to make some kind of accommodation with Greater Brazil. I'm a speck of grit in that particular oyster, so they sent me here. Out of sight, out of mind. They don't want to let me loose because I might cause more trouble."

"Would you?"

"I've seen enough trouble to last me the rest of my life."

"So tell them that. Tell them you want to go somewhere so far from Rainbow Bridge that they'll never hear from you again."

"You mean travel out to Saturn."

"Why not?"

"Because I'm not sure if I'm ready to take a step like that."

Macy tried to explain to Newt that leaving East of Eden and moving further out could mean giving up the idea that some day she might be able to return to Earth. "Greater Brazil wouldn't welcome me back unless I was in chains. But things could change. And if they don't, well, Greater Brazil isn't the only nation on Earth with a space programme."

"You'd go back to Earth if you could, but you can't go back right now."

"That's about the size of it."

"So while you're waiting for things to shake out the way you want, why not have some fun?" Newt said.

The next day, a warden came up to Macy as she was stripping off her pressure suit at the end of a session in the vacuum organism fields, and told her that her sentence had been commuted.

"What does that mean, 'commuted'?"

"It means that someone must like you a lot more than I do, because I don't think you've earned it. It means that you are to go to your cell and pack right now—there's a bus waiting to take you home."

Macy found Newt amongst the press of prisoners taking off and stowing away pressure suits, told him what had happened.

"I'd come visit when I get out," he said, "but they'd arrest me for it. They took away my right of entry into their crummy little city in case I corrupt the youth. But you can find me on the net. It isn't hard, just look up the name of my ship. *Elephant*."

"*Elephant*?"

"After the beast of burden. Don't you still have them on Earth?"

"I don't know. Maybe they're extinct."

"We have them, but they're small. Miniatures about so high," Newt said, holding his hand about a metre above the tabletop. "She's a good ship. Easy to spot, too."

"I'll talk to you when you're out," Macy said.

"You'd better," Newt said.

There was an awkward moment when they might have hugged or even kissed, but the warden told Macy that the bus wasn't going to wait forever, she should get her shit together right now.

"Remember what I said about having fun," Newt called after her. "I reckon they have a law against it in East of Eden."

On the long bus ride back to the city, sealed in a windowless cubicle, Macy had plenty of time to think about Newt's parting words. One thing she knew, she wasn't sorry about taking down Jibril. And she would do it again if the cosmo angel tried to cause her any more grief. She also knew that everyone in the settlement would know where she had been, and why, that all she could do was brazen it out as best she could. So when at last she reached Lot's Lot, she went straight to the refectory and ignored the frank stares of people as she walked past them to Jon Ho's café and sat at the counter and ordered an espresso and a shot of brandy.

"You didn't stop by your apartment?" Jon said.

"I guess I miss your coffee more."

"It might be an idea if you went there right now. And I'm sorry, but you better take this," Jon said, and set on the counter the half-full bottle of cherry brandy, with her signature on the tape wrapped around its waist.

"What's wrong?"

Jon wouldn't meet her gaze. "I really think you should check your apartment."

Someone was waiting outside Macy's door. It was the village's peace officer, Junpei Smith. He also had trouble meeting her gaze, telling her that he was very sorry, but the village caucus had discussed her probationary residential period during its last meeting, and the vote had gone against her.

It took Macy a little while to realise that she had been evicted. Junpei, apologetic and blushing, allowed her inside her apartment and she packed a few keepsakes and asked Junpei to put the rest of her possessions in storage and walked away, feeling a hot and tender sting of humiliation. At a lakeside café in the next village she nursed a beaker of green tea and decided against asking Ivo Teagarden for help because he'd probably give her a long lecture on how things were done and what she should do to get along. She didn't want to get along. She wanted her life back. Her independence. She called the administration office of the farms, because she knew that there was always a room or two free, set aside for visitors. That was when she found out that she had lost her job. The same story: a discussion in her absence, the vote gone against her. She would have to make a formal public apology to Jibril before she could be reinstated.

Her punishment hadn't ended after all—it had overflowed the confines of the rectification facility and spread like a stain into every corner of her life.

She finished her green tea, poured a finger of cherry brandy into the white china cup and allowed herself a few minutes of melodramatic self-pity while she sipped it, then called Ivo Teagarden and arranged to meet him. Not to ask for advice but to make a formal request.

He arrived a few minutes later, and as soon as he sat down on the other side of the table she told him that she wanted to leave.

"This is unexpected."

"I don't think so. I've lost my apartment and I've lost my job. There's nothing for me here."

Ivo Teagarden pursed his lips as he considered this. A second-generation Outer, ninety-two years old, he looked half his age, a vain and somewhat prissy man with a thick mane of black hair and a black spade-shaped beard, dressed as usual in a homespun knee-length tunic with strings of hand-carved stone and wood beads around his neck.

"I was hoping that your attitude would have improved while you were away," he said. "I hoped that you would have learned something about yourself, and how to live here."

"Is that what this was all about? To teach me a lesson?"

"To help you understand yourself and your part in our community."

"I think I have a very clear picture of my part in your community."

"It's something you can easily improve," Ivo said.

"By apologising to Jibril? I don't think so. I'd rather go back to jail."

"This isn't about Jibril, Macy. An old friend of yours will soon be visiting our city. Loc Ifrahim." Ivo waited for Macy to say something. When she didn't, he said, "Mr. Ifrahim claims that he is visiting us because he wants to try to explain the virtues of doing business with Greater Brazil. We suspect that he has other motives, and we would like to find out what they are."

Macy understood with a clean shock why her sentence had been commuted.

"You want me to do your dirty work. If I do, I get my job and apartment back."

"I can make no guarantees about your job or your apartment, Macy. That's up to your co-workers and the residents of your village. But if you help us, I will make sure that they know about it."

"You already know he's a spy. You don't need me to confirm it."

"We want to find out what he hopes to find out about us. If we know what he is interested in, it will help us build a picture not just of his intentions but also those of his masters. And that knowledge would be of great utility to the whole of the Outer System."

"I find out what he is planning, and you sell it on. Sorry, give it freely, for kudos."

"That's putting it very crudely."

"But you don't deny it's true. Suppose I don't cooperate?"

"This is a small community which can only survive as long as there is harmony. Sometimes, to avoid inharmonious conflict, it's necessary for an individual to make a sacrifice for the greater good. In this case, really it isn't much of a sacrifice, is it? In fact, you could look on it as a kind of redemption. A chance to make amends for your prideful stubbornness," Ivo said, and pushed back his chair and stood. "I don't expect you to come to a decision at once. Think about it, Macy. Think hard and well, but make your decision quickly. Mr. Ifrahim arrives here in just two days."

Macy took a long walk along East of Eden's long and narrow parkland floor, through a grove of olive trees, across flower-spangled meadows where sheep and llamas grazed, around a string of ponds, past enshelled groups of apartment blocks, the library, the theatre. She didn't believe that the whole business with Jibril, the silly confrontation, the trial, jail, had been engineered to force her to cooperate. Most likely, she thought, Ivo Teagarden and his cronies had learned about Loc Ifrahim's impending visit after she'd been sent to the rectification facility, and they'd engineered her release and the loss of her apartment and her job in a clumsy attempt to force her to do the right thing. On Earth, in Greater Brazil, the authorities would have presented her with a direct choice: follow orders or suffer the consequences. Ivo Teagarden and his cronies believed that they were morally superior. It was against their nature to order anyone to do anything against their will, or to make direct threats. But they didn't trust Macy, either. They couldn't be sure that she'd agree to help them. So they'd constructed a trap with only one way out, and probably convinced themselves that they were doing it for her own good.

That they were giving her a way of saving herself from the consequences of her own foolishness.

It didn't make the whole business any less distasteful—on the whole, she preferred honest brutality to devious and manipulative benevolence—and the more she thought about it, the angrier she got. Not with Ivo Teagarden, nor even with Jibril, but with herself. For being so naive. For failing to see that she would never be accepted or trusted by East of Eden and its citizens. For failing to understand that the city had been all this time a prison, her apartment a nicer version of the cell in the rectification facility.

She could stay here and do what they wanted, or stay here and refuse to do what they wanted and take whatever they threw at her. Either way, she'd be buried alive for the rest of her life. Or she could figure out a way of breaking free.

Getting away from Ganymede shouldn't be a problem. She was certain that Newt Jones would help her after he'd been released at the end of his short sentence, if only for the pleasure of thumbing his nose at the good citizens of East of Eden. But escaping from the city would be much more difficult. Newt couldn't get into East of Eden, and she couldn't get out. And besides, if she tried to contact him directly some AI would no doubt be listening in, and it would pass the information to Ivo Teagarden. As things stood, she didn't even dare look up the details of his ship on the net.

There was the delicate matter of timing, too. Loc Ifrahim was scheduled to arrive in East of Eden before Newt was released; Macy was going to have to tell Ivo Teagarden whether or not she was going to cooperate before she had any chance of working up a plan of escape. And she had a strong feeling that if she refused to help, her ass would be slung back in jail . . .

She ended up at the northern end of the city, in the cemetery park where, as in all Outer cities and settlements, the stores of carbon, nitrogen, phosphorous and other useful elements in East of Eden's dead were returned to the eternal loop of its ecosystem; bodies were dissolved by resomation and the fluid evaporated to a powder that was ceremoniously scattered around the roots of newly planted trees. The park was a peaceful narrow valley with wooded slopes rising either side of the lake that flooded its floor and, as in Rainbow Bridge's free zone, every kind of surveillance was forbidden within its boundaries. This was where Newt Jones had snuck into the city when he'd tried to smuggle in his illicit cargo, but Macy didn't know which of the six airlocks he'd used, or how he'd fooled the AI that controlled them; she should have asked him when she'd had the chance, back in jail. But the fact that he'd done it gave her hope. If he could get in, she could get out.

175

She climbed through stands of pines and wandered along the strip of rough heath that separated the trees from the footings of the curved roof, which was painted the fresh blue of a spring day on Earth. The air was warm. Butterflies tumbled around a flowering bush. White rabbits hippity-hopped through rough grass. Macy walked past the airlocks, each set in a fake rock face at the end of a sandy gully, studying the lie of the land around them, noting where paths ran, hollows and ridges, possible places of concealment. She went back down through the steep woods, crossed the lake on the slender span of a footbridge, and wandered past the airlocks at the top of the other side of the valley, then descended to a small grassy bowl circled by silver birches, her favourite spot in the park, and sat there for a long time, considering her options.

At last, she walked back into the central section of East of Eden, and put on her spex and called Ivo Teagarden, and told him that she would do what she had to do.

"As long as it is of your own free will, I'm delighted."

"It's my choice, all right."

"Good. You understand that until actual contact is made, your present position must remain unchanged."

"Loc Ifrahim has to see that I have been brought low. He'll think I want to help him because I'm desperate."

"You have a thorough understanding of the situation, Macy. Let's meet and talk. We have much to discuss."

Later that evening, Macy met with three of the refuseniks in a pumping station under the cemetery park's lake. A forgotten place where no one else ever went. A clandestine venue suitably dank and cold: puddles of water on the concrete floor, water dripping fat and slow from pipework slung overhead, the only light from graffiti that writhed across the walls like swarms of luminous serpents and spiders. After Macy had framed her request, Sada Selene, the leader of the refuseniks, shrugged and said, "Is that all?"

"It means a lot to me," Macy said.

The refuseniks went off to a corner and talked amongst themselves for a minute. Then Sada came back and told Macy, "We get the video rights."

"Why not?" It hadn't even occurred to Macy that her escape would be of any interest to anyone.

"We can definitely extract a little juice out of this," Sada said gleefully. "It's going to be a lot of fun."

Although she overtopped Macy by a half a metre Sada was only fifteen, and possessed by the artless enthusiasm and unquenchable confidence of someone who hadn't yet experienced any of life's hard knocks. Macy already had misgivings—the refuseniks' choice of meeting place suggested that they were confusing her very real problem with a trite situation in a cheap melodrama—and was worried that Sada and her friends would get carried away and attempt some grand gesture that would get her into even more trouble.

"Let's talk about practicalities," she said. "Convince me that you can help me."

Afterward, all she had to do was wait for Loc Ifrahim to arrive. She found a room in East of Eden's transients' dormitory and spent most of her waking hours in cafés in different villages, ignoring the sidelong stares of the other patrons. She supposed that by now everyone knew that she had been evicted and had lost her job, and tried not to care. Once, she was followed by a drone, but saw no sign of Jibril and yo's acolytes. On the evening of the second day of what she had come to think of as her internal exile, she opened the door of her mean little room and found Loc Ifrahim sitting cross-legged on the fold-down bed. He looked Macy up and down and told her she looked healthy and happy. "Much better than in those so-called performance pieces in which you have been such an unwilling participant. Prison must agree with you."

"It isn't called prison here."

"But that's what it is, isn't it? I believe you were beaten up," Loc Ifrahim said.

"I gave as good as I got," Macy said, wondering how he knew. She was surprised at how calm she felt. She closed the door and stood with her back to it because with the bed folded down there wasn't really anywhere else to go in the tiny room.

"Did they release you before the end of your sentence because it was unsafe for you to be there any longer? Or perhaps it was because they took pity on you."

Loc Ifrahim was dressed in canary yellow leggings and a black tunic. He still wore his hair in beaded braids, and his false smile was as bright and engaging as ever.

Macy said, "They let me out because they knew you would want to talk to me. Because they want me to find out why you came here."

"Then you can tell them that it's exactly what it seems to be. A simple fact-finding mission. Testing the waters. Believe it or not, we are still supposed to be establishing trading links with the Outers. As for visiting you, I have a little free time and thought I'd reach out to a citizen of Greater Brazil down on her luck in a strange place. Someone who has suffered a serious and very public humiliation. If you think it could help, I'll be happy to have a word with your tormentor."

"You could definitely compare notes about getting me into trouble," Macy said. "Why are you really here, Mr. Ifrahim? It isn't anything to do with fact-finding or trading links, is it?"

Loc Ifrahim studied her for a few moments, then told her to put her spex outside.

"They aren't switched on. Here, you can check," Macy said, and held them out.

Loc Ifrahim snatched them from her, stood up and cracked open the door, tossed the spex onto the floor of the corridor, shut the door and sat down again. "I was given a pair just like them," he said. "They contained a hidden transmitter and a tracking device."

"You're kidding."

"No, I'm not. They aren't very subtle here. Now you can explain to me how you think the good people of East of Eden have set you up, and what they want to find out. Don't worry. They bugged you, but they didn't bother to leave any bugs in this little cell."

Macy told the story as concisely as possible. It seemed to please the diplomat.

"They expect me to ask you for help, and expect you to betray me. An entirely understandable although rather transparent and simple-minded ploy. But why have you betrayed them to me?"

"I don't like being used. As you well know."

"I know that if you don't choose to help one side or the other, you'll rot here, Macy. They'll find some excuse to send you back to that 'rectification facility' of theirs. You'll grow old there. You'll die there, and no one will care. Or you can choose to help me, and I will help you in turn."

"You want me to pretend to work for East of Eden, but really I'd be working for you."

"Let's not get ahead of ourselves. I will see you again very soon, Macy. And when I do, I hope that you will have taken the time to answer a few questions. Here," Loc Ifrahim said, and stood up and handed Macy a data needle.

"What is this? A test?"

"Exactly," Loc Ifrahim said, and pushed past her and was gone.

178

The needle contained a list of anodyne questions about East of Eden, and twenty pages culled from one of the discussion groups about the Brazilian presence in the Jupiter System, with a curt note appended. *When we meet again, you can tell me if any of these comments seem important to you.*

After Macy had told Ivo Teagarden about the meeting and what Loc Ifrahim wanted from her, the old man took the data needle from her and told that he would have it checked. "I'll bring it back tonight, and then you can call Mr. Ifrahim and arrange to meet him again. This time, I expect that he will tell you what he really wants you to do."

She called Loc Ifrahim and set up a meeting for the next day. And after Ivo Teagarden returned the data needle and told her that nothing Loc Ifrahim wanted to know was especially secret, she could deal with his questions as best she could, she met Sada Selene in the cemetery park, and straight away told the girl about Loc Ifrahim's claim that her spex were bugged. "I'm sorry," she said. "It looks like I'll have to make other arrangements. Or give it up completely."

"This diplomat is really a spy. Yes?"

"More or less."

"So he could have been lying about this listening device," Sada said. "And even if he wasn't, we don't know that anyone was listening in. Or even if they *could* listen in, come to that. Where we met, there isn't a phone signal. That's why we met there."

"The listening device isn't a phone. And even if its transmissions were blocked, it could have recorded everything, and transmitted the recording later. We have to assume that they know, Sada."

"Well, it isn't a problem," the girl said. "There are plenty of other ways out of the city."

"If I'm going to do anything, I should do it on my own."

"Because you don't want to get us into trouble? I think it's a little too late for that," Sada said.

"I don't want to get you into *more* trouble."

"You really don't understand anything, do you?" Sada said, with a vehemence that surprised Macy. They were sitting in the little grassy bowl in the copse of silver birches. Now the refusenik girl bounced to her feet and paced around its edge. In her white suit-liner, with her pale skin and cropped, bleached hair, she looked like a skinny ghost. "I suppose you think that I'm a kid. Well, I'm not. I'm fifteen. So are my friends, everyone who wants to help you. And everywhere else but here, the age of majority is fourteen.

Everywhere else, we'd be treated like adults, not like children. So don't worry about exploiting us, Macy, or getting us into trouble. We can't *get* into trouble, not really. Because the city thinks we're kids. And we know exactly what we're doing, we all have our reasons for wanting to help you, and there's no way you can get out of here without our help," Sada said, and threw herself down in front of Macy and fixed her with a fierce dark gaze. "You don't know much, but at least you know *that's* true. Right?"

Macy laughed and shook her head.

"I'm deadly serious," Sada said.

"I don't doubt it. I ran away from home when I was only a little older than you. And that was very definitely a deadly serious thing to do. But it didn't put anyone at risk except my own self."

"No one will be in any danger if we do this properly," Sada said. "So let's talk about what we have to do."

They spent some time discussing alternative routes. Sada took it very seriously, assured Macy that she and her friends could make the necessary adjustments before tomorrow, and said that she would make sure that Newton Jones knew about the change of plan as soon as he was released.

"By the way, are you two in love? It would make a better story if you were."

"I think he's in love with the idea of having an adventure."

"Well it's still a great story," Sada said.

"Only if everything works."

"It will work. Trust me. Imagine I know everything and you know nothing."

"There's one more thing," Macy said, and explained what she wanted to do about the spex.

"It won't fool them for long," Sada said.

"Maybe it'll be long enough," Macy said. "And besides, I want to make a point."

1

When Macy Minnot told Loc Ifrahim that she'd completed the little test he'd set her, he suggested meeting in her room at ten the next morning. And turned up an hour early, planning to put her off balance and give her a hard time about the way she'd rolled over so easily. He didn't expect her to give up anything useful, of course; she would almost certainly have told her Outer friends that he'd tried to recruit her, and they would try to use her to feed him false information. But this wasn't really about intelligence-gathering; it was about causing the woman as much grief as possible to make up for the grief she'd caused him in Rainbow Bridge, and to show her that she couldn't escape the consequences of betraying the trust of her country. He'd already skilfully parlayed Jibril's persecution of Macy Minnot into something much more serious by feeding the cosmo angel tidbits about her past, and intended to get a great deal of pleasure from humiliating her and wrecking her life before he was through.

Except that she wasn't in her room, and her slate and some clothes and various small keepsakes were missing. Loc was about to leave when the door opened and Macy's handler, Ivo Teagarden, walked in. The old man didn't seem surprised to see Loc, saying, "What have you done with her?"

"Not a thing. I was about to ask you the same question."

"She called me. She was in some distress, told me to come here . . ."

Loc felt a twinge of unease. "Perhaps you should use the bug you planted in her spex, and find out where she is."

"I fail to see why that is any of your business," Ivo Teagarden said.

"Don't be a fool. You know exactly why it is my business. After all, it's the same business that brought you here."

Ivo Teagarden blinked at him, clearly having trouble processing this. Like all Outers, he wasn't accustomed to direct talk. If he had his way, Loc thought, they'd probably have to spend half an hour making polite conversation that mentioned everything but the plain facts of the matter.

"She asked me to come here, and she also asked you to come here," Loc said, as if to an especially dim child. "She played us. She made sure we'd be here while she went somewhere else. So we must find out at once where she is, and what is she doing."

With maddening slowness, Ivo Teagarden put on his spex and fitted a tipset glove over his left hand and played a brief arpeggio in the air. After a moment, he said, "She's in the cemetery park."

"Can you see her?"

"There are no cameras in the park, out of respect for our dead and people who visit them," Ivo Teagarden said. "Hmm. She isn't answering her phone."

"There aren't any cameras, so you're tracking her using the bug you planted in her spex. Don't bother denying it, just answer this: how can you be sure that's her? Suppose she gave her spex to someone else?"

"Why would she have done that?"

"Because she's trying to escape, and she wants you to think she's in this cemetery park when really she's somewhere else."

"She was planning to escape through one of the airlocks in the park," Ivo Teagarden said. "If she tries it, she's in for a surprise. Their AIs won't permit her or anyone else to use them without the intervention of a human supervisor. But perhaps I should send peace officers there, just in case. If she really did give her spex to someone else, they can talk to the person—"

"Who won't know a thing about where she is. Have your AIs look for her. Use the inputs from every drone and fixed camera in this rotten little hole."

"And why should I do what you tell me?" the old man said stiffly.

"Because she's played both of us for fools," Loc said. "Because I'd rather help you than let Macy Minnot escape."

She had escaped him once. He wasn't going to let her escape again. He wanted her to stay here, in this prison of a city, for the rest of her life. With a cold fuse of furious impatience burning inside him, Loc told the old man, "Hurry, damn you. We have to find her right away."

Macy was walking through the city's industrial zone, past workshops, refineries, bunkers, recycling plants, tanks and dump bins of raw materials . . . everything crammed either side of a broad central avenue with steep walls curving up to meet a strip of luminous ceiling overhead. She wore a suit-liner under loose-fitting coveralls. A day bag was slung over her shoulder. She was trying to look as ordinary and unconcerned as possible, trying not to spin into a fantasy of betrayal the fact that Sada had sent the youngest of the refuseniks to pick up the spex rather than do the job herself, suppressing the urge to break into a run.

Every species of robot, from giant trucks to squat machines the size of trash cans, glided to and fro. Some were fitted with cranes and forklifts, others with grabs and manipulators and cutting and welding equipment, and they all moved with swift and secret purpose from building to building, warning lights whirling for the benefit of the humans who worked here. Macy cut through a row of small workshops where people were unloading trays of freshly fired ceramics from a kiln, spinning shapes from lumps of clay on potter's wheels, pouring molten glass into a mould on a bed of sand, hammering sparks from a white-hot chunk of metal on an anvil. No one looked at her as she went past and she told herself that it was a good omen, then cursed herself for looking for portents. She'd be able to use the airlock or she wouldn't. The boy who'd collected the spex had been telling the truth when he'd said that Newt Jones had been released on schedule at eight o'clock this morning or he'd been lying. Newt would choose to come or he wouldn't. Nothing she saw or did now could change any of that.

On the far side of the workshops, a service road ran at the foot of a steeply slanted embankment of foamed composite. The tunnel that led to the airlock which Sada and her friends had supposedly fixed to allow Macy to pass through was set in the embankment about two hundred metres away. Macy paused as a robot truck laden with junked machine parts went past, then started across the road—and a drone dropped down through the bright air and hovered right in front of her, and Jibril and the pair of acolytes stepped out of the tunnel.

"You fooled Mr. Teagarden, but you didn't fool me," the cosmo angel said.

"I'm not trying to fool anyone."

Jibril's smile was duplicated by yo's acolytes, the three of them dressed paramilitary style in black coveralls like tall and slender mannequins stamped from the same mould.

"We're placing you under citizen's arrest, Macy," Jibril said, aiming something that looked very like a pistol at her. "Please do try to resist. I'd love to use this on you."

"I'd love to see you try," Macy said.

She stood with her back to the sheet-composite wall of a warehouse. A robot truck was trundling down the service road toward her. When it went past, she'd have a couple of moments to duck back into the workshops, try to find another way out of this place . . .

But Jibril must have spotted the truck too. The cosmo angel strolled across the road, yo's acolytes tagging close behind. "You can run if you want," Jibril said, "but you can't get away, Macy. It's a small city and it's ours. Go ahead, run. It'll be a lot of fun, chasing you down. It will make the record of your humiliation even better. A true work of art."

The robot truck slowed and stopped beside them. It was a low-slung transporter with a fat black sensor rod jutting at its front like a rhinoceros horn, a big bronzed capsule on its load bed, and a multi-purpose arm at its rear. The arm swinging up now like a mantis's forelimb. Something went off with a sharp crack and the three cosmo angels were knocked down, writhing inside the weighted net shot from the fat-barrelled gun clutched by the arm's terminal manipulators.

Something moved inside the capsule. It was Sada Selene, leaning at an oval hatch, beckoning to Macy, telling her to climb aboard. Macy swung up onto the robot's load bed and clambered through the hatch and Sada slammed it down and dogged it tight. She was bareheaded in a white pressure suit. Her eyes masked with spex. She sat down tailorwise, made a sharp gesture, and the robot truck moved off, turning right toward the central avenue.

"I guess there's been a change of plan," Macy said. She was braced at the rear of the capsule, looking out through the two-way mirror of the capsule's wall. No one seemed to be following them.

"This has always been the plan," Sada said, making tight gestures with her gloved hands, steering the truck via a link with her spex. A kitbag stuffed tight as a cocoon lay at her feet. An empty pressure suit was folded behind her.

"How did you know the cosmo angels had followed me?"

"Because we were following them. For people who think they're on the top rung of human evolution, they really are very stupid. The video of your escape will be a wonderful humiliation. Did you see their expressions when they realised that I was going to shoot them with the riot gun?"

"They are going to cause all kinds of trouble for you," Macy said.

Sada laughed. "I don't think so. You see, I'm coming with you. Your boyfriend has agreed to take me to the Saturn System."

"He isn't my boyfriend. And he had no right to agree to take you anywhere."

"I've been aching to leave this goldfish bowl for years," Sada said. "Nothing happens here and I can't bear it any longer. If I can't go up and out right now, I'll die of boredom. Don't look so fierce. We're going to have a lot of fun together."

The truck rolled out into the wide plaza in front of the main cluster of airlocks, passing robots loading or unloading other trucks with stacks of pallets, containers, crates, and tanks of raw materials.

"Peace officers," Sada sang out.

Macy saw them, a man and a woman riding fat-tired trikes toward the truck. A giant's voice ordered the truck to stop. Echoes blatted off the ceiling. The peace officers pulled up alongside, one on the right and one the left, matching the truck's speed.

"They're trying to take control," Sada told Macy, "but I'm blocking them."

The peace officer on the right pulled a gun, aiming it at the truck's sensor rod. A robot crane swung its arm around, plucked him from his saddle, and set him down on the roadway as his trike piddled to a halt. Another crane tipped a pallet into the path of the peace officer on the left of the transporter and she swerved to a halt and was left behind as the truck rolled on toward the open maw of one of the airlocks.

Macy looked all around, but couldn't see any trace of the refuseniks who must have hijacked the cranes. They could be anywhere, she realised, plugged into the robots via the city's net. Far off, she saw someone dressed in yellow and black bounding down the central avenue. He collided with a robot shaped like a trash can, lost his balance, fell flat on his ass and bounced up and ran on. He seemed to be shouting. Nearer at hand, the two peace officers had picked themselves up and were chasing after the truck too, but it rolled straight into the airlock and the inner door slid shut in their faces. A moment later the outer door slid back and the truck moved out onto a mesh road that cut across the dark plain toward the spaceport. Sada told Macy to hold tight as the truck swerved, bumped over the low curb, and headed across a dusty and gently undulating terrain.

"Another change of plan. You don't have to go to the spaceport because your boyfriend is coming to meet us. You might want to climb inside that pressure suit."

Macy stripped off her coveralls, feeling peculiarly vulnerable. The capsule was transparent and there was nothing outside its thin wall but killing cold and hard, radiation-drenched vacuum. High above, the sun's tiny disc burned close to Jupiter's skinny crescent. She stepped into the pressure suit, pulled its segmented torso up to her shoulders, punched her arms down the sleeves and sat down so that she could snap the cuffs of the overboots to the seals at her ankles.

All the while, Sada had been scanning the black sky, turning this way and that. She yelled and flung up an arm, pointing high overhead, and Macy saw a star moving swiftly across the black sky, growing brighter, resolving into the bug shape of a tug. The truck slowed to a crawl and stopped as the tug swept above it, jets flaring as it killed its forward momentum and settled toward them. Macy laughed. When Newt had said that his ship would be easy to spot, he hadn't been kidding.

Elephant was pink.

8

Apart from some bruising to his pride, Loc Ifrahim wasn't in any way damaged or embarrassed by Macy Minnot's escape from East of Eden. He spent some time finessing his report so that it laid the blame squarely on Ivo Teagarden and others in East of Eden, but he needn't have bothered. No one important took any notice of the incident: it was considered to be a minor footnote to an embarrassing but otherwise trivial affair. Four weeks later he was at last rotated back to Brasília, where he was rewarded with a small promotion and a place on the commission tasked with the responsibility of analysing information about the political players in the cities and smaller settlements of the Saturn System.

The commission was an excellent and exciting place to work, staffed by bright and fiercely ambitious young people committed to the urgent and supremely important task of bringing the Outer System under the control of Earth. Its offices were as hectically busy as an old-fashioned newsroom, with people tossing ideas back and forth around memo spaces, laboriously constructing or dissecting dynamic sociopolitical models, interviewing everyone who had ever visited the Outer System, and turning out reams of position notes and situation updates.

An entire floor was given over to the AIs, immersion tanks, and high-definition memo spaces of the Theoretical Strategy Group who were modelling every conceivable way of invading and securing the cities and settlements of the Outer System. Wargamers. Crews of earnest, pallid young men with no actual military experience who cleaved to the theories of various gurus and *éminences grises* with holy passion. They worked in a haze of stimulants, adrenalin, and testosterone, sleeping and eating in their cubicles as they ran enormous and intricate real-time simulations. Rivalry between crews was intense. It wasn't unusual for Loc to arrive at work on a morning to find some catatonically dazed or raving wargamer who'd tipped over the edge being led out by security guards; once, a huge fist fight erupted between rival groups and had to be quelled by riot police who tear-gassed the entire floor.

A vocal minority insisted that genocide was the only solution to the Outer System problem, and devised plans to smash the tents and domes of the cities and settlements with smart pebbles, or obliterate them with H-bombs, or eliminate their populations with bioweapons, poison gases, and gamma-ray flashover devices. But these extreme tactics were generally considered to be unworkable. The number of H-bombs required would seriously deplete Great Brazil's arsenal and leave it vulnerable to attack; the most hostile cities, such as Paris, Dione, were constructing missile-defence systems; most cities and settlements contained refuges and hardened buildings where the population could shelter if the main tents lost integrity, and parts of some cities were so deeply buried that they were impervious to conventional weapons; and in any case, the Outers were scattered so widely over the surfaces of the moons of Jupiter and Saturn that it wouldn't be possible to kill all of them, and a rump of survivors would most likely attempt revenge attacks against Earth. Besides, genocide was considered to be politically unacceptable and would destroy the valuable assets that for many were the only justification for going to war. The Outers had been engaged in every kind of theoretical and applied science for more than a century: the profits that could be made by plundering their data-bases and genome libraries, and seizing their scientists and gene wizards, were incalculable. And the intrinsic value of the cities and settlements was not inconsiderable, either. So most of the wargamers were engaged in what they called asymmetric or "quiet war" strategies that mixed propaganda, espionage, sabotage, and political coercion with conventional military tactics tailored to the unique conditions of the Outer System.

Robust predictive models generated by the wargamers and databases worked up by the intelligence groups were passed on to laboratories and think tanks where scientists, engineers and psychologists were developing hardware and techniques for covert and paramilitary operations, infiltration, sabotage, and dissemination of black propaganda. Politicians and officers from the three branches of the armed services were given one-on-one brief-ings. It was a rare day when a VIP didn't turn up, escorted through the fer-ment and hubbub of the offices by knots of aides like a great liner being manoeuvred into a berth by fussy, anxious tugboats.

With his extensive field experience and his many contacts, Loc quickly made himself indispensable. He strengthened his ties to Arvam Peixoto's crew, made many new friends, including senior politicians and members of the inner circles of several families, and became the go-to guy for anyone who needed a quick fix on some aspect of the intricate protocols, customs and rivalries of the cities and settlements of Jupiter's various moons, a snap opinion on one or another of the important political players, or the attitude and mood of the general population.

The work was important and timely. After the failure of the peace and reconciliation initiative, it was vital to gain direct control of the Outer System as quickly as possible, and the government was dominated now by those who believed that war was not only inevitable but necessary. A holy duty. Yet the programme to establish trade initiatives and cultural exchanges with the Outer System was being strengthened rather than abandoned because it provided a useful cloak for gathering intelligence and forging links with sympathetic cities on the moons of Jupiter and Saturn that could later be used as strongholds in the coming war.

A year after returning to Earth, Loc Ifrahim was on his way out again, this time to Saturn, to the little city of Camelot, Mimas. Like East of Eden, Camelot was an inward-looking city with a very high proportion of conservative first- and second-generation Outers in its population. Its mayor and several of its senators, laughably amenable to flattery and mild bribery, voted through a bill that granted Greater Brazil a permanent presence on Mimas, and gave their enthusiastic assent to plans to send an expedition deep into the atmosphere of Saturn—scientific inquiry fronting what was really a shock-and-awe demonstration of the latest model of combat singleship.

Schmoozing and sweetening the amiably corrupt politicians of Camelot was a full-time job, but Loc found time for his own private research, discovering that Macy Minnot had been adopted into the Jones-Truex-Bakaleinikoff clan. She was currently resident in their garden habitat, a tented crater on Dione, and was working as a biome designer. She had been doing some theoretical work on closed ecosystems, too, collaborating with a crew responsible for highly rated research on one of the extra-solar terrestrial planets, Tierra. He also discovered that the matriarch of the Jones-Truex-Bakaleinikoff clan, Abbie Jones, mother of the tug pilot who'd been instrumental in Macy Minnot's escape, was a good friend of the gene wizard Avernus. He forwarded that nugget of information to Sri Hong-Owen, out of spite. As for Macy Minnot, he had no particular plans to call on her at present, but he had no doubt that their paths would cross again. War was a quickening drumbeat, and when it finally came Loc was determined to make sure that she would be properly punished for choosing the wrong side.

Meanwhile, the *Glory of Gaia*, a modified freighter that was a carrier-battleship in all but designation, had arrived in orbit around Mimas. Operation Deep Sounding was about to embark into the depths of Saturn. Loc had much work ahead of him, capitalising on the operation's success by entering into negotiations for licensing the new fusion motor to municipalities and family trusts. The Brazilian government had no intention of granting any such licence, of course, but it would be an effective way of exacerbating tensions between the different generations of Outers and weakening civic cohesion. Four hundred years after the American Civil War, Loc and the other war-hawks held that this truth was still self-evident: a house divided against itself cannot stand.

PART THREE
CLOSE ENCOUNTERS

I

After the death of Father Solomon, the lectors and instructors were replaced by a squad of military trainers: lean, tough men who treated the boys with rough disdain and wore at all times pistols and shock sticks on their hips. There were no more exercises on the surface. Instead, the trainers introduced the boys to something they called drill, marching them around the gymnasium in close formation with rifles slanted on their shoulders, teaching them how to shift the rifles into various positions with precise, mechanical sequences of movement. The trainers continued the boys' training in use of weapons and sabotage and infiltration techniques, and the boys spent many hours in flight simulators, learning how to fly little rocket-propelled dropshells out of orbit in various strengths of gravity and land them safely on all kinds of moonscape. They spent a lot of time in immersion scenarios, too, practising how to talk and behave like the enemy. Previously, the scenarios had all been set in a detailed virtuality based on the city of Rainbow Bridge, Callisto. Now the boys were studying the structure, history, socio-economic conditions and cultural milieux of other cities, too. They'd had it easy for too long, their trainers told them. They'd been training for training's sake, but now their training had a purpose, and they must be forged and tempered so that when the time came they would be able to carry out their duties without hesitation.

The changes in their routines and the brusque treatment by their handlers bound the boys closer together. None of them blamed Dave #8 for what had happened; in fact, they were protective and solicitous toward him. Dave #7 tried to make a joke of it, telling him that at one time or another every one of them had dreamed of killing Father Solomon after being zapped by his shock stick. Dave #14 told him gruffly that orders were orders, he'd done what he'd had to do. Dave #27 told him that they were all of one mind and one heart. His had been the hand that had wielded the knife that had cut Father Solomon's throat, but any one of them would have done the same thing. And so all of them were guilty, and no one was more guilty than anyone else. Besides, Dave #27 said, it was in their nature to kill. "It is what we were born to do, and we have been trained for it all our lives. Is the lion guilty when it kills the lamb? Of course not, for it is only expressing its nature. It is the nature of lions to kill, and lambs to be their prey. We are like lions, and men are our prey."

"Even if that's true, the enemy is our prey," Dave #8 said. "And Father Solomon was not one of them."

"Perhaps he transgressed in some way that we don't know about," Dave #27 said. "He did something that could have threatened the success of our mission. Something that made him as dangerous as any of the enemy. But we don't need to know what it was. For we are merely the arm and the hand, brother, obedient to a will we must not question."

Dave #8 was not convinced or comforted by this. It was probably true that any one of his brothers could have done what he did; nevertheless, he was the one who had been selected. General Peixoto had asked Father Solomon to choose his most apt pupil, and Father Solomon had chosen him. Not because Father Solomon had believed that he was the best of all the boys, but because he'd thought that the general had wanted to kill one of the boys to make a point, and as far as he'd been concerned Dave #8 was the most flawed. And perhaps he had been right; perhaps he'd known what Dave #8 had suspected and struggled against all his life. Perhaps he'd known that Dave #8 *was* different, for all that he tried his best to be unexceptional, to look and behave exactly like his brothers. Perhaps Father Solomon had seen that mirrored in Dave #8's face, and so he'd chosen him out of all the rest, unaware that he hadn't chosen a sacrifice but his own killer. And so he had died, and Dave #8 had to live with his guilt and his growing certainty that he was not who he was supposed to be.

He did his best to atone by throwing himself into the new regime of training and education. He practised drill harder and longer than anyone else, and was the first to hit the floor for another punishing round of push-ups whenever one of the trainers detected a mistake or hesitation in the ranks. He tried to outshine his brothers in everything else, too. He wanted to prove that he was no different from them by being the best of them all.

And then one night he went to sleep as usual and woke up in another room, and realised that his punishment for being different and for having killed Father Solomon had come to him at last. He had been disappeared.

He was lying in a bed higher and softer than the narrow bunk in which he had slept every night of his life, in a small room lit by dim panels in the ceiling. His wrists and ankles were chained to the side rails of the bed and his face hurt. There was a dull ache in his nose, which felt as it had been packed with cotton wool, throbbing discomfort in his jaw and cheekbones, a maddening prickly itch across his scalp.

He lay there a long time, and for a long time nothing happened. It didn't matter. He'd been trained to wait, and now that the worst had happened all his anxiety and fear was gone and he felt only an oceanic calm. Presently, he became aware that the light in the room had brightened and a man was sitting beside his bed, and he came fully to himself once more as the man asked if he recognised him.

"Yes, sir. You are Colonel Arrães. One of our instructors. You taught us psychology."

"I also helped design your training programme, for my sins," Colonel Arrães said. "The way you were raised, the way you were taught, until things . . . changed."

Dave #8 dared to ask if he was being punished, and Colonel Arrães smiled and shook his head. He was a burly man with a bald pate and a kindly face. It was strange to see it in the flesh instead of floating in the visor of an avatar.

He said, "You are thinking of what happened to poor Father Solomon. You are in no way to blame for that. Both you and Father Solomon were caught in a power struggle in which one side asserted its right over another to take control of this project. But it doesn't matter who is in control, because the outcome is unchanged. You are about to begin the final part of your training. From now on, you will train alone, because in the end you will have to work alone. And because you will soon be put to work on a real mission, we have had to change your face. After all, we can't send out spies who all look the same, can we? How are you feeling, by the way?"

"I am fine, sir."

"You'll heal quickly enough. You have had your nose surgically broken, and your cheekbones and jawbone reshaped. Nothing serious. Minor plastic surgery, completely routine. You will no longer be called Number Eight, Number Eight. From now on your name will be Ken Shintaro. Do you understand?"

"Yes, sir. I am Ken Shintaro."

"Ken Shintaro is your cover identity," Colonel Arrães said. "Ken Shintaro, from Rainbow Bridge, Callisto. You will learn everything about him in the final part of your training. You will learn to live as him, but more importantly you will learn everything you need to know so that you can do the work we need you to do. Your work, your mission—that's what really defines you. You won't ever forget that, will you?"

"No, sir."

Dave #8 briefly wondered what his new face looked like, but it wasn't important. All that mattered was that the flaws that Father Solomon had detected would be hidden now, by the mask they had given him.

"I know you won't let us down," Colonel Arrães said, and stood up and told him that he had a lot to do before he was ready, but for now he should rest, and heal. At the door, the colonel paused and added, "I expect you want to know where you will be going."

"I am Ken Shintaro, from Rainbow Bridge, Callisto."

"Yes, you are. But you're going to Paris. Paris, Dione."

2

The engineers prepping the two singleships broke into a storm of applause when the pilots, a man and a woman dressed in close-fitting acceleration suits, were escorted into the hangar pod by a swarm of medics and briefing officers. The anthems of Greater Brazil and the European Union played one after the other and everyone stood to attention as best they could in the absence of gravity. An avatar wearing the face of the President of Greater Brazil delivered a brief prerecorded speech that touched on great moments of exploration and the questing and indomitable nature of the human spirit. Commander Gabriel Vaduva shook hands with the pilots in front of the roundel of Operation Deep Sounding while engineers and technicians applauded again, cheers and whistles and war-whoops, their enthusiasm genuine even though it was choreographed for the news channels. Then the security officer announced that the cameras were offline, the engineers resumed their work, and medics and technicians closed around the pilots for the final preflight checks.

The sleek black daggers of the two J-2 singleships lay nose to tail in their launch cradles. Engineers swarmed around them like ants grooming alletes about to fly the nest, making final checks and adjustments, loading the clandestine-op packages into weapons bays. The singleships were fully powered up, vibrating eagerly, each infusing the frigid air with crackling ozone and its own particular song. Cash Baker could feel the familiar music of his ship thrilling in his blood like a celestial choir. A complex harmonic resolving somewhere just above E-flat, braided from servomotors and flywheels, turbines, and the huge currents circulating in the superconducting magnets of its fusion torus.

Cash was spread-eagled in a dressing frame while a tech checked his acceleration suit for microscopic flaws that could cause pressure sores or hematomas. Woven from several hundred differently doped species of fullerene thread, quasi-living, self-regulating, the suit fitted as closely as a second skin from the soles of Cash's feet to the crown of his shaven head, leaving only his face exposed. At last, the tech signed off the suit and Cash was fitted with his face mask and the frame was elevated and rotated on its long axis and guided toward the holster of the lifesystem, a slot narrower than a grave that gaped behind the singleship's everted equipment pods. He glimpsed the other pilot, Vera Flamilion Jackson, suspended in her frame over her ship, and then his uplink came alive and he blanked out for a moment, came back with the comforting presence of his ship sinking through him and its control menu laid across the view of the crowded and busy hangar.

"Oh man," he said. "Let's get this thing on!"

"Ready when you are," Vera Jackson said.

The link cut out as the flight medics began their work, making sure that the alchemical marriage between the ship's control interface and Cash's nervous system was robust and there was no echo or leakage, running through the familiar series of tests on his visual, auditory, and proprioceptive systems, finally telling him that he was good to go.

He entered the lifesystem head first, like a breech birth in reverse. Smart gel flowed around him. The lifesystem connected lines that fed air and water and liquid nutrient, the hose that piped away wastes. A long smooth push gripped him from head to toe and then he was all the way in, cocooned in a thin layer of gel, and the ship's senses were fully meshed with his own, giving him a three-hundred-and-sixty-degree view of the final spurt of activity in the hangar. The equipment pods were closed away, the wings folded and retracted like an exercise in origami, and the ship sank further into its cradle, smoothly everting into vacuum.

Cash no longer had any sense of his body. It was a lump of meat in the sealed can of the lifesystem, sedated with muscle relaxants, fed by a drip, blood passing through a cascade filter to remove wastes, breathing and heartbeat and metabolic rate controlled by a bridge plugged into his autonomic nervous system. Its sole function was to sustain his brain. His mind. And as far as he was concerned, he wasn't inhabiting his skull right now. He had become one with his bird, his nervous system meshed with hers and extending into every part of her, her senses his own.

Launch was a little love pat from the cradle's electromagnetic catapult, a brief burp of attitude jets. Then Cash was falling away behind Vera Jackson's singleship, both of them swinging around the sharply curved shoulder of Mimas's heavily cratered globe. Saturn's fat crescent dawned, looking close enough to touch. Its rings, seen edge-on, were a dark line slashed across equatorial bands with delicate tints of butterscotch and peach, and cast a shadow grooved like a tire track across the turquoise and pale blue bands of the northern hemisphere.

There was another tremor as the singleship adjusted its trim. Cash watched the countdown flip back toward zero, yelled, "Geronimo!" and ignited the main engine, a long hard burn that would deliver him to Saturn, and to history.

The two singleships fell across the plane of the ring system, a little under half the distance between Earth and the Moon. Skating just a hundred kilometres above the broad bright arc of the A Ring and the narrow, eccentric braid of Huygen's Ringlet, soaring through sunlight across the wide gap of the Cassini Division, passing above the opaque and intricately braided B Ring, where ringlets of icy rubble backlit by the sun and divided by fine gaps dwindled away into shadow in one direction and in the other seemed to rise and converge in a narrowing arc or bridge that whipped around Saturn's hazy crescent. All this glory created from the rubble of a moon torn apart millions of years ago, ground fine and graded and ground again by gravity and simple Newtonian mechanics.

As Cash Baker and Vera Jackson passed the faint, narrow bands of the inner ringlets and rings, mission control transmitted a short burst of encrypted data that unpacked into the optical image of a ship some fifteen thousand kilometres behind the singleships but catching up fast—a fuzzy blob riding a bright spear of fusion fire that burned like a gypsy star against Saturn's nightside. One sidebar identified it as a shuttle, the SV *Happy Trails*, registered to a collective operating out of Paris, Dione; another tracked its orbital path back to Atlas, a tiny moon at the outer edge of the A Ring.

"Atlas was on the far side of Saturn when you guys set out," mission control said. "We think the ship was parked there—it must have kicked off when you did. It seems to have made its initial burn while it was hidden behind Saturn. It cut across the rings, and we only spotted it when it lit up again."

"You make it sound as if it was waiting for us," Vera Jackson said.

"It's possible. The mission profile is public knowledge."

"Are they talking?" Vera said.

"We haven't been able to raise the ship. According to chatter on the system's net, it's crewed by Ghosts."

Cash said, "A spook ship?"

Vera said, "Don't you ever read briefings? Ghosts are some kind of gang or cult whose members think they're guided by their future selves."

She was ten years older than Cash, ice-cool and fearsomely competent. When she and the other two European pilots had joined the singleship wing, Bo Nash had taken bets on who would get to fuck her first, and Cash had told him that it was more a question of who *she* would fuck first. Her hard-shell attitude made it difficult for anyone to like or get close to her, but Cash sure as hell respected her, one pilot to another.

"They're definitely connected to the government of Paris," mission control said. "We're right now sending its mayor some tough questions."

"Check out its beacon," Vera said.

She'd caught it on the broadband scanner, passed it through three increasingly paranoid filters to check for viruses, and copied it to Cash and mission control. A yellow circle with two dots and a curved line making a happy face; a rippling banner superimposed above it. *We Come in Peace for All Mankind* chasing *All These Worlds Belong to Us* around and around.

"Very cute," Cash said.

"Don't worry about it," mission control said. "They'll pass close to you but they can't follow you down into Saturn. Their ship is strictly for vacuum. You'll lose it just after you hit the edge of the atmosphere. Our thinking is that they're making a political point. It's just a fly-by. A stunt. So if they try to make contact with you by radio or line-of-sight laser, ignore them but bounce the message straight to me. Don't reply. Don't give them anything they can use. Is that clear? Now, let's get down to the final checks."

The two singleships were moving above Saturn's nightside now. The gas giant's black bulk eclipsed half the sky. The arch of the rings gleamed high above. Dawn was coming fast. Cash and Vera worked through checklists, tested guidance and control systems, made microscopic attitude adjustments. If they didn't hit a very precise entry profile they would either skip out of the atmosphere or descend too steeply and too fast and be incinerated.

All the while, Cash kept an eye on the shuttle. It had completed its burn and was drawing closer; if it kept to its present course and velocity it would pass them at a distance of less than a hundred kilometres just as they reached the outer edge of Saturn's atmosphere. Cash and Vera could fire up their motors and quickly leave the shuttle behind, of course, but they'd also miss the critical window for safe entry, and would have to abort their mission. So all they could do was keep to their course and keep watch on the interloper as they completed their final approach.

Ahead, the sun's tiny disc lit the leading edge of the gas giant's tremendous curve, a bridge of pearly light that quickly broadened into a crescent in which details of a vast cloudscape began to resolve. The two singleships were aimed at a pale oval between two latitudinal bands north of the equator—one of the long-lived storms that, anchored over a hot spot deep in Saturn's atmosphere, swept a clear area in the cloud decks around it. Details exploded out of the cloudscape as the singleships fell toward it, ripples and ruffles resolving along the boundary between the bands, intricate scrollworks formed by drag between opposing streams of atmosphere. Cash could see structures within the bands too, great ranges and banks of cloud. All this racing beneath the two singleships when the shuttle caught up with them, skimming past on a course that would cut a shallow chord through the uppermost fringe of the atmosphere before taking it out beyond Saturn. Cash glimpsed a flare as it shot past, cleaned up the video grab and replayed it, saw that it had dropped a heat-shielded pod strapped to a pair of solid-fuel retrorockets.

It was too late to do anything about it. He was already riding his ship through the beginnings of turbulence. Subtle vibrations, short sharp shudders as attitude jets fired to keep the singleship stable. It was travelling at hypersonic speed. Bands of cloud raced by far below and a high-pitched wail began to mount in volume and pitch and a pale glow brightened to a furnace intensity as friction transformed the kinetic energy of orbital motion into heat. Shock waves in the hot ionised hydrogen formed a stable shell in which the rainbow slicks of plasma streams flickered, the shock waves converging behind the singleship to a focal point like an incandescent diamond. Deceleration rose steadily: five g, ten, briefly peaking at just over fifteen. The light show slowly faded. Cash extended the singleship's wings. The atmosphere was thick enough now to use aerodynamic control surfaces rather than the attitude jets to maintain trim.

Cash was falling free through Saturn's vast skies at a steep angle, making slow S-turns to bleed off excess velocity. He eyeballed Vera Jackson's singleship falling ahead of him, about fifty kilometres to the east, looked for and failed to find any sign of the pod dropped by the shuttle, uploaded a status check to mission control and acknowledged the congratulations of the mission commander.

"On my mark," Vera said, and counted down from ten.

Cash deployed his drogue parachutes at zero and there was a thump and a tremendous corkscrewing jerk as the parachutes swung him around and checked his forward momentum, and then he was falling nose down through a vast clear ocean of hydrogen and helium at just under a hundred kilometres an hour, in a prevailing air current that was taking him eastward at about five times that speed. In about ten hours, if he kept falling at his present rate, he would reach the beginning of the amorphous boundary between the gaseous atmosphere and the deep ocean of hot metallic hydrogen that lay beneath, although long before then the singleship would have been crushed and scorched to a cinder by tremendous pressures and temperatures. Not even tough, heavily shielded robot probes had ever penetrated to more than half the depth of the gaseous phase of Saturn's atmosphere. The two singleships would fall for only three hours, dropping through the liquid-water zone before igniting their motors and departing.

If everything went well, they'd pass close to their target. And even if they missed it, the packages they planned to release contained autonomous drones that could ride the winds of Saturn for months while they tracked it down and searched for other anomalies.

Meanwhile, Cash had a few moments to enjoy the tremendous panorama wrapped around him. It was early morning. The sky was deep indigo and seemingly infinite, the sun a tiny flattened disc that glowered at the hazy horizon, the centre of concentric shells of bloody light that rose toward zenith. In every direction, the crystalline hydrogen atmosphere stretched for thousands of kilometres, broken only by a few wisps of cloud formed from frozen ammonia, looking just like ordinary cirrus cloud and tinged pink by dawn light. He felt like a king of this whole wide world, an emperor of air, and told Vera that this place was definitely made for flying.

"I hear that," Vera said. "Check out the storm. We're right in the pipe."

Below, halfway to the eastern horizon, a creamy ocean of cloud rifted apart around the storm's great oval eye. With interrupted arcs of cloud and clear air curved around it, it looked much like a hurricane back on Earth. In fact, everything seemed eerily familiar. Blue sky, white clouds, the sun gaining a golden hue as it lifted above the horizon. It took an effort to remember that the distance to the horizon was more than ten times that on Earth. That the storm was two thousand kilometres across. That the sky was hydrogen and helium a thousand kilometres deep, with cloud layers of ammonium ice above and decks of ammonium hydrosulphide and ammonium-rich water ice and water-droplet clouds below, endlessly blowing around this vast world.

Cash and Vera dropped slantwise toward the continent-sized storm. The parachute of Vera's ship was blazoned with the flag of the European Union. A blue rectangle vivid and alien against the muted creams of the cloudscape they were fast approaching. Vera caught a pinpoint signal on deep radar, too far away to resolve any detail but exactly where their target was supposed to be. A few moments later, Cash picked up another signal, about five hundred kilometres aft. Two small echoes. The singleship's guidance system tagged the dots with vectors. They were moving faster than the prevailing wind and they were moving under guidance, catching up with the singleships.

"We see them too," mission control said. "Stand by for advice."

Vera transmitted a snatched high-magnification shot of a drone riding atop a propellant tank. It reminded Cash of a photograph of an old space shuttle he'd once seen in a history text. Mission control came back, told them to stick to the mission profile, said that a formal protest had been lodged with the government of Paris, Dione.

"Imagine how grateful we are," Cash said, and proposed that they wait until the drones got close, then light up their motors and burn the fuckers out of the sky.

"We'd have to drop the parachutes first," Vera said. "And that would mean we couldn't complete the mission."

"So we sit here and hope these drones are tourists, just like we're pretending to be," Cash said. "I think not."

"Matter of fact, we do need you to sit tight," mission control said, and told them that everyone was working hard to construct workable solutions to a variety of scenarios.

"Just sit here and let them make the first move?" Cash said. "You have to be kidding."

"You heard the man," Vera said. "Hang tough."

Cash called up the navigation subsystem of his singleship and started to make his own calculations. The drones were still closing, and the two singleships were falling toward the edge of the volume influenced by the storm now, past a curving archipelago of plume clouds ten kilometres tall from their fluffy white tops to their trailing dark roots. There was a moment of bone-shaking turbulence as Cash passed through a fierce updraught before settling in a steady current circulating east and north, clockwise around the outer edge of the storm. A few dark clouds with the anvil shape of thunderclouds on Earth drifted ahead, caught in a slightly faster current.

The ambient temperature was −10° Celsius and steadily climbing. Pressure was rising too, already more than four atmospheres. Clear air stretched down to a reddish haze above a deck of dark brown clouds more than a hundred kilometres below. The target was less than a thousand kilometres ahead, its radar image beginning to resolve into separate signals. The sky above was almost exactly the blue of a summer's sky on Earth, and the small swift sun was considerably higher: daylight on Saturn lasted just five hours.

The singleships fell past the roots of the plume clouds and continued to fall toward the reddish-brown floor. Slowing now, because the parachutes were working more effectively as the atmospheric pressure increased, but still falling. In less than thirty minutes they would fall past the target; an hour after that, they would have fallen within a couple of kilometres of the top of the cloud deck below, breaking the manned descent record. Then they could lose their parachutes and light their motors and fly right out of there. Cash was looking forward to that part—the flying. But the two Outer drones were closing fast now, close enough to see that each was targeting one of the singleships.

Cash fired up the ship-to-ship laser and explained how they could escape and still make the rendezvous.

"We don't have enough fuel," Vera said.

"We won't be able to beat the record," Cash said, "but we'll be able to drop our packages and fly past the target and get back into some kind of orbit. The *Glory of Gaia* will have to come pick us up."

"And while we were waiting we would be sitting targets for any Outers who might want to take a shot at us."

"We're sitting targets right now," Cash said.

After a moment of silence, Vera said, "We'll have to clear it with mission control."

"I don't think we have time," Cash said. "This is a combat situation. Which means that as mission commander it's your decision."

He was watching the drone that had targeted his ship. It was shaped a little like a squid, its black body shell etched with a white skull grinning above crossed white bones, five blunt tentacles extended from beneath a hooded sensor cluster. He had a very clear picture of those tentacles splayed against the hull of his singleship in a fierce embrace . . .

"Let's do it," Vera said. "Link up—I'll push the button. Otherwise we might end up all over the sky."

"You got it," Cash said, and surrendered control. Vera started to count backward from ten, and Cash saw the drone detach from its booster, saw the spark of its motor, and told Vera to do it now.

She did it.

Cash's singleship bucked violently as the parachute detached and blew away like a leaf. For a brief moment he was in free fall. The drone skimmed past, attitude jets flaring as it tried to hook around, and then the singleship's fusion motor fired up with its characteristic double crack and the singleship flared downward, its nose gradually pitching up as Vera's ship pulled the same manoeuvre directly ahead.

His own bird juddered as it passed through the sound barrier, and control came back. He was flying, burning precious fuel as he chased after Vera, both of them drawing contrails through the clear air as they plunged eastward, accelerating through thickening atmosphere. The target was dead ahead, resolving on the radar into distinct signals. A ghostly signal shaped like a plumb-bob, a handful of rectangles sending back strongly, and a fuzzy cloud of activity around them.

"Drop the packages," Vera sang out, and Cash triggered the sequence, felt the shudder as black cylinders sprang loose on either side, tumbling end for end, sprouting parachutes and jerking away and vanishing into the vast sky.

They were almost on the target now. Cash glimpsed a scatter of foreshortened rectangles silhouetted against the vast white curve of the storm, and then Vera's ship began to pull up and he followed, continuing to gain speed, hooking upward, jolting through layers of crosswinds. The cloudscape directly below flattened out as he rose above it, becoming two-dimensional, darker bands on either side coming into view. The sky ahead darkened from blue to indigo to black. A few bright stars came out. It was so much like flying on Earth, although he was flying faster than anything had ever flown in Earth's atmosphere, and was still accelerating . . .

Cash whooped, pulled a barrel roll. The spark of the sun sank behind the planet's bulk and night flooded the cloudscapes below and stars came out everywhere else, with two moons standing one above the other directly ahead as the singleships cleared the outer edge of the atmosphere, reaching escape velocity of thirty-six kilometres per second and continuing to accelerate for more than five minutes, until their tanks were almost dry.

They were in orbit, falling in a long ellipse that would take them around Saturn once every two hours.

After the fusion motors cut off, Vera contacted mission control and ran through what had happened. Commander Vaduva came online and told them that they had done well, but must maintain absolute vigilance until they were picked up. Meaning that if any Outer ship attempted to rendezvous with them, they were to blow themselves up rather than be captured or taken as salvage. They began to transmit encrypted data, everything from second-by-second status reports during the mission to optical and radar images of the target. There was a long hour of checks and updates. The security officer played them a clip of the mayor of Paris, Dione making a bland statement that refused to take any responsibility for the actions of a few exuberant individuals, and told Cash and Vera that very serious diplomatic representations were being made at that very moment.

"I know what kind of representations I'd like to make," Vera said. "You and me, Cash, in a room with those Ghosts, we'd show them a thing or two about exuberance."

"I hear that," Cash said.

It had been a lot of fun, going toe to toe with the Ghosts, even though the encounter had ended in a kind of draw. Next time, he was determined to come out on top.

3

Highland cattle no bigger than Saint Bernard dogs, perfect miniatures with shaggy auburn coats and flexed horns, looked up from their grazing as Newton Jones came into the broad meadow. A few ambled out of his way; the rest stood and watched, jaws milling sideways, as Newt bounded toward the four people sitting around the hearth-glow of a memo space under a big sweet-chestnut tree, an outlier of the narrow belt of forest that girdled the outer zone of the garden habitat of the Jones-Truex-Bakaleinikoff clan. He dropped down beside Macy Minnot and said, "The warship picked up the singleships. It's heading back to Mimas."

"Let's hope this is the end of the stupid affair," Pete Bakaleinikoff said.

"Everything went perfectly," Newt said. "The Ghosts showed the Brazilians that they can't go wherever they want without being challenged. They scared them off, and they cleaned up the so-called science packages they dumped, too."

"Pure unevolved primate behaviour is nothing to be proud of," Pete Bakaleinikoff said.

"It was a silly stunt," Junko Asai said.

"Now it's over we should do our best to forget about it," Junpei Asai said.

Husband and wife leaned against each other with fond familiarity, dressed alike in collarless white tunics and white trousers. Junpei wore plum-coloured lipstick and layers of bead necklaces; Junko had a carefully trimmed strip of white beard under his lower lip and many rings on his fingers. They had been married for almost fifty years, had six children, fifteen grandchildren, and four great-grandchildren, a casual fecundity that Macy, from a country where only the rich, lottery winners, and criminals had more than one child, thought amazing. They were also two of the smartest people she had ever met. In partnership with Pete Bakaleinikoff, they operated a cloud of optical telescopes more than twenty-thousand kilometres across that sat in a stable orbit at Saturn's trailing Trojan point. Junko and Junpei had designed the elements of the telescope cloud and the AI that coordinated its operation; Pete Bakaleinikoff had underwritten its cost and supervised analysis of the data that it collected. For the past five years they had been studying Tierra, a rocky terrestrial planet about one and a half times the diameter of Earth that orbited inside the life zone of the star Delta Pavonis, mapping its single supercontinent and sprawling ice caps, its Mars-sized moon. There was life on Tierra: oxygen, water vapour and methane in its atmosphere; seasonal colour changes along the shoreline of the supercontinent. Currently, the telescope cloud's best resolution yielded about a hundred kilometres to a single pixel, but its owners were continually refining and tweaking their instruments and analytical programmes.

Newt flew missions that maintained and updated the cloud; Macy had become involved through Pete Bakaleinikoff, Newt's uncle. Pete was also interested in long-term closed ecosystems of the type that would be required by a multi-generation starship that might take two or three hundred years to complete its journey, in which everything would have to be continually recycled with as close to one hundred percent efficiency as possible. It was the kind of problem that was meat and drink to Macy, and Pete had enlisted her help in constructing and running a variety of robust experimental systems.

Macy was fascinated and amused by the trio's enthusiastic accumulation of pointless data. Tierra wasn't the first Earth-like extrasolar planet to have been discovered; it wasn't even the tenth. And even if the telescope gang could finesse their instruments to the point where they could resolve more than fuzzy blotches that might or might not be the Tierran equivalent of lakes, forests, grasslands and deserts, it wasn't likely that anyone would ever visit the planet in their lifetime. The best they could hope for would be a fast fly-by by some microprobe, but even if one could be constructed at whatever unimaginable cost and effort, it wouldn't reach Delta Pavonis for more than fifty years. Still, Macy often felt an undeniable frisson while studying pictures of the distant world, and her work on closed-cycle ecosystems was about to give her kudos rating its first big boost. With Pete Bakaleinikoff and Junko and Junpei Asai, she was going to attend a conference on research into extra-solar planets and interstellar flight. Newt had interrupted a discussion about how best to present their data.

He told Junko, "We shouldn't forget about it; we should build on it. After all, they're still here. They haven't gone away. Their warship is right now headed back to orbit around Mimas, and there are more ships on the way. We can't pretend that their presence doesn't matter, that we can carry on as if they don't exist. Ignoring them isn't an option."

"It is a serious situation," Pete said. "And a stunt like this, the equivalent of beating our chests like gorillas, hooting and howling, it is not to me a sensible way of dealing with it."

"So what if it *was* like a stunt?" Newt said. When he became excited about something, a tender blush crept across his cheeks and his gestures became extravagant. He was blushing now, and flinging his hands about as if trying to conjure something from the air by sheer force of will. "You have to admit that it did something useful. It defined a limit. It told the Brazilians that they can't move around with impunity. That they can't do what they want. That there are people prepared to stand up to them."

"It is hardly a secret that many of us are opposed to their presence," Junko said.

"Although most would prefer to talk to them in a sensible fashion than antagonise them," Junpei said.

"It was a keen manoeuver," Newt said, his enthusiasm undented. "The Brazilians must have taken notice of that. They know now that we may not have big ships and the latest in fusion-motor technology, but we definitely know something about flying."

"By 'we' I hope you mean Outers in a general sense," Pete said. "I hope you don't plan to take credit for any part of this."

Newt laughed. "You're worried I might be involved in some way? I wasn't involved."

"I'm glad to hear it."

"It was the Ghosts' mission from first to last. If I had been in charge of it," Newt said, "I would have made sure that I had back up. I wouldn't have missed the opportunity to claim salvage on those singleships after they ran out of fuel."

"Luckily, we have only to explain to the Brazilians why they were buzzed by a bunch of kids who believe that they are obeying instructions from their own future selves," Pete said.

"At least they did something," Newt said.

"You bet," Pete said. "They hooted and howled. They threatened a peaceful scientific mission."

"Help me out here," Newt said to Macy. "*You* should be happy that someone showed those guys what's what."

Macy said, "You really want my opinion?"

"Didn't I just ask?"

"Last week you told me that my opinion didn't count because I hadn't lived here long enough to understand how things really worked."

"I said that?"

"Words to that effect."

"Well, I'm sure that you must have some idea about whether or not the Brazilians are going to mind their manners from now on."

"Brazilians and Europeans," Macy said. "It's a joint expedition."

Newt shrugged.

"I'm sure they'll see this thing just as I do. That it was a silly stunt and no real threat at all," Macy said.

"No real threat? Is that why the singleships turned tail and ran?"

"Maybe they did run away. Or maybe they escaped from an ambush without firing a shot. Reacted to a threat in a peaceable and sensible manner."

Newt stared at her, then shook his head slowly. "These are the people who tried to kill you once upon a time. And you're taking their side?"

"You asked me for my opinion," Macy said. "I gave it."

"You think that we should just let them roam around the system at will, doing whatever they want?"

"That's a different question. You want my opinion on that, too? I think we can't even *ask* them to stop roaming around. We can tell them that they need our permission to go into orbit around Dione, or land here. It's the same deal if they want to land anywhere there are people. But as far as I understand it, no one has the right to tell anyone where they can or can't go anywhere else in the system."

"In fact, the Ghosts broke the rule of free passage when they endangered the Brazilian ships by flying so close to them," Junko said.

"It put the Ghosts in the wrong and the Brazilians in the right," Junpei said. "It was not helpful."

"I can see that I'm in a minority," Newt said. He didn't seem displeased by the idea. "Well, maybe that will change soon enough. There are a couple of other bits of news I came out here to tell you, seeing as you're off the net, thinking about science. One is that Marisa Bassi will be visiting the day after tomorrow. He's going to talk about Dione's response to the arrival of the new ships from Earth."

"If he's hoping for support, he's looking in the wrong place," Pete said. "Paris can do what it wants. That's its right. But we agreed to maintain a position of neutrality. And that's our right."

"The other thing I have to tell you," Newt said. "Some people think that we shouldn't remain neutral, given that the situation will change once those new ships arrive. They think that we should consider supporting Paris. They petitioned for a poll—had enough signatures to get one, too."

"You youngsters, you're as bad as Marisa Bassi," Pete said. "Stirring up trouble when there's no need. I don't suppose your mother is too pleased about this."

"I haven't asked her," Newt said, bouncing to his feet. "One thing I do know. Whether or not we support Marisa Bassi, staying neutral isn't a luxury we can afford any more."

After he'd gone, Junko smiled fondly at Macy and said, "The way you two bicker. Anyone would think you're in love with each other."

"I don't think Newt cares for anything but his own reputation," Macy said.

Macy had long ago realised that Newton Jones's nonchalant, devil-may-care attitude only lightly masked a deep and abiding desire to escape from the shadow of his mother's fame. It was no easy task. When she'd been a year younger than Newt was now, Abbie Jones's mother and father had been killed in a blowout and she had inherited sole use of a ship, which she'd equipped for long-range voyages. She'd explored the moons of Uranus. She had been the first person to set foot on Enka's nitrogen snows. And she'd embarked on a solo expedition that took her through the Kuiper Belt to the edge of the cometary zone and set a record for the furthest distance any person had ever travelled from the sun—more than seventy trillion kilometres—that had yet to be broken.

Journeying out beyond the heliopause, into the outer dark where comets more widely separated than planets travelled in long, lonely orbits, Abbie Jones was gone for more than four years, was believed by most to have long since died when her ship at last limped back to Saturn. It was her last expedition. She married, and with her husband and two dozen other pioneers founded a commune on Uranus's largest moon, Titania. She lived there for six years, until the little commune imploded because quarrels and personal differences between its founding members had been magnified by isolation and hardship. And then she and her husband and children had returned to Dione, and had helped to build what was now the garden habitat of the Jones-Truex-Bakaleinikoff clan.

She was the senior member of the clan now. A powerful matriarch, remote and forbidding. Newt, the youngest of her four children, was defined not by what he could do but by whose son he was: everything he did was measured against the yardstick of his mother's achievements and usually found wanting. That was what he was struggling against, in what he cheerfully and knowingly admitted was a classic example of filial rebellion, driven not by malice but by a kind of sweet, rakish desperation. His sisters and his brother had come to an accommodation with their heritage, but Newt had cast himself as the rebel, the outsider. Living a restless, marginal life piloting the clan's tug, hauling cargo to any and every destination in the Jupiter and Saturn Systems, falling in and out of love, dreaming up all kinds of hare-brained, semilegal or illegal schemes to make credit or gain kudos. He'd had numerous brushes with the law and always refused his mother's offers of help: every narrow escape or fine or short spell of community labour added incrementally to his small reputation as a daredevil pilot and smuggler. And then he'd helped Macy Minnot and the young refusenik, Sada, escape from East of Eden.

Although this adventure had won him considerable kudos, although he believed himself to be a rebel's rebel, Newt had brought Macy and Sada directly to his clan's home. He'd pretended that he wanted to introduce Macy and the refusenik girl, Sada, trophies of his daring escapade, to his mother and the rest of his family, but in fact he had nowhere else to take them. The clan owned the tug he piloted; the clan's garden habitat was his only home amongst all the cities and settlements of the Saturn System; he had needed his mother's influence to cancel the warrants that East of Eden had issued for his arrest and for the arrest of the two refugees he'd liberated. Sada had soon moved to Paris, Dione, where she had taken up with the Ghosts, the gang who'd just attempted to wreck the Brazilian and European mission into the depths of Saturn's atmosphere. Macy had stayed on at the garden habitat, working for Newt's father, Strom Bakaleinikoff, who supervised the regulation and gardening of the habitat's ecosystem.

Macy liked Strom, who was not only as sweet-natured as Newt but was also unambitious and unassuming, content with his lot and possessed of a profound knowledge of ecosystem engineering. She had learned much from him, and he had encouraged her collaboration with his brother, Pete. As for Newt, he seemed more or less indifferent to Macy once the excitement and fuss surrounding her escape had died down. It was insulting, really, especially as he had a reputation for having a woman in every port. She understood why he hadn't tried to make a move on her during the long voyage from Jupiter to Saturn, Sada right there with them in the close confines of *Elephant*, everyone in everyone else's pocket. But he'd shown no real interest in her afterward, either; it was as if she was a trophy he'd brought back and left to gather dust on some high and half-forgotten shelf.

She wouldn't have minded so much if she hadn't found him, his frank good humour, boyish charm, and helpless vulnerability, so damnably attractive. They'd settled into a combative relationship, quarrelling and sparring, their banter teetering between teasing and flirtation, but sometimes Macy would feel a raw unrequited ache at the back of her throat when she looked at him, and then she'd get angry because of his friendly indifference. She'd had a couple of flings while working on the ecosystems of new oases, nothing serious as far as she was concerned, nothing at all to do with getting back at Newt for the affairs he'd had since he'd brought her to Dione. But although she'd made a kind of life for herself with the clan, it had about as much direction as Newt's, and she still felt that she was an outsider. Felt that she could see more clearly than most, with her outsider's viewpoint, the tensions growing within and between the cities and settlements of her new home.

Reaction to the renewed interest of Earth in the affairs of the Outer System roughly split down generational lines. Older Outers, including almost all the surviving members of the original exodus, argued that it would be in everyone's interest to reach an accommodation with Earth. Despite the failure of the biome project at Rainbow Bridge, they still hoped for some kind of reconciliation. For the sake of peace, for the exchange of ideas and goods that would benefit both parties.

Outers in their teens and twenties and thirties were more suspicious. They dismissed the promises made by Greater Brazil and the European Union, were enraged by the imminent arrival of a ship from the Pacific Community, whose mission and intent were completely unknown, and believed that the aims of Earth and the Outer System were so different from each other that war was inevitable, and that Outers should make a stand before Earth was able to strengthen its presence by falsely seducing foolish peaceniks, as they had already seduced the city of Camelot, Mimas. A significant proportion called for preemptive strikes against the warship in orbit around Mimas, and the Pacific Community ship and a Brazilian resupply ship that were approaching the Saturn system.

A third group also believed that war was inevitable, but that it would be impossible to fight off or defeat an invasion force without causing massive damage and loss of life in the cities and settlements of the Outer System, which were peculiarly vulnerable to attack. A single strike by a simple kinetic weapon would wreck the integrity of any city, cause explosive loss of pressure, kill thousands. Rather than directly confront Earth, this third group believed that it would be better to make control of the Outer System as difficult as possible. To practise nonviolent resistance, and move as much infrastructure and as many people as possible to oases scattered across or tunnelled into the surfaces of most of Saturn's moons.

So far the Jones-Truex-Bakaleinikoff clan had remained neutral, cleaving more or less to the middle way, but now a significant minority of its younger members had forced a new poll on whether or not the clan should support Paris's protests against Earth's presence in the Saturn System, scheduled to take place after Marisa Bassi's visit. The mayor of Paris had a private meeting with Abbie Jones and other senior members of the clan, then gave a short, informal address to everyone else, saying that they were in the midst of a grave situation that would grow graver still unless immediate action was taken. He urged the Jones-Truex-Bakaleinikoff clan to add its voice to those asking for the immediate and unconditional withdrawal of Earth's so-called scientific expedition from the Saturn System, and asked it to volunteer one of its members for service on a panel, drawn from every city and major settlement, that could negotiate with Earth on behalf of everyone in the Saturn System. In his opinion, only a united front could win a favourable outcome, for otherwise Earth would contrive a series of unilateral deals like those it had already made with Camelot, Mimas and several small settlements, split the Saturn System into a patchwork of quarrelling factions, and take them over one by one.

It was a modest, conciliatory performance that was rewarded with polite but tepid applause. Most of the young members of the clan looked disappointed; they'd been expecting a stirring call to arms. Afterward, at the reception on the lawn in front of the sprawling Great House, Macy Minnot floated past knots of people and clumps of flower-starred mimosa bushes toward Marisa Bassi, who was holding court near one of the buffet tables. She'd been told that the mayor wanted to meet her, and had decided to confront him directly.

Marisa Bassi was much shorter than the Outers around him but he had a powerful, vital presence and was as broad-shouldered and thick-necked as a street tough. When Macy reached him he grabbed her right hand with his, fastened his left hand on her right elbow, and said with loud and apparently unforced enthusiasm, "The famous refugee from Earth! I'm so pleased to meet you at last! You and I, you know, we have something in common. You defected to the Outer System, and so did my father. I see you didn't know that, but it's true. It was forty years ago, when the European Union first attempted to reach out to us. My father was one of the civil servants sent from Earth to attempt to draw up an agreement. That didn't work out, but he fell in love with my mother and he defected so that he could be with her. A true Romeo and Juliet story, but with a happy ending! So I am only one generation removed from Earth, and here you are, having defected just as my father defected. A historic occasion, don't you think?"

Macy managed to pull free from his grip, saying, "I think that of the two of us your father might have had the better deal."

"But surely you have a much better life here than in Greater Brazil. After all, you have been able to join one of our most distinguished clans. You are free to do what you choose. You are no longer a chattel, but a citizen."

"I meant that your father chose to defect. I was kind of railroaded into it."

"My father defected because he fell in love with my mother. And when it comes to falling in love, does anyone really have a choice?" Marisa Bassi said, smiling at the aides and well-wishers and hangers-on gathered around him. "Perhaps your defection was not as romantic as my father's, Macy, but it was most certainly heroic. That's why I would very much value your opinion about my modest little proposal. Please, don't be afraid to tell me exactly what you think."

"It was definitely a clever speech. You want us to think that if we support you we'll be helping to bring about a peaceful end to the confrontation between the Outer System and Earth. But seeing as you've already made a bad situation worse by making heroes of the Ghosts who pulled that silly stunt, I can't help wondering what this is really about."

"Would you rather I congratulated the Brazilians on their skill in evading a trap?" Marisa Bassi said, clearly amused by Macy's presumption.

"You didn't have to say anything."

"And my silence would have given tacit support to the Brazilians. Everyone believes that I am obsessed with war. But war is not inevitable. Not if we present a united front and make sure that the people aboard the *Glory of Gaia* know that they are not welcome here and that they are not as free to move about our system as they might suppose. That doesn't mean that we can't reach an agreement with the Brazilians and the Europeans, or even with the Pacific Community for that matter. But we cannot—we *will* not—negotiate with anyone as long as there is a warship in our sky. We will not negotiate under duress. It is important that we make that very clear." Marisa Bassi gripped Macy's hand and arm again, aiming his forceful gaze straight into her face. "But listen—I did not come here to argue with you. I came to ask you a favour. It's nothing, really. All you would have to do is speak about Greater Brazil. I would like you to let the people here know about the tyranny endured by the people there. How the so-called great families accumulated wealth and power by acts of violent piracy. How ordinary people live like slaves, with every aspect of their lives controlled and no say in the political process."

"It sounds to me like you think that you already know all about it," Macy said.

"But you know the details. You are the authentic voice of the oppressed. You don't have to make any speeches. You can talk to a sympathetic interviewer. A simple friendly conversation. And people could ask you questions, and you could answer them in any way you liked. No restrictions, no censorship, none of the apparatus of control that you no doubt remember and fear. Don't answer straight away. Think about it. And I hope you will make the right decision, Macy."

"You can have my answer right now, Mr. Bassi. It's no. Because I don't want to be part of your propaganda machine."

"I want you to tell the truth. Our people deserve to know it, so that they can make up their minds. That's how we do things here, Macy. People are given unconditional access to information, and they use that information to decide how to vote. Here, people are free. They are not owned like animals, as they are in Greater Brazil."

"It isn't quite like that."

"If you think that we have some wrong-headed ideas about Greater Brazil, don't you want to explain how things really are?"

"I guess I should be flattered that you think I could be useful to you," Macy said. "And I don't have a problem with telling the truth. No, the problem is that people like you, the ones who want to cause trouble, have already made up their minds, and no amount of truth is going to change that."

Marisa Bassi wasn't so easily put off, and told Macy to think it over. "I will ask you again, and when I do I hope you will have changed your mind. Much is at stake," he said, and turned his attention away from her and asked a new arrival to the group around him, Ismi Bakaleinikoff, what she thought of his modest little proposal, and Macy realised that she had been dismissed.

Yuldez Truex, the foppish leader of the little group of youngsters who wanted the clan to align itself with Paris, caught up with her as she drifted away, telling her that she had made a mistake by not accepting Marisa Bassi's offer there and then. "This is a fine opportunity for you. If you do it, you'll not only gain some kudos; you'll prove that you actually have some loyalty to us, too. But if you don't, well, everyone will say that you can't bring yourself to tell the truth because at heart you're still loyal to Greater Brazil."

Macy laughed. "Since when does being loyal mean agreeing with you?"

"I'm trying to give you some good advice," Yuldez said. "When the fighting starts, anyone whose loyalty is in doubt could find themselves in a good deal of trouble."

"Who are you loyal to, Yuldez? The clan, or Marisa Bassi?"

"I want us to do the right thing," Yuldez said. "And you should do the right thing, too."

"As soon as I've figured out what that is, that's just what I aim to do," Macy said, and before Yuldez could reply Newt loped up and said, "Is this kid troubling you again?"

"He's no trouble," Macy said.

"At least I can count on *your* vote," Yuldez said to Newt. "I know that someone who was cheering on the Ghosts won't want us to surrender without a fight."

"Macy and I need to have a private word, Yuldez, so why don't you run along? I'm sure you have plenty of other people you need to charm."

After Yuldez had moved off, Newt told Macy that the kid had been born with a sharp tongue. "He used to tease kids younger than he was, liked nothing better than to make them cry. I keep hoping that he'll grow out of it, but I'm not sure that he ever will."

"So you think I'm some little kid who needs protecting?"

"That's not exactly what I meant. And you don't have to say what you're going to say next. The bit about learning how to stand on your own two feet and how taking a tumble now and then is all part of the learning process. Because you always say it when you get pissed off because someone tries to help you out."

"There's pretty much no point in saying it because you never take any notice of what I say," Macy said. "But I really don't need any help dealing with pissant hotheads like Yuldez."

Newt grinned. "I guess you think you can deal with Marisa Bassi on your own too."

"I thought I already did. He asked me to do him a favour—"

"And you told him you didn't want to be part of his propaganda machine. One of his aides streamed the whole conversation straight to the net. About thirty seconds into it people started phoning me, and I watched the rest," Newt said, and pulled a pair of spex from his shirt pocket, swung them to and fro. "You can watch too, if you want."

"The son of a bitch ambushed me," Macy said. She felt as if all the air had been knocked out of her.

"If you ask me, you're already part of his propaganda machine," Newt said. "What are you going to do about it? Not that I'm offering to help, of course. Let's say I'm mildly curious."

"I don't know. But I guess trying to stay outside of this mess isn't an option anymore."

After the incident that very nearly wrecked Operation Deep Sounding, the volume of diplomatic bluster grew louder on both sides. The Brazilian ambassador at Camelot, Mimas dispatched to every city and settlement in the Saturn System a clip in which he protested the reckless action of the crew of the SV *Happy Trails* and warned that any further attempt to interfere with the lawful passage of Brazilian ships anywhere in the system would be met with appropriate force. The mayors, senators, selectmen, and prefects of those cities and settlements that had voted to adopt a neutral stance responded with a variety of emollient messages that all made a point of noting that the Ghosts were outside their jurisdiction. The mayor of Paris, Dione made a long and impassioned speech in which he claimed that any activity by the so-called joint expedition was a legitimate target for peaceful protest, boasted that he had authorised the installation of various defence systems around his city, including gamma-ray lasers and rail guns capable of firing canisters of smart gravel, and said that he would not hesitate to take action if the Brazilians and Europeans made any move that might be perceived as a threat to his city's safety and sovereignty. Pundits on both sides were still analysing the implications of this challenge when, in her first public appearance for more than a year, the gene wizard Avernus released a short address to the net.

She spoke with straightforward directness to a locked camera that framed her head and shoulders. A brown-skinned, white-haired old woman wearing no makeup or jewelry, lacking any cosmetic cuts. And yet she radiated charisma. She was as famous as any scientist living or dead, and older than almost anyone else on Earth or in the Outer System. She had been born on Earth at the beginning of the twenty-first century. She had survived the oil wars and the water wars and the general chaos of the first great round of climate change, and after the Overturn had been one of the leaders of the rebellion that had led to the great exodus to Mars and to the moons of Jupiter and Saturn. She had created the first vacuum organisms, designed a variety of ecosystem packages adopted by most of the Outer System's cities, settlements and habitats, redesigned the human body for life in low gravity, developed the first longevity treatments, and much more. Her fame had survived the decades when she had more or less withdrawn from the public eye, and had transmuted to rich and strange rumours and legends. So this breach of her famous reclusiveness instantly captured the attention of everyone in the Outer System and everyone of any importance on Earth, although analysts, commentators, and psycholinguists who afterward took it apart word by word agreed that, while she spoke with admirable clarity, the content of her address was mundane and platitudinous.

Avernus spoke of the different paths that the nations of Earth and the colonies of the Outer System had taken after the Overturn, each driven in a different direction by the different problems that they had had to overcome. But despite these differences, she said, the recent histories of the peoples of Earth and of the Outer System were underlain by the same indomitable human spirit, often reckless yet also often admirable, that spurred heroic attempts to understand and improve the human condition and fix its imprint on the future through endeavours that were staggering in scale and ambition.

Time and again we fail, she said. And each time we fail, we rise up again and continue, determined this time to fail better. We do this because we have the great gift of being able to see farther than the compass of our little lives, and it is because we want to preserve what is best from those lives that human beings, whether from Earth or from any of the moons of Jupiter and Saturn, must put aside all differences and unite in common cause. In this spirit, she asked the Outers to refrain from antagonising the expedition currently in orbit around Mimas, reminded her audience about the importance of developing trade links, and alluded to the great things that the two branches of humanity could achieve through cooperation: a truly utopian future in which Earth was finally and fully healed, and the entire Solar System was colonised by a peaceful and harmonious plurality of city-states. As for the immediate future, she called for the establishment of an entity similar to the United Nations of old, where representatives from every inhabited moon in the Jupiter and Saturn Systems, and every nation of Earth, could discuss their differences. Finally, she announced that for the duration of the present crisis she would take up residence in Paris, Dione, where she hoped to make a contribution to the process of peace and reconciliation.

The speeches of Avernus and Marisa Bassi defined the polarisation of the Outer System. On the one hand there were those who wanted to bridge the historical divide between the Outer System and Earth through cultural exchange, trade in goods and intellectual property, diplomacy, and cooperation in projects that would benefit everyone. On the other, there were many who not only distrusted the motives of the three great political powers of Earth but also felt that Earth itself was irrelevant, a spent force whose show of military strength was a futile reflex. Who boasted that the future belonged only to the Outer System, which was at the brink of a cultural and scientific revolution that would drive the next stage in human evolution.

As in the Outer System, so on Earth. In the Brazilian Senate, supporters of the green saint Oscar Finnegan Ramos argued with great passion for a continuation of the efforts to establish trade links. But the majority believed that the Operation Deep Sounding incident proved that the Outers were a growing threat to the people of Earth, and there was a major setback for those arguing for peace when, in secret session, the head of national security presented evidence that various cities on the moons of Saturn were stockpiling weapons of mass destruction, including genetically engineered plagues and a variety of nuclear weapons, and that Marisa Bassi had commissioned a feasibility study on the possibility of perturbing the orbits of certain short-period comets, echoing the infamous plan by Martian colonists to target Earth with a Trojan asteroid. When portions of this evidence were leaked to public forums, there were riotous demonstrations against the Outers in every major city in Greater Brazil and the European Union, and the government of the Pacific Community announced that its expeditionary force to the Saturn System would ensure that the tragic mistakes of past history were not repeated.

"The plain fact is that the opponents of peace have already made up their minds, and will use anything to buttress their claims," Oscar Finnegan Ramos told Sri Hong Owen. "And so they stir up fear and hatred. Unreasoning prejudice. As long as people fear their enemy they will believe that he is capable of any atrocity. These rumours about plagues and planet-killers are rumours only, but in the present climate they are a very effective way of demonising the Outers. And we are disadvantaged because we cannot stoop to the level of our opponents by spreading false counterrumours. We must cleave to the truth because otherwise we will become like our enemies, and traduce our own cause. At the same time there is no point being right, logically, morally, historically . . . Being right in every sense, but losing."

Sri had come to the green saint's hermitage in Baja California at his request. He had been receiving so many visitors because of the growing crisis that a temporary runway had been constructed outside the little town of Carrizalito. Sri and her two sons had flown there directly from the Antarctic, and then she'd had to wait at a control point while Oscar finished talking with a delegation of scientists from the European Union. Someone had tried to poison his water supply a month ago, and the level of his security was higher than Sri had ever known it. Armoured vehicles and soldiers at the airport. Checkpoints along the road from Carrizalito. A trim, deadly corvette cutting back and forth a couple of kilometres out at sea. And despite having been thoroughly searched at the control point, she'd had to submit to the attentions of a wolf patrolling at the edge of the dunes before it allowed her to walk the rest of the way to Oscar's hut.

Now, as Sri and Oscar strolled along the beach in the warm whip of the wind, the wolf followed them at a discreet distance, salt white sunlight glittering off its mirror-finish hide as it stalked through combed stands of dry grass along the crests of the dunes. Sri had once seen one of the combat machines chase down a deer in the grounds of the factory where they were constructed. The executives who had laid on the demonstration had made bets about how long the deer would last as the wolf hazed it back and forth, playing with it as a matador plays a bull until at last the deer could run no more and stood splay-legged and trembling, foam dripping from its muzzle, and the wolf took it down with a single flechette that struck it just below the base of its skull and severed its spinal column.

Sri was acutely aware that the wolf up on the dune crest could do the same to her in a moment, but never once looked toward it as she and the green saint walked along the tideline. Oscar poked at flotsam with his staff as he talked about parallels with the brief and one-sided war with Mars, rehashing old arguments.

"A hundred years ago, there was no doubt that we should have gone to war," he said. "The Martians tried to decimate Earth. We had to retaliate, or they would have tried it again. We could have occupied Mars, used it as a stepping stone to Saturn and Jupiter. Instead, we wrecked the entire planet like a toddler throwing a temper tantrum. And now I see it beginning to happen all over again."

He lifted a tangle of kelp with the iron-shod point of his staff and slung it away across the sand, and immediately apologised to Sri for his ill temper.

"I have had a bad day. A series of bad days. Too many people who should know better believe that this will be no more than a police action. They call for pacification, purification, prevention. What they will get instead is outright war, plain and simple. It may well destroy the Outer System cities completely, and then there is the risk that the surviving Outers will retaliate. That they may succeed where the Martians failed. On days like this I wonder if the radical greens weren't right after all. I wonder if Gaia might be better off without us. In time, some other species might start to look at the stars and wonder. Bears, perhaps. Or raccoons. Perhaps they will manage things better . . ."

They walked a little way in silence. When Oscar said they should turn back Sri felt something relax inside her, like a muscle uncramping. The meeting was coming to an end; perhaps the old man would finally come to the point. But they were halfway back to his hut before he broke his silence and said, "How is your connection with Arvam these days?"

"I'll be happy to take a message to him."

It cost her a great effort not to look at the machine that slinked along the crest of the dunes.

"If I want to speak to my nephew I can call him. I dandled him on my knee when he was a baby, saw him grow up. He was a fearless child, bright and forthright . . ." They walked a little way while Oscar looked at something in his head. At last he said, "I know that the superbright project has ended. I was wondering if there were still formal interactions between your staff and his."

"There are meetings now and again about potential new projects."

Sri felt a tingling caution. She still didn't know just how much Oscar knew about the superbrights—the real superbrights, not the chimps. And she didn't know if he knew or suspected anything about the other programme.

"It would not be unusual to meet with his people."

"Not at all. What do you want me to do?"

"It isn't much. And you're going to Brasília anyway, yes? These intelligence hearings."

"I was subpoenaed," Sri said. "I submitted a report immediately after my return, and now I have to go through it word by word in front of the security committee, under oath. It's not exactly a sign of trust."

"I'm not accusing you of aiding our opponents," Oscar said. "They're looking for any and every excuse to hurt the Outers. I know you have no choice in the matter."

"They're interviewing my son, too. Everyone who visited the Outer System in the last five years."

"How is Alder? And Berry, too."

"Alder is running his own office now, looking after the ongoing application of several of my old projects. Berry is still interested in natural history."

"Alder is sixteen, yes? As precocious as his mother. You should have brought them with you, instead of leaving them in Carrizalito."

"Perhaps next time."

"I have something that I think Berry might like to see. Which reminds me—this little favour. Someone in my nephew's intelligence-analysis team is sympathetic to our cause. He tells me that his colleagues are under considerable pressure to produce reports that conform to the prejudices of their master rather than to the truth. He wants to give me the raw data which forms the basis of the report that the teams are presently preparing. I plan to have the data analysed by my own team, to see whether or not the conclusions by my nephew's people conform to truth or to prejudice. And as you and your people have formal lines of communication with Arvam's people, it seems to me that you would be the best person to take charge of the data and bring it to me in a safe and discreet fashion."

Oscar gave Sri the name of the man who wanted to help him, told her that he was a senior officer within Arvam Peixoto's intelligence unit who would be able to invent a suitable excuse for meeting either with her or with one of her people.

"I'll do it myself," Sri said.

"Good. Then you will bring it to me yourself, as soon as you can. We must counter my nephew's black propaganda and challenge his claims before they take root, yes?"

"I'll do what I can."

Sri knew that she should take this straight to Arvam, tell him everything, let him decide Oscar's fate. It was the right thing to do for all kinds of reasons, not least her own safety, but Arvam was getting ready to depart for Saturn, and had no time and little patience for anyone opposing him. If he found out about this silly plot he would almost certainly use it as an excuse to humble and humiliate Oscar, strip him of any influence he might still have in the family, and cause as much damage as possible to the peace and reconciliation faction. And if Oscar's reputation was ruined, then Sri's would be tainted by association. Besides, she still felt a vestigial loyalty to her old mentor. So she would save him from his foolishness by doing nothing. She would wait a few days, she thought, and then send Oscar a message, tell him that she had failed. She'd find some way of dressing it up to look like it wasn't her fault; perhaps she could have Yamil kill this officer, make him disappear . . .

"It's all right to be afraid," Oscar said, mistaking the nature of Sri's silence. "These are dangerous times. I know that you are safe enough in your research facility in the Antarctic, but you should take care, my dear, when you are in Brasília. You might even consider whether it is wise to be taking your sons with you."

"Alder has been subpoenaed too."

Oscar's gaze clouded for a moment. "Oh yes. Of course. I'm sorry, my dear. I'm very distracted, these days."

"You don't need to worry about me. I can look after myself."

"You always were the best of my pupils."

"I will never forget the debt I owe you," Sri said.

She realised with a pang of sorrow and pity that their long relationship was at an end. After this, anything she still owed him would be cancelled. He would owe her, in fact. He would owe her his honour and his life, although he would never know it.

"There's something I want to show you before you leave," Oscar said. "The thing I think Berry will like. It won't take a moment."

The green saint led Sri along the beach to a wire enclosure above the high-water mark.

"You're trying again with the turtles," Sri said.

"Not exactly. Two females I released last year returned and laid eggs. When they hatch, they will produce the first generation of truly indigenous Kemp's ridley sea turtle for more than a century and a half."

Oscar smiled with genuine, innocent pleasure. He looked strong still. Stooped like an ape, his broad shoulders mottled pink and brown from a recent round of phage treatment that had destroyed incipient sun-cancers. Indomitable and enduring.

"When everything seems hopeless," he said, "hope is what we have left. And sometimes it rewards our faith in it. Go now, my dear, and do what you must."

Sri and her sons flew to Brasília, and everything went wrong almost at once. On the road out of the airport, two police cruisers intercepted and boxed in Sri's limousine. Yamil Cho told the driver to pull over and said that he would ask the police what they wanted, but when he climbed out two officers slammed him against the side of the limousine, patted him down, and took away his pistol and handcuffed him. Watching all this through the tinted windows, Berry wanted to know if the police were going to shoot Yamil, and Alder said of course not, city police wouldn't dare interfere with family business, it was all a stupid mistake.

An officer opened the door beside Sri and told her to get out.

"You'll regret this," Alder told him.

"Hush," Sri said, and climbed out into hot sunlight and the rushing slipstream of vehicles speeding past. She was wondering if Arvam had found out about Oscar's plan and had decided to put an end to it by disappearing her. She felt quite calm, but there was a high singing in her head and a looseness in her knees as the officer gripped her elbow and guided her to one of the cruisers and told her to get in the back.

A trim young man in a black suit was sitting on the bench seat, turning his cool smile to Sri as she settled beside him, apologising for the melodrama. "Unfortunately, we can't reach out to you through the normal channels."

The cruiser creaked on its suspension as the officer climbed into the front seat, and then it cut out past the limousine and accelerated hard, its siren wailing.

"Don't worry," the young man told Sri. "Your sons and your secretary will be soon be on their way to your apartment."

"And where are you taking me?"

"Euclides Peixoto would very much like to ask you a favour," the young man said.

The police cruiser drove to the southern edge of Brasília, climbed a winding street lined with lush vegetation and the high walls of the houses of the rich to the secluded villa where Euclides Peixoto kept one of his mistresses. Euclides was waiting for Sri in the inner courtyard. His mistress, a plump, motherly woman in her forties, set out a jug of iced coffee and plates of sweet pastries on the tile-topped table between their chairs, and left them alone.

Euclides assured Sri that the place was completely secure, regularly swept for bugs and guarded by a hand-picked cadre. No one would ever know that she had been here; they could talk freely. "What I want you to do," he said, "is tell me about the favour that my uncle wants from you. Tell me everything."

"You already know everything. Otherwise you wouldn't have kidnapped me."

"You're angry. And no doubt more than a little afraid. I understand. But there's no need to be afraid. Have I harmed or threatened your sons? No. I allowed them to go on to your apartment, with your secretary. Have I harmed or threatened you? No. I have invited you here because I want to help you. I want to save you from a terrible mistake. So, go ahead, tell me about this favour. And don't leave anything out."

Sri knew that Euclides knew that Oscar had asked her to collect the damned data needle. Perhaps he, or more likely someone else in the family, who knew how deep it went, had bugged Oscar's hermitage. Or perhaps the person who was supposed to give it to her had been discovered, or was a double agent. It didn't matter. All that mattered was that Euclides, when he'd had his fill of cat-and-mousing her, was going to ask her to betray Oscar.

224

It was the only possible reason why she had been brought here. She'd thought it through during the ride in the cruiser, examined it from every angle, and she knew exactly what she was going to be asked to do, and knew that she'd have to do it. She had been planning to protect Oscar from the consequences of his own foolish meddling, but that was impossible now. He was already doomed. All she could do was try to save herself, and her sons, and her work.

So she fixed her gaze a few centimetres to the left of Euclides Peixoto's face and, as dispassionately as she could, explained that Oscar was suspicious about the report concerning the Outers' capabilities and wanted her to reach out to a man inside Arvam Peixoto's intelligence team who was prepared to leak the raw data on which the report was based. She knew that she had no choice, but that didn't make it any less distasteful, or shaming.

"After you collected this data needle, you were supposed to take it straight to Oscar," Euclides said. He lounged carelessly in his low chair, bare chested, wearing only white trousers. His right arm was sheathed from shoulder to elbow in tattoos—stylised eagles and jaguar heads that looked vaguely Mayan.

"I was supposed to go straight back to him after I finished my business here," Sri said.

"Straight to Oscar. No one else is involved."

"No one else."

For a long moment, the only sound was the splashing of the fountain in the centre of the shaded courtyard. Sri could feel her heart thumping in her chest.

Euclides said, "Would you have done it? Would you have taken it to my uncle, laid it at his feet like an eager puppy?"

"I was considering my options."

"You're a very clever woman, Professor Doctor. I'm sure that you had already decided what to do. Were you going to tell Arvam about the traitor?"

"I was thinking of having him killed. The traitor."

"Before or after he gave you the data needle?"

"Does it matter now?"

"It matters to me that you are completely candid."

"I didn't intend to take the data needle to Oscar. And I wasn't going to tell General Peixoto about it, either."

"You were going to protect my uncle from the consequences of his own foolishness. How admirable."

Sri waited out his silence, his bright and mocking gaze.

"It seems to me that my uncle has always been old," Euclides said. "He has a rich and glorious history, but now, much as I hate to say it, he's grown afraid of change. As far as he is concerned, the past is more important than the present. Because the past is fixed and familiar. Because there is so much in the present that he can no longer control or understand. See, that's why he's retreated to that hermitage of his. He's shrunk his world to a manageable size. Beachcombing. Those turtles. His vegetable garden. I don't mean to criticise. Quite the opposite. For someone of his advanced age, hobbies like that should be more than enough to occupy his days. And yet, as you well know, he can't stop meddling. He's no longer of the world, but he can't leave the world alone. Even though he no longer understands how things really are, he believes that he can still make a difference. Who is the traitor, by the way? You neglected to give his name."

"Manuel Montagne."

Sri felt nothing except a faint astonishment that she felt nothing. She had sentenced a man to death, and she felt nothing.

"Manuel Montagne," Euclides said, relishing the taste of the name in his mouth. "Lieutenant Colonel Manuel Montagne. A member of Arvam's personal staff. Well, you needn't feel guilty or remorseful, Professor Doctor. I already know that this Montagne values his own stupid moral qualms more than loyalty. I already know that he is a traitor. The question is, of course, does Arvam also know?"

"I have been absolutely honest with you," Sri said. "Remember that."

"You made the right choice, and I am pleased that you did. You are an asset, Professor Doctor. Not just for your skill and ingenuity, but because my uncle only suspects that you are a traitor. He does not yet know."

"I have always served the family to the best of my ability," Sri said.

"Glad to hear it. Now, pay attention. This is what you will do. You will meet with Colonel Montagne, but you will not take the information that he gives you to my dear uncle. You will instead give him the information that I wish him to have. I know what you're thinking," Euclides said. "But don't you worry, Professor Doctor, I have no intention of harming you or your sons. As long as you do what I ask, that is. And I have no intention of harming my uncle, either. No, I want to prevent him from making a fool of himself. So this is what you will do. You will give him intelligence information that will show clearly that the Outers are not only planning an attack on our assets in the Saturn System, but they are also arming themselves to attack Earth. If he has hard evidence that the Outers are planning to go to war, it may convince him to give up his foolish attachment to the lost cause of peace and reconciliation."

"I very much doubt that it will do anything of the kind. He failed to stop a war a century ago, and that makes him more determined to stop this one."

"It's true that my uncle is a very stubborn man," Euclides said. "And very clever, and very cunning. The way he's testing your loyalty, with this little errand? But maybe I'm just as cunning. Once you've delivered the intel, I'll expose his man, Colonel Montagne. And the good colonel will give up the plot, by and by, and there'll be a scandal, and Oscar will be disgraced."

"What about me?"

"You will have shown loyalty to the family rather than to a deluded old man. And you know he's deluded. What he doesn't understand, this isn't just about Earth versus the Outers, true humans versus so-called posthumans. It's a war of the generations. On both sides, we have been ruled by the very old for too long. They resist change. They see only what they want to see. Well, it is time to change all that. In fact, it is an historical inevitability. So I would advise you to give up your sentimental attachment to your mentor, Professor Doctor. Don't try to save him from himself. He'll only take you down with him."

"I suppose I must let you know when I have arranged to meet with this colonel."

"No need. I'll know all about it before you do. We're keeping a very close watch on him."

"Does General Peixoto know about him? About this?"

"Arvam doesn't need to know anything about this," Euclides said. "He's far too busy on that ship of his, getting ready to leave for Saturn. He has a lot of work. A lot of preparations. He shouldn't be bothered with something like this. You understand?"

"Oh, I think I do."

Sri knew that Euclides needed her to deliver the data needle, and that when she had done it, despite his assurances, her usefulness would be over, and she would most likely be killed.

"You'd better," Euclides said. "Oh, before you go. One more thing. The family thinks it would be best if you stayed in Brasília for the time being."

"I plan to return to Antarctica immediately after the deposition," Sri said. "Like General Peixoto, I have much work to do."

"I'm sure there's nothing in your little kingdom of ice that you can't supervise just as easily here as there," Euclides said. "You'll be allowed to travel to my uncle's beach hut, of course, but you'll come straight back. And you'll stay right here. You and your sons."

"My sons have nothing to do with this."

"The family is concerned about your safety, and theirs. They will be safe here."

"They will be hostages, you mean."

"They will be safe. I promise. No, not another word. It has been decided, and what has been decided cannot be undone. Great changes are in the air. We need to keep everyone close in the next few weeks. Everyone important to us. And you, my dear Professor Doctor, are more important than most."

"I've served the family faithfully," Sri told her oldest son. "When we went to Jupiter, it was because I wanted the biome to succeed. I went with the best of intentions. And at the same time I was working for Arvam. Again, with the best of intentions. What else could I do? If I had shown any hint of disobedience, if I had refused either Oscar or Arvam, I would have been punished. Stripped of all I've worked for. But despite my loyalty I'm condemned anyway. I've been forced to betray Oscar, and afterward, well, you can be sure that I won't be rewarded for it."

"You did the right thing," Alder said. "The only thing you could do, in the circumstances."

"I know. But it doesn't make it any better."

Sri and Alder were walking in the grounds of the Peixoto family library. What had once been the Jardim Botânico, before the Overturn and the civil wars. It was early evening. Lights were flickering on along paths that wandered between flower beds and long, lush lawns and stands of trees. The afterglow of sunset lingered low in the west but otherwise the sky was clear and the first stars glimmered in the darkening blue and the freshly minted crescent of the Moon was slung like a cartoon smile above the library's scattering of black cubes.

It was one of Sri's favourite places on Earth. After Oscar Finnegan Ramos had plucked her from an obscure posting in an agricultural research facility and gifted her with one of the famous scholarships that allowed the recipients to work on anything they pleased, she'd spent three years here, cultivating her first truly original ideas, beginning to understand how she must shape herself and her career so that she could win from the world her heart's desire. Right there, on the bench in front of a clump of palms and hibiscus, she had finally realised how to crack an electron-transfer problem in the novel artificial photosynthesis system she'd been trying to develop, a problem that for weeks had remained stubbornly opaque no matter how much she turned and twisted it. She remembered that she'd been watching emerald green hummingbirds floating on blurred wings about the brash red hibiscus blossoms when the answer had come to her unannounced and fully formed, a true moment of epiphany, a pure and unalloyed happiness unmatched until the birth of her first son.

Sri still maintained apartments in one of the accommodation blocks used by visiting scholars, and loved to walk in the gardens around the library. But now the dear familiar maze of paths and landscaped knolls and ridges felt like a cage, and the warm, humid, darkening air pressed against her like a shroud.

"Euclides isn't working alone," Alder said.

"No. He couldn't have devised something like this. He's the visible portion of some deeper plot by a faction of the family. They support the war, and they want to humiliate Oscar. To undermine his authority. That much is plain. And I think that they also want to undermine Arvam, too."

"Are you sure he isn't a part of this?"

"Euclides made it quite plain that he isn't. That he doesn't know that a member of his staff is passing information to Oscar. No, they'll use this against Arvam, too, when the time comes, to make sure that he does not grow too powerful after winning the war. And of course, they'll also use it as an excuse to eliminate me. It's all very neat. Admirably so. A bullet that can strike three targets at once."

"Why would they want to eliminate you?"

"Because my loyalty is in question. Because I know too much. Because I have outlived my usefulness. Because I have given them everything they need to prosecute their war, and they no longer need me."

Sri spat out the words like bitter seeds.

"You expected a reward, but instead you feel that you have been punished," Alder said. "You are upset because you feel that you have been treated unfairly. But it's an abiding principle that ordinary people who serve the rich and powerful must always be prepared for sudden and unexpected reversals. For the rich and powerful can be unthinkingly cruel and capricious. They can change the lives of their servants on a whim, and think nothing of it. So it's possible that as far as Euclides and this shadowy faction are concerned, you're simply a go-between. A pawn in the game they are playing with Oscar and the general."

"A pawn they are thinking of sacrificing."

"If the game is close to the end, perhaps you can win promotion instead."

"Euclides told me that the family wants me to stay here. That I am forbidden from returning home. If they can cast aside twenty years of my work on a whim, then surely they can cast *me* aside on a whim, too. Without a pang of regret. I cannot rely on charity, or sentiment. No, if I am to survive this I need to make a move of my own. And besides, there is the other thing."

Alder understood at once. "Avernus."

Ever since the fiasco in Rainbow Bridge, Sri had vowed that if war came, *when* it came, she would make sure that she was rewarded for her loyalty and hard work by being given sole access to Avernus and her secrets. That prize was hers, and hers alone. Only she was worthy of it; only she deserved it. The thought of one of her grasping, foolish rivals poking and prying into Avernus's work, learning and using the gene wizard's secrets, filled her with bitter helpless anger.

She said, "It would be better to kill Avernus and destroy her works than let some lesser fool ruin or pervert them."

They walked through the hot and deepening twilight. Irrigation machines woke amongst the lawns and sprawling flower beds, clicking as they spat arcs of water high into the air.

After a little while, Alder said, "This isn't one of your tests, is it? You already know what you want to do, you want me to work it out . . ."

He was ten centimetres taller than Sri now, and although he still had a boy's coltish awkwardness she could see quite clearly the lineaments of the handsome, elegant man he was becoming. He was dressed, like her, all in black. A black short-sleeved shirt, pleated black trousers, black boots with pointed steel-tipped toes. His honey-coloured hair cropped short save for a long lock at the right temple, tumbling past his forehead to the tip of his sharp cheekbone. He was no longer a boy. He was an ambitious young man, thoroughly familiar with the processes of politics and power, and the compromises and negotiations required to further his mother's interests and protect her research.

Sri felt sorrow and pride mingling in her heart, even though she'd always known, as she'd encouraged Alder to take on more and more responsibility, that it would be at the cost of his innocence. It was the price paid by everyone with any power, but it did not make it any easier.

She said, "I don't want you to work out anything. I want to keep you safe, and that means you can't know what I may or may not be planning to do. But I will need your help. Politics, plotting, flattery and all the rest—it isn't what I do. And besides, you're involved in this as much as I am. Even if I survive, our lives will be utterly changed. And if I make the wrong move, well, at best you and Berry will not only be orphaned but also disinherited."

Alder laughed, and immediately apologised. "I'm sorry, but it sounds so very dramatic."

"Nevertheless, it is true."

"I really think that I could help you more if you trusted me—"

"Don't ever think that I don't trust you. This is not about trust. It is about keeping you safe," Sri said. "If you know too much, you will never be safe, so don't *ever* ask me about my plans again."

"I'm sorry," Alder said again.

"You'll need to go away," Sri said. "Somewhere that puts you out of reach of Euclides."

"What about Berry?"

"I'll look after Berry. You will have to look after yourself until I call on you for help."

"Of course."

Sri stopped. Alder stopped too, and turned to look at her, tall and grave.

"Promise," she said.

"I swear it."

She leaned forward, rose on tip-toe and kissed him on the lips. "Good. It may take a year. Perhaps longer. But not forever. I will contact you when it is safe, and then I will need all your skills of diplomacy and negotiation. It won't be easy, but it's the only way we can survive this."

"You have taught me that nothing important is ever won easily," Alder said. "And although Euclides and his faction may have power over you, you are more powerful than you think or they realise. You have done very important work for the family. You are a great gene wizard. The greatest the family has ever known. That counts for something."

"Let's hope so."

5

The Jones-Truex-Bakaleinikoff clan held their polls publicly, in the Athenian manner. People voted by placing a white or black glass disc in the ballot box, and the vote was carried or defeated by a simple majority. Newton Jones was one of the last to vote on the proposal to support Paris, Dione. Smiling at Macy as he picked up a black disc and dropped it into the box. Ten minutes later the tally was announced. Black outnumbered white by a slim majority. The proposal had been defeated.

On his way out of the room, Yuldez Truex said to Macy, "I don't suppose you'll be happy until you see Brazilian storm troopers marching in here."

"You lost fair and square by more than one vote," Macy told him. "Quit blaming me and try to get over it."

The next morning, she was working in the garage, loading a rolligon with insulated boxes containing bags of seeds, cultures of microorganisms, and flasks of nematodes and springtails and worms, when she received a summons from Newt's mother. Abbie Jones lived in a solitary tower west of the keep. It had the sleek and finned shape of a space rocket from the time three centuries past when such things were no more than unrealised dreams and it was clad in seamless black fullerene polished to a shine that held tenebrous reflections of the formal garden around it. Beds of lilies, pale grasses, ornamental thistles with silvery foliage, all bordered with clipped box. Gravel paths. A bower of sprawling white roses. A square pond with flagstones set around its four edges and fat koi carp patrolling beneath lily pads like coins scattered across the surface of the black water.

Macy had met and talked with Abbie Jones several times, but never before alone, and she had never before visited the matriarch's tower. She was received by a small robot with three spidery legs and a transparent plastic carapace much scuffed by age. It led her into an elevator that rose to a room near the top of the tower, where Abbie Jones sat on a cushion studying a slate before one of the big round windows set at the four quarters of the compass. She was as pale and slender and tall as Newt, dressed in a plain tunic of unbleached cotton and trousers of the same material. Her long white hair was brushed back from her face and held in a kind of loose net that hung at her right shoulder. She set the slate aside and asked Macy to sit, asked if she'd had breakfast.

"Yes, ma'am."

"Well, do you like coffee?"

Macy said that she did and sat on the cushion opposite the old woman as the little robot clattered off to the elevator. The room was small but light and airy. A case of books was set against a wall between two of the windows, facing the frame of a handloom in which a long heavy cloth patterned in red and black stripes hung half finished. The round windows looked out across the green and white garden to the patchwork of fields and wooded lots and meadows that spread to the rim forest under the bright light of the chandeliers and the high angles of the tent.

Abbie Jones said that she hoped Macy didn't mind the interruption to her work; Macy said that it wasn't anything that couldn't wait.

"You're going out to quicken a new habitat."

"Yes, ma'am. Out on the plain south of Carthage Linea. There's a crew of robots building a bunch of them there."

"Please. My name is Abbie."

"Okay."

"You've been quickening oases for a while now."

"About eight months."

"You like the work?"

"Very much."

"I'm glad. Everyone should find something they love doing. Then work isn't work. It's a part of themselves. Of who they are."

"I see you like to weave."

"It helps me to relax when I've had enough of trying to run this place. We're a non-hierarchical democracy that puts decisions about anything and everything to the vote. But someone has to make sure that those decisions are implemented in a fair and transparent manner. And someone must also deal with day-to-day problems and snags too small to be worth the collective wisdom of the people."

The little robot returned carrying before it a wooden tray set with a coffee pot and a pitcher of milk, straws of sugar, bone-china cups and saucers, and a plate of thin honey-coloured biscuits. It set the tray on the floor between the two women and its sensor band swivelled through one hundred and eighty degrees and it stepped backward to a spot by the bookshelf and hunkered down with a hydraulic sigh. Abbie Jones poured coffee into the cups and asked Macy if she took cream or sugar.

"Just black is fine."

Abbie Jones took a sip of coffee and looked at Macy over the rim of her cup. "You voted against making an alliance with Paris."

"The majority did."

"Do you suppose that Marisa Bassi has taken the way you voted as a sign that you do not want to help him?"

"He can take it how he wants." Macy paused, then said, "If Marisa Bassi knows how I voted, if he didn't just guess but he's flat-out certain, then someone who was present at the vote must have told him that I dropped a black disc in the box."

Abbie Jones inclined her head, smiling faintly.

"I think I know who," Macy said. "Don't worry, I'm not going to cause trouble over it. Unless you want me to."

"If necessary, I will deal with it myself."

"How do you know that Marisa Bassi knows about the way I voted?"

"He called me just before I called you. He presented various arguments about why we were wrong to refuse to support him. And he said that he knew you had voted against the motion, and suggested that you might have been poisoning the minds of some of the clan with what he called pro-Brazilian propaganda."

"Is that why I'm here?"

Abbie Jones shook her head. "I am not accusing you of anything. I asked you here because I thought it was only fair to let you know what he said. Has he spoken to you?"

"No, but I bet he will. Most likely he'll ask me to help him again. And if I don't agree, he'll probably make a speech accusing me of being some kind of spy."

"If you need any help, you have only to ask."

"That's good of you. But I think I have a way of cutting the ground from under him."

"The offer stands."

"I thank you for it," Macy said. "But if you don't mind, let me try my idea first. I'm sort of committed to it, anyway."

After a small silence, Abbie Jones said, "Sometimes something happens to someone that changes their life forever. Something divides their life into two. Into before and after. Everything that happened in the before, even those actions and decisions that could be held accountable for causing the divide, becomes afterward remote. Like a dream, or a story told about the life of someone else. And everything that happens afterward is different from everything that went before, because the person is never again the same. That's happened to you, I think."

"My life has changed, that's for sure. I'm not sure yet how it's changed me."

"It happened to me, too. The same abrupt change. Before I set out on my long voyage through the Kuiper Belt, I had a modest amount of fame in the

234

small circle of people who were interested in the outermost reaches of the Solar System. A little kudos. Nothing more. But when I came back I was for a short time the most famous person in the Outer System, and my fame attracted rumours that I had encountered something strange in the outer dark. An alien or the ghost of an astronaut from a lost expedition. A true artificial intelligence grown from the seed of an ancient robot probe. A profound hallucination that regressed me through a parade of past lives. Something that made me something more than human. That gave me a godlike perspective on the little comedies and tragedies of ordinary lives. It was all nonsense of course, but understandable nonsense. People like dramatic explanations for dramatic situations and dramatic changes. And it was certainly true that my life had been changed, utterly and forever. I will not deny that spending four years alone might have had something to do with it, but the fact is that I discovered nothing out there that I didn't expect to find, and if I changed then it was no sudden thing that changed me but the simple day-by-day evolution that everyone experiences. The voyage itself made me famous, and fame alone cut my life in two. Into the before and the after. One of the reasons I set out with my husband and some of my friends to found a settlement on Titania was to escape from the goldfish bowl of fame. And we were all very young then, and had the arrogance of the young. We believed that we could not fail at anything. But we did. We were too far from everywhere else and we were divided by petty disagreements magnified into vicious grievances by our loneliness. And so we came back, and my husband and my children and I made a new start, and here we are." Abbie Jones dipped a biscuit in her coffee and took the smallest bite. "The point being, I was wrong to think that I could find a way back to the life I had had before I became famous. No one can go back to what they were in the before. Because there is no longer any before."

There was another small silence. Both women sipped their coffee. The ancient little robot stood quiet and still by the bookcase, a pinlight in its sensor band glowing red. At last, Macy said, "I kind of ended up here through a series of accidents. It definitely wasn't planned. But I'm not looking to go back to what I was. At one time I thought it might have been possible. I hoped it was. But now I know that it isn't."

"That's good. It means you are free to find out what you've become."

"I'm an outsider. I know that. Maybe I'll always be one. But I'm trying my best to make a place for myself here."

"You are also more famous than you once were. It can be useful, if you accommodate yourself to it. Or it can become a burden, if you are not careful.

235

A constant fight against the expectations of other people." Abbie Jones took a sip of coffee. "We can look back at the place where our lives changed. At what defines us. Not everyone has that advantage. Some people must struggle all their lives with the question of who they are, and never find a satisfactory answer. My youngest son, for instance."

Macy didn't say anything, but she knew then, with cold iron certainty, that the matriarch knew exactly what she was planning to do.

"Newton is restless," Abbie Jones said. "He tries out different things. Different ideas, different attitudes. As someone else might try on different clothes. He hasn't yet found something that satisfies him."

"I'm sure he will."

"He doesn't want to be known as the son of Abbie Jones. He wants to be his own person. He hopes to find something that will lay a line or boundary across his life. Something that will define him ever afterward. As you and I are defined by what happened to us. He is not stupid, and he is brave enough, although it is the kind of bravery that hasn't yet been tested. The kind of bravery that could be mistaken for bravado or recklessness. And he is also easily led."

"I wouldn't try to make Newt do anything he didn't want to do. I wouldn't even know how to try," Macy said.

She wondered if Abbie Jones was probing her, trying to find out if she knew what Newt got up to on his solo trading trips to the various cities and settlements of the various moons. Who he met, who he talked to, what they talked about. Well, she didn't. Oh, Newt liked to drop hints and teasing suggestions, but Macy, who didn't know half as much about how things worked out here as she would have liked, lacked the context to sort out facts from his usual brags, boasts and tall tales, let alone fit them into any kind of sensible story. And besides, his mother, who was ferociously well connected, and respected, too, with deep reserves of karma, a power in the world, probably knew more about Newt's escapades than Macy did. So maybe this was a warning; maybe Abbie Jones thought Macy was somehow plugged into Newt's fantasy world . . .

"Well, in this particular case I hope that you are successful," Abbie Jones said. "Not only for your sake. If Marisa Bassi is able to convince the right people that you are some sort of spy, the reputation of the clan will be damaged. We'll be made to look like fools for taking you in, or worse."

"I won't let you down."

Macy drove out across the dark plain, past fields of vacuum organisms, past a low range of hills where every New Year people from habitats and oases round and about used explosive charges and drills and chisels to sculpt from the rock-hard ice fantastically detailed statues and frescos of real and imaginary animals, castles, temples, palaces and fantasy landscapes, some in the natural, sombre colours of the ice, others frosted white or sprayed with coloured water. The road swung around the far edge of this gigantic fantasia and ran in a straight line northeast toward the network of ridges and scarps associated with Carthage Linea's gigantic trough. Saturn's crescent slowly climbed beyond the horizon. The road cut through a series of ridges softened by a mantling of dust created by several billion years of micrometeorite impacts, and Macy swung away from it and drove north, driving up a long slope that gave out at an abrupt scarp that dropped to a dished plain where a scattering of oases and shelters glittered in vivid shades of green like exquisitely detailed pieces of jewelry.

Macy thought of a smart rock hurtling out of the black sky: as long as it was travelling fast enough, it didn't have to be very big, striking one of those little tents and vaporising it, punching a fresh crater in the landscape. She imagined rocks targeted at every settlement, dozens of rocks smashing down on Dione, pounding it hour after hour . . .

She followed a narrow road that switchbacked down the scarp, drove out across the plain toward the new oasis. A crew of construction robots had just completed the tent and its infrastructure, and the Jones-Truex-Bakaleinikoff clan had won the contract to quicken it. *Elephant* was parked on the far side, its shocking pink hull vivid against the tan and umber landscape. Macy pulled up next to the tent's service lock, fastened her helmet and climbed outside, and started to haul insulated boxes and drums onto a sled. She hadn't been working long when Newt came around the flank of the tent, loping along eagerly. The chest plate of his white pressure suit was decorated with the dark-blue sky and blowsy suns of Van Gogh's *Starry Night*.

"I'm sorry I'm late," Macy said. "Something came up."

"You could have called."

"I knew you'd wait. And I'm not that late."

"Can't you unload this stuff when we get back? You're going to make us even later."

"I don't want to leave them in the rolligon. If its battery gives out, the cold will get to them."

"The battery won't give out."

"If you give me a hand, it'll take half as long."

Newt helped her load the rest of the rolligon's cargo onto the sled and they pulled it into the big airlock and cycled through. The space under the slanting sides of the tent was divided into two by a sinuous ridge decorated here and there with faceted outcrops of black basalt and covered in a layer of artificial topsoil derived from particles of smectite clays and siderite that had been ground to glassy sand and conditioned in a bioreactor. A gardening robot had laid it down a few days ago. After checking the viability of its microflora and biota and making any adjustments she felt necessary, Macy was going to seed every square centimetre with a mix of fast-growing grasses and clovers. She would return two weeks later to plough in the catch crop to provide green manure, and leave the soil ready for the mature plant cover.

She shucked her helmet and told Newt to sit down, she had something to tell him.

"Are you backing out?" he said, after he'd taken off his helmet and perched on the edge of the sled.

"I still want to go. But you should know that your mother knows about us."

"She knows what you're planning to do?"

"Maybe. I don't know. She didn't ask me about it, and I didn't ask her. But she made it plain that she knew you were helping me."

After Macy had given Newt a summary of the conversation, he said, "It was Yuldez, wasn't it?"

"Who told Marisa Bassi? I think so."

"He asked me for a ride last night. Turned up as I was getting ready to leave, said I could drop him off at Paris on my way to pick up the cargo. I told him it was too far out of my way, he could get the train. I guess that's what he did."

"And early the next morning Marisa Bassi calls your mother. It fits."

"Let me deal with him."

"Your mother said *she'd* take care of him. Besides, it isn't as if he gave away any real secret. Everyone in the clan knows how I voted."

"He wanted to get you into trouble."

"Marisa Bassi would have gone after me anyway, when he realised I wasn't going to cooperate."

"This plan of yours had better work, then. Are you going to tell me exactly who it is you're planning to meet?"

"You'll see soon enough. When we get to Enceladus."

6

Euclides Peixoto called Sri a few hours before she was due to appear before the Senate Intelligence Committee. She was taking breakfast with Alder and a clutch of aides, lawyers and councillors, rehearsing her testimony. After she walked out onto the terrace, Euclides told her that the meeting with the traitor, Lieutenant Colonel Manuel Montagne, would take place at three o'clock in the afternoon.

"This afternoon?"

"Don't worry, Professor Doctor. You have plenty of time," Euclides said, and told her that she was to walk west along the central promenade by the Lago Paranoá. The traitor would be waiting for her at the far end.

"And then?"

"And then it will proceed as arranged. He has no reason to suspect you, and my men will of course be watching. In the unlikely event that there is trouble, they will intervene at once. But I am sure that you will do your best to make sure that there is no trouble, yes?"

"Don't gloat. It demeans both of us."

"You're in no position to take a moral tone with me. After you collect the data needle, you will meet with one of my aides. You will exchange the needle for one with the salted data, and that's what you will take to my uncle."

"That's all I have to do," Sri said, although she knew that it wasn't. She had plans of her own now.

"That's all. You made the right decision, Professor Doctor. You won't regret helping us."

At the Senate Intelligence Committee, Sri read out her answers to questions that had been given to her in advance, and after a little light cross-examination the chairman thanked her for her help and told her that she was discharged. Then it was Alder's turn to give his sworn deposition; sitting beside him, Sri was proud of how fearless he seemed as he stood before the four senators and their advisers and recited his answers in a clear and calm voice.

Afterward, bodyguards drove Alder back to the apartment, and Yamil Cho drove Sri across the city to the rendezvous with Colonel Montagne. Through a dense traffic of bicycles and bicycle carts towing improbably large loads, army and civilian trucks, buses and jitneys so crowded that they looked like heaps of people locked together like army ants around a morsel of food. Past monolithic superquadras that blotted out much of the sky and cast the tree-lined avenues in perpetual shadow. Apartments and shops were crammed into the broad terraces of their lower floors and tiers of farm platforms rose high above, clad in racks of solar panels and topped by windmill generators whose giant blades heliographed shards and splinters of sunlight.

Sri loathed Brasília. She loathed the brutalist architecture. She loathed the heat and the bone-dry air and the dust that blew from the planalto and turned the sky blood red. Most of all, she loathed the crush of people on the streets, the proles with their cheap garish clothes and unreconstructed and imperfect bodies and faces, sheer overwhelming numbers of them, far too many people crushed together out of necessity and ideology. The land was for Gaia; the cities for people. It was the culmination of a trend that had begun with the invention of agriculture. Now almost everyone on Earth lived in a city, and the cities no longer sucked the life out of the surrounding countryside, no longer drew on water and food and mineral resources for a hundred or a thousand miles around, but were self-contained, recycling water and garbage, growing food in farm towers and on rooftops and elevated platforms. Urban islands isolated like pockets of plague from the regenerated and reconstructed wildernesses that surrounded them.

The stink of the street infiltrated the limousine's air-conditioning and clung greasily to Sri's skin. Sweat and cheap perfume, incense from altars and shrines, the smoke of the cooking fires of street vendors, the sweet tang of burnt gasohol. Music in a dozen clashing styles thumped from sound systems that adorned the vehicles all around, from loudspeakers above shops and the stalls along the sidewalks under the huge trees that lined the avenues. People lived their lives right out in the open, like animals. All along the broad sidewalks they were having their hair cut or their teeth fixed, being tattooed or scanned, eating, watching puppet shows or acrobats or dancers, listening to itinerant preachers ranting at street corners, praying at roadside shrines dedicated to a zoo of totemic spirit animals. To the proles, Gaia was not a scientific concept, the intermeshed totality of the Earth's biomes, but an ancient goddess, powerful yet vulnerable. Through their chosen spirit animal they prayed to Her for intercession in their lives, prayed for forgiveness of the great wounds that humankind had caused, and prayed for her renewal. In their rude shrines, She was depicted as Aphrodite rising naked from the sea on a scallop shell, or a many-armed dancer, or a maternal figure vast and fertile, or a laughing child dancing through a sun-spangled forest.

An amazing chasm of ignorance, no way of filling it, Sri thought as she stared at the carnival streets through the smoked glass of the armoured limousine. Sometimes she dreamed of plagues that would winnow humanity to a sustainable level. Of a green, wild planet in which just ten million people roamed the plains and forests, sailed the clean blue oceans. Tall strong intelligent people who lived lightly on the land, linked by a planetary net, carrying civilisation in their heads. A utopia in which everyone was like her. Billions had been killed by climate change and the wars for water and agricultural land, and billions more had died during the Overturn, but it had not been enough.

The frigid empty landscapes of the moons of Saturn rose in her mind's eye. The gardens of the cities and oases. Green cathedrals celebrating the triumph of rationality.

She became aware that the traffic was slowing, bunching up. Arpeggios of horns. The shouts of frustrated drivers. The animal roar of a crowd packed into a plaza, spilling into the road. Yamil Cho used his headset to talk with someone, then told Sri that there was a small problem, but it should be negotiable.

"Is it some kind of meeting?"

"I believe it's a war riot, ma'am."

"A riot?"

"People get stirred up by propaganda and eventually their anger finds an outlet. They burn effigies, chant slogans. Usually nothing serious. The news channels cover them like they cover futsal matches."

"I don't watch the news channels."

Sri remembered something that Oscar had told her long ago, when she had complained one day about the sheer numbers of people who contributed nothing to the world, who were no more than fleshy vessels for the blind reproductive urges of their genes. According to him, mob behaviour had evolved soon after human beings had first crowded together in cities. Mobs were ugly and vicious but they were also purposeful, congregating around a wound in the populace's psyche like white blood cells around an infection in the body. They were safety valves for frustration and dissatisfaction; they united a population against a real or imagined enemy. Mobs have always been with us, Oscar had said. Every kind of government had been tried, but the mob was a constant of civilisation. Rulers believed that they were in control, that they had been elevated above the herd and governed by common consent or brute force or divine right, but in reality they were merely servants of the mob.

Yamil Cho talked into his headset, then told Sri, "The police assure us that we will be quite safe as long as we stay in our vehicle. I will get us out of here as soon as possible, but it is best to behave inconspicuously."

"We are inside a limousine, Mr. Cho. We are hardly inconspicuous. And besides, we must not miss the rendezvous. Get us away from here right now."

"I will do my best," Yamil Cho said, and began to edge the limousine forward.

The crowd surged around a giant people tree in the centre of the plaza. People trees were a legacy of Avernus, cut by her before she had left Earth for the Moon, before the Overturn. They were planted in every city. Their abundant sugar-rich sap could be tapped to make syrup or wine or beer and their seed pods could be crushed to make biofuel; they produced protein-rich nodules at the junctions of their branches, their bark yielded several spices and an antibiotic, or could be boiled to make a kind of paper cloth, and their nutritious leaves could be eaten raw. People could live out their entire lives in them and never want for anything. Many holy men and women did just that; it was a rare tree that was not inhabited by a mendicant or a seeress.

This one had something hanging from the very end of one of its broad lower branches. As the limousine crept past the outer fringe of the crowd, Sri saw that it was the corpse of an albino man, head flopping broken-necked against his shoulder, clothes tattered, a placard fastened to his chest with two words lettered in what looked like blood. *Against Nature*. People were beating at the corpse's feet and legs with sticks as if it were a piñata. They were pelting it with stones and fruit. Even shoes. They were pulling off their shoes and throwing them at the corpse.

Had they mistaken him for an Outer, or was he a surrogate for their inchoate rage against the posthumans? Sri realised that it didn't matter. What mattered was the mob's fury.

A small flock of police drones and one-man copters hung at different levels above the stepped terraces and setbacks of the superquadra that surrounded the plaza on three sides. Yamil Cho explained that the police usually didn't intervene directly in situations like this because it generally inflamed the mob.

"They are pumping pheromones to make the rioters more peaceable."

"It doesn't seem to be working," Sri said.

More and more people were crowding into the plaza, like ants swarming a sugar lure. People tried to stare through the limo's mirrored windows, a parade of leering, confused, angry, tearful faces. Fists battered the limo's body, drummed on its roof like rain. It rocked on its sturdy suspension like a small boat in a choppy sea. Out across the crowd, small knots of fighting were beginning to break out as the mob turned its rage on itself. Something thumped on the window a few centimetres from Sri's face; pieces of fruit slid down the glass, leaving a slimy trail. And suddenly the limousine was the centre of a barrage of fruit and stones. A man battered at the windshield with a stake torn from a roadside stall. Yamil Cho aimed a grazer at him and the man dropped the stake and fell to his knees shrieking in agony as the weapon's beam triggered his pain receptors. Others surged forward and started to rock the limousine from side to side, and were thrown back when fifty thousand volts surged through the limousine's body.

Yamil Cho advised Sri to buckle her safety harness. As she clipped her-self in place, the limousine pulled out around a truck painted with pious slo-gans and mounted the sidewalk, scattering pedestrians and smashing through stalls as it picked up speed. Yamil Cho talked calmly to the police as he aimed the limousine with pinpoint precision. As it slewed back onto the road, a copter beat down overhead, lights flashing and siren wailing, and other vehicles began to clear out of the way.

A few blocks later, they were driving through normal traffic, past a normal street scene. Yamil Cho thanked the copter and it stood on its nose and sheered away, heading back toward the riot.

"Are they common, these war riots?" Sri said.

"There's at least one a day now, ma'am. And not just in Brasília, either."

"It can't be stopped," Sri said.

"They generally burn themselves out pretty quickly," Yamil Cho said.

"I mean the war can't be stopped, Mr. Cho. The people have spoken. They want it."

"Yes, ma'am." Yamil Cho drove for a block, then said, "If I may be so bold, I think you're doing the right thing. Not because war is inevitable, but because it's the right thing to do."

"Thank you, Mr. Cho," Sri said, surprised and touched. She had never before heard the man express an opinion.

The place where she was supposed to meet with Lieutenant Colonel Mon-tagne was in the broad park of grass and clumps of trees that ran beside the long lake which centuries ago had been created by diverting three rivers. Sail-boats were out on the water, colourful as a flock of butterflies, tacking back and forth in the hot breeze. Sri walked along the central promenade past stalls and benches and clumps of picnic tables. Families. Sweethearts strolling arm in arm. Children sitting rapt before a puppet show.

No one was waiting for her at the far end of the promenade, but a scrap of paper had been screwed into the mesh seat of the very last bench. A street address was written on it.

"It's a good precaution," Yamil Cho said, when Sri returned to the lim-ousine, hot and out of temper. "This fellow knows what he is doing."

"Playing silly games won't help him."

"Of course not."

"Are we still being followed?"

"We lost the first team when we went past the war riot, but another team was waiting for us right here. I can lose them easily enough along the way. Just say the word."

Sri shook her head. "I want them to follow us. I want Euclides Peixoto to know that I did exactly as he asked."

The new rendezvous was a street-corner luncheonette near the Cemitério da Esperança, no different from a thousand such. Tables and chairs scattered under the broad shady branches of a people tree, a stall that sold coffee and fruit juice, fried doughnuts and empadinhas. Sri took a seat and when the waiter came over ordered a glass of mango juice that she had no intention of drinking—the stuff would be a gross cocktail of bacteria and impurities. After a couple of minutes a young black-haired man who was not the waiter brought the glass to her table and set it down on a paper napkin.

"I am a friend of Colonel Montagne," he said. "Do you know that you are being watched?"

"I suspected it," Sri said.

"What you need is in the fold of the napkin. You understand why we must take precautions. It is not for our safety, but for yours."

For a moment, Sri felt the urge to tell him that this was a charade, that Euclides Peixoto was planning to salt the information, and in any case the green saint they no doubt revered didn't need it, this was just his way of testing her loyalty. This young man and Colonel Montagne probably believed that they were changing history, but they were caught up in a game they didn't understand, out-thought and out-manoeuvred, doomed. She could save their lives with just a few words. The impulse rose up in her like a sickness, making her dizzy and light-headed, and then it was gone. She was in control of herself again.

"I want to say that it is a marvellous thing to meet you, Dr. Hong-Owen," the young man said, with a sudden bright smile. "You are doing great and important work. I can't express my admiration for your bravery in coming here, and for standing in front of that committee of old fools and telling them the truth about our brothers and sisters."

"Brothers . . . ?"

"We are all of us children of Gaia. Here on Earth, and on all the other worlds. This war the old men want—you and I know it is quite artificial. They want to deny evolution. They have remade the world for their own benefit and they are frightened of change because they know that change will unthrone them. I have read your work, Dr. Hong-Owen. That you are on our side—it makes me happier than I can say. I know that you will ensure our little gift reaches the right person," the young man said, and turned and walked away through the tables and chairs into the swirling crowds moving along the broad sidewalk.

A bumblebee-sized drone sped after him, flashing in the sunlight for a moment as it flew out of the shade of the tree, above the heads of the crowd. Sri carefully folded the paper napkin, slipped it into her pocket, and walked back to the limousine.

When Sri returned to the apartment, she found her sons playing a kind of water polo in the pool out on the big terrace. She stood in the shadows by the French windows, watching them splash and shout. Alder was quick and cunning, but Berry, graceful and strong in the water, had control of the ball for most of the time. Unlike Alder, he'd been conceived by natural means after Sri had seduced Stamount Horne, a one-eighth-consanguineous member of the Peixoto family who at that time had been second-in-command of the security service.

Truthfully, Stamount had allowed himself to be seduced. He had almost been Sri's match in intelligence, cunning, and ambition. They would have founded a fine and powerful dynasty, but five months after Sri had allowed herself to conceive Stamount had been killed during a campaign to clear out a troublesome tribe of bandits that had been sabotaging the trans-Andean railway. Sri would always mourn him. She wore on the third finger of her left hand an intricate latticework ring of bone grown from a culture of his osteoblasts, and in honour of his memory had never once cut Berry, who had inherited his father's good looks but little else.

Berry was a cheerful child as long as he was given what he wanted as soon as he asked for it, but his intelligence was no more than average, he was lazy, and lately he had been exhibiting a streak of careless cruelty; after a couple of unfortunate incidents with his playmates, fortunately the children of servants, Sri had decided that he could not be trusted to be left alone with any child smaller than himself. Yet he was always deeply and unconditionally affectionate and loyal to his mother and to his brother, and Sri loved him in turn and was more patient and tolerant with him than with anyone else, knowing that he would always be dependent on her, would always need to be protected from the consequences of his foolish and impulsive nature. He left the pool when she called to him and dutifully trotted over and told her about his visit to one of the city's farms. She let his happy babble wash over her, allowed herself to relax. She was committed now. No turning back, no need to anguish over it.

But later, in bed, with Yamil Cho moving over her, as smoothly muscled as a snake, his skilful tongue and lips and fingers forcing her to bite her lips to keep from crying out, a face flashed in the hot dark behind her eyelids: the doomed young man who had delivered the data needle.

7

"There it is," Newt said.

Elephant was falling around Saturn, closing on Enceladus, and Mimas had just risen past the hazy edge of the gas giant. One window in *Elephant's* memo space showed an enhanced optical view of the *Glory of Gaia's* oval black shell hanging sharp and clear against the heavily cratered surface of the little moon; another showed the radar display. Something small and fast tracked past the Brazilian ship's fat radar echo. Merging with it for a moment, moving past. Macy asked Newt if it was one of the combat singleships.

"Most likely one of the entourage," Newt said. "There are always two or three of our ships keeping a close watch on it."

He pulled back the optical view to reveal two sparks hanging at different levels behind the Brazilian ship.

Macy said, "Are those the same size as *Elephant?*"

"More or less."

"It's a big ship."

"And there are two more coming our way."

"Have you ever done that? Hung around it. Kept watch."

"I might have buzzed it once or twice."

"That won't scare them off."

"Of course it won't. But we have to remind them that plenty of people don't want them here, and we like to keep a close watch on everything they do. So we buzz them. We try to futz their telemetry and radar. Light-bomb them. Just generally annoy them every way we can, and hopefully annoy them and sap their morale. I guess you think it's pretty childish."

"I think that none of you has ever been in a real honest-to-goodness shooting war."

"So when things kick off, I should just hope for the best and sit it out, uh? Or even worse, give in before anything happens, like the folk in Camelot."

"I just hope you aren't harbouring romantic notions about surviving some kind of close encounter with a singleship, coming out a hero. Because you won't."

"Know why I voted against siding with Paris?"

"I don't suppose it was to please me."

"Aside from the fact that Marisa Bassi is a blowhard more interested in his reputation than reality, I know we can't defeat Earth by playing it at its own game. We have to be smarter than that," Newt said. "And you might want to think about this. If there is a war, you're going to need a good place to hide. Because the Brazilians are bound to come looking for you. Maybe then you'll change your mind about sitting it out."

Macy knew that he wanted her to ask him what he was planning, him and his friends here, there, and everywhere in the Saturn System, but she also knew that he was flirting with her, teasing her. Having fun. So she said, "One of the things I learnt in the R&R Corps, no plan survives contact with the enemy."

Newt laughed. "I guess you never had any really good plans."

Enceladus was a bright, white snowball. Its low-relief surface was painted with layers of fine ice crystals that reflected almost all the sunlight that fell on it and were constantly renewed by geysers in the tiger-stripe terrain of its south pole, where pods and leads of liquid water immediately beneath the brittle surface boiled violently when fractures exposed them to the freezing vacuum, driving plumes of ice crystals more than four hundred kilometres into space. Most of this fell back to the moon's surface; the rest escaped its gravity well, going into orbit around Saturn and adding material to the E Ring. Enceladus was just five hundred kilometres in diameter, so small it should have frozen solid billions of years ago, Newt told Macy, but the water was rich in ammonia, which lowered its freezing point by almost a hundred degrees Celsius, and radionuclide decay and tidal stresses provided enough thermal energy to keep it liquid. So there was still plenty of geologic activity on the little moon; as *Elephant* circled toward Baghdad, Newt pointed out patchworks of complex, fractured terrains, compression ridges, smooth, recently resurfaced plains, softened craters crossed by faulting . . .

The domed city came up above the horizon, standing on a lightly cratered plain whose contours were softened by layers of bright frost. And then they were down, and took a bus from the platform spaceport into Baghdad. The city's tent stood on aerogel and fullerene composite foundations fitted inside the low ramparts of a small impact crater, and its interior had been flooded with melt water to create a circular lake with shellfish reefs, kelp forests, mangrove islets and vast rafts of giant water lilies. From green islands at its centre rose a spiky city of skeletal spires scaffolded from fullerene spars, bearing platforms and terraces planted with trees or pieced gardens, studded with capsule houses painted in vibrant colours, knitted together by a web of slender bridges and slides, zip lines and cableways.

Following the instructions she'd been given, Macy led Newt to a café at the base of one of the outermost towers, where he forked up a plateful of vegetable tagine and drank several cups of mint tea as he made calls to various factors, talking up his cargo of handloomed denim cloth and eight varieties of coffee. Later on he'd sit down with one of them and haggle for an hour or two, using stochastic comparisons with similar exchanges recently recorded on the Bourse and laying off favours and promises on future interest in other goods to get the best deal on the spices and pharm yeasts he wanted to take back to Dione. The Outer System's economy was driven by thousands of deals like this, and by trading in kudos, the elaborate system that tracked and indexed everyone's social esteem and contributions to the common good. At bottom, it was more like a game than a serious monetary system. Traders bluffed each other like poker players; some deadlocked deals were even resolved by a throw of dice.

Macy slouched in her sling chair, sucked down sweetened mint tea, and tried not to think too much about why she'd come here. Politics was a game too, and she was painfully aware that she was a naive and inexperienced player who had only a vague idea of the rules. All she could do was declare her hand and play it by ear. Rely on the kindness of strangers.

It was early evening. The chandelier lights dimming, the panes of the city's tent darkening and gradually obscuring the snow-white moonscape outside. Fat, sluggish waves rolled across the lake, under a flexing tessellation of giant water lily pads. Above it, half a dozen flyers were engaged in a kind of aerial ballet, skimming low over the lake, soaring up, twisting around each other like bats under the black sky, under Saturn. Low gravity made human-powered flight possible in habitats and cities on all of Saturn's moons. It was a popular sport; Macy had tried it several times in the Jones-Truex-Bakaleinikoff habitat, gliding from platforms fixed high on one or another of the tent's support struts. On Enceladus, where gravity was so vestigial that human beings weighed no more than ravens or crows on Earth, people flew all the time. They wore wing suits, or like some of the flyers at play above the water had somatic tweaks that gave them membranous folds of skin which stretched from wrists to ankles, and modified their muscle fibres and the oxygen-bearing capacity of their hemoglobin so that they could fly for hours.

Newt finished his business calls, gossiped with a couple of friends, finally took off his spex and told Macy that her mysterious contact was late.

"Not very."

"If they don't turn up, will you tell me what this is all about?"

"They'll turn up."

"When you're done, there are a couple of bars I know you'll like. One right under water, in the middle of a kelp forest," Newt said. "You swim down, come up in this kind of bell of air."

"If you get drunk, how do you swim back?"

"It serves tea. All kinds. You drink tea and nibble this and that and kick back. Watch the fishes through the glass."

"Sounds like fun. What's that?"

A man's voice rose up from somewhere high in the neighbouring tower, an ululant chant floating out into the darkening air, the evening settling all around.

"The call to prayer," Newt said. "You don't have Muslims in Greater Brazil?"

"Sure we do. I've just never met one."

A shadow flickered over the broad terrace as a flyer swooped past, cruciform in a green wingsuit, catching an updraught and beating up and out over the lake.

"This is a very spiritual city," Newt said. "There are Muslims, Christians, Hindu, Jews . . . There's a Buddhist temple in Camelot, Mimas. Some of the people who organised that Permanent Peace Debate in Paris, they're Buddhists, too."

"What were those monks again? The ones who keep the ryokan up in the rimwall of Dido Crater?"

Macy had gone there six months ago with Newt, Pete Bakleinikoff, and Junko and Junpei Asai. In a garden of moss and bamboo they'd soaked in a hot pool carved from a block of siderite, sipping rice wine and nibbling tiny pickled vegetables, talking telescope business, contemplating the stark empty moonscape beyond the ryokan's tent.

"Shinto," Newt said. "Some of the Buddhists are Shinto, too. The people who have Japanese ancestry, anyhow."

"But none of the clan has any particular religion that I've noticed."

"We're filthy rationalists," Newt said. "You were religious, I guess, at one time."

"At one time."

"But not now."

"No."

"What happened? Did you lose it when you ran away and saw what the wide world had to offer?"

"I lost it before I ran away," Macy said. "I guess that's *why* I ran away."

The flyer in the green wingsuit came back toward the terrace, skimming in above the water, swooping up at the last moment to make a neat landing at the far end. Her suit folding around her like a cloak as she ankled toward them, pulling off goggles, shaking black hair loose around her shoulders.

Newt looked at her, looked at Macy, began to laugh.

The flier was Avernus's daughter, Yuli.

Macy and Yuli talked inside a pod with a halflife fur floor and a plexiglass shell, hung high at the edge of a cluster of lighted towers. When Macy started to explain what she wanted to do, Yuli interrupted her, saying, "I understand everything."

"Everything?"

. "It is quite simple. Marisa Bassi wants you to talk about Greater Brazil. About Earth. If you refuse, he will brand you a traitor. A spy. If you agree to be interviewed by one of his stooges, you will be contributing to his endless round of martial propaganda. You believe that we can help you find a way out of this trap. That by talking with my mother, you can answer Marisa Bassi's public challenge without being beholden to him or contributing to his cause."

"I came out here as part of the peace-and-reconciliation effort. To promote understanding between Greater Brazil and the Outer System. I still believe in that, and I'll talk to anyone who wants to listen about Earth. I'll do my best to answer any questions as honestly and fully as I can. But Marisa Bassi only wants to hear about how the great families grab all the wealth and power and oppress everyone else. Horror stories he can use to justify himself."

"Tell me: can we stop the war?"

"No, probably not."

"My mother thinks otherwise. That is why she has made herself into a hostage in Paris. She has set herself up in direct opposition to Marisa Bassi. She is using her kudos and all her contacts here and in Greater Brazil and elsewhere on Earth to try to stop the inevitable. And she believes that because our enemies would very much like to capture her alive, they will not strike at Paris while she is there. We have tried to persuade her that she has overestimated her importance and underestimated their ambition and aggression. And their fear of us, of what we might soon become. She will not listen to us. She thinks we are too pessimistic. But she has agreed to talk with you."

Yuli sat cross-legged on the warm blue fur, slight and slender in her green wingsuit, unbound black hair falling around her heart-shaped face and over her shoulders. Her skin was snow white and her eyes chlorophyll green. She looked about eight, but she was exactly Macy's height, and her green gaze was bold and serious. Coolly analytical. There were rumours that she wasn't Avernus's biological daughter (and if she was that in itself would have been a miracle, given Avernus's great age) but a construct or a clone. Or that she was really much older than she looked but had been cut so that she didn't age. Whatever she was, she was definitely spooky.

"I don't think I can change your mother's mind," Macy said.

"I don't expect you to change her mind. Only she can do that, when she is in full possession of all the facts. And perhaps not even then. But we must try to make sure that she is informed. She quit Earth a century and a half ago. She has tried to keep up, but she knows that there are serious gaps in her knowledge. That's where you can be of great help. My mother would like to hear the truth. Raw, unmediated. She would like you to answer her questions as fully and honestly as you can. Will you do that?"

"Like you said, it's why I came here."

"You can't come to Paris because Marisa Bassi might arrest you. And my mother won't leave Paris. But it isn't a problem," Yuli said, and pulled a pair of tipset gloves from the pouch pocket of her wingsuit. "Put these on. Also your spex."

"You want me to do this right now?"

Yuli laughed, and for a moment looked exactly like an ordinary little girl. "Of course. We guessed what you wanted and decided that we would accept before you asked to meet me. And as you want to tell the truth, you will surely need no preparation."

"It goes out on the net."

"Streamed directly as it happens, raw and unmediated."

"I guess you really did figure out everything I was going to ask you."

"I know that war is inevitable. I know that it will change everything. I don't yet know how. I can only hope that in the long run it will change things for the better. And the best hope for the best outcome is that my mother not only survives but also evades capture. That she comes to her senses and quits Paris before it's too late. We are trying everything in our power to convince her. Even this."

"Do you ever worry that some people might mistake your direct manner for rudeness?"

"The truth should not insult anyone. I am desperate. So are you. We can both help each other. Now, I think you should lie down. And don't try to move your avatar until you have become used to the time delay."

"Where are we meeting, your mother and me?" Macy said, pulling on the tipset gloves.

"One of her gardens," Yuli said, and put on her own spex.

Macy's spex blanked as soon as she lay down, and then the telepresence link meshed. She was lying on warm soft fur, and she was inside an avatar that was standing in front of a transparent wall, looking out across a vast gulf of crystalline air toward a churning smog-yellow tornado spout that dwindled toward a lumpy red-brown cloud layer far below. It was midday. The tiny disc of the sun shone overhead in a sky as blue as Earth's and flecked with wisps of white cloud. A flock of tiny sharp-edged rectangles hung off to one side of the giant tornado.

Macy called up the avatar's virtual control stick and turned from the view to see where she'd ended up. A big square room with transparent walls and a faintly gridded but otherwise transparent floor, the topmost of a stack of floors in a tall, cylindrical building that hung in midair. A giant glass test-tube ringed round top and bottom with transparent bladders and studded with attitude jets. Other avatars stood here and there on this floor and on the floors below, like man-shaped chess pieces poised in the middle of a game. One stirred and walked toward her with a delicate swaying motion, and a voice in her ears said, "I am Avernus. Welcome to Deep Eddy."

Macy introduced herself, asked if this place was real.

"Oh yes. Quite real. We're floating in Saturn's water belt, about three hundred kilometres below the edge of the atmosphere," Avernus said. "Those white clouds are water vapour, and the storm is mostly water vapour, too, a standing vortex driven by a hot spot in the liquid-hydrogen zone far below. It cools as it rises, but it is still much warmer than surrounding atmosphere, and dissipation of heat drives cloud formation, just like a hurricane on Earth. Also, the winds that circle it sweep away the smog created by Saturn's anaerobic chemistry, giving us this splendid view. We can see for about a thousand kilometres in every direction."

Macy asked if the rectangles hanging out in the air were other buildings; Avernus said that it would be easier to show her than to explain.

"We'll go there as soon as we have finished here. The Brazilians tried to investigate this place during that silly stunt when they flew their singleships deep into Saturn. They didn't quite succeed, but I know they will be watching this now, so what better place for our meeting? I no longer have anything to hide. If they want to find out anything about my work, anything at all, all they have to do is ask. This is not a factory for dreadful weapons, or a hiding place for monsters. It has no function at all, except as a place where people can come to contemplate this beautiful world, or to meet. And that's why we are here, of course. To meet, and to talk. To begin with, tell me how you came out here."

"It's kind of a long and complicated story."

"I have plenty of time."

They talked for almost an hour. Macy told Avernus about her escape from the Church of the Divine Regression, her raggle-taggle life in Pittsburgh that had ended when she'd joined the Reclamation and Reconstruction Corps.

Her work in the ruins of Chicago and her promotion after she had saved the life of Fela Fontaine, how she had joined R&R Crew #553, and how she had won a place on a construction crew and gone to Rainbow Bridge, Callisto, by default. Avernus asked many questions. Macy couldn't tell the gene wizard much about politics and the rivalries of the different families, but she tried to answer all the other questions as directly and truthfully as she could.

At last, the gene wizard said, "I promised to show you the rest of Deep Eddy. If you let me take control for just a moment . . ."

There was a kind of blink, and then Macy's viewpoint was hanging above a long rectangular carpet woven from patches of black and deep crimsons, flecked here and there by tiny patches of white. Slow ripples propagated along its length and its edges beaded with the black spheres. Floats. Beyond it, two more rectangles were silhouetted against the blue sky.

"It's a garden," Macy said. "You've made gardens out here!"

"I call them reefs," Avernus said.

The two of them were patched into one of the little robots that cultivated the reefs, and Avernus sent it trawling low over the floating meadow. Apart from their dark pigmentation, designed to maximise collection of sunlight, the plants of the reef looked remarkably like terrestrial plants. There were mossy hummocks, patches of tall thin blades that looked like grasses, dense tangles of ferny branches or black straps metres long. Things that looked a little like sunflowers, with short fleshy stalks topped by dishes that concentrated the feeble sunlight on a silvery node at their centres. Cottony tangles of dew catchers that trapped water vapour when the reef drifted through a water-droplet cloud, irrigating nearby plants in exchange for nutrients drawn off from their roots. More than fifty different species crammed edge to edge, rooted in a mesh saturated with a kind of tar of simple carbonaceous compounds, using photosynthetic energy to transmute the tar into useful organic molecules. Floats with black skins a few nanometres thick absorbed solar energy and heated the pure hydrogen inside, providing just enough lift to stop the reefs from sinking as constant winds spun it around Deep Eddy. When the reefs were swept through one of the streamers that extended from Deep Eddy's margins, they were drenched in methane and ammonium brought down from higher, colder layers of the upper atmosphere. Microbes in the tarry "soil" absorbed these vital nutrients, and so the reefs grew and extended.

"To begin with, they were all seeded with the same mix of species," Avernus said. "They have since found their own different equilibria. We don't interfere in their development, except to try to keep them on station. And to cut one in half, when it grows big enough. We started out with just ten. Twenty years later, there are more than a hundred times that number."

"Nobody lives here."

"Not that I know of."

"You just made it to see if you could make it."

"I'm interested in exploring the endless possibilities of what Per Bak called self-organising criticality. The complex and delicate equilibria that arise from the symbiotic interdependence of chaos and order that we find in sand piles, free markets, and ecosystems. On my best days, I think that I might be aspiring to something like art. But in any case our worlds would be drab and poor places if we created things only for reasons of utility. I enjoy making my gardens, and I hope people can find their own pleasure in them. Only a few people knew about Deep Eddy before we met. Now its address and the protocols for accessing its avatars have been made public. Anyone can visit it. Even people from Earth. *Especially* people from Earth. I want them to understand that there is nothing but my little gardens, and the planet's wild beauty."

Macy saw something that looked very like a centipede move at a glacial pace through the undergrowth, stalking a clutch of fat worms that were grazing on a dense tangle of black straps. She said, "Your gardens are beautiful, too."

"Thank you. And thank you for your candour. I want to think about what you've told me. And then perhaps we can meet in another garden, and talk again."

"I'd like that," Macy said. But the link had already dissolved and she was looking up through the transparent lenses of her spex at the fullerene girders and darkened panes of Baghdad's tent.

Sitting cross-legged by the transparent wall of the capsule, silhouetted against strings of lights wrapped around clustered towers, Yuli said, "I've collated the first rolling polls. Do you want to know what people are saying about you?"

8

Sri's parting with Alder was awkward and oddly formal. For his sake, she tried her best to appear cool and calm and businesslike, and he was quiet and withdrawn, clearly anxious about what lay ahead. The dangers of the immediate future, and the treacherous reefs of power and politics that he would have to navigate on his own in the weeks and months to come.

As soon as Sri left for her meeting with Oscar Finnegan Ramos, Alder would be driven to a business meeting at the offices of Sri's lawyers, where two men were waiting to smuggle him out of the building and take him to a safe house. His appearance would be altered by minor plastic surgery and a couple of simple tweaks that would darken his skin and change the colour of his eyes and then, travelling under a carefully faked identity, he would make his way by road and rail to Buenos Aires, where he would rendezvous with a chartered plane that would fly him to Antarctica. This subterfuge was necessary not only because of the security order that prevented him from travelling anywhere outside Brasília, but also because in a few hours Euclides Peixoto's men would almost certainly want to arrest and question him.

Sri had been gifted the site of the Antarctic research facility by the government of Greater Brazil many years ago, she had spent much of her modest fortune developing it, and last night she had signed everything over to her eldest son. Her legal team had assured her that any challenge in the civil courts to the transfer of title would be thrown out. It was possible that Euclides Peixoto and his friends and allies might attempt to confiscate the facility by adding a rider to some bill passing through the Senate, or try to take control of it by main force. But even if they could find enough allies to win a vote, legal challenges would drag on for years, and it was highly unlikely that they would risk exposing their hand and damaging their reputation by staging an armed assault on private property.

So Alder would be as safe there as anywhere else, and would take charge of the research facility and preserve and protect Sri's work. She planned to return in triumph as soon as possible, of course, but that didn't make it any easier to say goodbye.

"I wish I could take Berry with me," Alder said.

"He'll be much safer with me."

Last night, Berry had been put to sleep and packed into a hibernation coffin that had left the apartment complex in the truck that each evening hauled away trash for recycling.

"I'll miss him," Alder said. "And I'll miss you."

Sri felt a yearning tenderness deep as hunger, wanted to sweep her brave and beautiful son up, crush him to her and never let him go, but she could not allow herself to show any weakness or doubt.

"We will survive this," she said. "We will survive, and we will go on to do great things together."

"I won't let you down."

"I know you won't."

Sri flew directly to Baja California in a helicopter piloted by Yamil Cho. They landed near the control point and Sri followed the path through the dunes to Oscar Finnegan Ramos's hermitage.

A wolf squatted at the point where the path funnelled between steep sand ridges. The nervous systems of the wolves had been Sri's first successful synthetic design. She'd based them on the long, quick-firing fibres of mantid shrimps and the visual information-processing of turkey vultures, and in a tradition several centuries old she'd built a back door, accessed through the olfactory system. Before leaving the helicopter, she'd dabbed onto the web of skin between her thumb and forefinger a spot of oil containing a tailored indole. Now she placed her hand in the slot of the wolf's ID system and indole molecules latched onto tailored receptors in the machine's olfactory bulb, deactivated its internal checksum system, and opened a secret pathway that gave direct access to task priorities. When she touched the signet ring on her little finger to one of the wolf's motion-detecting lenses, the patterned flash of light from the LED in the ring instantly reprogrammed its targeting system.

The wolf rose on strong multi-jointed limbs and shot its weapons systems from their sheaths. Baring its fangs. Sri knew that the machine was under her command, but the display of firepower was still unsettling. She told it to stand down the security system to which it was linked, and then walked on toward the beach, floating on her cold resolve.

Seated on a tree trunk salt-whitened and stripped of bark, Oscar Finnegan Ramos was using a short-bladed horn-handled knife to whittle a whistle from a finger of wood. As usual, he wore only a pair of shorts. He looked up as Sri and the wolf approached, his dark eyes blank as windows in an empty house.

"I thought it would be you," he said. "At least you had the decency to come here yourself. You didn't send one of those psychotic creatures that you keep on the Moon."

"I always wondered if you knew about them."

"Whose idea is this? Yours or my nephew's?"

"It's all mine."

"Once upon a time you were able to take the long view. But you've grown so very impatient in the past few years. It will be your undoing sooner or later."

"This is my only chance to save my life and the lives of my sons."

"You should never take chances in a game as deep and dangerous as this. You should always know exactly what you are doing, why you are doing it, and what the consequences will be. And, forgive me, but you seem very uncertain about what you think you need to do. Are you sure that you have thought it through?"

"I know exactly what I must do. Don't make this hard."

"By which you mean, 'Die quietly. Don't make a scene. Don't make it hard for me.'"

"Will it be hard for the man who gave me the data needle? The man you sacrificed?"

"I must suppose that Euclides manoeuvred you into thinking that killing me was the only way you could save yourself. He has forced you to do what he wants you to do, and made you think that it is entirely your idea." Oscar's smile was gentle and serene. "If you have any doubts, then perhaps it is because you know this, but have not yet thought it through."

"I've thought it all through, most carefully."

Sri felt very calm, but she had to thrust her hands deep in the pockets of her blouson to hide the trembling that she couldn't bring under control. When Oscar pared a final few flakes from the whistle and put it to his lips and blew a long low note, she felt her scalp freezingly contract, wondered if he had just activated some kind of backup security system. But nothing happened. The hot wind still blew, bending the grass on top of the dunes; low waves still unrolled far down the beach, falling from left to right; out to sea, the corvette was silhouetted against the burning water like a cut-out. No doubt people aboard it were watching this encounter, but it didn't matter. The wolf had control of the local security net and the statite thousands of kilometres above, and it had deactivated the ship's weapon systems, too.

Oscar smiled at her. "I have lived a very long time. And anyone who lives even half as long as I knows that you live every day with death. Death is your constant companion. Always just around the corner of your thoughts. Even on a beautiful day like this. I had thought that when it came, I might welcome it. I was wrong," he said, and threw his little knife in a straight hard trajectory at Sri.

The wolf shot the knife out of the air with its chunker, and Oscar tumbled backward off the tree trunk and then he was up and running, weaving this way and that. The wolf went after him, but had trouble getting traction in the soft dry sand. When Oscar jinked around the fencing he'd erected to protect the latest batch of turtle eggs, the wolf ploughed straight into it, poles clattering off its shell, netting wrapping around two of its legs and bringing it to its knees.

"Kill him!" Sri yelled into the hot wind. Frightened and angry, her thoughts cut loose, tumbling. Oscar was swarming up a slope of sand on all fours. Wings of sand cascaded around him.

"Just do it! Kill him!"

The wolf reared up. There was a tremendous flash of light and Oscar was blown sideways out of a fountain of sand and smoke. He rolled down the slope in an untidy bundle and lay still on his back.

Sri called Yamil Cho, then walked up the beach and made sure that her mentor was dead. As she stood up, the helicopter stooped in low over the dunes in a roar of over-driven turbines, landing on the hard pan of sand at the edge of the water.

It took off as soon as Sri climbed inside. Beach and sparkling ocean tilted outside the cabin. The corvette was drawing a wide white wake in sparkling blue water as it turned toward the shore.

"The shuttle?" she said as she fell into the seat beside Yamil Cho.

"Prepped and ready," Yamil Cho said.

"Berry?"

"Already aboard. We'll be there in twenty minutes."

The helicopter was turning end for end as it rose. Sri saw the dunes stretched out along the shore, the dry brown flanks of the mountains. She saw the thin white line of the road, a thread of greasy black smoke rising where the control point had been. The sun shone with serene beneficence in a perfect blue sky. It occurred to her that it might be her last day on Earth.

PART FOUR
TREMORS OF INTENT

I

After Operation Deep Sounding, Cash Baker and the other singleship pilots were kept busy flying so-called science missions around Saturn's moons. They mapped variations in gravity and radio fields and overflew every major city and settlement, probing them with radar and sidescanning microwave arrays, shooting high-resolution videos. Much of the data could have been acquired remotely or by using drones, but the overflights were meant to be deliberately provocative, establishing the dominance of the Brazilian and European joint expedition, testing the capabilities of the Outers' traffic control and defence systems. According to the psy-ops officers, every overflight contributed to an ongoing hydra-headed programme aimed at promoting fear and hostility within the Outer community, destabilising its social and political structures, exacerbating divisions between belligerent factions and those still trying to prevent war, and panicking those communities as yet undecided into declaring neutrality. Most of the pilots were sceptical about the strategy. Luiz Schwarcz said that it was like hitting a hornet's nest with a stick and hoping that at some point they would start stinging each other instead of you. "When it comes down to it, Outers are Outers. They'll stick together against a common enemy despite their differences."

"If you're gonna fight someone, there's no point tweaking his nose or throwing insults," Colly Blanco said. "You just go ahead and do it. Make sure you throw the first punch."

"I'd volunteer for a first strike," Cash said.

"We all would," Luiz said. "It's why we got cut. It's why we're here."

"Instead of which, we're sitting here with targets painted on our asses while psy-ops dicks around with black propaganda and denial-of-service attacks," Colly said. "And if one of the tweaks decides to take a pop at us, we could be in trouble. All they need to do is throw a bunch of high-speed gravel at this damn hulk of a ship. Some of it is bound to get through, do to us like the Martians tried to do to Earth a hundred years ago with the goddamn comet."

"It was an asteroid," Luiz said. "The Chinese used the comet against the Martians. But you have a point."

"Ice, rock, fucking *cow flop*, it don't make no difference when it's coming at you at ten thousand klicks per," Colly said.

Three days later the resupply ship, the *Getúlio Dornelles Vargas*, entered orbit around Mimas. The Pacific Community's ship wasn't far behind, and four more Brazilian ships had just left Earth orbit. Three were headed to Jupiter; the fourth, the *Glory of Gaia*'s sister ship, the *Flower of the Forest*, was bringing General Arvam Peixoto to Saturn.

After the *Getúlio Dornelles Vargas* laid up alongside the *Glory of Gaia*, Cash Baker was summoned to a meeting with two secret service agents who told him that he had been selected for a clandestine mission.

"You can't discuss or disclose anything about this with anyone else," one of the agents said.

"That includes the mapping specialist you're bunking with," the other agent said. "It also means that if you are captured we will deny all knowledge of you."

Cash dealt them his best grin. "Aren't we all friends here? Why don't you just tell me what you have in mind?"

A couple of hours later Cash was buttoned up inside his singleship, watching from several perspectives as a dropshell was loaded into the starboard slot in place of the weapon pod. The dropshell was about the size of a coffin, little more than an open cockpit set in front of an ion motor, with small but powerful solid-fuel boosters slung either side. It reminded Cash of the ancient sports car that his great uncle Jack had lovingly rebuilt, hand-machining replacements for rusted-out components, sculpting new bodywork from resin laminate and painting it with fifteen hand-rubbed coats of cherry red lacquer. Uncle Jack had driven that old car at the head of every neighbourhood parade, Thanksgiving, Homecoming, and Earth Day, until one fine summer's day, exactly a year after his wife had died of rampaging lymphoma, he'd fuelled it up and taken it out, tried to take a bend at more than a hundred and fifty kilometres an hour, and smashed it to smithereens and killed himself.

The passenger arrived at the very last minute, while Cash and the techs were running through final preflight checks. He was already wearing a pressure suit, but the ship's microwave scanner saw right through it, revealing a tall, skinny young man, picking up the asynchronous pulses of microhearts in his femoral and subclavian arteries: he was an Outer. The secret service agents hadn't told Cash word one about his passenger, had told him that all he had to worry about was delivering him to the right spot. But there was no doubt in Cash's mind that he was some kind of turncoat. A spy maybe, or an assassin.

The passenger was zipped into the dropshell and the slot was sealed, Cash finished the checks, and without any ceremony the singleship sank into its cradle and was everted into vacuum. Cash used the attitude jets to get some distance from the *Glory of Gaia* and lit the singleship's fusion motor, quickly outpacing the Outer tug that tried to follow him as he headed inward toward Saturn.

The mission had been scheduled to begin during the final approach of the Pacific Community's big ship; hopefully, Cash's singleship could slip through the system while everyone was distracted. At present, trailed by a little fleet of sightseers, including a Brazilian drone, it seemed to be heading into a wide orbit around Saturn, but a final burn could put it anywhere else; in the pool Colly Blanco had set up, Cash had his money on Titan. Meanwhile, his singleship fell across the ring system, and gained velocity and altered course as it hooked past the edge of Saturn's banded cloud oceans. As he headed outward, Cash risked pulsing the sky with deep radar. There were only a couple of Outer ships crossing the ring system, and neither of them had a chance of intercepting him. But that didn't mean that there might not be a few nasty surprises lurking out there, like spooks in a pitch black basement . . .

He sped past the C Ring, with its gaps and its narrow, broken and braided ringlets, past the opaque sheet of the B Ring, and on out across the wide, star-filled gap of the Cassini Division. The A Ring spread beyond, with his target, Atlas, just outside its sharp edge.

Cash prepped for the drop, ran a final set of checks, and opened the slot where the dropshell rested. Atlas grew from star to speck to lumpy dot. It was a peanut-shaped chunk of water ice with a semi-major axis just forty kilometres across, yet its faint gravity braided complex ripples and clumps and kinks at the edge of the A Ring and kept the Keeler Gap open. Despite its small size, a crew of construction robots had paid it a visit and built no less than three small habitats, powered up and pressurised, waiting for hardy settlers or hermits. Or refugees, if there was a war. There were enough untenanted habitats scattered across Saturn's seventy-odd moons (most of them, like Atlas, irregular chunks of water ice) to house the populations of the system's cities twice over.

The proximity alarm sounded and Cash kicked into hyper-reflexive mode, made a microscopic adjustment to the singleship's trim as Atlas rolled toward him. He glimpsed a string of craters along one edge, the largest containing the emerald glint of a habitat, and the counter rolled back to zero and he fired the rail gun. Atlas flew past beneath the singleship's keel and at the same instant, with the tiny moon shielding the singleship from optical or radar observation, the dropshell shot away with a brief flare of its boosters. It was thoroughly stealthed, and Cash soon lost radar and optical contact as it angled away from the singleship. His best guess was that it was heading on out toward rendezvous with Dione.

Cash turned his bird end for end and began the long burn that would take him back around Saturn to Mimas. A quick check of the telescope showed that, some fourteen million kilometres away, the Pacific Community ship had made its own course correction. It looked as if he was going to be out ten bucks. It wasn't headed for Titan or any of the other inner moons. No, it was rising above Saturn's equatorial plane toward the largest of the flock of tiny, eccentric outer moons, Phoebe.

2

When news about the Pacific Community ship's destination broke across the Saturn System's net, Loc Ifrahim was stuck in a small, rat-infested habitat on Dione, attending the Eighteenth Conference on the Great Leap Up And Out. Delegates had travelled from every inhabited moon of Saturn and Jupiter to talk about interstellar travel, from practical discussions of closed ecosystems, long-term hibernation, and mapping of extrasolar planets by deep-space telescope arrays, to esoteric raps about teleportation, downloading of minds into data storage, and all kinds of theoretical ways to beat the light-speed barrier. Loc was babysitting a scientist from the Air Defence Force, and had orders to reach out to delegates from those cities and settlements still hoping for some kind of reconciliation between Earth and the Outer System, and to do his best to put the fear of God into the rest. As far as he was concerned, things had started badly and had gone rapidly down-hill from there.

The habitat was a fat shaft cored out of Dione's icy regolith east of Ilia Crater, adjacent to the railway that ran all the way around the moon's equator. A broad ramp with chambers and rooms set off it spiralled from top to bottom of the shaft, and its walls were landscaped with grottos, terraces, and cascades of ferns and mosses, waterfalls of lianas and flowering vines. Constructed as a venue for meetings and conferences, the place had no permanent inhabitants; its environmental systems were controlled and maintained by an AI and a crew of robots, and its hanging gardens were groomed by rats cut for intelligence and dexterity.

Loc had been extensively briefed about the people attending the conference, but no one had bothered to warn him about the rats. At the meet-and-greet reception on the first day, he'd been standing off to one side of the crowd, watching the complex social interplay with professional interest, when something had scuttled out from beneath a citrus bush. A black rat fully half a metre from nose to tail and wearing some kind of harness, running straight past his slippers. Loc recoiled, instinctively aimed a kick at the thing, missed, and swung right around in the vestigial gravity and stumbled off-balance into the railing at the edge of the terrace. He would have pitched over and plunged more than a hundred metres to the treetops that filled the bottom of the shaft if one of the Outers hadn't caught hold of his tunic and hauled him back.

It was a loathsome humiliation made worse when Loc saw Macy Minnot amongst the onlookers.

He'd already spotted her name on the list of delegates, had been planning to have a quiet word with her at some point. One on one. Setting the record straight. But now he had to make the best of a bad situation, so he straightened his tunic and ankled over to her and gave her his best smile, saying, "Ms. Minnot. How strange that we should meet again like this."

"This is Loc Ifrahim," Macy Minnot told the man standing beside her. "Mr. Ifrahim, my friend here is Pete Bakaleinikoff."

Loc widened his smile by a notch. "The designer of the telescopic array. And the uncle, I believe, of Newton Jones."

"You've been keeping track of me," Macy Minnot said. "Should I be flattered or frightened?"

"I don't think you should be flattered *or* frightened," Loc said. "If I may be frank, I am not especially interested in you."

"I'm glad to hear it," Macy Minnot said.

Her auburn hair was clipped short, she was wearing a loose white T-shirt printed with a butterfly projection map with continents and oceans that were not Earth's, and she seemed completely at home amongst the Outers, lifting her chin to give Loc that level, defiant look he remembered all too well. No doubt she was relishing his discomfort and was planning to tell everyone that he'd always been a clown, just look at the way she'd managed to get the better of him at Rainbow Bridge. . . . He hadn't realised until that moment quite how much he hated her, and decided then and there to put her in her place.

"Still, if you have a moment to spare," he said, "I would of course love to catch up. Perhaps over a drink or two, to show there are no hard feelings."

"I'm not sure if I should be seen talking with you right now, let alone in private," Macy Minnot said, returning his smile. "People might think I'm consorting with the enemy."

Loc told her that he was fostering trade and cultural links and promoting peace and reconciliation, a thankless task perhaps, but an essential one. He mentioned some of the many new friends he'd made on Mimas, explained that he had come here in the hope of making many more.

"I'm accompanying Colonel Angel Garcia. Perhaps you've heard of him? A very eminent scientist. I'm sure that you and Mr. Bakaleinikoff would enjoy meeting him. And I have no doubt that he would be delighted to hear all about your telescope."

"You friend is free to talk with anyone and everyone," Macy Minnot said. "That's why we're all here."

"I'll tell him that. I can see that you are eager to go about your business, but before I go, perhaps you can tell me," Loc said, struck by sudden inspiration, "if there's any truth in the rumour that Avernus will be attending this conference?"

"What rumour would that be?" Macy Minnot said, her expression suddenly guarded.

Her companion, Pete Bakaleinikoff, said, "She's only ever been to one of the conferences. The first."

"Confidentially, we're most anxious to establish contact with her," Loc said. A complete lie, of course, but Macy Minnot couldn't possibly know that, that was the beauty of the thing. Oh, the fun he was going to have, messing with her head. "As you have talked with her publicly and at length, perhaps you might know of a way of reaching out to her—"

A hand fell on his shoulder, bore down. Loc turned, looked up at a skinny young man whose pale angular face and disordered crest of black hair was familiar from intel reports, and said, "Mr. Jones. A pleasure to meet you at last."

Newton Jones ignored him, saying to Macy Minnot, "Is this scunner who I think he is?"

"He wants me to help him get in touch with Avernus."

"Did you tell him that if he hops on a rail car and runs over to Paris, he'll probably find her there?"

"I was about to tell him that you don't reach out to her; she reaches out to you," Macy Minnot said.

She looked a trifle piqued. Some trouble there, between the maiden and her white knight.

"I have good and important reasons to contact Avernus," Loc told her, but the moment was gone, and so was his enjoyment. "Unfortunately, Marisa Bassi has made it very clear that Brazilians and Europeans are not welcome in Paris, which is why I was hoping she might be here."

"I'm surprised, Mr. Ifrahim. I thought you'd be all for war."

"It won't be the first time you've been mistaken about my motives, Ms. Minnot," Loc said and sketched a bow. "I do hope we can talk later."

And maybe he could try to fake her out without Mr. Newton Jones interfering.

Macy Minnot waited until he had gone past before she called to him.

"I hope you don't have a problem with rats, Mr. Ifrahim. They do all the gardening here, and generally keep the habitat ticking over. They're pretty hard to avoid."

Loc couldn't let her have the last word. "I'm quite able to rise above all kinds of minor annoyance, Ms. Minnot."

The thing was, he really did have a problem with rats. He hated them because they reminded him of his childhood in the shanty town at the edge of the ruins of Caracas. The dingy two-room apartment whose front door opened straight onto the congested street. The ripe smoky stink of the recycling heaps that rose above the crumbling buildings, and the flies that swarmed everywhere in the sticky summer heat, big green flies walking over food and people's faces, swarms of tiny black flies that got in your hair and eyes and nose.

Like all the other kids in the neighbourhood, Loc had earned pocket money by salvaging scraps of rebar and wiring from the heaps, scrambling amongst the monstrous trucks that brought in rubble from the old city, destroyed in an earthquake twenty years ago and now being turned into parkland. Loc had escaped it all after he'd passed the civil-service examinations, had hauled himself up the endless rungs of the diplomatic service by hard work and relentless ambition. But no matter how far he'd risen the smell of burning garbage or the sight of a fly or cockroach or rat could bring memories of his wretched childhood crowding back. Rats had infested the recycling heaps. There had been a bounty on them, a couple of cents for every corpse. Some of the older boys had organised themselves into gangs that hunted them down, but Loc had never taken part. He'd hated rats then, and hated them even more now, and he had plenty of time to reacquaint himself with that visceral revulsion here. The organisers of the convention had stashed him and Colonel Angel Garcia in the worst level of the habitat, just above the hothouse basement that was the engine room of the habitat's ecosystem, where giant banyan trees knitted a dense maze of glossy leaves and branches above a floor of deep, rich mulch, and provided a home for a small army of rats.

As for the conference, the colonel was tedious company, Macy Minnot was avoiding him, and the discussion groups were dismayingly chaotic. No chairman, no formal presentations, no panels of distinguished scholars, just unruly mobs sparring and squabbling around memo spaces. Someone might spin out an idea for a few minutes, then someone else would interrupt and embellish it or demolish it, or start up an entirely new line of argument. More often than not, two or three people would be talking at once, trying to shout each other down. No consensus ever seemed to be reached on anything, everything was in flux, and in any case most of the business of the conference seemed to take place outside the timetabled discussions and workshops; it was not only a talking shop, but also a social event where delegates could meet old friends and make new ones, hike trails laid out in the extensive ice gardens on the surface, get drunk or stoned, get laid. There seemed to be an awful lot of semi-clandestine sex. And because Loc was excluded from the social and sexual *ronde*, he was having a hard time trying to understand just how seriously the Outers took their crackbrained schemes to launch robot probes or even manned ships to various stars, to create new kinds of human beings, to find ways of living forever.

On top of all this, the small contingent of Ghosts attending the conference seemed to have decided to spend most of their time harassing him. Following him about and making loud and provocative remarks about his appearance, jostling him when he stood at the back of one of the discussions, interrupting Colonel Garcia whenever the man tried to speak. Loc was certain that they were responsible for the crude attempt at bugging the room that he and the colonel shared, but when he'd made a complaint to the organisers of the conference he'd been told that they didn't have to power to intervene, and besides, hadn't he heard of a little thing called freedom of expression?

On the third day of the conference, a couple of hours after the Pacific Community ship went into orbit around Phoebe, the Ghosts cornered Loc and started to tell him exactly how they were going to kick everyone from Earth out of the Saturn System. He managed to keep his temper, stalked out of the discussion with the Ghosts jeering at his back, and spent the rest of the day in the squalid little room that he shared with Colonel Garcia, surfing news sites. Here was a fuzzy video of the ship landing, snatched by an Outer tug passing within twenty million kilometres of the little moon. Here was a much sharper picture of the ship sitting in a big basin under a towering cirque of cliffs, taken by one of the telescope arrays that monitored traffic. Small smudges a few pixels in size were circled—people in pressure suits, apparently. As yet there was no comment from the government of the Pacific Community, but there was plenty of chatter across the Outers' news boards. Predictably, Marisa Bassi, the mayor of Paris, Dione, had denounced the landing, and the usual hotheads and firebrands were making a lot of noise, too. Early polls reported a ninety-eight percent disapproval rating.

It wasn't one of the worst scenarios—the Pacific Community hadn't gone into orbit around an inhabited moon, or attacked one of the Outers' cities or settlements, or shot up or captured one of their ships—but it was still pretty damned serious. Yet when Loc placed a call to the embassy in Camelot, Mimas and requested that they charter a ship to take him and Colonel Garcia off Dione, he was told to stay where he was. He was to protect the colonel from any blowback and talk to friendly delegates, reassure them, tell them that the Brazilian and European joint expedition strongly disapproved of the seizure of Phoebe, contrast its good intentions with the Pacific Community's naked aggression.

Loc had no intention whatsoever of putting himself in harm's way. Colonel Garcia could look after himself, and there was no point talking to any Outers, no matter how friendly, until this clusterfuck of a situation had cooled down. So he stayed in the room, following developments on Phoebe and across the Saturn System, until hunger drove him out early in the evening.

He was almost immediately ambushed by one of the Ghosts, a tall leathery woman named Janejean Blanquet, who got right in his face and told him that if Earth thought that it could take over one of their moons, it could fucking well think again.

"Maybe no one happens to be living on that rock, but it's still *our* rock. We'll take it back, little man. You wait and see."

She'd cornered him near the bottom of the ramp that spiralled through the habitat's core, bamboos and a wall of black stone on one side, a drop to the banyan jungle at the base of the habitat on the other. No one else was about, no one Loc could appeal to, no one to witness this latest assault on his dignity. He tried to reason with the woman, smiling his nicest smile, saying that she was threatening the wrong person, that he had nothing to do with the Pacific Community, its ship, or its plans, but she was drunk or stoned, and out for blood.

"We'll kick their asses off that rock and maybe we'll kick *your* ass right here and now if you dare to stick around," the woman said, leaning in to poke a bony finger at Loc's chest. Her pupils were shrunken to pinpricks in her jittery blue eyes; her breath was foully metallic. "You get off of our moons and out of our sky before we blow you away."

Loc tried to slide around her, but she was as quick as a snake, stepping right up to him, poking at him again. He grabbed her wrist and twisted it, she howled and clawed at his eyes, and he drove her backward through a thicket of bamboo, pinned her against the wall. For a moment, caged by rustling stems of bamboo, they stared at each other. Then the woman spat in Loc's face and raked his face from cheek to chin with her filthy nails, and he grabbed hold of her lacquered crest of snow-white hair and slammed her head against the stone wall and did it again and again, until her eyes rolled back and she went limp in his arms.

A wave of revulsion and panic surged through him and he shook her off and pushed backward. The woman fluttered bonelessly to the floor. Loc saw blood and bits of matter on a facet of black stone, blood on the tips of his fingers when he touched his stinging cheek.

All right. None of this was in any way his fault, but there was no way he could explain it, no way he could expect a fair hearing. The only thing he could do was get out, get as far away from here as quickly as possible.

He looked all around, leaned at the rail and squinted up past the thread of braided light pipes strung through the axis of the shaft, listening for any sounds of alarm, then scooped up the Ghost's limp body. She was as light as a bird. The back of her head was slick with blood and looked dished. Blood soaked the neck of her white coveralls. Her eyes were half closed and she was breathing with an irregular rattling snore. Hide her down amongst the roots of the banyans? No, the goddamned rats would find her at once. Loc staggered forward, shuffled up the spiral until he reached one of the little terraced gardens, and dumped her behind a stand of flowering bushes, then called Colonel Garcia and told him to meet him at the room. The man started to protest but Loc cut him off and told him that something had come up: they needed to discuss it privately, and at once.

As he pulled off his spex he caught the ghost of his reflection in a panel of wet black rock: his rakish profile, his wolfish grin. A fat surge of adrenalin was kicking in. Everything seemed a little brighter, more real. He hadn't felt so alive since Rainbow Bridge.

Loc was stuffing his possessions into his crash case when Colonel Garcia came into the room. "This had better be important," he said. "I was in the middle of a very interesting discussion about recreating organisms from pure information."

"I was attacked," Loc said, and gave a quick precis of his version of what had happened. "We can't stay here. They'll lynch us."

"The woman who attacked you—she is dead?"

Colonel Garcia was a small, ugly man with a pot belly. He was staring, slightly pop-eyed, at the scratches on Loc's cheek.

"I don't know," Loc said. "She was still breathing when I left her."

"You left her? Where? If she is badly hurt, we must see to her—"

"It doesn't matter if she lives or dies," Loc said. "They'll lynch us anyway. We have to get out of here. Then we can call for emergency retrieval."

"No."

"No?" Loc stared at the colonel. He couldn't believe what he'd just heard.

"No. Whatever it was that happened between you and this woman, this so-called Ghost, it is not grounds for emergency retrieval. We are guests," Colonel Garcia said primly. "We are here thanks to the generosity of the government of Camelot, who supplied the ship that brought us here, and the organisers of this conference, who invited us. This is what we will do, Mr. Ifrahim. First, you will take me to where you left this poor woman and we will summon medical aid. Then we will inform our hosts about what happened."

Loc laughed. He couldn't help it. It bubbled out of him, a kind of squeaking noise fuelled by disbelief and anger. "You want me to give myself up to the *Outers?*"

"We must do the right thing. We must endeavour to make sure that this does not turn into a serious diplomatic incident. If you are innocent, you have nothing to fear," Colonel Garcia said.

Loc laughed again, and swung his crash case in a wide arc and smashed its hard edge into Colonel Garcia's face. The man squeaked in shock and reeled backward, clutching at his broken nose, and Loc swung the case again, a solid blow to the side of his head. The colonel slid loose-limbed to the floor, blood bubbling in his nostrils, blood running from the triangular gash above his ear. Eyelids fluttering as he tried to focus on Loc.

"You brought this on yourself, you stupid sanctimonious son of a bitch," Loc said. "You were going to get me killed."

"Don't," the colonel said weakly, and tried to raise his hand as Loc slammed the crash case down again.

3

Cash Baker was about a million kilometres out from Mimas and the *Glory of Gaia* when he spotted a brief flare of fusion exhaust dead ahead: a transport moving off at a fast clip. He raised mission control and asked for an update, but although the laser line was tightly focused and strongly encrypted they refused to tell him who was piloting the tug or where it was going. One thing was sure. It wasn't heading out toward Phoebe and the Pacific Community ship: it was heading inward, around Saturn.

One of the Outer ships trailing above and behind the *Glory of Gaia* sidled toward Cash as he approached. A squat tug, lit up with slogans from stem to stern, it launched several waves of tiny drones that fanned out across Cash's trajectory and flared in random bursts of hard white light and radio noise. Cash was in no mood for games. He punched straight past the fireworks display, flipped the singleship end for end and decelerated with pinpoint precision, gliding beneath the great curve of the *Glory of Gaia*'s hull at a little under 0.1 metres per second, lining up with the cradle that slid out like a drawer in a morgue's rack and settling into it with a couple of brisk squirts from his attitude jets.

The two secret service agents were waiting in the hangar and escorted him straight to a cubicle as soon as he'd been unhooked from his bird. They assured him that the status of the mission hadn't changed after the Pacific Community had seized control of Phoebe, but they wouldn't or couldn't tell him anything about the transport. Fizzing with impatience, stinking and itchy in his acceleration suit, Cash spent one of the longest hours of his life going through the flight record line by line, and as soon as the debriefing was over he headed straight to the pilots' mess.

Luiz Schwarcz and Caetano Cavalcanti were playing chess. Cash sat across from them and said, "Maybe you can tell me about the transport that just now ran off full tilt. Did I miss the outbreak of war?"

Luiz moved a pawn one space and said, "You didn't hear?"

"I've been out," Cash said. "Didn't you miss me?"

"There's been an incident," Caetano said.

"On Dione," Luiz said. "Some trouble with a diplomat and the scientist he was escorting."

"Bunch of bullshit," Caetano said as he studied the board.

"The Outers killed the scientist, the diplomat got away, and the transport is going to pick him up," Luiz said.

"I thought we couldn't land on Dione," Cash said. "In case the mad mayor tries to take us out with his famous defence network."

"The guy that needs rescuing is on the run from the Outers," Luiz said. "The only way he can get off Dione is if someone goes in to fetch him off. The transport is carrying a squad of marines in case there's trouble on the ground."

"It's going in without any support?"

"Of course," Luiz said. "We don't want to rile up the Outers any more than we have to. Are you sure you want to do that, C?"

"You bet," Caetano said, and let go of the knight he'd just moved.

"Then you won't mind if I do this," Luiz said, and moved a rook straight down the left-hand side of the board and took a pawn.

"Shit," Caetano said.

"Sounds like a hairy mission," Cash said.

"It's pretty bad," Luiz said. "Before it goes in, the transport is going to have to hang at least one orbit so it can locate and confirm the pick up point. And if the Outers don't take a pop at it then, you can bet they'll be scrambling to get on its tail when it goes in. It's definitely going to have to throw some fancy evasive moves on the way out."

"Who's flying it?"

"That would be Colly."

"The little son of a bitch," Cash said. "How did he get to be so lucky?"

4

Macy was eating dinner with Newt when two Ghosts walked into the refectory. A man and a woman, both dressed in white, faces hardened by grim and determined expressions, they looked around at the tables scattered amongst stands of greenery. Then the woman touched the man's arm, pointed at Macy. Newt started to rise as they came across the room and Macy told him to sit down, she'd handle them.

"If they've come to give you a hard time because of that ship landing on Phoebe, you tell them to go to hell," Newt said.

"I tell you what, I'm going to hear what they have to say for themselves before I decide what to do," Macy said, irritated by his presumption.

The two Ghosts loomed at the table. "Macy Minnot," the man said. "We are here to arrest you for the murders of our friend and colleague Janejean Blanquet, and of Colonel Angel Garcia. Stand up. You are coming with us."

"You have to be kidding," Macy said.

She was too astonished to be afraid or angry, but Newt was giving the man a look of naked aggression.

"On what grounds?" he said. "And more to the point, by what authority?"

"By the authority vested in us by the mayor of Paris, for the defence of Dione and the rest of the Saturn System," the woman said.

"As for the grounds," the man said, raising his voice, speaking loudly for the benefit of everyone in the refectory, "Janejean was left to die after her skull was fractured in a brutal assault. Colonel Garcia was found dead in his room, also brutally assaulted. The diplomat Loc Ifrahim has fled from this habitat. We believe that Macy Minnot aided and abetted him. She will come with us, for questioning."

Macy said as calmly as she could, "If Loc Ifrahim killed these people, I want you to know that I hope that he answers for it. I really do. But you should also know that you're making a bad mistake by thinking that I have anything to do with this, just because of who I am."

"I've been with her all day," Newt said, getting to his feet. "And I can round up at least twenty people who can say the same."

The woman reached behind herself and in a fluid movement pulled out a taser and shot him. He went down at once, twitching and jerking. The man produced a pistol and raised it above his head and shot out a chunk of the ceiling, the noise loud and hard. People dived for cover or sat frozen as a cloud of dust rolled down over them.

"You can walk out with us or we can knock you down and carry you," the man told Macy. "Your choice."

The two Ghosts muscled Macy out of the refectory, up the habitat's spiral walkway, and out through the tunnel to the station, where a rail car was waiting. Four pressure suits lay on the floor at one end of its compartment, next to a long shape wrapped in a sleeping cocoon which Macy supposed was the body of Janejean Blanquet. At the other end of the compartment a floor panel had been removed and a cable snaked out of the hole to the slate resting on the lap of a woman sitting beside it. She was a Ghost too, dressed all in white like her friends, with golden eyes and long hair the colour of tarnished aluminum. As soon as Macy was shoved aboard, the woman poked at her slate, and the doors closed and the rail car accelerated out of the station into the naked moonscape.

Macy sat on one of the low cushions and the man squatted in front of her. "We're not going to kill you. You'll get a fair trial at Paris, even though you don't deserve it. You and Loc Ifrahim."

"Have you taken him prisoner too?"

"Some of my friends have found him. We're on our way to pick him up."

"I guess that's why this car is heading east, away from Paris."

The man smiled, revealing even black ridges instead of teeth. "Don't worry. We'll get there eventually."

"Not if my friends catch up with you first."

"You and your friends are living fossils. You're the past from which we're rising," the man said.

"Tell me something. Was it your idea to kidnap me, or was it Marisa Bassi's?"

"Was it your idea to kill poor Janejean, or Loc Ifrahim's?" the man shot back.

Macy met his hard stare, but didn't see any point in telling him again that she'd had nothing to do with the woman's death.

"That's what I thought," the man said.

He stood up and wandered over to the woman with the slate, who told him, "It will take forty minutes at full speed. It's going to be tight."

"Make it less. Let's see how fast this thing can really go."

The three Ghosts spread their equipment across the floor, squatting there like grasshoppers, knees up by their ears, as they checked each piece. The man saw Macy staring, aimed his pistol at her, laughed when she looked away. The Ghosts had taken her spex. No one knew where she was; she had no way of calling anyone for help. If she was going to get out of this, she would have to figure out how to do it by herself. One thing she knew, she wasn't going to get any kind of fair trial. Marisa Bassi was no doubt planning a carnival of anti-Brazilian propaganda starring herself and Loc Ifrahim. She'd tweaked his nose by siding with the peaceniks and talking publicly with Avernus, and now he was going to get his revenge.

The rail car hurtled along the elevated railway. It was one of several hundred that travelled endlessly along a superconducting magnetic track powered by geothermal bores tapping into residual heat deep in Dione's core and wrapped around the moon's equator, a great circle three and a half thousand kilometres long. Right now the rail car was running parallel to sheer slopes broken by abrupt scarps and spattered with small impact craters, one of the long ridges created by compression faulting when Dione's interior had cooled. Saturn hung low in the black sky, sinking toward the western horizon as they sped east, toward the hemisphere that permanently faced away from the gas giant.

At last the Ghosts packed up their equipment, fastened themselves into their pressure suits, and ordered Macy to climb into the spare. It was a child's suit, and a bad fit. She had brought her customised suit to the conference but it had been left behind when she'd been kidnapped.

"I won't be able to walk far in this," Macy said, as one of the Ghosts helped her to adjust the joints.

"You won't need to walk," the Ghost said.

The rail car glided to a halt. The Ghosts locked their helmets over their heads and the man casually pointed his pistol at Macy as one of the women checked the seals of her suit and her helmet; then the door slid open and air puffed out into black freezing vacuum. Macy stepped out of the rail car onto a narrow walkway but ignored the man's order to start climbing down the rungs set in one of the legs of the nearest of the A-frame pylons that supported the track. When he moved toward her she turned and grabbed hold of his arm and pulled him backward. They fell four metres with swooning slowness and she was able to jerk his pistol from his grasp before they hit the ground with a thump much harder than she had expected. She kicked away and pointed the pistol at the man's faceplate and told the two women, framed in the doorway of the rail car above them, that she'd shoot him if they didn't drop their weapons right away.

"I don't think you will," the man said. He started to push to his knees, froze when Macy put a round in the ground right in front of him.

"The next one will go straight through your helmet," she said. "I swear."

"That's enough," someone else said, and half a dozen figures riding trikes appeared against the black sky above the crest of the ridge that ran parallel to the elevated railway track, all of them aiming a variety of weapons at Macy.

She looked at them, then tossed the pistol to one side. A woman laughed as the people on top of the ridge drove down the shallow slope. One of them swung off its trike, stooped over Macy, and pulled her up by her wrist.

Macy recognised the face inside the fishbowl helmet centimetres from her own. It was Sada Selene, the refusenik who had helped her escape from East of Eden.

The Ghosts carried Janejean Blanquet's body down from the rail car with solemn and reverential care, lashed it to the loadbed of one of their trikes, wheeled around, and took off and quickly left the stranded rail car far behind. Macy rode beside Sada, bouncing along in the middle of the pack as they followed the railway east for a few kilometres before turning away and climbing a long slope that, paved with giant irregular polygons and smoothed by billions of years of infalling dust and micrometeorite erosion, rose in a gentle grade toward a narrow gap pinched between low, rounded bluffs—the scar of an impact that had hit the top of the ridge at a glancing angle.

Macy was used to seeing moonscapes mediated by her pressure suit's AI: geographical features tagged, contours limned, deep black shadows softened by microwave radar, a fully zoomable ability that allowed her to examine distant objects in immediate close-up. But the AI in the pressure suit she'd been given had been hacked, and without its interpolations everything looked bare and bleak and nakedly hostile. She remembered one of the ancient hymns that the members of the Church of the Divine Regression had sung to praise the God who had hidden His secrets in the landscapes of pi. This one sung only at Christmas. *Earth stood hard as iron, water like a stone.*

Her suit phone had been hacked, too, leaving only a single short-range channel. As they sped along, Sada told her that everything was going according to plan. When Macy asked her what the plan was, one of the other Ghosts, a man, told her that she'd see soon enough and several of the others laughed. So Macy changed the subject, asked Sada how she'd fallen in with the Ghosts. The girl explained that she'd always been a physics junkie and maths geek, that she had become interested in the Ghosts after she'd come across requests for proofs of novel assertions in special relativity they had posted on physics boards. While working on one of the assertions she had uncovered a hidden cipher that, when she'd cracked it, had yielded an encryption key that allowed her to communicate directly with Levi, the leader of the

Ghosts. Finding and cracking the cipher had been an initiation test: she had passed; she had been led into deeper mysteries. Soon afterward, she'd begun to plan her escape. She'd been too young to leave East of Eden without the permission of her parents, but when Macy had asked for her help she'd seized the chance to hitch a ride to the Saturn System.

"And I thought you helped me because we were friends," Macy said ruefully.

"We were. We are," Sada said. "Although I think you made a bad mistake, Macy, when you posted that conversation with Avernus on the net. It made you look as if you were siding with the appeasers."

"I thought it made it clear that I think that war is inevitable," Macy said.

"It made it clear that you think we're going to lose," someone said.

"I don't think we can defeat an overwhelmingly superior force, if that's what you mean."

"We'll win," Sada said cheerfully. "We'll drive our enemies back to Earth and take charge of human destiny. You are riding with people who will never die."

"Is that written in the stars?" Macy said, and immediately regretted it.

Silence hummed in her ears. After a moment, someone laughed.

Sada said patiently, "It's a basic principle of general relativity that anything travelling faster than light violates causality. It follows a closed time-like curve. It's a snake that eats its own tail. Any faster-than-light machine is also a time machine, and that means that signals can be sent from some future event into its own past. So what we know about the future is as real and true as physics."

This was at the heart of the Ghosts' creed. Levi, their reclusive leader, claimed that he received messages from his future self, who had travelled faster than light to an Earth-like planet orbiting the star beta-Hydri and was transmitting past-directed signals to a time before he had set out. According to Levi, the messages he received were necessarily vague, because his future self did not want to unmake his own history, erase himself by switching the universe onto a different track. But the fact that he could receive them at all was proof that in the future he and his disciples would gain access to technology that permitted faster-than-light travel, and use it to colonise the stars. They were the chosen. As long as they followed the correct path, they would complete the closed timelike curve and fulfil their destiny.

Macy thought that people who'd convinced themselves that they wouldn't ever die were likely to get themselves killed sooner rather than later, but she kept her opinions to herself. She knew from bitter experience, from being raised inside her mother's church, that there was no point arguing with Sada, that the young woman's belief system was as hermetic as the closed timelike curves at its heart. Besides, Sada had once been a good friend, even if her motivations turned out to be more than a little suspect, and Macy hoped that she could use whatever was left of that friendship to help her survive.

The little party drove through the gap at the top of the ridge into a jumbled boulder field where chunks of ice of every size, some as big as houses, all of them capped with black dust and sculpted by micrometeorite erosion into smooth shapes, sat on a shatterground several kilometres across and cut with forking crevasses that sloped downward and ended at a sudden drop, the edge of a low cliff. The trikes stopped and everyone climbed off. Beyond, a lightly cratered plain stretched north and east.

Sada stood shoulder to shoulder beside Macy and pointed to a bowl-shaped crater halfway to the horizon. "Just inside the rim, in the wedge of shadow," she said. "You see it?"

"No."

"It's blazing away in infrared."

"I can't see in infrared. Someone hacked the AI in this piece-of-shit suit."

"Trust me, it's right there in plain sight. Just over six klicks away."

"*What's* there?"

"The rolligon."

"The one that Loc Ifrahim stole?"

"What else?"

Around them, Ghosts were busy about their trikes, unpacking equipment. What looked like rocket-propelled grenades, needle-nosed metre-long tubes painted yellow and black, with attitude jets set around their main thrusters. Fat shoulder-launchers with underslung grips and flip-up ranging sights.

Macy had a freezing sense of dismay. "You want to *kill* him? What kind of justice is that?"

Several kinds of laughter rang in her ears.

"He's bait," a man said.

"The enemy have sent a ship to rescue him," a woman said. "We're going to shoot it down."

"We're going to show them who owns this sky," another woman said.

"You're going to witness the first shot in the war," Sada said, sounding happy and excited.

The Ghosts loaded four missiles into four shoulder-launchers, checked guidance systems, unfolded and aimed a microwave radar dish at the western quadrant of the sky. Macy stood to one side of their businesslike bustle, elbows and knees chafed by her ill-fitting suit, her right foot slowly freezing because of a glitch in the suit's thermal management system. She turned this way and that, scanning the boulder field and the shallow slopes that rose on either side of it for possible escape routes. She was pretty sure that the Ghosts would not only fail to shoot down the rescue ship but would also make themselves a target for its counterattack. When that happened, she intended to try to put as much distance between them and herself as quickly as possible, although she was bleakly aware that she didn't stand much of a chance. She was being watched by Sada and the man with the pistol, and any attack would be over in a couple of seconds. And even if she somehow managed to get away, she had less than six hours of air—and a very long hike back to the railway . . .

It happened with almost no warning, and very quickly. A stir amongst the Ghosts, someone shouting something about a bogey at eight o'clock high, four of them stepping forward and raising shoulder-launchers in the same direction. The missiles spurted away one after the other, thrusters igniting as they sped out above the plain, stars dwindling into the black sky. Macy, following their track, spotted another star drifting high in the west, and then the entire plain lit up with a soundless flash like sheet lightning that tore the sky in half. Something was falling and on fire—it had to be the rescue ship, stricken, slanting eastward, slamming down somewhere beyond the horizon.

A white-hot plume climbed into the sky and everything around Macy instantly gained a sharp shadow. Then a shock wave raced across the plain, throwing up an expanding wall of dust. The ground heaved and Macy sat down hard as her feet flew out from beneath her. Several of the Ghosts fell down too, and all around rocks and small boulders which had stood for two or three billion years where they had last fallen were running down gentle slopes toward the edge of the cliff. There was a moment of quiet, and then the first wave of ejecta from the impact slammed down.

The rescue ship had crashed into the surface of Dione at a steep angle, smashing a new crater into the icy regolith. Most of the debris from the ship was thrown more or less straight up, but chunks of ejecta excavated by the impact flew outward in every direction, describing long curves in vacuum and low gravity. All around Macy, flying shrapnel knocked plumes of dust and shards from boulders or struck the ground at shallow angles and spent their velocity in loosely cemented dust and ice gravel. A chunk of ice smashed into one of the trikes and sent it tumbling end over end across the boulder field. Two of the Ghosts were killed where they stood; another took off in great loping strides and was struck down and vanished in a plume of dust.

Macy had been under fire before. Instinct kicked in: she pushed up from the ground and flung herself toward the black shadow beneath a large undercut boulder. She was almost there when Sada smashed into her and they both flew sideways, sliding down a short slope that funnelled toward one end of a crevasse. Macy used her boot heels as brakes, ploughed to a halt in a shroud of dust, and grabbed hold of Sada's shoulder harness as she went past. She lay still for a moment, trying to get her breath. High above, fugitive stars glittered in the black sky—sunlight reflected from pieces of the ship thrown up by the impact and turning over and over as they fell back, everything large and small falling at exactly the same rate, a perfect demonstration of Galileo's famous law. An attitude motor was still on fire as it tumbled down, a chalice of burning fuel that struck a ridge, flamed out, and sent a ring of secondary debris scything outward. Then things were falling all around, a constant random rain of brief and eerily silent explosions. Macy rolled sideways past Sada and dropped over the edge of the crevasse.

She floated down a short distance, struck a steep slope with a blow that shivered her entire body inside the pressure suit, and used the friction of her gloved fingertips to slow herself, gliding down a long way to the bottom. Screams and shouts were ripping through the short-range channel and she switched it off. In the sudden silence, she became aware of her harsh breathing, the quick surf of her pulse in her ears.

Although sunlight burned along the edges of the crevasse it was pitch black at the bottom because there was no air to refract the light, but the darkness was no hiding place because the Ghosts were equipped with infrared vision and Macy's suit was not perfectly insulated. And she knew that its small bubble of heat and air could not sustain her forever. There was plenty of power in its batteries, but in a little over five hours she would exhaust its air supply. If she was going to escape she had to get moving, right now.

She risked blinking the suit's lamp at its lowest setting, saw a wandering floor with walls bulging out above. She walked as far as she could, groping her way in the dark to the far end of the crevasse. It was easy to scramble up it in the vestigial gravity. She clung at the lip, blinking in the wash of weak sunlight. Everything around her was as still as a black and white photograph.

As she pushed up over the lip of the crevasse someone stepped out of the deep shadow cast by a big boulder twenty metres away and aimed a crossbow at her with one hand and tapped the side of its helmet with the other.

Macy switched the radio on.

"You're coming with us," Sada said.

"I don't suppose there's any point asking you to pretend you didn't find me."

"Turn around and walk west," Sada said. "The rolligon's on the move. We have to catch up with it before people come to find out what happened here."

"I can see that Loc Ifrahim might be useful to you, Sada, but I'm no one special. And I didn't have anything to do with your friend's death."

"I don't suppose you did. But we've been asked to bring you back with us all the same."

"You can save yourself a lot of trouble by telling Marisa Bassi right now that I won't help him."

"You'll be able to tell him yourself soon enough," Sada said.

5

The spy had been trained to expect and to deal with every kind of trouble, from routine identity checks to hostile interrogations. But at the end of the journey that had taken him halfway around Dione, from the spot in the badlands of Padua Linea where he had landed the dropshell to the city of Paris, he simply swung down from the robot tractor on which he'd hitched a lift, loped through the glare and bustle of the freight yards to the nearest airlock. He cycled through, stripped off his pressure suit and folded it into its carry bag, slung the carry bag over one shoulder, and walked straight out onto a quiet industrial street.

When he phoned the social services AI, it accepted without demur that he was Ken Shintaro, twenty-two years old, born in Rainbow Bridge, Callisto and currently on a wanderjahr that had just brought him to the Saturn System. After they achieved majority at age fifteen many young Outers spent a year or two travelling. They hitched rides between different moons—by custom, every ship had to accept at least one passenger on every journey. They worked in menial jobs, sampled different cities, different cultures. Most returned home; some settled in their adopted cities; a few never settled at all, and kept travelling. As for his identity, a demon had infiltrated the Jupiter System's net several years ago and set up a tranche of false identities, waiting to be used like clothes hanging in a closet. Any person or AI with the appropriate authority could access Ken Shintaro's medical and genetic records, his commonplace educational and employment record, his unexceptional level of karma. Everyone else could check out his bio, patched together from samplings of the bios of ten thousand real Outers. A fake life authentic in every detail. The gene markers, fingerprints and iris records used for identification were his own; identical to his brothers; identical to all the ghost identities planted in the net.

Ken Shintaro was given subsistence credit, allocated a one-room apartment in an old block near the industrial zone, and offered a selection of menial jobs. He chose the first on the list—general labourer in one of the farm tubes—checked into his tiny apartment, and stripped off his funky suit-liner and took a long shower, wearing a facemask while he stood under a nozzle that shot streams of water over him, and the gridded floor sucked the water away. He'd used a shower like this on the Moon, but the water behaved differently in Dione's much lower gravity, clinging to his skin like a thick gel.

After the shower, he shaved the face he'd been given: Ken Shintaro's face. Rounder than the faces of his brothers, the nose broader and flatter, the skin sallow, a spiky crest of blond hair. But his eyes were unchanged, and so were his teeth. He ran the tip of his tongue over that familiar terrain of peaks and steps now, and spent a little time walking up and down in his room, testing the thin hard mattress in the sleeping niche, unfolding the table and folding it back. Convincing himself of its reality, of the reality of the city that lay open to him. He had been training for this mission all his life, and now he was here, and everything was at once familiar and strange, and it was time to get to work.

He selected from an array of innocuous messages one that confirmed he had arrived in the city safely and on schedule, and mailed it to a blind account that was being monitored by the intelligence unit in the embassy in Camelot, Mimas. There was a message waiting for him, equally innocuous, a brief video of children splashing in the shallows of a swimming pond from which his spex extracted and decrypted hidden text. He had been tasked with a new secondary mission: to locate and, if possible, facilitate the extraction of two people kidnapped by agents working for Marisa Bassi and who, it was believed, were being held somewhere in or near Paris. He committed their details to memory, deleted all traces of the message.

The demon which had set up the fake IDs had also set up accounts for various small amounts of credit and kudos under various names. He used one of these to purchase the supplies he needed: common chemicals, the kind of equipment used by many Parisians to brew their own varieties of wine and beer. He established fermenters full of nutrient broth in a disused access tunnel, seeded them with ordinary yeast, and returned three days later, when the yeast cultures had thickened, and added microdots containing phage virus that had been hidden under his toenails. The phage infected and transformed the yeast cells into chemical factories. One culture metabolised urea and produced a simple but powerful plastic explosive. Two more pumped out virus particles. A fourth produced ordinary wine. He freeze-dried the two varieties of virus suspension. He used the plastic explosive to build small but effective bombs that he stashed in hiding places in various parts of the city, ready for emplacement. He bottled the wine and set the bottles on a shelf in his room, in case anyone should think to check why he had purchased brewing equipment. Then he scrupulously cleaned and sterilised the fermenters and packed them away.

All this took a week of hard work. And as Ken Shintaro, he had to work for six hours every other day in the farm tubes, too. But there was no time for rest because he had a fixed deadline: the arrival in the Saturn System of the *Flower of the Forest*, already on its way from Earth.

He'd downloaded several demons into the city's net the day after he'd arrived. Now they began to make themselves known. The bourse on which citizens traded goods and karma fell over several times. Traffic on the net slowed to a crawl at random intervals as demons consumed much of its processing power with vast, futile calculations. There were problems with power distribution. Temporary brownouts, and then a rolling blackout that spent most of one day migrating from neighbourhood to neighbourhood.

The city began to realise that it was under attack. The mayor appealed for calm and vigilance. Like all recent arrivals, Ken Shintaro was interviewed by a peace officer, but his cover story was armour-plated.

Ken Shintaro liked to walk around the city. He visited many apartment blocks and public buildings. He loitered in the park near the compound where Avernus and her crew lived. He saw Avernus several times, and once managed to get inside the compound by volunteering to help unload a pallet of supplies. After that, he went by the compound every day. He took long hikes outside, too. He walked through the vacuum organism farms. He watched ships arrive and depart at the spaceport. He visited several shelters within a day's journey of the city, often staying the night before returning.

There were several cafés and bars and saunas frequented by Outers on wanderjahr, places where they could swap stories, gossip, and exchange information about jobs and free rides, but Ken Shintaro kept himself to himself. He was affable, yet somewhat remote. A quiet, studious, serious man. He worked hard at the farm, and was scrupulous about doing his share of the small maintenance tasks for which the residents of the apartment building were responsible.

This was how he first met Zi Lei, although at the time he didn't really take much notice of her. They were both members of a team of six residents who'd been given the job of changing the dust collectors in the block's central air plant, which involved putting on hooded coveralls and masks, hauling out the hoppers at the base of the plant's cyclone shaft and scooping the matted dust into bags for composting, replacing the hoppers, and then vacuuming the workspace. Afterward, Ken Shintaro shared tea with the others, listened to them gossip for a little while, and then excused himself. Two days later he ran into Zi Lei again, at the Permanent Peace Debate.

This had started out as an ordinary public forum set up by a small group of citizens to criticise and counter the flamboyantly belligerent speeches and tactics of Paris's mayor, Marisa Bassi, and develop and promote alternatives to his policies. It had been running continuously ever since. Twenty-four hours a day, seven days a week. Anyone could take to the platform and speak until a majority of the audience decided that he or she had spoken for long enough. Approval was signalled by silence, more or less, although most of the time at least half the audience seemed to be paying no attention to the speakers, engaging instead in private conversations and arguments, distribution of donated food or self-published pamphlets (Paris had reinvented the printing press, newspapers, and books), or zoning out in some private virtual nirvana. Disapproval began with jeers and slow handclapping that spread from those who had actually been listening to the speaker to the rest of the audience, who stopped whatever it was they had been doing to express their dislike for someone to whom, until then, they had paid no attention. Embattled speakers who refused to give way were subjected to mock arrest by the debate's volunteer peace officers, dragged from the stage, and ejected from the building. Sometimes the peace officers had to do this several times in succession, when the ejected speaker ran around to another entrance and attempted to regain the stage.

Approval and disapproval seemed to be dispensed at random. Some speakers were jeered as soon as they stepped onto the stage; an old man who spoke in an invented language was given twenty minutes of reverential silence. And anyone could interrupt the speaker with a question or comment at any time, and it wasn't unusual for an interruption to last far longer than any speech.

Ken Shintaro discovered the Permanent Peace Debate while following the man who was its *bête noire*. He'd spotted Marisa Bassi in one of the green markets, and felt something like a *coup de foudre*. He knew all about the mayor of Paris from his training sessions, had watched hours of footage of his speeches and had studied a dramatised biography, but seeing him in the flesh for the first time was still a shock. He watched from a parallel aisle as the man moved through the market at the centre of an eager crowd, acknowledging jeers and cheers with the same good humour, shaking hands with stall-holders, accepting every offer to taste samples of cheese or slices of fruit, sip little cups of coffee or juice, stopping to listen to anyone who wanted to talk to him. At last he disengaged himself from the hustle and bustle of the market and, trailing half a dozen aides, crossed a park and entered a tunnel in a high curved wall that led down to the base of an amphitheatre.

Ken Shintaro slipped in behind him. People were thinly scattered amongst dimly lit tiers of sling nets that encircled and rose up above the circular stage. A few people clapped as Marisa Bassi made his entrance, others stood up and cupped their hands to their mouths and booed, but most paid him no heed. Some were talking in small groups or studying slates, some seemed to be asleep, and the rest were watching the man who, shuffling in slow circles through the spotlights that knit across the stage, was talking in a tired, hoarse voice about lost dreams of utopia, tears swelling in his eyes and slowly running down his cheeks, sparkling in his grey beard. His amplified voice echoed under the high roof, mixing with the aviary chatter of the audience.

Marisa Bassi was telling the people around him that he hadn't come to speak, just to listen: he liked to take the temperature of the debate every now and then. Yes, just like a doctor—why not? He had the health of the city always at the front of his mind. Someone asked him when the sabotage to the net would be fixed and he said that he had his best people working on the problem, but their enemy was very subtle.

"I know you," someone told Ken Shintaro.

His heart jolted and he turned to see a woman standing at his elbow. She was exactly his height, fine-boned and very slender. Black hair cut straight across her forehead. As her restless gaze moved over his face, he thought of the chickens someone kept in the apartment block's communal gardens, pecking at dirt, and then he recognised the woman. She lived in the apart-

288

ment block too; they had worked together on the air-plant detail; her name was Zi Lei.

He manufactured a smile and asked her about the theatre, and she began a long explanation about the Permanent Peace Debate, leaning close to him because noise was rising from the tiers of sling nets as people started to shout at the man on the stage.

"You tell me something useful!" the man shouted back. He stood with his hands on his hips, slowly turning in a circle, his face shining in the spotlit glare. "You tell me one thing we can do that is useful! None of you know anything!"

"He is angry because he can't win their hearts," the woman, Zi Lei, said. "Anger is bad. Like black air."

He asked Zi Lei what people were trying to do here. He was interested because Marisa Bassi was clearly interested, standing with his arms folded across his chest, watching as the man shouted at the audience and the audience shouted back. After a few moments, the mayor said something to the very tall woman next to him, something that made her tip back her head and laugh loudly.

Zi Lei said something about the communal mind, many of her words lost in the full-blooded baying of the audience. The man in the spotlight threw up his hands and walked off the stage and sat down, and Zi Lei darted forward and leapt to the centre of the stage. Ken Shintaro wondered if he was supposed to follow her. No. He stayed where he was, watching as the jeers and shouts of the crowd died away. A tiny drone floated down, amplifying Zi Lei's voice as she said that there were too many bad vibrations in the theatre and nothing could be done until they were cancelled. Someone started to object but several young men and women near the stage stood up and called for quiet.

Zi Lei stood still in the crossing beams of the spotlights. Her skinny chest rose under her black vest as she took a deep breath and she locked her hands together at her throat and let out a kind of pulsing hum, *ohmmmmmm-ohmmmmmm*, taking in a breath with each *oh*, the hum continuous, machine-like, and now members of the audience were humming too, a great engine of sound that continued for more than two minutes before people began to clap. Zi Lei stopped abruptly, bowed, and walked off the stage, passing Ken Shintaro without looking at him.

He followed her outside, curious and excited. He didn't understand what had happened but felt that it was important. Something that he hadn't been briefed about. A discovery of his own. When he caught up with her and asked her what the humming meant, she pulled a folded sheet of paper from a pouch slung on her hip and thrust it at him, crumpling it against his chest. As soon as he took it from her she darted away, crossing the plaza in three bounding leaps and disappearing between the stalls of the green market, gone.

The sheet of paper was densely printed on both sides. There were many exclamation marks. Some words were printed in capital letters or in red or yellow ink. He puzzled his way through it several times. It seemed that wise aliens were watching humanity but were repelled by the disharmony in the universal vibrations that pervaded the Solar System. If these could be tuned correctly, then the aliens, who were called the Edda, would make themselves known. Then they would uplift humanity into a new state of grace.

A search of the net yielded copious amounts of material that Zi Lei had posted about the Edda, as well as a journal detailing her reactions and feelings to the messages she claimed to have received, and comments from people who appeared to treat the whole thing as a piece of fiction, a work of art. He knew from his extensive briefings that Paris was famous for its artists, storytellers, and theatre, and he supposed that Zi Lei's tracts about the Edda and her journal were part of some kind of elaborate fiction, and that her performance at the Permanent Peace Debate had been something to do with it too— although the way she had briefly united the audience was, as far as he was concerned, strange and frightening. Suppose there was some kind of harmonic that could tune peoples' minds, make them think as one, like the drills of the last days of his training . . .

Ken Shintaro had to work at the farm the next day. There was much to do. Three greenhouses were full of dying crop plants that had to be ripped out and dumped outside in freezing vacuum as a precaution against the spread of disease. Engineers were taking samples from every microalgal monoculture, too; oxygen production was down eight percent. He overheard two of the engineers discussing the problem. One of them said that it was even worse in Xamba, Rhea, where they'd had to switch over to electrolysis of water to supply oxygen; the other said that on Tethys, both Athens and Spartica had lost their dole-yeast cultures.

His brothers at work, softening targets for the final assault.

When he returned to his room he found another copy of Zi Lei's text folded in half at the foot of the door, weighted by a teardrop of heavy transparent plastic. A message had been written across the crowded print in red block capitals: *Are you one of us?*

The next day, she came up to him and asked him if he had read her exegesis. It took him a moment to realise that she meant the pamphlet; she was already hurrying on, breathless and choppy as her prose, explaining that she had first met the Edda in dreams, and now she saw their agents here and there.

"I thought at first you might be one of them. I thought you might be a spy."

For a moment, he felt a jolting convulsion in his chest. It was as if Zi Lei could see right into his skull. See his secret self. Then he realised that she meant the Edda, and calm rolled down from the top of his head and he said, "I'm a visitor. I was born in Rainbow Bridge and I am on a wanderjahr."

"I know. I looked you up," Zi Lei said. She was smiling, showing small teeth white as grains of rice.

They were standing in the park near Avernus's compound. A few people stood in front of the entrance of the square building, brandishing laser pens that branded glowing slogans in the air. *Help us in our hour of need. A plague on the houses of Earth. Peace is not the answer.* They wanted Avernus to join the war effort and create weapons. *Give us guns, not flowers.*

Zi Lei asked again if she had read her exegesis; and he said truthfully that he had read it several times but didn't really understand it.

"It's all there, if you read it properly," Zi Lei said, and added that she had work to do, and walked away.

He didn't see her for two days, and he missed her. Not as much as he missed the familiar company of his brothers, the routine and order of his childhood, but with the same kind of sweet ache, and his heart lifted when he found a mango outside his door and a folded sheet of paper underneath it with a scrawled note. *You look tired. This will help.*

He saw her that evening, at the Permanent Peace Debate. He sat beside her but she didn't speak to him for a long time, frowning with concentration while three women on the stage discussed a text that hung in the air, taking suggestions from the audience, modifying it. It was some kind of declaration of peaceful intent. At last Zi Lei shuddered all over, said that she had been trying to smooth out the harmonics but it was no good, something was resisting her, and she stood up and walked out.

Ken Shintaro hurried after her, found her sitting on a bench at the far side of the plaza outside. She was very pale, and her hand trembled as she wincingly cupped her forehead. "It is such hard work," she said.

"Let me help you," he said.

He bought her a bowl of noodles. He told her how much he had enjoyed the mango. She didn't say anything for a while, stirring with her chopsticks the noodles coiled in the bath of rich oil-flecked broth. He felt a pleasurable tenderness, watching her. Remembering how he had looked after his brothers when they had fallen ill or had been hurt in the gymnasium, how they had helped him. He urged her to drink some of the broth, smiled when she managed a few mouthfuls and declared that she felt a little better.

"It is such hard work," Zi Lei said. "But it is very important. Only I can stop the war, you see."

He listened patiently to her monologue about resolving tangled harmonies, and the fleet of beautiful ships waiting deep inside Saturn, waiting for humanity to prove itself worthy of joining the great Galactic civilisation.

"I have been shown secret visions in my dreams. I have sworn to use this secret knowledge for the good of all humankind. It is hard, very hard, but I will do it."

"I have secrets too."

He just blurted it out. And yet he wasn't horrified or shocked by the violation of his training. Instead, he felt only a kind of giddiness. Happiness, relief.

Zi Lei stood and told him that she had work to do and leaned across the table and kissed him hard on the mouth. They stared at each other with shared astonishment. Then she clapped a hand over her mouth and loped away.

After work the next day, as he was walking toward the apartment building, a woman came up to him and said that she was a friend of Zi Lei.

Ken Shintaro said that he was pleased to meet one of Zi Lei's friends because he hoped that he was a friend of hers too.

"That's what I want to talk about."

They sat at a tea stall. The woman introduced herself: Keiko Sasaki. She said, "You haven't been in Paris very long."

It was a statement of fact that seemed to require no answer. Keiko Sasaki was a slender young woman with a calm, matter-of-fact manner. When she asked him if he was planning to stay here long, he shrugged.

"I know how it is. I was on a wanderjahr myself two years ago," Keiko Sasaki said, and listed several cities, including Rainbow Bridge. She mentioned people she had met, places where she had worked. He nodded and smiled as she talked, wondering if this was a test, if she was trying to trick him into revealing that he knew less about Rainbow Bridge than he should.

"Of course, it was easier then," she said. "There are almost no flights between Saturn and Jupiter now, what with the fear of war. You must be worried about getting home."

"Not really." Mention of the war made him wary. He sucked tea from his bowl, picked a stray bit of twig from his teeth and set it in the saucer.

Keiko Sasaki sipped her tea too. At last, she said, "You met Zi Lei at the Permanent Peace Debate, I think."

"We first met when we worked together. We live in the same building."

He was wondering if Keiko Sasaki had been following him.

"You know that she is not well. She works too hard. She worries about war. And she is not taking her medication . . . Did you know that she is schizophrenic?"

He shrugged because he didn't know what to say.

"I'm Zi's friend, Ken. I'm also her health worker, appointed by the city to monitor her welfare after she self-harmed herself two years ago. She is supposed to be taking part in a programme of cognitive therapy designed to help her analyse and deal with her anxieties and fantasies, and she is also supposed to be taking medicine to counteract a serotonin imbalance. At present, she is doing neither because she claims that she is in the middle of a period of intense creativity," Keiko Sasaki said. "She has the right to make that decision of course. I can only advise her. But while she's usually amenable to reason, right now she is in a manic phase and is very vulnerable. And the current situation is feeding her fantasies."

"The current situation?"

"The fact that we may at any moment be at war."

His suspicion that this wasn't really about Zi Lei, that the woman was some kind of peace officer, hardened into certainty. He had been told that there was a high probability that he would be discovered. It had been emphasised over and again during his training, and he'd spent every waking moment after entering the city wondering if he was being watched by people who knew that he was not who he was pretending to be. A constant state of anxiety and suspicion, of always wondering if passersby were watching him, if the ordinary exchanges with people at work, in the green markets, and with his neighbours in the apartment block were more than they seemed. A constant low-level dread; constant analysis and self-monitoring. Now all that fell away and he felt that he was sitting at the centre of a great ringing calm. He didn't feel angry or afraid; in fact, he felt relieved that the inevitable had happened. His immediate impulse, which he immediately suppressed, was to ask Keiko Sasaki how she knew, when he had been found out, what had given him away. But until she gave him a clear and obvious signal that she knew all about him, both of them were doomed to play out their roles.

Keiko Sasaki said, "Zi thinks of you as a friend. An ally."

"I hope that I am."

"Good. Then can I ask you to do something? Not to help me, but to help Zi."

"I can try."

"If you want to be a good friend to Zi, if you would like to help her, it would be a good idea if you didn't encourage her fantasies. Listen to her, but don't ask questions. Try to talk of other things. And maybe you can keep her away from the Permanent Peace Debate, too."

"She does good there."

"It was a useful safety valve when it started, but it's a parody of itself now. It's become the focus of malcontents and fantasists. A place where they can let their emotions run away and elaborate their paranoid fantasies. In some cases that's just what they need. But in Zi's case, encouraging her fantasy, which is what happens every time she gets on that stage and gets people to hum along, isn't good for her at all. She doesn't see that people make fun of her. She only sees what she wants to see. She sees validation. And that drives her deeper into her fantasy, and increasingly alienates her from ordinary life. At the moment, she's so deep inside it that she won't even talk to me. She thinks I'm some kind of spy or enemy agent trying to prevent her straightening out the vibrations. But she talks to you, she likes and trusts you, and that's why I'm asking for your help."

"I'll do everything I can," he said.

After a moment Keiko Sasaki returned his smile. "Zi needs friends. And if you can be a true friend to her, you'll also be a friend to me."

"We can talk again," he said from inside his great still calm.

He knew that they were talking in plain code. Zi had nothing to do with this, except that she was the excuse for contact.

"I'd like that," Keiko Sasaki said. "You're a good person, Ken. I'm sure we have much to talk about."

He considered his options as he walked to his apartment. They had made clear to him that they knew what he was. They had the power to end the game at any time. It was quite possible that they knew all about his hard work, all the little tricks and traps he had set up, but he couldn't check anything because they might have set traps of their own. And he couldn't abort the mission, either. His controllers could recall him, but he couldn't reach out to them for help. Which meant that he had just two options. He could try to drop out of sight, leave the city and live a fugitive existence, flitting between untenanted habitats and shelters, erasing all trace of his presence each time he moved on. It would allow him freedom of movement, but it would limit his sphere of action, reduce the number of targets he could strike to those few outside the city. Or he could stay in the city and continue to play the game. Keiko Sasaki could try to play him, and he could try to play her while continuing to make his plans to hit the most important targets that he had been assigned.

The second option seemed better. He had much useful work still to do before the *Flower of the Forest* arrived. And soon after that there would be so much confusion that surely he could slip away, and perhaps he could take Zi Lei with him. The thought of escaping with her comforted and calmed him.

Meanwhile, he had to pretend that things had not changed. He went to meet Zi Lei at a bar in the long park that slanted in the upper part of the city. It was built on a platform perched in a big redwood tree. He swarmed up the steep ropeway and there she was, sitting at the tiny counter, and he felt his heart lift and turn as he sat happy and breathless beside her.

6

It was generally agreed that war was imminent. The Brazilian flagship, the *Flower of the Forest*, was due to arrive in the Saturn System in only a few days, and a smaller, unidentified ship was following close behind. Meanwhile, the singleships, tugs and drones belonging to the Pacific Community and to the Brazilian and European joint expedition flew unchallenged everywhere around the moons and rings of Saturn, and the life-support, communications, and transport systems of every city were under attack.

One day, Paris's net fell over completely, and rioting broke out in several places before it was restored. Many people, including every notable scientist, gene wizard and environmental engineer, received messages asking them to surrender. Brief blackouts rolled through random sectors of the city. Five percent of the output of its fusion generators had been diverted to the ancient electrolysis facility to supplement oxygen production by the microalgal cultures, whose productivity had fallen to sixty percent of optimum values. The virus infecting the crop plants in the city's farms had been identified, but it had mutated into several different strains and there was still no effective cure.

War fever tightened its grip on the city and its population.

Everyone was issued with an emergency breathing kit: a small air cylinder attached to an inflatable helmet with a self-sealing neck ring. In theory, anyone caught in a part of the city that explosively decompressed could pull the helmet over their head and twist the valve on the cylinder, giving them two minutes to find shelter. In practice it was all but useless. Explosive decompression was not a trivial event like a plumbing accident or a tire puncture. In a large space like the city's tent it would create an instant hurricane blast. People would be knocked off their feet, struck by flying debris, blinded by fog as water vapour precipitated out of thinning air. People not immediately rendered unconscious or injured by falls or flying debris would probably be too dazed and disorientated to pull on their breathing kit, and even if anyone managed that, they would suffer decompression bruising over their entire body, quickly followed by death caused by sudden exposure to temperatures low enough to freeze oxygen.

But in what everyone was learning to call the current situation, panaceas like the emergency breathing kits assumed totemic significance completely out of proportion to their actual usefulness. Wardens appointed by the mayor's office were given the power to do stop checks on anyone at any time, to make sure that they were carrying their kits, to ask them to account for their movements. The wardens wore red armbands and carried plastic 9mm pistols and shock sticks that the city's manufactories had stamped out from designs more than a century old. They guarded every transport hub and the entrances to every public building and apartment block, patrolled the markets and parks, and stood at the barricades which had been erected at every major intersection in the city.

Because he was a visitor caught up in the city's self-imposed siege, Ken Shintaro was challenged by wardens at almost every checkpoint. In the feverish climate everyone was suspect to some degree or other, but non-citizens were top of the list. So far the city's council had not acted on calls for their internment, but many of the wardens seemed to think that they were just one step away from being enemy combatants, and several times Ken Shintaro had been roughed up or strip-searched in public by these zealous guardians of the city's new regime. Parisians, having set themselves up as the symbol of resistance to Earth's three major powers, were growing increasingly bitter about those cities like Camelot, Mimas or Xamba, Rhea, not to mention almost all the cities and settlements in the Jupiter System, whose populations had voted to declare that they would offer no active resistance to any incursion. Of course, Paris's population could easily disperse amongst the hundreds of empty refuges and oases scattered across Dione, but evacuating the city would be as bad as capitulating to the enemy; they could retain their sense of defiance only by staying where they were, and that meant suffering a constant fear of attack, massive casualties, and defeat, and at the same time denying that defeat was an option.

So they had made themselves sacrifices laid on the altar of their principles. Citizens had to be eternally vigilant, eternally suspicious of their neighbours, alert for any sign of panic, disaffection or disloyalty. Every outsider was a potential enemy, as was anyone who ventured any kind of opinion that contradicted the common mindset that gripped the population, or complained, however mildly, about the privations, or had in the past offended someone who now had been given authority.

Ken Shintaro endured the constant low-level harassment with stoic good humour. A bemused smile; a benign vagueness when challenged; an unquestioning eagerness when asked to agree with some patriotic declaration. Behind this mask, the spy had to stay vigilant, constantly self-monitoring himself, making sure that his expression was always pleasant and his attitude helpful, forcing himself to seem as rabidly enthusiastic during the evening rallies as everyone around him. It had been easy to pretend to be like everyone else when everyone expected him to be like them, but now that everyone's behaviour was in some degree abnormal he had to work hard to make sure that he did or said nothing suspicious, and he sometimes wondered what it might be like to shed his mask and let himself go.

Soon, when the war started, he would have his chance. Meanwhile, he had to pretend to be as crazy as everyone else.

In order to protect the city's freedom, habeas corpus had been suspended, the city's council had been given emergency powers by popular vote, and the council had granted the mayor, Marisa Bassi, the kind of absolute authority that would make most dictators weep with envy. Strict food and water rationing was introduced. Ordinary life was displaced by emergency and safety drills, classes in weapon handling, street fighting and first aid, and work in the volunteer labour brigades that were constructing barricades, hedgehogs, shelters, pillboxes and trenches inside and outside the city. Participation in all these activities was mandatory, and although attendance at the rallies held each evening in the main park was not, almost everyone in the city who hadn't been assigned to some duty elsewhere turned out anyway, packing the park from edge to edge, listening to poets declaim, musicians play, and mixologists perform, all this building up to the concluding address by Marisa Bassi, who each and every night whipped the crowd into a patriotic ferment.

The theme of the mayor's speeches was always the same. No surrender. They will not pass. Get out of our sky. An ardent defiance and aggression backed by patriotism and naive enthusiasm rather than any real military strategies or capabilities. The city's ground defences extended for several kilometres around its perimeter but they were rudimentary and unsophisticated, and although the squads of volunteers who practised hit-and-run guerrilla tactics or manoeuvred on trikes, rolligons, flying belts and platforms out on the plain to the north and east of the city looked impressive, they were poorly armed amateurs who stood no chance against experienced marines and fighting drones. The city's much-vaunted defence system, the missiles and rail guns hidden in bunkers on the surface, the smart rocks and killer satellites in orbit, weren't much better, as incursions by enemy ships had already proven. And once the defences fell over, the city would have to fall back on twentieth-century techniques of trench and street warfare to counter troops armed with twenty-third-century technology.

But although Paris couldn't possibly survive a sustained attack for more than a day or two, the few realistic voices in the debate about war and the practicality of defending a tented city were drowned out by the clamour of the mob. A sense of barely suppressed hysteria heightened the city's daily life. Children played war games and raced around everywhere more or less unchecked; some formed gangs that supplied wardens with food and drink and ran messages or small errands. Adults were gripped by the same excitement, but despite their public declarations of loyalty and a willingness to fight to the death most people were scared and upset and apprehensive. There was an increased awareness that the city's tent and ancillary domes were no more than fragile bubbles of light and heat and air in an immensity of freezing vacuum. Although everyone was supposed to be in a constant state of alert, people drank more and took more drugs, quarrelled, brawled, and indulged in reckless and sometimes public promiscuity.

Two days before the *Flower of the Forest* was due to rendezvous with its sister ships around Mimas, Marisa Bassi declared martial law.

The first Ken Shintaro knew of it was when his neighbours woke him at six in the morning, banging at his door, shouting, demanding to be let in. He scanned the room to make sure that nothing was out of place, unlocked the door. Several people crowded in at once, led by Al Wilson, the man who organised the apartment building's maintenance rota.

"When did you last see Zi Lei?" Al Wilson said.

He had been trained to tell the truth whenever it didn't conflict with his mission. He said truthfully, "Yesterday."

A woman was looking in the shower stall. A man was rifling through the closet. Another man was fingertip-searching the sleeping niche. All the people in the room were wearing red armbands. He could feel their excitement and hostility. They gave him hard, hostile looks. They were clearly ready to do him harm. His heart beat a little faster and his scalp prickled. The cool air tingled over every square centimetre of his skin. A man standing in the doorway said, "Why did you change your lock, friend? The pass key didn't work."

Another rule from his training: if you are asked an awkward question, you do your best to ignore it. Pretend that you haven't even heard it. Change the subject. He said, "Has Zi done something wrong?"

The man in the doorway said, "That's our business. And you should put some clothes on."

"I was sleeping."

He moved and reacted slowly and tentatively, his eyelids drooping as if he hadn't yet shaken off sleep, but he was fizzing with barely contained energy, had already worked out what to do if it came to it. Disable Al Wilson by chopping him in the throat and step past him and kill the man in the doorway, with his grabby gaze and scrap of beard under his lower lip like a pubic graft. Break his neck and then do the others. He could see it very clearly for a moment, and realised that he had shifted his stance, ready to act. Luckily, none of the intruders noticed.

"Maybe we should take him in," the woman in the shower stall said.

"He isn't on the list," Al Wilson said.

"He's from Rainbow Bridge," the woman said. "Lots of peaceniks there. They *collaborated*. They let those people into their city. They *started* this."

Al Wilson ignored her. He had a finicky, harassed manner, as if he was surrounded by obstructions that must be navigated with infinite care. He said, "We need to find Zi Lei. You're a friend of hers. Perhaps you know where she is. Where she might be."

"She isn't here."

"You can't be as dumb as you look," the man in the doorway said. "Drop the act and tell us what you know."

"I don't know where Zi is," Ken Shintaro said, giving the man the innocent look he practised every day in the mirror, like all his expressions. "What is this about?"

"It's about treason," the man examining the sleeping niche said. He was kneeling now, running his fingers under the lip of the niche.

"It's for her own safety," Al Wilson said.

"The crazy bitch has gone to ground," the man in the doorway said. "If we find out you know where she is, we'll back for you."

"If you find out anything, let me know," Al Wilson said weakly. His seniority made him the leader of this little gang, but it was clear that the man in the doorway would take over if there was any trouble.

Ken Shintaro said, "Is this for her safety?"

"It's for the safety of the fucking city," the man in the doorway said.

Al Wilson made flapping motions. "Let's go, people. We have a lot of work to do."

He locked the door on their backs and shed Ken Shintaro. He carefully searched the room in case someone had planted a bug. He checked the net, found the announcement about martial law, found another that said that Marisa Bassi would be addressing the city at eight a.m., a third stating that the Permanent Peace Debate had been closed down. This was not war, then. It was a local problem, a heightening of the city's fever. And Zi Lei was caught up in it somehow.

She didn't answer when he called her. All right, he would check all the places in the city that she had shown him, starting with the Permanent Peace Debate. He would find her and help her. He righted everything in the room and took a shower, first hot then cold. As he was dressing, Keiko Sasaki called. She asked him if he had seen Zi Lei and he told her that people had come to his apartment, looking for her.

"They think she's part of the peace movement," Keiko Sasaki said.

"Well, she is," he said, thinking of Zi Lei standing on the stage of the theatre and making her humming noise, the audience ranged above her humming too. He was impatient to end this call because he wanted to get out and about and see what was happening, but he didn't know how to do it without arousing suspicion.

"I'm petitioning to have the warrant for her arrest waived," Keiko Sasaki said. "It will take some time, though, because almost everyone who's been arrested has someone petitioning on their behalf. If you happen to see her, Ken, if she comes to you asking for help, will you try to keep her out of trouble? Keep her in your room, or somewhere safe, and tell me at once. Tell me if you see her. Will you do that?"

"Yes," he said, because it seemed simplest to agree. "I have to go now," he said, and cut the connection.

He went past the amphitheatre that hosted the Permanent Peace Debate. Peace officers and wardens wearing red armbands were guarding every entrance. At the café where he and Zi Lei often ate breakfast together, the man who gave him his cinnamon oatmeal and beaker of coffee told him that he should be careful, they were arresting people all over the city.

"About time," another customer said.

"We're a democracy," someone else said. "We shouldn't arrest someone because we disagree with them."

Which started one of the noisy debates that the citizens of Paris loved— everyone with contradictory opinions, everyone trying to talk over everyone else. He ate his breakfast, sitting quietly in the middle of the noise. The café's customers were still arguing when he left.

He drifted slantwise through the city, checking the places where he had been with Zi Lei. Neighbourhood green markets were besieged by people desperate to buy fresh produce. Many small businesses were closed. Cafés and bars that had stayed open were doing roaring business. Freed from its ordinary routines, the city had a raffish carnival air. Kids chased each other through the vines and broad branches of a huge banyan tree in one of the parks, screaming as they leaped and tumbled, making noises like guns and explosions, dying dramatically in slow motion before scrambling up, reborn, ready to resume the fight. People stood outside doorways talking, passing flasks back and forth. People watched as a man spray-painted *traitor* in ragged black letters across the door of an apartment on a set-back terrace. Small groups of wardens wearing red armbands stood at the intersections and at the entrances to public buildings, scrutinising every passerby.

He kept his gaze averted as he passed through checkpoints, trying to look humble and harmless, hiding the hot flame of excitement that burned in his breast. Soon he would be able to shed Ken Shintaro completely and show his true self to these people.

At last his seemingly random wanderings brought him to the compound where the gene wizard Avernus was staying. There was a mutinous crowd in front and peace officers stood in a line across the gate. He asked a woman at the fringe of the crowd what was happening and she told him that Avernus and her gang of peace-lovers had been arrested.

"They won't let us in," she said, and raised her voice, shouting at the peace officers. "Show us what those traitors were doing!"

He asked where the traitors had been taken.

"I heard the correctional facility," a man said.

"That's what they want us to think," another man said. "I reckon they stashed them someplace secret. So if it comes down to it they can use them as bargaining chips with the enemy."

"We'll never make any kind of bargain with the enemy," the woman said, bristling.

"It's definitely somewhere outside the city," a third man said. "I have a cousin who works in the warehouses. He saw them being loaded into a couple of rolligons."

The woman said, "We should paint a big target out on the plain and put her and all the other peace-lovers in the bullseye and see how they like it."

Ken Shintaro edged away from the small crowd and was walking back through the city when at exactly eight o'clock his spex rang. A civic alarm. Everyone around him had stopped and was putting on spex. When he fitted his own pair over his eyes, he found that Marisa Bassi was making the same speech on every channel. The mayor talked about the vote that had united the city in defiance against the invaders. He talked about the necessity of rounding up troublemakers for the sake of the city's safety and the inevitable loss of certain individual rights during this period of tension. He asked everyone to stay calm and do their duty by carrying on with their lives and their work.

"I know many of you want me to take the fight to our enemy. I say, let them leave now, and we will not follow them or attempt to exact any retribution. But if they do not leave at once, they should prepare to face the consequences. They should prepare to face a people united in their determination to fight to the death in the name of freedom."

A group of wardens started clapping at the end of this. He wondered if he should clap too, but everyone else, on the street and in the café under a big sweet-chestnut tree, were resuming their conversations or walking on to wherever it was they had been going. So he walked on too, and soon realised that he was being followed by the man who had stood in the doorway of his room while it had been searched.

The man made no attempt to conceal what he was doing, walking about twenty metres behind him, stopping when he stopped, moving on when he moved on. His spex identified the man as Ward Zuniga, thirty-one, a construction worker, no partner, a very small cloud of friends.

He sat in a park and passed some time reviewing his plans, finding nothing out of order. Ward Zuniga sat nearby, got up when he got up, followed him to a café and sat nearby while he ate noodles, followed him back to the apartment building, up the walkway to the door of his room.

"I'm on to you," Ward Zuniga said. "I know what you're doing."

"What am I doing?"

"Why are you smiling? What's so funny?"

"I suppose I am excited by what happened today. Like everyone else."

"You? You're not like everyone else."

"I'm not?"

He could kill the man and drag his body into his room, but what then? He would have to go into hiding, and it would be very difficult to move around the city because people would be looking for him.

"You're an outsider. A collaborator," Ward Zuniga said.

He realised that the man was talking about Ken Shintaro, from Rainbow Bridge. He felt almost sorry for him—his reek of testosterone, his unfocused aggression, the pathetic scrap of beard dabbed on his chin.

"I understand," he said. "You must be wary of strangers at a time like this."

"Are you shitting me? Because if you are, it'll come right back at you."

They stared at each other. It was one of those moments when things can go down either of two different roads. Then Ward Zuniga pointed with his forefinger, right in Ken Shintaro's face, and said, "I'll be seeing you."

Ken Shintaro blinked and stepped back, hands raised to his chest in a defensive gesture.

Ward Zuniga smiled. "Yes sir. I have plenty of time for you," he said, and turned on his heel and floated off along the walkway.

Later, after midnight, he woke to a faint scratching at his door. It was Zi Lei. She fell into his arms and while he held her he looked over her shoulder, checking the walkway and the courtyard below. No one was about.

"You don't have any clothes on," she said, after he had pulled her inside and shut the door.

"I was asleep."

"Oh, I don't mind. I'm above such things," she said.

"You're shaking," he said, and snapped the tab on a beaker of green tea and gave it to Zi Lei, then pulled on his trousers and sat with her on the floor.

She held the beaker in both hands, taking small quick sips, and told him that she had known at soon as the vote was called that there would be trouble, that her mission had marked her out, that she must hide. She'd spent all day in a storage room beneath the building, waiting until everyone was asleep before sneaking out to find him. She was a spy now, a real spy, she said. The Edda were in direct contact with her; they had implanted themselves in her head. She had shed her birth identity. She was in the process of becoming something else. She had changed, and the city was changing too. Soon everything would change, she said, then yawned unselfconsciously and said that she had much to do but first she had to rest, she was so very tired.

"I know," he said, and took the beaker of tea from her and set it down.

Zi Lei yawned again and began to tell him about the new solar order, a sleepy but steady and unpunctuated flow of words circling around and around until he leaned forward and seized her and did the one thing that he knew would shut her up: kissed her full on the lips.

She gave a squeak of surprise, then yielded. They leaned against each other, his face on her shoulder, her face on his. Her exquisite trembling slowly relaxed and he felt something wet his bare chest—tears. She had a rank but not unpleasant odour like old sweat, the comforting smell of the room where he had practised day after day with his brothers.

"I've been so afraid," she said.

"You don't have to be afraid now."

"The truth—it's such a burden."

"I know."

He felt a tender swelling in his chest, a mix of pity and helpless love. He knew that he had to use her to help complete his mission, but told himself that what he was about to do was for her own good. Besides, he couldn't keep her here. If Ward Zuniga found out, he'd have to kill the man, and then there would be real trouble.

He looked into her face. The hypnotic he'd stirred into the green tea had done its work. She was half asleep, her pupils huge black pools.

"You're strange," she said. "A strange man. Not like the others."

"We aren't like the others."

"No . . ."

He told her that she must do something for him, and she sleepily agreed, opening her mouth like an obedient child, letting him place the capsule on her tongue, swallowing it. He massaged her throat to ease it down, told her that he had to go out for a moment, she could sleep now.

"Hold me first," she said.

He gathered her up in his arms and laid her in the sleeping niche, then went out and woke Al Wilson. Betraying her would earn him trust and kudos, and besides, it was for her own good. She would be safe in prison, and with a little luck she would be held in the same place as Avernus and all the others from the Permanent Peace Debate.

7

When the guards unlocked the door of her cell, an hour before breakfast, Macy was already awake and working through her second set of sit-ups. She didn't ask the two women, who waited just outside the door while she stepped into her coveralls and slippers, where they were taking her. By now, after six weeks of incarceration, she was used to being roused at odd hours of the day or night, being taken to the bare little office for yet another round of questioning. Long sessions with different pairs of interrogators. Wearing a tight MRI cap so that they could tell if she ever deviated from the truth while they worked through their interminable lists of questions.

Macy always tried her very best to stick to the truth. There was no point in lying because she had nothing to hide. She'd spoken at length with Avernus about her life on Earth and how she had ended up in exile in the Outer System, and during the interrogation sessions she was led through that story over and over again. She talked about her childhood, how she'd run away from the Church of the Divine Regression and ended up in Pittsburgh, how she'd joined the Reclamation and Reconstruction Corps. She talked about how she'd been selected for the construction crew, her training, her work on the biome at Rainbow Bridge. The whole sorry saga of Ursula Freye's murder. Her defection, her life in East of Eden until she'd escaped, her life with the Jones-Truex-Bakaleinikoff clan . . .

The only time she refused to answer her interrogators' questions was when they touched on Newton Jones and the other people in what had become her extended surrogate family. She refused to speculate or comment on their beliefs, whether they supported the peace movement or whether they supported Marisa Bassi and every other true and righteous Outer who wanted to drive the ships from Earth out of the systems of Saturn and Jupiter. If they wanted to know anything at all about anyone in the clan, she told her interrogators, they should damn well go talk to them.

They asked her about Loc Ifrahim, too, just as they no doubt asked him about her. Macy told them what she knew as dispassionately as possible. Trying to stick to the facts, trying not to colour or distort them with her deep dislike for the man. Going over everything again and again, until she began to doubt that any of it was real; until it seemed as remote as a story she'd once experienced in a virtuality. She was never threatened with physical violence, the food wasn't bad, she exercised as best she could in her cell, read books on the little slate they'd given her, and tried to stay alert. But it was getting harder and harder to keep the numb languor of jail at bay.

When she'd been arrested, she'd thought that she would be subjected to a show trial, but that didn't seem likely now. And although she supposed that Newt and others in the Jones-Truex-Bakaleinikoff clan must be petitioning for her to be charged or released, she doubted that they would be successful. Her guards let slip that Marisa Bassi and Paris's council were busy with preparations for war and the problems created by sabotage to the city's farms and its net. It seemed that she and Loc Ifrahim were being kept in limbo, bargaining chips whose value was dubious and might never be tested.

The last couple of sessions had been a little different, in a spooky, creepy kind of way. Her two interrogators, a man and a woman this time, had been as polite as ever, but instead of going over the old ground yet again they'd asked her if she had any knowledge of a long list of sabotage techniques and had showed her pictures of two or three hundred people, a few she knew, most she didn't, asking her the same questions about each and every one before dismissing her. Now, as she was escorted into the brightly lit office, she felt a small shock of recognition when she saw who was waiting for her. Sada, lounging in one of the sling chairs, smiling up at her, flapping a hand toward another chair, telling her to sit.

Macy sat. A small bone-white ceramic knife lay unsheathed on the table between her and Sada, haft and blade all one piece. Perhaps it was there to tempt Macy into trying to do something foolish. Or to remind her of what might happen to her if she refused to cooperate. She did her best to ignore it.

Sada studied her and said, "You look a lot better than I thought you would."

"How did you think I would look?"

"You look fit and well. Rested, even. That's good."

"And you look like a hundred klicks of rough road. Maybe we should swap places. You look like you could do with some downtime and you can get plenty of that here."

Sada stretched in her chair, as unselfconscious as a cat. "I *could* do with some rest. I've just come back from a long, hard trip."

"You'd like it here. I've been in jails a lot worse. I wouldn't even call this a jail, really. It's more like a hotel where they don't let you have the keys to your room."

"A long, hard trip," Sada said again. "Working on something that will make sure that everything comes out the way it's supposed to. Working for the future, you might say."

She was dressed in a white vest laced to the tops of her small breasts, white leggings. Her hair cropped short. Small iron rings sewn along the arc of her left eyebrow. A tattoo of the constellation Hydrus sprawled across her cheek. She really did look exhausted, her skin chalky, her eyes darkly pouched and red-rimmed, and she looked absurdly young, too. A child in fancy dress, smiling expectantly at Macy, no doubt hoping to be asked where she'd been, what she'd been doing. Macy let the silence stretch. She wasn't going to play that game.

"I can't really tell you about it, but you'll see soon enough," Sada said. "Everyone will. I don't feel guilty about how things ended up, you know. Because this is how things are meant to be. We're part of something bigger than our little stories, Macy. Something huge and strange and wonderful."

"If you came here to justify what you did to me, tell me that you had to do it for the greater good, I'd as soon skip the coffee and go back to my cell," Macy said. She said it with some force, but without anger. She didn't feel any anger toward Sada, only sorrow. Sorrow that the girl had lost her way. That she had been caught up in someone else's deeply dark and dangerous fantasy.

Sada picked up the knife, turned it back and forth. Its blade was hooked like a velociraptor's claw. Skinny rainbows slid along its cutting edge, which was no doubt sharpened to the width of an atom.

"Why I'm here," the girl said, "Marisa Bassi has a favour to ask of you."

"You're working for Marisa Bassi now?"

"We have always worked *with* Marisa Bassi. He is a potent instrument."

"I've been asked to cooperate by all kinds of people, Sada. Now they've sent you. I'll tell you what I've been telling everyone else. I had nothing to do with the deaths of your friend or Colonel Garcia, and you have no evidence to the contrary. So charge me and let me stand trial, or let me go."

"It isn't only about poor Janejean now. They say you're a spy. You're suspected of espionage. Working against the city."

"They can say anything they like about me, but that doesn't make it true."

Macy did her best not to flinch as Sada leaned forward. The girl rested the point of the knife on the tabletop and turned it back and forth. "You're accused of espionage. And because habeas corpus has been suspended they don't ever have to let you go if they don't want to. They can keep you here forever without having to charge you. But I can help you, if you'll let me."

"Marisa Bassi asked for my help once before," Macy said. "He asked me to tell the truth about life in Greater Brazil. And I did. Maybe it wasn't what he wanted to hear, because it wasn't full of stories of exploitation and slavery and horror. It wasn't useful propaganda. But it was the truth."

"You said that you've been in worse places than here," Sada said.

"Once or twice."

"Talk about those places, Macy. Talk about life on Earth and this time tell the whole truth," Sada said, lightly stabbing the tabletop at the end of each sentence. "Explain what it's *really* like, living under the thumb of a self-selecting elite. Tell the truth about the repression and cruelty. How ordinary people are treated like slaves. How free speech and free thought are ruthlessly suppressed."

"I've already told the truth," Macy said. "If they haven't taken it down, you can look it up on the net."

"You want us to win the war, don't you? You can help, in a small way, by reminding people about their enemy. By stiffening their resolve."

"By spouting propaganda."

"Only our enemies would look it at that way."

"You want me to lie," Macy said. "I say what you want me to say—what Marisa Bassi wants me to say—and you'll let me go. Is that the deal?"

"He told me to tell you that he loves his city. That he'll do anything to save it. That if he had to, if he thought it would boost people's morale, he'd give you a show trial and execute you as a spy. Instead, he's giving you this one last chance to help the city, and to help yourself."

"Ask Mr. Bassi this," Macy said. "He'll lie, overturn the law, lock up people who don't agree with him, kill them . . . What exactly is he trying to save?"

"As far as we're concerned? It's the future of the human race," Sada said. "Little things like freedom, change, diversity. The kind of things you enjoyed while you were living with Newton Jones and the rest of his clan. Please, Macy. I want you to think very hard about cooperating because this really is your last chance."

"Yes or no, right now?"

"Right now."

"Something has happened, hasn't it? First questions about sabotage, and now this . . . Has the war begun?"

"Not yet. But it will, very soon. And when it does, no one will want to hear what you have to say. Think about that. Take your time. I'll leave you alone for a little while if you like. But I need your answer before I leave, and you won't be asked again."

"No," Macy said.

"No?"

"Tell him I've already told the truth and if he doesn't like it too bad. Tell him I won't lie for the greater good. Because how can it be good if it needs lies to support it?"

"This is your answer?"

"There can't be any other as far as I'm concerned."

"I'm sorry it has to be this way," Sada said, and flipped the knife through the air and caught it and sheathed it at her belt and swung up from the sling chair in one flowing movement.

The two guards stepped up behind Macy and hoisted her to her feet. She said, "I'm sorry, too. Because I shouldn't have let you get caught up in this."

"It is what it is because it is how it should be," Sada said. "You don't understand that now, but you will."

Macy and Loc Ifrahim were being held with several other high-profile prisoners in what had been until very recently a research facility some twelve kilometres northeast of Paris: a single-storey blockhouse under a small dome set amongst fields of vacuum organisms pieced across the dusty plain inside Romulus Crater. Apart from the interrogation sessions she'd been kept in her cell, but now she was taken outside and saw that a big cage of fullerene struts strung with razor-wire mesh had been erected where plots had been planted out with tweaked fruit bushes and bean plants. At least fifty people were crowded inside. Like Macy, they were all wearing bright orange coveralls. Some sat at low tables or stood in little groups; others lay in hammocks or on the ground, arms over their faces to blot out the glare of the floodlights. Two drones hung at different levels in the air in front of the mesh, fans whirring in their delta wings, tasers and dart guns slung under their bellies, camera eyes gleaming red as flecks of blood.

The guards told Macy that they needed her cell for a new prisoner and unceremoniously thrust her through the gate and locked it behind her. As Macy looked around, a woman with wild white hair stepped up and struck her across the mouth and shoved her backward, pinning her by her shoulders against a wall of the toilet block and screaming into her face that this was all her fault, *all her fault*, her voice a rising shriek, her spittle spraying Macy's cheeks. Macy reared back and thumped her forehead into the bridge of the woman's nose as hard as she could. The woman squealed and let go of Macy, and Macy braced against the wall and kicked her square in the belly. The woman reeled backward and sat down hard. Sat with her hands flat on the ground on either side of her and her head bowed, blood running slow and thick from her broken nose, fat drops dripping onto the front of her orange coveralls. Someone told Macy enough, it was over; someone else put a hand on her arm. Macy ignored them and stepped forward. She was breathing hard. The side of her face was hot and swollen. Everyone in the cage had turned to watch her. The woman glared up at her through a curtain of white hair.

"Hate me if you want," Macy told her. "But we're both stuck in this thing together. It'll be easier if we try to get along."

"They took me from my children," the woman said. Her eyes were bright with unshed tears. Bubbles of blood and mucus clung to her nostrils. "They took me right in front of my *children* . . ."

People helped her up, led her away to another part of the cage. No one asked Macy if she was all right. She spotted a man she knew slightly—a construction engineer, Walt Hodder. A calm, competent man in his sixties, a solid and highly respected citizen, chair of the city's transport committee, he'd argued eloquently for caution in the city's public forum and had talked to Macy several times over the net after her interview with Avernus. When she went up to him, he told her that everyone here was associated with the peace and reconciliation movement—they'd all been arrested at more or less the same time. Give Marisa Bassi credit: he knew how to organise a coup. Paris's council had declared a state of emergency. Peace officers had closed off all airlocks and shut down the railway system. The city had been locked down. There had been nowhere to run. Avernus and her daughter and her crew had been arrested. So had two councillors prominent in the peace movement. "For their own safety," according to Marisa Bassi. Gangs of people had made citizen's arrests and some had been pretty brutal, Walt Hodder said. The peace officers and wardens who had closed down the Permanent Peace Debate had run everyone inside through a gauntlet. Anyone who tried to resist had been beaten down. There were people here with broken arms and ribs, broken jaws and noses, concussions . . . No one knew what would happen next.

"I guess the right side lost the argument," Macy said.

Outside the razor-wire perimeter, one of the drones had dropped down to aim its camera directly at her face. She turned away from it. She wished now that she had asked Sada what she'd been doing. Setting up some kind of stupid stunt, no doubt. But what?

"If Bassi gets his way, everyone will lose," Walt Hodder said.

8

Soon after the *Uakti* crossed Phoebe's orbit, some thirteen million kilometres out from Saturn, two singleships sharked in on it and precisely matched its delta vee, laying off ten kilometres on either side. A laser blink transmitted a message addressed to Sri Hong-Owen, ordering her to relinquish control so that she could be safely escorted to the *Glory of Gaia*. A few seconds later a drone attached itself to an access port just forward of the shuttle's tail fin and spliced into the control bus. The shuttle's attitude jets swung through fifteen degrees on its horizontal axis and the main motor began to cycle through its preignition sequence.

"I believe we should prepare for a course change," Yamil Cho told Sri.

Sri had been on edge ever since he'd spotted the singleships closing in on them. Now she felt the first flutters of real panic. "They told us that they were escorting us to the *Glory of Gaia*. And that's exactly where we were headed. That's what I agreed to do. So why are we changing course?"

When she'd fled Earth, Sri's first and best hope had been to surrender to Arvam Peixoto. They'd had several full and frank exchanges as they headed

311

out toward Saturn, Arvam aboard the *Flower of the Forest*, Sri following behind in the stolen shuttle. She had told him everything she knew about the plot fronted by Euclides, and what she'd had to do to escape it. He'd told her that he couldn't condone Oscar's assassination, but he admired the bold recklessness of her move: it would almost certainly expose the plotters, and in any case the old man's time would have soon come by one hand or another. At last they'd reached an agreement. Arvam would allow Sri to live in exile in the Saturn System and would do his best to protect Alder and the research station, and Sri would devote all of her skill and expertise to his service. She would unriddle Avernus's secrets, and make Arvam a very rich man. But now, at the moment of placing her life into his hands, giving herself whole and entire, she was scared that she had made a serious mistake.

Yamil Cho was unruffled. "We were headed toward Mimas because the *Glory of Gaia* is in orbit around Mimas," he said. "If we are no longer headed toward Mimas, then something must have changed since we last checked the *Glory of Gaia*'s position."

He conjured a long-range optical view in the memo space between their acceleration couches. The little moon was a small black spot centred on the pencil line of the rings, silhouetted against the umber bands that girdled Saturn's equator. A tiny spray of sparks was moving away from it. Yamil Cho zoomed in until the sparks resolved into clusters of blocky pixels. Registry tags popped up over each one, identifying the *Glory of Gaia*, the *Flower of the Forest*, the *Getûlio Dornelles Vargas*, and half a dozen Outer ships that were trying to follow them.

"Where are they going?" Sri said. "Where *we* going?"

"It is too early to tell. But our three ships do appear to be heading in different directions."

Sri studied the cluster of bright pixels under the *Glory of Gaia* tag. "Dione," she said at last. "The mayor of Paris, Dione made his city the centre of the resistance to our presence. Arvam will want to deal with him personally. His vanity will demand no less."

The main engine lit and acceleration pressed them into their couches.

"So this is war, then," Yamil Cho said.

"War, or something very like it," Sri said. "It seems that we have arrived just in time."

PART FIVE
A SMALL, QUIET WAR

I

The *Glory of Gaia* was a big ship, one of the largest ever built, but it was crammed with equipment and supplies and was carrying more than twice its normal complement. Senior officers doubled up in cabins; junior officers hotbedded in life capsules; specialists and technicians slept and ate and spent their off-duty hours in little encampments in corridors or in their cubbyholes or weapon blisters and turrets. The specialists' wardroom doubled as the sickbay because the sickbay, which lay conveniently close to the ship's spine, had been converted into a self-contained fighting bridge containing a triumvirate of strategic AIs and immersion tanks for the ship's combat team, and the combat team slept in their tanks because there was no room for them anywhere else. Everyone breathed a common air filled with the stink of cooking and farts and unwashed bodies, and everyone knew everyone else's business because they all lived in each others' pockets—no one except the highest-ranking officers and security officials was ever out of sight or sound of at least two other people.

And then the *Flower of the Forest* made its rendezvous with the *Glory of Gaia* and the *Getûlio Dornelles Vargas*, and two detachments of marines who had been slumbering like fairy-tale knights in hibernation coffins in the *Glory of Gaia*'s zero-gravity gymnasium were revived and had to be fitted somehow into the already overcrowded quarters. Security personnel, technicians and senior officers shuttled back and forth between the three ships. Everyone knew that they were getting ready for battle even before General Arvam Peixoto gave an address to all ranks, telling them to prepare for action and assuring them that everything was in place to guarantee complete and total victory.

"The enemy does not yet realise it, but we are already engaged in a small, quiet war of attrition and diplomacy, of propaganda and subtle sabotage. Their morale has been sapped. Their reserves of air, food, and power are depleted. Half of their cities have indicated that they will offer no resistance. Several more are close to surrender. The rest will try to give us a fight, but in every case we will prevail. Not because we have might on our side, although we do, but because our cause is right and just, and each of us carries the proud flame of righteousness and justice in our hearts."

Watching this in the memo space in the pilot's mess, Cash Baker told Luiz Schwarcz, "I guess we can forget about being rotated back home."

The *Glory of Gaia* had been orbiting Mimas ever since it had arrived in the Saturn System. Now it fired up its motors and broke away, heading toward Dione, some two hundred thousand kilometres outward. Paris, Dione was expected to put up the fiercest resistance; General Peixoto would direct the campaign against it personally. The *Flower of the Forest* broke orbit too, heading toward Rhea. The small caravan of local ships which had been dogging the *Glory of Gaia*, skimming as close to it as they dared at random intervals, firing off clouds of noble gases and using lasers to print in letters fifty metres high brightly glowing slogans, launching drones the size of beetles that tootled across hundreds of empty kilometres on whispers of gas and blew apart in harmless firework displays or attached themselves to sally ports and used them as loudspeakers to transmit the screams of babies or wailing sirens into the interior, fired up their motors too. Falling behind one by one into the starry black as the *Glory of Gaia* and the *Flower of the Forest* steadily accelerated. The last fired off a huge cloud of neon and printed a final farewell: *SO LONG, SUCKERS*.

Despite numerous housekeeping regulations about securing everything in zero gravity and strictly enforced disciplinary measures that punished anyone caught breaking them, when acceleration established a pull down the *Glory of Gaia*'s axis all kinds of junk came loose or dropped from where it had drifted to or had been carelessly left. Cash Baker, Luiz Schwarcz and the other pilots were in the hangars, helping the techs police a litter of loose tools, bolts, snips of wire and plastic and metal shavings, wrappers, and blobs of coolant and grease, when Vera Jackson came in and announced that there was going to be a special briefing in five minutes.

"Is it on?" Luiz said, voicing everyone else's thoughts.

"Not yet," Vera Jackson said. She was grinning, though, so something was definitely afoot. "Not exactly. You and Cash leave that crap to your crews and come with me."

Arvam Peixoto and several aides were waiting for them in the briefing room. The general laid out the mission in his customary blunt manner. The Pacific Community's base on Phoebe had just received an anonymous warning that they had six hours to evacuate their position: someone had aimed a chunk of ice at them from Ymir, one of the most distant of Saturn's small, irregular moons.

The general pulled up photographs in the room's memo space, fuzzy long-range views of a pitted slab, and said that the Pacific Community had fired a missile at it, but the missile had been shredded by kinetic weapons as it made its final approach.

"The ice has a defence system mounted on it, which makes it a hard target," the general said. "The Pacific Community ships can't do anything other than a fast flyby because it is coming right down their throats and they don't have the advantage of the new fusion motor. So we are going to help them out by intercepting and destroying it as soon as possible. It will show that Greater Brazil and the European Union are good friends of the Pacific Community, it will demonstrate our technological superiority, and it is an excellent opportunity to find out what the Outers are capable of. One of you will carry one of our last resort H-bombs; the other two will deal with the defence systems mounted on the ice. We're still gathering data on it. As soon as we know what we need to know we will devise and send you a detailed plan of action. Meanwhile, you will launch immediately. The sooner you get there, the better the chance of destroying this thing, or significantly altering its trajectory. Do you all understand? Good. If you have questions, ask them now."

Luiz asked if anyone knew who had fired off the ice.

"I'm sure they will make themselves known soon enough," the general said. "Anyone else? No? Then go with God and Gaia, and go swiftly."

Within ten minutes, Cash was in the hangar, purged and plugged, fitted into his acceleration suit. He shook hands with Luiz Schwarcz, Vera Jackson, and his tech team, and then he was zipped into his bird and jacked in. Just like any other routine run, except for the flutter of excitement in his chest, the way he'd felt as a kid whenever he'd set off with his two cousins into the sewers to hunt rats or possums.

As soon as his bird had dropped from its launch cradle, falling away from the *Glory of Gaia* at twenty metres per second, it began to pitch and roll, hunting for the point where it would catch up with its target. All Cash had was a set of coordinates: the chunk of ice was so far out and so small that it was beyond the detection limit of his radar and optical systems; even Phoebe was no more than a smudge of pixels. Luiz's and Vera's singleships hung close by to starboard, turning in unison. To port, the massive, bristling bulk of the *Glory of Gaia* occluded a large portion of the sky. Behind it were the few Outer ships still in pursuit, and beyond them was the misty bulk of Saturn.

Cash had a few seconds to take all this in, and then the singleship's motor fired up. He was on his way.

Phoebe was an unmodified primitive object that had been captured by

Saturn when it had wandered in from the outer reaches of the Solar System. Its wide orbit, with a semi-major axis of some thirteen million kilometres, more than thirty times the distance between Earth and the Moon, was not only inclined to the gas giant's equatorial plane but was also retrograde. The icy missile fast approaching it had fallen at a slant across the entire system and the three singleships were catching up with it from behind, climbing above Saturn's equatorial plane and aiming at a point where their path would intersect with their target. Luiz said that this was the opening salvo of the long-awaited war, but Vera reckoned that it was a shot across the bows aimed by a bunch of hotheads.

"The tweaks don't have a consensus about anything," she said. "There's no central control, just a bunch of small groups with different agendas. And that's how we'll defeat them. After we move in on one or two hostile cities and show what we can do, the rest will surrender on any terms we care to make."

"If this thing hits where it's aimed," Luiz said, "it won't matter who was responsible for it. It'll be war. Everyone who wants to fight will try to get in their shots right away. There won't be time for your domino theory to take hold."

"It isn't going to hit where it's aimed because we're going to make sure it doesn't. Jettison any thoughts to the contrary, mister."

"Permission to make another point, Colonel?" Luiz said.

"Don't be a smart-mouth, Schwarcz," Vera said. "You know you can say anything you like to me as long as it isn't seditious. Since I'm in a good mood, you can even insult my mother."

"I was thinking that they could have fired off any number of missiles at Phoebe, and told us about just this one."

"It's possible," Vera said. "But so far Phoebe hasn't spotted anything else, and neither have we. Best leave speculation to the tactical crew, Schwarcz. They do the thinking, we do the doing. You want to be less like them and more like me and Baker. You still awake, Baker?"

"Aye aye," Cash said.

"Bullshit. You were daydreaming about the girl you left behind. Well as far as you're concerned she's long gone, fucking someone else and making babies. You're out here on the finest and most important mission you've ever flown, and you will stay frosty unless I tell you otherwise."

"Aye aye."

But it was hard not to zone out. Cash's radar and microwave and optical sensors were sweeping a vast bubble of space with the regularity of a ticking clock, but there was nothing in any direction for fifty thousand kilometres except for the other two singleships. The traffic moving between Saturn's moons and the chatter on the Outers' communications network was dwindling behind them, remote as the lazy drone of a beehive on a summer's day. So he fell through empty space with nothing to do but run system checks and stargaze until the *Glory of Gaia*'s tactical crew sent a brief, heavily encrypted package that contained a detailed survey of the target.

The optical image wasn't much of an improvement over the ones the general had shown them, but radar scans showed that the chunk of ice was roughly oval, one hundred and twenty metres long and thirty metres in diameter. Grooves cut down one side suggested that it had been sheared away from a bigger mass. A one-shot chemical motor was buried in a pit in the trailing end, and the tactical crew aboard the *Glory of Gaia* claimed that two faintly radar-reflective spots on either side of the midpoint were most likely attachment points for a pair of lightsails. The motor would have contributed most of the ice's delta vee, with a modest contribution from laser beams aimed at the sails, which would have made final course corrections after launch.

"Amazing that no one spotted it," Vera said. "With the motor burning and lightsails reflecting gigawatts of laser light it must have been quite a sight when it got under way."

"A tiny speck of light in a very big ocean of dark," Luiz said. "The volume inside Phoebe's orbit is something like one point seven times ten to the power twenty-one cubic kilometres. And this came from much farther away."

If there had been lightsails they were long gone, ejected after the ice had achieved its final velocity. And so far the tactical crew hadn't been able to identify the defence system that had taken out the Pacific Community's missile; Cash and Vera would have to probe the ice very carefully before Luiz delivered the H-bomb. And they'd have to do it quickly. By the time they matched delta vee with the ice, they would be less than an hour out from Phoebe.

Cash, Vera and Luiz discussed tactics until turnover, when they flipped their ships end for end and began to decelerate. They had been travelling much faster than the ice to catch up with it, and now they had to shed a substantial portion of their velocity, a hard burn that peaked at three *g* and was followed by small course corrections to make sure that the three singleships were flying in precise formation, Cash and Vera about twenty kilometres apart, Luiz trailing several hundred kilometres behind. Their target grew dead ahead, a giant bullet slowly rotating, showing pits and craters across its surface. Still no sign of the defence system. Phoebe hung way beyond it, a faint sliver that in telescopic views resolved into a craggy globe with bright-floored craters spattered amongst long linear grooves and scablands of loose material that had drifted to the bottom of slopes. One tremendous impact had created a basin more than forty-five kilometres in diameter, its rim a broken cirque more than four kilometres high, half the height of Everest; a gigantic bite out of the little moon that gave it a lopsided, flattened profile. The Pacific Community had built its base in a secondary crater near the huge cliffs of the basin's cirque; Luiz said that the chunk of ice would strike Phoebe close to the basin or even inside it.

"The people who sent it on its way knew exactly what they were doing."

"We also know a thing or two," Vera said. "Ready with your proxy, Cash?"

"Aye aye."

"On my mark."

The two proxies shot ahead of Cash and Vera's singleships, closing on the ice. Cash was flying his by wire, plugged into its sensorium. Watching the foreshortened bullet-shape grow, radar overlaying and giving depth to optical and infrared images. He could see the pit at the trailing end where the motor was buried, make out hollow spheres that had to be fuel tanks ringing it. The putative anchor points for the lightsails were sharp spikes on either side, and there was a faint image of a pair of broad hoops or girdles running from stem to stern . . .

The proxy was slowing, less than ten kilometres from the ice, when Cash lost contact with it. No warning, just like that. Vera's proxy was dead too. Both of them riddled by some kind of kinetic weapon, falling blindly past the ice now. Luiz, hung way back, transmitted to Cash and Vera a single video frame that showed two specks blurring away from the ice's trailing end, said that the hoops must be rail guns. "They can fire forward or aft, and their ends are flexible so they can cover large arcs of sky. And they must be made out of some kind of superconducting fullerene, which would explain why it is so hard to spot on radar."

Vera said it didn't matter what they were was made of because she was going to cook them right now, and she and Cash brought their X-ray lasers online and raked the ice port and starboard, burning long shallow troughs into the hoops, curtains of vaporised material exploding away. Then they fired dumb missiles at the trailing end of the ice and the missiles sped in unhindered and blew out the motor in a blink of hot light. Although the ice appeared to lie defenceless before them, Cash and Vera hung back and sent in another pair of proxies, and as the proxies snarked in there was a stutter of activity across the surface of the ice, sharp plumes of dust flying up from craters as a swarm of tiny drones hurled themselves at the proxies and the singleships.

Cash fired a broadside of flechettes, discharged chaff to confuse the drones' targeting systems, triggered the power cycle of the gamma-ray laser, activated the systems that would bring the ship's fusion motor back up to full power. All this in less than a second, as he kicked into hyper-reflexive mode. Everything seemed spaced and deliberate: the ship's systems were frustratingly slow to react to his commands. Flashes when flechettes struck five of the drones; more flashes when flechettes struck the ice. The rest sped on, would continue to fall forever in long, eccentric orbits around Saturn. The surviving drones were accelerating toward Cash, cutting through the random radio chatter, flashing lights, infrared sources and explosively inflated radar-reflective bubbles of the chaff. His gamma-ray laser fired and took out a drone, expelled the one-shot power source, cycled a fresh one into place, and fired again and took out another drone. It cycled once every tenth of a second, but in Cash's accelerated state it seemed way slower than his father's old pump-action shotgun and the drones were closing fast, too many of them for the gamma-ray laser to take out before they hit the ship.

Cash had just enough time to feel a fat wave of horror and anger. It was like being a pilot in a plane a moment before it struck the ground, or the driver of a car just before it crashed. A sick realisation that he'd screwed the pooch, that this wasn't meant to happen—he was supposed to be a hero, not a casualty.

There was only one thing left to do and he did it. Even though he knew it probably wouldn't save him, he had to try. He flipped on the singleship's motor, full power, but the incoming drones blew up as he shot past them. An intense flash of electromagnetic radiation seared the singleship's hardened sensor systems; the outer edge of an expanding cloud of hot diamond shrapnel slammed into its stern.

Most fragments buried themselves harmlessly in layers of frangible armour, but a few penetrated to the hull, where expended kinetic energy turned them to plasma that burnt through the composite skin and sent secondary particles showering into substructures around the motor and its fuel tanks. The shock of the multiple impacts and surges from overloaded optical systems and damaged control ganglia and processor arrays flooded through the ship's control interface with a white flash and a sudden roar. The battle AI performed an emergency disconnect and pumped eight milligrams of sevofluorane into Cash's oxygen supply and put him out before feedback could fry his motor and sensory synapses.

When he came back, a shade over fourteen minutes had elapsed since the strike. The damage in the stern of the singleship was a numb tingling in his calves and feet. He had a bad headache and he was blind and a taste like burnt plastic filled his nose and mouth, very like the taste he'd had for days after all his teeth had been pulled and replaced with contoured plastic ridges at the beginning of the J-2 programme. After a moment of disorientation, his training kicked in. He'd been through simulations of multiple malfunctions of the ship's systems hundreds of times. He tried and failed to access the ship's visual and radar displays, then pulled down status reports, stepping on his dismay when he saw the huge blocks of red scattered across system readouts. The motor was damaged but still burning at about four percent maximum thrust; the battle AI was doing its best to carry out the last order he'd given before he'd been put under. Cash overrode the AI and shut down the motor carefully, then completed his survey of the singleship's status. One of the three fuel cells that provided backup power was down and one of the tanks that supplied the attitude jets with propellant was dry, most likely holed. He'd lost every kind of optical display, too. Most of the cameras were intact, but overload had burned out the main bus and all the processors. Radar was more or less working, aside from a hole of about thirty degrees; when he used it, Cash discovered that he was already more than two thousand kilometres beyond Phoebe. No sign of the ice, or of the other two singleships, but hell, the singleships were stealthed, and maybe the H-bomb had taken care of the ice . . .

He tried to raise Luiz and Vera, and that was when he discovered that the communication package was crippled by fatal faults in both the antenna of the microwave transmitter and the ganglia that controlled the aim of the modulated laser. Shit. He was dumb, half-blind, and running on minimum power, with a severely reduced supply of propellant for his attitude jets and a damaged motor that he didn't want to fire up again until he knew exactly what was wrong with it; he'd been lucky that it hadn't flamed on him when he'd been hit, leaked plasma through a warp in the containment fields and scorched the ship hollow. The singleship's repair mites were already beginning to clean up the gross damage, but it would take them a long time to diagnose the faults in the fusion motor, and even longer to fix them.

After a few moments' thought, Cash launched one of the proxies. Now he could at least see again. Phoebe's flattened disc hung behind him; beyond it, barely visible at maximum magnification, were the two singleships, separated by several hundred kilometres and closing fast on the little moon. There were points of light twinkling between the singleships and Cash saw a brief pinpoint flare that had to be an explosion: it looked like Luiz had delivered the H-bomb to the ice and vaporized the son-of-a-bitch, and now he and Vera must be chasing down the biggest chunks still heading toward Phoebe, blowing them to gravel and steam or knocking them off course . . . So they'd survived the drones, but even if they knew that Cash was alive they couldn't rescue him. Only the *Glory of Gaia* and its tugs were equipped for retrieval.

The *Glory of Gaia* was too far away, but maybe he could raise Luiz and Vera, appraise them of his situation. The proxy was equipped with more than a dozen analysis packages, including a laser spectrograph. He aimed it past Phoebe and started blinking it on and off, three long flashes, three short flashes, three long. The pilots had been taught Morse code for situations like this, and he was grateful for the foresight of the training team. Three long, three short, three long. SOS. Save Our Souls.

Cash kept sending for a long time.

No one responded.

2

Soon after news sites began to report that the Brazilian ships had quit Mimas and that someone had aimed a slab of ice at the Pacific Community squatters on Phoebe, rumours of a murder quickly spread through Paris. In the feverish atmosphere, it was like accelerant sprayed on a burning building. Within minutes, hundreds of citizens had converged on the scene.

A man had dragged a woman into his apartment, raped and killed her, then tried to kill himself by cutting his wrists. He'd staggered from the scene of the crime drenched in his own blood and the blood of his victim; his immediate neighbours and wardens from a nearby checkpoint had restrained him; he'd sobbingly confessed. The facts were plain enough, but wild stories quickly multiplied and spread through the angry crowd. The woman was a spy who had tried to seduce and murder the man, and he'd killed her in self-defence. The man was an assassin, and explosives had been found in his apartment. Someone shouted "Traitor!" and the cry was taken up by the mob. When peace officers tried to take custody of the man, the crowd surged around them and beat them to the ground. The man was stripped naked, lashed to the trunk of a tree in a nearby park, and strangled by a cable looped round his neck and tightened by a dozen people hauling on it. More peace officers arrived and attempted to cut the body down, but the mob attacked them and they retreated.

The spy walked past the scene an hour later. The battered and bloody body was still tied to the tree in the middle of the trampled park, guarded by a party of men and women half-drunk and armed with staves and kitchen knives. It shocked and excited him. The air of grim hysteria was heady. He knew that it would not be long now. The *Glory of Gaia* was only a few hours from entering orbit around Dione. Everyone in the city knew that war was almost upon them.

He'd been out and about, making final preparations. Everything was in place. His little tricks and surprises were primed and ready. He'd encrypted a file containing dozens of hours of conversations recorded by the bug he'd planted in Avernus's compound and downloaded to his spex when he'd passed by every day, and had mailed it to a blind account maintained by the Brazilian embassy in Camelot, Mimas. Now all he had to do was wait, wear the mask of Ken Shintaro for just a few more hours. He went back to his apartment because it seemed safer than wandering the feverish city. Ward Zuniga was on duty at the checkpoint set up outside the entrance of the apartment building, and he forced Ken Shintaro to strip naked. Vindictive, prejudiced and petty, revelling in the opportunity to use his new powers to cow and bully those he disliked, he made it plain that unlike decent, dull Al Wilson he hadn't been fooled when the spy had given up Zi Lei.

"I'm on to you," he said, flinging Ken Shintaro's clothes at him. "I know you're up to something, mister."

Ken Shintaro endured this in silence, although the secret pressed hard at the back of the spy's throat, aching to be released. It would not be long now. At the rally that night the crowd was angry and restless, riven by crosscurrents of rumour. Videos floating above packed heads showed over and over again footage of the strike on Phoebe. Brazilian singleships had altered the ice-slab's trajectory and smashed it to fragments with a low-yield nuclear weapon, but a few chunks had reached their target. A sudden stutter of bright flashes stitched a line across the equator of the misshapen moon, lofting clouds of dust that quickly obscured the dimming glow of small fresh craters. The crowd cheered every time the impact was shown, cheered Marisa Bassi when he claimed that the strike had been organised by agents sponsored by the city. He showed them video clips of the crew of agents at work on tiny Ymir's sharply curved surface. A razor-edged line of explosions cutting away an oval chunk of ice. Pressure-suited figures manoeuvring a fusion motor into a floodlit pit, laying a rail gun track across a pitted slope that angled to a sharp edge against a naked starscape. The ice riding a long spear of chemical flame, great sails shining on either side so that it looked like a close triplet of stars as it accelerated away toward Phoebe.

Cheers and screams and whoops, a tremendous baying rising under the high angles of the tent as five men and women dressed all in white joined Marisa Bassi on the stage: the heroes who had thrown the ice at Phoebe. The spy stood near the back of the crowd, buoyed by the press of bodies all around him yet feeling as if he was the only real person in a fantasy scene. A woman nearby was screaming wildly, all emotion and no meaning. A young man and an older woman were kissing passionately. One man said to another that the city was going crazy and a third thrust his face close to the face of the man who'd spoken and yelled that he was a traitor; there was a scuffle until the two men were pulled apart, shouting at each other, and all the while Marisa Bassi continued to speak and the crowd hooted and bayed.

No one wanted to go home after the rally ended. Public spaces were full of people arguing and laughing and carousing. Crowds spilled out of bars and cafés. A quartet of drummers filled a park with their beat as dozens of people danced around them, leaping high in the air. A circle gathered around a couple having sex, cheering and clapping. Wardens at checkpoints were passing around bottles and pipes, or accepting drinks and tokes from passersby.

The spy observed all this with a cool, rational gaze, as if everything was part of an exhibition got up to illustrate every variety of human vice and folly. He was in an exalted state. He was very close to the culmination of his life. He had been trained and educated for this since birth. He had been made for this. And now it was about to happen. He would not fail because he could not allow himself to fail. As he drifted through the riotous city, he felt his brothers at his back. He quivered with the thrill of secret knowledge.

He was stopped at a checkpoint because one of the wardens recognised him and insisted that he give an account of his movements. The man was drunk or stoned, and another warden was aiming his pistol at passersby and roaring with drunken laughter when they shrank away or shouted with indignation. The spy explained that he had been at the rally and like everyone else he could not sleep. The warden nodded and said we should all get some rest because we will soon be at war, but because we'll soon be at war none of us can. The spy smiled at this lame sally and was half-disappointed that the warden hadn't asked him what he had been doing earlier. *Sabotaging the city*, the spy would have said, and then he would have killed the warden and taken the pistol from the drunk and killed him and everyone else in range, and kept on killing until someone killed him.

The warden forced him to drink from a flask that was going around and told him to get lost. He got lost, and when he was out of sight spat the mouthful of liquor into a flower bed and wiped his mouth on the back of his hand. The mask was still in place, but he could feel it dissolving into his own face. His smile was no longer the vague beneficent smile of Ken Shintaro but a feral grin that grew stronger when a woman noticed it and stared at him. He stared right back until she turned and hurried off, and he marked her haunch and stride like a hunter measuring his quarry for the kill.

Thirty minutes later, the city's net fell over. For a moment, there was an eerie silence as everyone stopped what they were doing and attended to the same message: a call from one of the spy's demons. Surrender now, it said, and then it popped out of existence along with everything else, from basic phone service to the newly grafted defence applications. For a few seconds people stood still, trying to get their spex to work, and then they began to realise that everyone else's spex weren't working either—that this wasn't a harmless prank but something awful and unprecedented—and there was a growing roar of shouts and shrieks, people arguing, people issuing orders that no one was ever going to obey.

And then the lights went out all at once. It was night out on the surface of Dione, so the darkness was sudden and absolute. Noise doubled and redoubled, a great shout of despair that was hardly checked when a few seconds later the city's secondary control system kicked in and the street lights came back on again at half-strength and everyone looked wildly around as if expecting the enemy to step out of the shadows that were now tangled everywhere.

The spy was standing at the edge of the park at the middle of the city. He drank in the sounds of dismay and confusion. Soon the panic would spread and grow as people realised that a series of small explosions had knocked out the railway that linked the city with the rest of Dione, crippled the main air-conditioning plant, and taken down key parts of the power grid and the water and sewerage system.

The first stage of his work was over. Everything had gone according to plan here, and he did not doubt that the work of his brothers had thrown sand in the infrastructure and civic mechanisms of other cities on other moons, damaged their food supplies, tainted their water, and ruined the recycling systems that kept their air fresh and clean. Most would quickly surrender because their populations would be too busy surviving to offer any resistance, but Greater Brazil and its allies wanted to make an example of Paris because it had been at the forefront of the resistance. Very soon the second stage in the fall of the city would begin, and the spy had to be ready for it.

He felt an electrical hyperclarity as he set off toward the airlock he'd been using to get in and out of the city, at the edge of the warren of industrial chambers excavated in the rock-hard water ice beneath the northern edge of the city's main tent. The spy had chosen it because it was little used and close to his place of work, and he'd stashed his pressure suit there.

All he had to do was get outside and wait until the real attack began. He was halfway to the airlock when he saw Ward Zuniga.

This was at one of the barricades that had been strung across the city's grassy avenues. Set up between two apartment blocks, it was built from water-filled plastic blocks, and topped with tangles of smart wire. Ward Zuniga and another warden, both wearing pressure suits with helmets hooked to their belts, were standing at the narrow opening to one side of the barricade, stopping everyone who filed through, telling them to either report for duty or get to a place of safety as soon as possible.

There were two other avenues that ran straight through the city; it would have been easy to backtrack and take another route. Instead, the spy glided straight on, seeing Ward Zuniga's face brighten with recognition, hearing him tell the other warden that here was one of the strangers they needed to lock up out of harm's way.

"You're right," the spy said loudly, stepping so close to Ward Zuniga that he could smell the stale alcohol on the man's breath. He felt ten metres tall, utterly invulnerable. "You should lock me up. All of this, it was me. I did it."

Ward Zuniga blinked as he tried to process this, and the spy snapped forward and plucked the man's pistol from his holster and stepped back. It took less than a second. Ward Zuniga was groping for the pistol that wasn't there, panicked and puzzled, trying to understand what had just happened. The other warden went for her shock stick, and the spy struck her with the grip of Ward Zuniga's pistol, a hard, fast blow to her temple that put her straight down.

"You were right about me all along," the spy told Ward Zuniga and aimed the pistol straight into his face.

The man closed his eyes. He was trembling all over and his hands were half-raised, fingers spread wide as if trying to push something away, and the spy couldn't shoot him. It might have been different if this had been in the gymnasium where he had practised killing so many times in so many ways, or if Ward Zuniga had tried to run, like Father Solomon, or if he hadn't been dull, decent Ken Shintaro for too long. Whatever the reason, he couldn't kill the man in cold blood. He was aiming the pistol squarely and steadily at the bridge of Ward Zuniga's nose and his forefinger was curled around the trigger and he told himself to do it, do it now, but he couldn't.

"I'm going to spare your life because you're going to die anyway," he said. "In the moment of your death, remember that you could have stopped all this. You could have saved the city. Instead, you let me go."

"Please," Ward Zuniga whispered. "Please."

His eyes were still squeezed shut when the spy brushed past him and broke into a run on the far side of the barricade, leaping along in huge bounds. He went past two men who turned and stared, heard one of them shout something. The whipcrack of a shot parted the air close to his head and he saw a warden standing in the middle of a cross street, one hand bracing the other, staring at the spy over the sight of his pistol.

The spy bounced high on his next stride and the warden's shot punched his left shoulder and sent him tumbling. He pushed to his feet, his whole shoulder and arm numb from the tremendous blow, hot blood running down his arm. He'd dropped Ward Zuniga's pistol when he'd been shot. It lay on the clipped grass of the avenue a few metres away. Behind him, people were shouting, telling him to surrender as they advanced slowly and cautiously toward him. Kneeling in the gap of the barricade. Flattened against the walls of the apartment blocks on either side. Darting from shadow to shadow. Shots began to snap and crack through the air. A round struck a long gouge in the turf centimetres from the spy's feet and he ran forward and scooped up the pistol and kept running.

The numbness in his shoulder thawed and fire spread through the nerves and veins that laced the joint of his arm and his neck. He hardly noticed it. His every cell sang with a thrilling exhilaration, a reckless glee. There was another barricade ahead, in front of the place where the grassy avenue divided around the root of a soaring buttress. He pushed with all the strength in his legs, bounding higher with each stride, soaring headlong above intricate coils of smart wire that unwound with startling speed and snapped at his heels. He struck the safety rail of a maintenance walkway that jutted from a corner of the buttress and grabbed it with his one good hand and used his momentum to vault the walkway and land on the far side of the barricade, in the middle of three wardens so startled by his sudden appearance that they didn't try to stop him as he dodged around them and ran on.

After that, it was a straight chase to the airlock. He slammed the door on his pursuers and leaned against it for a moment, breathing hard and grinning like the devil. Something hammered on the far side of the door and there was movement behind the little inspection window set in it, but the AI was stupidly loyal to him and wouldn't let anyone in, and he knew it would take several minutes to cut through the door.

His wounded shoulder throbbed and burned; his left arm hung limp. He could open and close his fingers but they had no strength. He pulled off the loose shirt he wore over his suit-liner, ripped a seam with his teeth, and tore off two strips of cloth. He used one to plug the wound and wrapped the second around his shoulder and neck to hold the pad in place, feeling broken bone scrape under bruised skin as he tightened and tied it off using his teeth and right hand.

Someone outside fired two shots at the little window in the door; the slugs left black smears on the diamond pane.

He pulled the pressure suit from the locker and stepped into it, howling to let out the pain as he threaded his left arm into the sleeve. He zipped himself up and locked down his helmet, his breath harsh in the aquarium calm and smell of warm plastic behind the faceplate, and told the airlock to open its outer doors and stepped out onto a broad apron at the base of the tent's coping wall.

A warren of trenches and bunkers, part of the city's defence system, stretched away west and east across the floor of Romulus Crater. The sun was an hour from rising. Saturn's big crescent spread saffron light over the platforms of the spaceport, industrial tents and blockhouses, fields of vacuum organisms.

He used the suit's comms package to ping the capsule that he'd made Zi Lei swallow, but received no reply. It should have immediately bonded with her stomach wall, so he doubted that she'd eliminated it. Either she was being held in a place that blocked transmission, or she wasn't in or close to the city but somewhere below the horizon.

After a moment's thought, he asked the comms package to send a ping once a second, and cut to the west and began to climb alongside a cogged railway that ascended the shallow slope of the crater's rim, parallel to the slant of the city's tent. He hadn't climbed very far when the ping was answered. Simple triangulation, multiplying his height above the crater floor by the radius of Dione and taking the square root, gave him the distance to the horizon. A little over twelve kilometres. He pulled down a map. There was a small research facility exactly that distance from the city, to the northeast. He looked out across the vacuum organism fields, used the faceplate's zoom feature, and saw the facility's tiny, luminous bead gleaming against the black sky at the dark curve of the horizon. He walked a few steps down the slope, and the transmitter's signal cut off when he lost sight of the facility.

All right, then.

He doubled back, swinging north along a contour-line road to skirt around the defences. He passed several parking lots and hangars, all of them empty; every vehicle must have been commandeered by the citizen volunteers of the defence force. So he had to travel on foot, loping along in balletic bounds. He was moving toward the first of the vacuum organism fields when his suit's motion detector beeped. He swung left and right, saw two rolligons speeding toward him along a mesh roadway. The city's GPS was as dead as the rest of the net, so they must have spotted him visually. He told himself that it might have happened even if he hadn't provoked a chase through the city, and cut straight into the field of vacuum organisms.

It was planted with things like giant sunflowers, thousands of them in long straight rows, fat stalks twice his height each bearing a kind of silvery dish, every dish aimed in the same direction, east, in anticipation of the rising sun. He crossed the field in less than five minutes and climbed the low wrinkle ridge beyond the far edge, saw two rolligons ploughing parallel paths through the rows of vacuum organisms as they sped toward him, and raised his pistol and took aim.

It wouldn't fire. Out here, just before dawn, the temperature was −200° Celsius. Some vital part had frozen.

He stowed the pistol and bounded down the far side of the ridge, picking his way through a debris field flung from a small impact crater, pausing in the black shadow of a big block balanced near the crater's rim, leaning out to take a quick peek.

The two rolligons glittered at the top of the ridge. A line of figures stretched out on either side, moving slowly downslope toward him.

He was neither afraid nor particularly worried. He believed that he could sneak from shadow to shadow, out of sight of anyone watching from the rolligons, cut around the end of the line of searchers and head out east across the crater floor. He pulled up a map of the immediate area, was plotting a new route to the research facility when he saw a flash in the black sky to the west of Saturn's crescent, and for a moment his fierce confidence faded. If the people searching for him had put up a platform or flitter so that they could scan the area from above he could be pinned down and shot like a stray animal. But the suit's radar told him that the object was more than thirty kilometres away, moving across the sky at more than three hundred klicks an hour and braking hard—the flash he'd seen must have been the flare of a jet. He used the faceplate's zoom facility and saw a vehicle shaped like a broom shoot past high overhead, glittering in the light of the sun that was still minutes from rising. A moment later, the vehicle's bristling head broke apart into two dozen space-suited figures: marines, jetting away from their transport in a spreading wedge aimed roughly at the spaceport.

The spy's confidence kicked back in at once. He leaned around the edge of the block again, saw that the search party was bounding back up the ridge toward the rolligons, and set off in the opposite direction, skirting around the crater, clambering up the next wrinkle ridge. Its crest was higher than the first, and he could see the rolligons speeding away across the field of vacuum organisms back toward the city, could see flashes on the plain beyond.

War had come to Paris.

Sparks winked high in the black sky as kinetic weapons aimed from somewhere beyond the horizon used boosters to kick themselves toward their targets, plunging down and striking trenches and blockhouses and throwing up fountains of dust and white-hot debris. A tug dusted off from the far edge of the spaceport and was struck by a missile fired from the marines' position. Its upper part was blown away in a brief red flare; the remainder, motor still lit, rolled across the plain in a vast pinwheel of dust and flame. Lumpy shapes dropped straight out of the sky: battle drones inside protective impact bags. The machines tore open the bags even as they bounced and rolled through vacuum organism fields, raising themselves up on tall tripod legs and running forward. Several were struck by missiles fired by the city's defence force and vanished in brief clouds of dust and machine parts. The rest raked the slope in front of the city with miniguns and heavy-calibre kinetic weapons and rockets as they galloped along. A phalanx of construction robots rumbled out toward the advancing drones, and the drones picked up speed, leaped onto the big machines, and ripped them apart with reckless savagery. Several of the construction robots erupted in huge explosions as bombs planted in them went off, but a second wave of battle drones was already arcing down, rolling across vacuum organism fields and hatching out and running forward to reinforce the marines.

All this in the utter silence and clarity of hard vacuum.

The spy turned and went on down the far side of the wrinkle ridge. Without ceremony, the shrunken disc of the sun appeared at the horizon to the east and flung a tangle of shadows across the cratered plain. A minute later, the spy saw movement ahead and sought shelter in the shadow inside the bowl of a small crater and peeked over its low rim as two rolligons sped along a road a kilometre away, heading toward the research facility. He scanned the empty landscape and pushed out of the crater, and was promptly knocked down when the ground bucked beneath him.

South, a pinpoint light flared and faded, for a moment brighter than the sun. Although the spy's faceplate turned into a mirror a microsecond after the light struck it, he had to spend a little time blinking away after-images swollen by fat tears before he could use the suit's map and figure out where the explosion had been and what had happened: something had hit or otherwise critically damaged one of the city's fusion plants and the pinch field had let go.

The two rolligons had stopped. One stood at a slant where it had braked hastily and the other had run off the road. The spy bounced to his feet and chased after them as they straightened up and set off again. The war was well under way now, but he still had to complete his mission. He still had to find Zi Lei, and take custody of Avernus and the traitor Macy Minnot.

3

When the lights came on, burning raw and bright under the dome's polarised panes and angled truss work, most of the prisoners in the cage were asleep. It was a little after midnight. Men and women stood up or swung out of their hammocks, asked each other what was going on. A few started clapping in a slow steady rhythm, but it quickly petered out. Everyone was nervous and jittery. Several minutes later the ground shook, a brief sharp heave. Then it shook again. Everyone was on their feet now. One man was shouting that the guards were getting ready to kill everyone by evacuating the air; a woman was screaming the names of the children she'd left behind in the city; another woman stood in the centre of the cage and began to chant a mantra and a dozen or so people stepped up and joined in, their mingled voices rising under the dome of the tent. Other people stood along the perimeter of the cage that faced the blockhouse and began to shout in chorus, asking for their pressure suits.

Macy told Walt Hodder that they had the right idea. "If the city or anywhere else in the crater is hit by missiles or kinetic weapons, debris could be lofted a long way. As I know from experience. So even if we're not a target, we need to get out of here. Or at least suit up."

Dread and excitement burned low in her belly. She was convinced that the war had finally started. That everything was about to change. She wondered where Newt was, hoped that he was sitting safe in one of the storage basements of the clan's habitat. Because if he got it into his head to fly some crazy mission in *Elephant*, he'd almost certainly be killed.

Walt Hodder thought for a moment, then said, "The gates are the weakest point in the perimeter. If we can organise some kind of lever-and-pivot system we could raise them up off their hinges."

"You want to try to break out? What about the drones?"

Walt Hodder studied the two machines which hung in the air at different levels outside the razor-wire perimeter. "Making noise doesn't seem to be getting the guards' attention, but I'm sure that an escape attempt will. Then we can try to talk to them."

"If they don't use the drones against us. Or taser us or shoot us full of tranquilizer."

"I doubt if they'll listen to reason, either. But we have to try. For a start, we can break up the plumbing. The pipes could make useful levers."

"And I think those benches will supply the pivots," Macy said. She felt a lot better now that she had something to do. "Let's find some willing volunteers."

The frames of the benches on either side of the tables were bolted to the cage's floor. A dozen people rocked one from side to side until they had loosened the bolts, giving enough play to insert a pipe ripped from a shower in the toilet block and pry the frame free. Walt Hodder reckoned that they'd need to use two benches as pivots for pipe levers wielded by as many people as possible to lift one gate out of true. They were working on the second when someone shouted. It took Macy a moment to realise what had happened: the drones had fallen out of the air.

Someone wondered what it meant and Macy said that it meant they should work faster. They were prying at the second bench when two people in white pressure suits, helmets hooked to their waists, toting pulse rifles, came out of the square structure that housed the facility's garage and airlocks. One of them was Sada Selene. She and her companion galloped across the compound without looking at the prisoners and entered the blockhouse.

Macy and the others redoubled their efforts. They'd just managed to rip the bolts loose from one side of the bench's frame when several muffled shots sounded one after the other from somewhere inside the blockhouse. A moment later someone ran out, a young man with a neatly trimmed beard, one of the people who had interrogated Macy. He made it halfway across the compound when two shots cracked out and he collapsed face down, blood darkening the back of his green shirt. The woman who had shot him, one of the Ghosts, skinny and absurdly tall in a white suit-liner, walked over to the cage, stood beside one of the drones, pointed her pistol at the people who were trying to pry up the bench, and told them to stop what they were doing. Macy and everyone else backed away and the woman raised her voice and told everyone in the cage to sit down.

Someone dared to ask if the war had started and the woman gave him a contemptuous look. "What do you think? Sit down. All of you."

Avernus and her daughter, the five members of her crew, and Loc Ifrahim came out of the blockhouse, all of them with their wrists plasticuffed in front of them, followed by Sada and her companion, and two men in white suit-liners. The party halted in the middle of the compound while Sada walked over to join the woman with the pistol.

"They were breaking up the furniture," the woman said.

"They're trying to escape," Sada said, and slung her fat-barrelled pulse rifle over the shoulder of her pressure suit and called out Macy's name.

Macy stood up and walked to the wire, aware that everyone in the cage was watching.

"This is your last chance," Sada said. "I can take you to a place of safety."

"What about everyone else?"

"They'll be safe enough here. We already have enough hostages, as you can see, but I'm making this offer as a friend."

"I'll come with you if you let the others go."

"No. They might get it into their heads to cause trouble."

"Then I'll stay here. With my friends."

"The war has started, Macy. And for the moment, the Brazilians are winning. They've just about overrun the city's ground defences, and they'll be here pretty soon. Your only chance of escaping them is to come with us."

"So you're running out on Marisa Bassi. And taking hostages to negotiate favourable terms of surrender."

"We don't plan to surrender," the woman with the pistol said.

Sada laughed. "You don't know what we did, do you? All of you were locked up in here when it happened, and I suppose the guards didn't bother to tell you. How the war started, Macy, we threw a chunk of ice at the squatters on Phoebe. The Brazilians blew it up with an H-bomb, but some of the fragments got through. They made a *beautiful* string of craters when they hit."

"They won't stop chasing you, Sada. It doesn't matter how many hostages you have, they won't forgive you for that."

"They should thank us. They wanted an excuse to start the war and we gave it to them. And we'll win it, too. If not now, then in the long run. How else will we reach the stars and send messages back to ourselves unless we win?"

"I'd wish you luck," Macy said. "But I don't think there's enough luck in the universe to help you."

"Well, I don't mind wishing *you* a little luck," Sada said. "Maybe it'll help you escape ahead of the Brazilians. If you do, I'm sure we'll meet again."

When Sada and the woman with the pistol turned away, everyone in the cage stood up and began to shout. The Ghosts ignored them and chivvied their prisoners toward the garage. And all at once the two drones rose from the ground and swooped after them. One of the men collapsed, clutching at the dart that had suddenly sprouted from his neck, and there was a brief milling confusion as the Ghosts ran and rolled and tried to shoot the drones down, and the drones shot at the Ghosts with tranquilizer darts. Very few missed their targets. The prisoners screamed and howled in horror and triumph. Sada ran for the airlock and a dart struck her just above the neck ring of her pressure suit and she took a faltering step and fell flat. Avernus's crew tried to shield the old gene wizard and her daughter, and were struck by darts and swooned to the ground. The woman in the pressure suit hit one of the drones with a shot from her pistol and as it spun down out of the air its companion fired a dart into the woman's chest plate and fired another into her cheek. She pawed at it and fell to her knees and tried to raise her pistol, then keeled sideways and lay still.

Everyone outside the cage was down, apart from Loc Ifrahim and Avernus and Yuli. The surviving drone dropped down in front of the three of them as they stood with their wrists cuffed, looking all around them, and a man stepped out of the entrance to the garage and airlocks and told them to remain absolutely still.

"I'm a diplomat," Loc Ifrahim said. "A non-combatant taken prisoner and held here illegally."

"I know who you are," the man said. He was bareheaded in a pale grey pressure suit scuffed with black dust. His face was pale and expressionless. His eyes were masked with a pair of spex.

Loc Ifrahim said, "If you know who I am, then you know that I'm on your side."

"You are not the only reason why I am here," the man said. He moved about the fallen Ghosts, picking up their weapons and throwing them one after the other in high tumbling arcs onto the roof of the blockhouse. He stooped over Sada and picked up her pulse rifle and walked to the perimeter of the cage and studied the prisoners, his gaze moving from person to person, settling on the woman who had started the chant.

"Zi Lei," he said. "I've come to save you."

4

The spy entered the research facility through the airlock beside the garage. He cycled through into a locker room where a small army of bright orange pressure suits hung along two walls, shucked his helmet, and put on his spex and sorted through his zoo of demons. One forced the local net to handshake with his spex and two more slipped through and began to peel back the layers of security that protected the facility's AI.

Within ninety seconds, the spy had access to every camera in the surveillance system in the dome and the blockhouse. He saw people lying dead or unconscious in offices inside the blockhouse: clearly there had been some kind of serious quarrel or mutiny. He saw Avernus and her daughter and the diplomat Loc Ifrahim standing in the compound outside the blockhouse, handcuffed with five other prisoners and guarded by men and women in white suit-liners and white pressure suits. He saw prisoners inside a razor-wire enclosure, all of them sitting on the ground except for one. It was Macy Minnot, talking to a young woman in a white pressure suit who stood on the other side of the wire. He couldn't see Zi Lei, and inspected the seated prisoners one by one and there she was.

A strong wave of pleasure moved through him. For a moment, studying Zi Lei as she sat cross-legged in orange coveralls, her dear familiar face, he forgot about his mission. He even forgot about his injured shoulder. It was hurting badly now, but he wouldn't let the suit treat it with painkiller because he needed the clarity that painkiller might dull.

Then one of the demons handed him control of the two drones that floated in the air, monitoring the prisoners inside the wire. After that, it was simply a matter of selecting targets and letting the drones do the rest.

It took less than a minute to knock down everyone outside the razor-wire enclosure except for the diplomat and the gene wizard and her daughter. The spy should have called for a retrieval crew then, and made sure that his targets were secure until pickup. He didn't. He wanted to free Zi Lei first. He wanted to make sure that she was safe. He wanted to make sure that she could reach a place of safety before the retrieval team arrived.

So he stepped out into the compound and got rid of the weapons dropped by the people who'd been knocked down by tranquilizer darts, and called to Zi Lei. They stood with only the razor-wire between them and he told her how glad he was to have found her safe and sound, and started to explain that he would free her and let her take one of the rolligons. But instead of bubbling over with gratitude and relief, as he had imagined she would, she was furious and close to tears, and the other people in the enclosure, clearly mistaking him for someone fighting on the side of the city, were all shouting at him, demanding to be freed.

He told them to be quiet and when they didn't obey he jacked the stock of the pulse rifle against his hip and blasted a chunk of the mesh floor of the enclosure. In the ringing and shocked silence he told Zi Lei that he had done everything for the best of reasons. Staring straight at her as he tried to project his candour and concern, and also keeping watch, through the link with the surviving drone, on the three handcuffed prisoners behind him.

"I asked you for help," Zi Lei said. "I trusted you, and you gave me up to the peace officers. Why should I trust you now?"

"You don't have to trust me. You don't have to believe anything I tell you, except for one thing. I came here to help you."

The spy would have said more, but the prisoners were growing mutinous again. Some called out to him; others, including Macy Minnot, had begun to pry at the gate with lengths of pipe. Trying to lever it off its hinges. He fired another shot into the floor and told them all to stand back. This wasn't like any of the simulations and scenarios he had practised. There was no script. He wasn't acting this out but living inside it, excited and hopeful and exasperated and upset. Zi Lei was upset too, begging him not to hurt anyone.

"The war has begun and you have to get away from this place," he told her. "There are two rolligons in the garage. Take one of them. Drive out of the crater and keep driving. Find a shelter or an oasis and wait there. I'll find you when this is all over. I promise."

"What about my friends?"

"This is about you and me, Zi. They'll have to take their chances."

"Free them, Ken. Free all of us. This is why we were brought together. Don't you see? They are working through you right now, but you're resisting it. I know you're a good man. Let them do good, through you."

He realised that she was talking about her fantasy of the Edda, and it broke his heart.

"I have one more thing to do. Just one more thing, I swear. And then we can be together, and I can explain everything."

"I won't leave without my friends," Zi Lei said, and turned from him and floated away from the razor-wire.

The spy called after her and told her that they would leave together, and when she didn't reply he brought the drone across the compound to the wire. He couldn't think of any other way of dealing with the prisoners. He had to neutralise them before he opened the gate and freed Zi Lei and made Macy Minnot his prisoner; otherwise they'd probably try to rush him, and then he'd have to try to kill some of them or all of them. And even if he could do it he didn't think he could bear it, afterward. He would explain it to Zi Lei later. He would explain everything.

He saw the two of them climbing into one of the rolligons, driving out of Romulus Crater across a rolling plain, past craters and ranges of wrinkle ridges to one of the oases scattered everywhere. They'd wait out the war there. Just the two of them. He would take the people he'd been ordered to locate to a shelter and secure them and send a message to the retrieval crew, and then he would drive off with Zi Lei. He knew it was a fantasy but he didn't care. He wanted it to be true and that was all that mattered.

"What I have to do—it's for us," he said.

A moment later, the drone began to take down its targets.

5

Walt Hodder clutched at the dart that sprouted on his chest and his eyes rolled up and he collapsed beside Macy. Everywhere in the cage men and women were falling where they stood or running and falling head-long. Outside the razor-wire the drone rose higher, turning this way and that with tiny precise flicks, targeting people trying to hide under tables or behind those who had already fallen.

Zi Lei was shouting at the young man who stood masked and resolute, begging him to stop hurting her friends. And on the other side of the compound, Yuli bounded over to the woman sprawled unconscious in her pressure suit and jerked out the dart lodged in her chest plate and ran straight at the man. He staggered when she leaped onto his back, dropped the pulse rifle and clawed at her. But she had already danced away, poised on the balls of her feet, watching calmly as he pulled out the dart she'd stabbed into his neck. He took two wavering steps toward her and fell to his knees, groping vaguely for the pulse rifle. She snatched it up and slammed its stock against the side of his head, and he toppled over and lay still.

The drone was slanting along the razor-wire fence, taking down the last of the prisoners. Yuli flipped the pulse rifle end for end and fired from the hip. The drone jolted sideways in the air, one wing sheared away, and spun to the ground. Her second shot kicked smoking pieces of the machine across the compound; her third shattered the casing of the gate's lock.

As Yuli and Macy dragged the gate open, Zi Lei ran out and knelt by the man and cradled his head in her lap. His spex lay askew on his face and a thread of blood crept from one nostril and edged across his cheek, shockingly bright against his pale skin. He didn't look at all menacing now; simply young and helpless, a callow knight who'd failed his first serious test. Zi Lei bent to listen to his stertorous breathing, her black hair falling around his face like a wing, and looked up when Macy asked who he was.

"Ken. Ken Shintaro. From Rainbow Bridge, Callisto. He's on a wanderjahr."

"You know him from the city?" Yuli said.

Zi Lei nodded. "He must have come here to save me. He wanted to make things right after he let the wardens arrest me."

"I doubt that very much," Yuli said flatly. She was holding the pulse rifle in both hands, pointing it off to one side of where Zi Lei knelt with the unconscious young man. Telling Macy and Avernus, "It's plain that he's either a traitor, or an infiltrator working for the Brazilians. He didn't come here to make anything right. He wanted to capture us, for exactly the same reason that the Ghosts wanted to take us away. We're valuable assets. Spoils of war. That's why we weren't shot full of tranquilizer like everyone else."

"A higher power was working through him, but he didn't realise it," Zi Lei said. "He had to give me to the wardens so that I would be brought here. And when I was brought here he came to rescue me, and saved everyone else."

"I believe I had something to do with that," Yuli said. "And I'll deal with him, too, if it comes to it."

"Remember who you are," Avernus said sharply. "We are not like those who consider themselves our enemies. We will not hurt or kill anyone."

"I could take care of him," Zi Lei said.

"I don't think so," Yuli said. "It's too dangerous to take him with us, and it's too dangerous for you to stay."

Avernus said to Zi Lei, "You trusted him, and he betrayed that trust. Think very carefully, my dear. Can you trust him now? Truly?"

Zi Lei looked down at the unconscious young man she was cradling. After a long moment she looked up again. Her eyes were starry with tears but her face was set as she shook her head left and right.

"We'll lock him up here, with the Ghosts," Avernus said. "He'll be quite safe. And no doubt his friends will find him, sooner or later."

"If he doesn't get free first, and cause more trouble," Yuli said.

"What about Loc Ifrahim?" Macy said.

"The diplomat? I suppose the Brazilians wanted to rescue him," Yuli said.

"I mean, where is he?"

Yuli looked all around, then sprinted across the compound. Macy chased after her, through the locker room to the inner door of the airlock.

It had been jammed shut. Through the port, they could see Loc Ifrahim fastening himself into an orange pressure suit. Yuli banged on the port with the stock of the pulse rifle; he lowered the helmet over his head, grabbed Sada's ceramic knife from the floor—he must have used it to cut his plasti-cuffs—and hit the release switch for the outer door and was veiled in a brief mist as it swung open. He turned and mockingly waved bye-bye and stepped through, and the door swung shut on his heels.

By the time Macy and Yuli had found pressure suits that more or less fitted them and pulled them on and gone out through the garage, there was no sign of him. They climbed a walkway that curved up the side of the research station's dome and looked all around but failed to spot the fugitive. Beyond the dark patchwork of vacuum organism fields, the long, low ridge of the crater's rim swept across the horizon. The upper part of the city, angled against the rim's shallow slope, shone like a splinter of glass. Tiny lights flared and faded around it.

"One thing I know," Yuli said over the short-range band, "you can't stay here a minute longer. Neither can my mother."

"First we need to make sure everyone is safe."

"Let me do that. I'll make sure everyone gets away from here. Even the guards and the Ghosts. But it will take time for them to shake off the effects of the tranquilizer. And there is no time. You must leave right now, and take my mother to a place of safety. I assume you know somewhere suitable—you've lived here long enough."

"I can think of one or two places," Macy said.

"Find a good place to hide," Yuli said. "Then we can work out how to get my mother off this moon. Which she should never have visited in the first place. It's time to regroup and rethink."

"What about you?"

"You think I'm a little girl," Yuli said. "I'm not. It would be better to think of me as a monster. Let's go inside. It isn't going to be easy, persuading my mother to see sense. I'm going to need all the help I can get."

6

Arvam Peixoto wanted to oversee the endgame of the battle of Paris from the ground, and insisted that Sri Hong-Owen accompany him. He allowed her to bring Yamil Cho, his one concession, and they flew down from orbit in a transport that carried technicians, marines, and a brace of battle drones in its belly. It came in fast and low, skimming above the plain south of the conjoined rims of Remus and Romulus Craters, then pitching up and climbing past long fans of fallen rubble and terraced cliffs and setting down near a small pressure dome that had taken a bad hit—the spars of its framework were twisted and warped and broken, the few surviving panes frosted white.

The transport's belly door dropped open and the technicians and marines rolled out in three armoured personnel carriers and sped away along the rimtop highway. The city's surviving fusion plant had been secured and the technicians were going to check out its control systems, reaction chambers, heat exchangers, and transformers, and search for booby traps and any attempts at sabotage. Sri and Yamil Cho rode with Arvam Peixoto in a fourth APC to the transport hub at the top of the city's tent, with the two battle drones pacing ahead and behind.

Arvam explained that the perimeter defences had been rolled back and pretty thoroughly stomped on, but there were still pockets of resistance inside the city, and a fair number of snipers who were taking shots at any invader who strayed into their cross hairs. He was animated and exuberant, pointing out a shallow crater where some small engagement had taken place, breaking off to talk to his aide, listening to something on his phone, then telling Sri that it wouldn't be long now. The marines had fought their way into the railway station at the top of the city and the freight yards at the bottom—it was just a matter of advancing both fronts toward the centre and then mopping up.

"We're trying to open a line of communication with the mayor so that we can ask him to surrender," Arvam said. "We've already been contacted by two different officials who want to sue for peace, but as far as we can tell they aren't plugged into the command structure. We don't even know if there *is* a command structure; it's possible that not even the mayor can stop the fighting."

He took a call on his phone and then studied his aide's slate, telling the woman to organise defensive positions around the compound and make sure that the park on either side of the river was thoroughly searched and surveilled, turning back to Sri.

"The fighting was bad outside, and it will be twice as bad inside. This is their city. They have hiding places, spiderholes, they know how to move from place to place without being spotted . . . But don't worry about any of that. I have some good news. Avernus's compound has been secured. So cheer up, Professor Doctor. You're on the winning side. You've put yourself on the front line of history. Because history is definitely being made today. When Paris falls, the other cities will fall too. It's a brutal lesson, but necessary. And with any luck you'll get all you want, and more."

"You have Avernus's compound, but you don't have Avernus."

"Not yet."

"We don't even know if she is still on Dione. If she's alive or dead."

"Wherever she is now, alive or dead, you get first look at her last home. And pretty soon you'll have access to all the places where she worked her magic. If she *is* dead, figuring out all her secrets should keep you busy for the rest of your life," the general said, and turned away to take another call.

Sri was having a hard time hiding her growing misgivings. As far as she was concerned, everything hinged on finding Avernus alive, but the battle for Paris was now in its final stages and there was no sign of the gene wizard, no clue as to where she'd been taken after she and her daughter and crew had been arrested by Marisa Bassi. And there was no sign of the spy who had infiltrated Paris weeks before, either. He'd planted a bug in Avernus's compound and had mailed hours of recordings just before Paris's net had fallen over, but so far he hadn't made himself known to the invading force. Meanwhile, Sri was at Arvam's mercy, his to use as he saw fit, his to discard when he decided that she was no longer useful. And Berry, still sleeping in his hibernation coffin, was his too. A hostage Sri had willingly given up as a guarantee of her cooperation. At least Alder was safe. The thought of her brave, capable son alive and well in the sanctuary of her fortress of solitude, protecting and continuing her life's work, was her only comfort.

The APC ground through a gap cut in a slumped ridge, and the city was revealed. Its long tent, ridged and faceted, ran down the inside slope of the crater rim to the crater floor, bending like an elbow at its midpoint and stretching away amongst a jumble of small domes and blockhouses. Swirling layers of smoke pressed against the tent's huge panes down its entire length, obscuring the buildings and parks inside. Paris was burning. Sri felt a stab of excitement and apprehension. Avernus was somewhere down there. In the city, or out on the plain of the crater's floor. Must be. Had to be.

The APC drove down a ramp into a big airlock whose outer doors had been wrenched away. The inner chamber was marked by scorch marks and gouged by shrapnel and small-arms fire. Most of the lights had been shot out. Everyone in the APC sealed their pressure suits and disembarked, moving carefully in the slight, dreamlike gravity, and cycled through a small auxiliary airlock and emerged in a covered plaza. The battle drones stooped through the airlock one after the other, and then the party set off down a stalled escalator encased in a glass tube that slanted to one side of a horseshoe-shaped waterfall, the source of the river that ran down the centre of the city.

The pumps that drove the river's recirculation had either been damaged or switched off. The waterfall was dry, and so was the riverbed that ran away downhill between meadows and stands of trees where small fires smouldered. A squad of pressure-suited marines was guarding the beginning of a road that meandered off through the trees. Arvam Peixoto unlatched his helmet and tossed it to his aide, shook hands with every one of the marines and took their lieutenant off to one side and talked to him for a few minutes before clapping him on the shoulder and walking back to Sri and the others.

"We're clear to go all the way to the bottom," the general said. "You can all unlatch your helmets, by the way. The air's perfectly breathable."

The marines had rounded up half a dozen two-seater trikes with fat, low-gravity tires and composite frames painted bright primary colours. Sri rode pillion behind Yamil Cho, following Arvam Peixoto and his aide down the steep white road. The two battle drones loped alongside, their cowled bodies swivelling this way and that. Trees strung with platforms and nets and cableways flowed past, sprawling stands of flowering bushes, glimpses of meadows. Tiers of smoke hung at different levels under the framework that supported the faceted ridges of the tent's roof, drifted around banks of lights suspended from the roof. There was a strong odour of char and burnt plastic. Something was on fire amongst trees close to the road—a wrecked battle drone collapsed amongst uprooted trees, burning with a fierce heat that Sri felt against her exposed face as they sped past. She thought of the entire forest catching fire; the entire city. She mentioned this to Yamil Cho, and he told her that no one would have time to put out fires. "They are either fighting or hiding from the fighting."

The road forked and they turned left, rumbling over a bridge that humped above the river. Two bodies in civilian clothes were tumbled against each other in the dry river bed below the bridge's span. Blood dyed a long pool of water caught amongst rocks. On the other side of the river, a white flat-roofed building was on fire. Dense black smoke tumbled from a big hole knocked in its walls and thinner streams of smoke issued from every one of its windows. Bodies were scattered across a broad plaza.

They cut away from the road, following a short track between stands of puffball pines that fell away to reveal a one-storey building with blind white walls. Sri's heart gave a little kick. She recognised it from surveillance photographs: the compound where Avernus and her crew had lived until they had been arrested.

It looked untouched. A smart-wire barrier had been strung across its square entrance and at one corner several marines in armoured pressure suits stood or crouched, watching the city burn.

Everyone climbed off the trikes and Arvam Peixoto took Sri by the arm and steered her past the marines, followed by his aide and Yamil Cho and two battle drones. One of the marines told him that the area was still unsecured, but the general shrugged off the warning and gestured grandly toward the city and told Sri that if Avernus was hiding there she would soon be found.

Beyond a big park of trees and grass crossed by white paths, the centre of the city was framed by the arch where the sloping section of the tent met the section that lay more or less flat on the crater floor. Open-plan low-gravity helices and honeycombs of public buildings and apartment clusters, cased by the transparent organic shapes of secondary tents, stood amongst parks and plazas on either side of the broad dry river bed, with the gridded blocks of the older part of the city stretched away behind them. Threads of smoke rose everywhere, feeding a thickening haze. Sharp snaps and banshee whoops and rattling fusillades came from near and far. Arvam pointed to several places where the fighting was fiercest and explained that the citizens of Paris had set up barricades at intervals down the main avenues and at the bridges across the river. Every building was defended and groups of fighters were using service tunnels to move about under the city.

"My men have to risk their lives to clear each block, and after they move on the sons of bitches pop up behind them and start firing. They started most of those fires, too," Arvam said. "It looks like they'd rather destroy their city than surrender it, which is why we need to end this as soon as possible."

There was a falling whistle truncated by a flat bang as something struck amongst the trees behind the compound. Then a sprawl of white roses at the edge of the park in front of the compound vanished in a fountain of red flame and black smoke. Smouldering pellets of dirt floated down all around

Arvam laughed. "Mortars! They're using mortars on us!"

The battle drones rose up, weapons pods everting their sheaths, as a third explosion blasted everyone with stinging dirt. Yamil Cho pulled Sri down; the aide crouched; Arvam drew his pistol and loosed off shots in the general direction of the park. A moment later both drones started firing, fire flashing from the fretted barrels of their recoilless guns, the noise tremendous as streams of explosive slugs laced with red tracers hosed out across the park and converged on a building at the far edge. A wall disintegrated; the flat roof collapsed. A small figure scooted out and was caught by intersecting lines of gunfire and torn apart and flung aside.

The drones ceased fire at the same moment. Standing still as statues with smoke drifting from the muzzles of their guns. Arvam Peixoto broke the ringing silence, his voice sounding flat and shrill as he shouted at the marines who were guarding the compound, ordering them to get down there on the double and clear out the buildings along the perimeter. They jogged past, spreading out in a line, and another mortar whistled down. The explosion tossed one of them into the air and he tumbled limply and lay still. The drones started firing again, taking out the front wall of the building next to the one they'd already demolished, stopping in unison.

Two marines knelt over their fallen comrade. One looked at Arvam and shook his head and the general told him to leave the man there. "Freeze him and leave him. You've got a war to win."

The marines pulled out a body bag, rolled the dead man into it, and sealed it up and pulled the tag to start the chemical reaction that would lower the temperature inside to 2° Celsius.

"I want those buildings taken out right now," Arvam told his aide.

The pair of drones fired TOW missiles to the right and left, smashing holes in the buildings along the far perimeter of the park, setting the remains on fire. The marines bounded away across the park as debris began to drop out of expanding clouds of dust and smoke.

"This is the diehard element," Arvam said. "Dead-enders. Suicide jockeys. Even if we get a line open to Marisa Bassi, I doubt they'll surrender. But we have to try. After all, we are not barbarians."

"They didn't do too badly for civilians armed only with mortars," Yamil Cho said.

He must have been amped up by the brief firefight; he wouldn't usually speak out of turn.

"A lucky strike," Arvam said lightly. It seemed that nothing could dent his invincible good humour.

"Perhaps they recognised you," Sri said, angry because he'd put her in the line of fire.

"Perhaps they did." Arvam seemed pleased by the thought. He shaded his eyes with his wrist and watched as the marines disappeared one after the other between two smouldering buildings, then told Sri that he had a little job for her: he wanted to see if Avernus had left behind anything of interest.

There was a spray of pockmarks on the wall by the entrance to the compound, but it was otherwise undamaged. A short tunnel with doors at either end led to a courtyard garden roofed with irregular panes of diamond tinted pink and yellow and set in a spiderweb of fullerene composite. Sleeping pods were scattered amongst stands and beds of tropical plants. A colonnade along one side sheltered several open-plan rooms; rugs and cushions had been dragged out and scattered across the garden or thrown into the bowl of a fountain where water pulsed from the top of a chunk of black rock and rippled down its sides. Someone had daubed in red paint a chicken-foot symbol in a circle on the white wall facing the colonnade.

Printed books lay in heaps on the floor of one room. When Sri picked one up, it fell open to the first page and a young man's voice said, "Whether I shall turn out to be the hero of my own life, or whether that station will be held by someone else, these pages must show . . ." A sentiment that so precisely echoed her present situation that she felt a little shock, as if someone had crept up behind her and suddenly spoken into her ear.

It took only a few minutes to ascertain that nothing was left of Avernus's personal possessions apart from the books and a clear shard of plastic that Yamil Cho passed to Sri. It came alive when she touched it, showing a looped segment of a panning shot across a cavern floor crowded with strange organic shapes. She put it in one of the patch pockets of her pressure suit and walked twice around the garden and saw nothing unusual. She did not know what she had been expecting to find, but she felt disappointed. The plants were common or garden species—saw-toothed palmettos, bamboos, a cluster of dwarf date palms, flowering acacias. A fig tree sprawled over the wall opposite the entrance. Yamil Cho found a small lizard clinging to one of the branches, its skin the exact shade and texture of the smooth grey bark, changing to jagged pulses of scarlet and black when Sri plucked it from its perch and snipped off one of its toes and dropped it in a sample tube. A pale cricket twice as long as her thumb crouched in a cage woven from bamboo slivers. Sri tapped the cage and it sang a clear pure snatch of melody.

"Mozart, I believe," Arvam said, surprising her.

"I saw ones like this in a green market in Rainbow Bridge," Sri said. "They're common to all the moons."

"Take it," Arvam said. "And check everything else."

"The plants are just plants. Nothing special."

"The lizard looked like an ordinary lizard until you disturbed it."

"Chameleonism is hardly a novel cut."

Arvam stared at Sri for a moment, then took the slate that his aide held out to him and turned his back on her.

She set to work with a cold fury, snipping samples from everything and dropping them in tubes that Yamil Cho labelled. They'd worked halfway across the courtyard garden when there was a sound like a huge door slamming deep underground. A sudden breeze bent bamboos and shook waxy leaves; needles pushed into Sri's ears; the doors of the short entrance tunnel slid shut. Overhead, the spiderweb roof creaked and groaned and the pastel colours of its diamond panes brightened as beyond them veils of smoke were sucked away, revealing the lights hung under the roof of the tent, stark against the black sky.

Across the garden, Arvam Peixoto shoved the slate at his aide, ordering the man to find out where the breach had occurred, and Sri realised that Paris had just lost its air.

7

It was a long walk to the city, across rolling, lightly cratered terrain, through pieced vacuum organism fields. Every few minutes Loc turned and scanned the fields for any movement or flash of colour, but it seemed that he had managed to escape free and clear. He told himself that he'd had no choice, that he'd been woefully outnumbered and running away had been his only option. He told himself that he'd get his revenge. He'd surrender to the first Brazilian soldiers he encountered, find their commanding officer, explain that he knew where to find Avernus, and insist on leading the search for her. The gene wizard was a great prize; he was bound to be rewarded handsomely after he captured her. The thought of that, and ideas about what he'd do to Macy Minnot after she was handed to him for questioning, kept his spirits up as he loped along in the ill-fitting prison-issue pressure suit with only his elongated shadow for company.

Loc had been walking for almost an hour, and had used up more than half his air supply, when he left the last field behind and crabbed down a slope of rubble to a mesh roadway that ran across dusty and rubble-strewn flats toward the crater rim, curved across the horizon like a range of low hills. The city's long tent slanted up a shallow slope, bright as a splinter of sunlight under the black sky. On either side of the city and along the rim's flat crest thready plumes of dust spurted up and dropped straight back—some kind of bombardment going on. Everything sharp and small and vivid, the explosions soundless.

He hadn't been following the road for very long when he came upon the twisted remains of a rolligon that had been struck by a missile. Fragments of composite panelling and glass and quick-frozen bodies and pieces of bodies were strewn all around a fresh crater, but a quick search failed to turn up any kind of weapon, so he went on at a steady lope. At last he left the roadway and headed out across open ground toward the spaceport, where two transports sat gleaming fat and beautiful in the level light of the newly risen sun, their blunt noses blazoned with the green and blue flags of Greater Brazil and the European Union. The radio in his pressure suit had only one short-range channel, and there was no traffic on it. So he couldn't contact the attacking forces and let them know who he was and what he wanted to do; he could only hope for the best and march forward with his hands raised in the universal sign of surrender.

Loc was approaching a cluster of small blockhouses at the edge of the raised landing field when dust snapped up to his left, little spouts of dust walking in a line toward him. He realised that he was being shot at and backpedalled and fell flat on his back. It probably saved his life. Before he could get to his feet, something smacked into the ground a few metres away and a soundless flash sent a flat fan of debris scything above his head.

He crawled backward to the shelter of a bank of ice rubble and sat there until the pulse of adrenalin had faded away and he was no longer trembling. It was clear that he couldn't risk trying to reach the transports; he didn't have any way of talking to the Brazilian troops and he was wearing an orange pressure suit with black numbers stencilled across its chest that marked him as an escaped Outer criminal. No, he was going to have to find a way into the city.

Loc had less than an hour of air left now, and it took most of that time to navigate the chevron berms and traps and trenches of the defences that the citizens of Paris had so laboriously constructed and so quickly abandoned. He had to climb in and out of more trenches than he cared to count, but he had one piece of luck when he found five bodies flung out around a fresh crater. They'd all been carrying guns, and one was still functional.

By now he could see that the freight yards at the tip of the city had been flattened, and that the airlocks were guarded by battle drones that would no doubt shred him without compunction if he got too close. Luckily, he'd visited Paris soon after he'd been posted to the Saturn System, had spent some time touring its perimeter, gathering information that without doubt had been of vital importance when the invasion plans had been drawn up. There were plenty of other ways in through the secondary domes and tents, and after a little thought he cut to the east, where a row of farm tubes lay at right-angles to the main tent.

The airlock at the end of the first farm tube was barricaded by a pile of big ice blocks, and the farm's roof had been ripped open: the rows of bushes and plots of corn inside frozen solid in near darkness. The next farm tube was intact, green and lighted, but its airlock was barricaded too, and so was the next, and the one after that. Loc choked down his panic—he had about ten minutes of air left now—and after a few seconds' thought found a service ladder, swarmed up it, and with huge loping strides ran along the top of the curved roof. Rows of fruiting bushes were visible beneath the transparent panes, vivid heartbreaking green that triggered a pang of homesickness. He took one last bounding stride and pushed off in a huge arc that took him across the two-hundred-metre gap between the farm tube and the main tent, a record-breaking leap on Earth but nothing extraordinary in Dione's low gravity. His aim was just about perfect. He struck a slanted pane full length, rebounded and tumbled backward onto the walkway below, and caught the rail and lay still for a moment, his heart pounding in his chest and his breath loud and harsh inside his helmet.

The steep quilting of the tent stretched away on either side. Here and there faint featherings of vapour jetted into the black sky—air venting through joints stressed by explosions or through small holes drilled by kinetic and energy weapons. It was a stark reminder of his own perilous situation, that his suit had only a few minutes of air left. As he crabbed along the walkway each breath seemed harder to take than the last and it wasn't easy to stay calm, especially when the hatch of the first access point he found wouldn't open because the mechanism had been disabled from the inside. He moved on, panting from the exertion of trying to force the hatch, his heart pounding in his chest, and tried the second hatch. It swung open silently and smoothly and he swarmed inside and pulled it shut behind him. There was a sharp hiss as the tiny compartment pressurised, and he yanked off his helmet and took great gulps of cold fresh air before he opened the inner hatch, scrambling out onto a walkway tucked between the slanting roof of the tent and the flat roof of one of the square apartment blocks that had been part of the original city before it had been extended up the slope of the rimwall.

Thirty seconds later Loc was at street level, standing at the mouth of an alley, clutching the pistol he'd taken off the dead man and looking up and down a broad avenue lined with big chestnut trees. Smoke shrouded the roof of the tent and dimmed the chandelier lamps. Inverted whirlpools in the smoke marked the locations of small leaks. The sound of small-arms fire crackled near and far, punctuated now and then by the crump of an explosion or the brief scream of an energy weapon. To his left, apartment blocks receded into a grey haze; to his right, a barricade blocked the avenue. Something had ploughed through it and bodies in pressure suits lay on either side of the gap. Good. It meant that the attackers had taken the position and advanced deeper into the city; it meant that he was behind friendly lines. All he had to do was find someone to whom he could safely surrender. He thought about taking off his pressure suit because the damn thing made him a highly visible target, but remembered the smashed farm tube and the small leaks in the tent's roof and decided that it would be better to keep it on in case there was a major blow-out.

He reached the barricade in three long strides and crouched behind a tumble of water-filled plastic blocks. The dead men and women had been stripped of any weapons they might have carried. Most had been shot in the head. Loc was nerving himself to run down the avenue to the next barricade when someone shouted behind him. He turned and saw two men standing in the middle of the rubble-strewn street, aiming pulse rifles at him. Both of them were Outers; both were wearing pressure suits with helmets hanging from their belts like grotesque fruits.

"I'm a friend," Loc said quickly, and raised his hands.

"I think you better drop that pistol, friend," one of the men said. He was in his forties, with receding blond hair cropped close to his skull. "And lose that knife I see in your belt, too."

Loc stooped and set down the pistol and the ceramic knife and straightened. The blond man told him to move to one side, and his companion stepped forward, scooped up the pistol, and stepped back. "Maybe you can tell us what you're doing here, and why you're wearing a correctional facility suit," the blond man said.

"He looks like one of the enemy to me," his companion said, giving Loc a hard stare.

Loc ignored him and told the blond man, "I was in the correctional facility, yes. Some of us volunteered to fight, but on the way here our rolligon was hit by a missile. I'm the only survivor."

"Yeah? How did you get into the city?" the second man said.

"I walked."

"Past the fuckers who took the yards?"

"I came in through one of the maintenance locks up on the roof."

"Ease up on him, Ward, you can see the man's with us," the blond man said, and slung his pulse rifle over his shoulder and came forward and shook Loc's hand. "Al Wilson."

"Corey Wilcox," Loc said. It was the name of one of his interrogators.

Al Wilson introduced his friend, Ward Zuniga, explained that they were one of the hit-and-run teams that were harassing the enemy behind the battle line. "Look up," he said.

A drone hung high above the avenue, its sleek triangle hazed by drifting smoke.

"How we spotted you, Corey," Al Wilson said. "How we spot the enemy, too. But we're done with that now. It's time to make a stand."

"Why don't you point me toward the enemy?" Loc said. "I want to kill as many of them as I can. For my dead comrades."

"I reckon you'd do better if you came along with us," Al Wilson said.

"Do I get my pistol back?" Loc said, smiling at him.

"Later on."

"Right now, you can take point," Ward Zuniga said. "Go on. Through those apartments across the street."

They cut through the apartment block. In its central courtyard the bodies of men, women and children sprawled amongst wreckage fallen from the shattered canopy. All the windows overlooking the courtyard were broken and ribbons of smoke drifted from most of them. A short passageway on the far side led out to another broad avenue where people were rebuilding and reinforcing a barricade and cutting down a grove of small trees in an island garden at a T-junction to improve sight lines.

Al Wilson talked briefly with a young woman and followed her to the far side of the barricade; Ward Zuniga grabbed Loc's arm and told him that he could get to work right away. He pushed him toward a group of men and women who were filling hollow plastic blocks at a water bowser and dragging them to the base of the barricade, where they were passed from hand to hand up a chain of people to the top.

The water-filled blocks weighed little in the low gravity but were awkward to move. As he worked, sweating hard inside his pressure suit, Loc felt giddy with anger and barely suppressed hysteria. He'd trekked across the hostile surface of the moon, he'd been shot at by his own people, he'd barely had time to find a way into the city before his air ran out, and after all that he'd ended up working for the tweaks. But there was no chance of making a run for it: there were too many people milling around the barricade and the mean-eyed fellow, Ward Zuniga, was sitting on a block with his pulse rifle laid across his lap, watching him. So Loc had no choice but to toil to and fro until at last there was a stir in the little crowd around him. He looked up and saw a stocky man walking amongst the people, shaking hands.

It was the mayor of Paris, Marisa Bassi. Loc, who had once met the mayor at a reception, turned away and busied himself filling a block with water, frightened that he would be recognised. As the mayor drew closer, Ward Zuniga stood up and shook hands with him, and Loc took the chance to edge away. He found Al Wilson talking with another man, the two of them consulting a slate. Al Wilson was full of good humour, telling Loc that Marisa Bassi had been captured by enemy soldiers just two hours ago, but he'd manage to escape and make his way to the Bourse and broadcast a final message of defiance.

"It's wonderful news," Loc said. "But what is he doing here?"

"Organising the last stand, of course." Al Wilson showed Loc the slate—an aerial view of the city patched from the viewpoints of those drones still aloft—and explained that the enemy had entered at the top and bottom and was moving toward the centre. "We booby-trapped most of the buildings in the centre and then we used service tunnels to cut behind the enemy, here. When the two enemy lines meet, the whole area will go up in flames. We'll stand fast and deal with the survivors when they retreat."

Loc had a falling sensation. "How do you know they'll come this way?"

"Because our people will lead them here." Al Wilson clapped Loc on the back. "We still have a chance at winning the battle. And even if Paris falls, the war won't end until we drive these swine off Dione and out of the system."

Flasks were being passed around. People toasted each other, drank. Loc took the opportunity, while work stopped for a moment and everyone was distracted, to start moving sideways through the crowd. If he didn't make a run for it now he would never get another chance. He would die here, trapped amongst fools prepared to give up their lives in a grand but ridiculously stupid gesture. But before he could reach the edge of the crowd Ward Zuniga stepped in front of him and shoved a flask at him and told him to drink up, it looked like he needed some courage.

Loc wiped the top of the straw, sucked up a slug of foully sweet fruit brandy, and handed back the flask and asked for his pistol.

"I'll give it you when the time comes. Meanwhile, you can get back to work," the brute said, clearly enjoying himself.

Loc was dragging a block toward the barricade when another stir of excitement passed through his fellow workers. Some clustered around slates; others scrambled up the barricade. A flash of red light lit the smoky distance and there was a ragged sound of thunder. The ground trembled gently. All around Loc, people cheered and clapped. The trap had been sprung. The fools had blown up their own city in a vain attempt to save themselves.

Beyond the litter of felled trees at the T-junction a tall curtain of thick black smoke swirled into the avenue, and out of its rolling base came a man riding a fat-tired trike at speed, braking so hard in front of the hedgehog of angled girders at the foot of the barricade that the trike briefly lifted onto its front wheel. The man bounded off and swarmed up the steep face of the barricade, shouting over and over again that the enemy was right behind him. Half a dozen people reached down and hauled him over the top. He was very young and very tall and very skinny. His white pressure suit was splashed with blood at the thigh and his eyes were wide and staring as he looked about and said breathlessly that the enemy would be here at any moment, could someone please give him a fucking gun.

Marisa Bassi strode amongst the people at the bottom of the barricade, tearing slates from their hands, shoving them toward the barricade.

"This is our moment!" he shouted. His voice was hoarse and he was unshaven and haggard, but he was full of energy. Someone handed him a pulse rifle and he lifted it above his head in a two-handed grip. "This is our moment! What we do here may live on in infamy or it may live on in glory but I promise you that it will not be forgotten! You will not be forgotten! Fight not for your lives but for the city and for the freedom of all our worlds!"

Marisa Bassi held his stupid pose while people cheered his blowhard rhetoric to the echo. Loc ducked away when the mayor's gaze passed over his face; then Al Wilson was at his side, sweating and cheerful, handing him a pistol. Other people were pressing behind, so Loc had no choice but to scramble up the blocky face of the tall barricade—he knew that he would be shot down like a stray dog if he tried to run.

He found a footing next to Al Wilson at the top of the barricade. People crouched side by side, peering through chinks along the top of the barricade, lowering helmets over their heads and locking them in place, checking their weapons. Loc reached for his own helmet, but remembered with a chill that his lifepack was almost out of air. A muscle under his jaw was jumping and there was a fine tremor in his arms and legs and he felt that at any moment he might faint. The curtain of black smoke drifted down the avenue with dreamy slowness and battle drones stepped out of it so quickly that it was as if they had materialised out of thin air.

For a moment, nothing happened. Then the drones exploded into motion and everyone except Loc started to fire at them as they pounded forward in a threshing of long spiky limbs. Explosions thudded along the walls of the buildings on either side of the avenue and the drones were caught in a vast loom of sticky threads, a web that contracted the instant after it formed and lifted them into the air.

Everyone was firing through chinks in the barricade, the noise tremendous. Compressor guns started up with a loud roar. Chains of people passed up cylinders of polished concrete that were fitted into the fat breeches of the guns, and with percussive thumps the guns flung the cylinders straight into the struggling tangle of machines, smashing carapaces and shearing away limbs. But the drones were already chopping free of the threads that bound them, bringing their own weapons to bear. Heavy rounds knocked chunks from the grassy roadway, sparked from angled girders, struck the barricade. Water spouted from shattered blocks and people fell backward, shot through the head or chest. One man howled and whirled around, spraying his neighbours with blood hosing from his half-severed arm. Al Wilson grunted in surprise, spun in a half-circle to show Loc the raw meat where his face had been, and collapsed.

Loc tumbled after the dead man, letting himself bounce loose-limbed to the base of the barricade. Someone stepped on his hand as they scrambled up to take his place and he bit down on a scream. He looked around without moving his head and then slowly and carefully pushed to his feet and started to creep to the edge of the barricade. But before he was halfway there he was grabbed from behind and lifted and turned and dumped on his back. He stared at Ward Zuniga's angry face and jerked up his pistol and fired and kept firing as the man fell backward, smoking holes blown in his pressure suit by the explosive rounds, the noise of the shots lost in the ragged fusillade along the top of the barricade and the industrial roar and thump of the compressor guns.

Loc scrambled to his feet and ran, didn't stop until he reached the entrance of the nearest apartment block. He glanced back, saw a battle drone leap clear over the top of the barricade. It was missing several limbs but turned with balletic grace as it flew through the air and killed three people with precise head shots before a round from one of the compressor guns smashed it sideways. Then the centre of the barricade blew apart in a smash of flame and smoke that sent bodies and parts of bodies cartwheeling into the air. Loc turned and ran down the short passage into the apartment block's garden, tripping over the body of a woman, falling flat on his face and bouncing straight up and running on through the passage on the other side, almost into the arms of a marine in an armoured pressure suit.

Loc shouted that he was a friend, then caught himself and shouted it again in Portuguese as the marine brought his short-barrelled carbine up on its sling. Loc saw himself in the silvery mirror of the marine's faceplate. His orange pressure suit was spattered with blood and his face was the face of a madman.

"I'm a diplomat! A prisoner of war!" he screamed, and a huge wind got up out of nowhere, showering them with dust and debris and leaves stripped from threshing trees. Loc's ears popped. A banner torn from its moorings eeled down the street and wrapped itself around the marine, and Loc jerked up his pistol and fired into the mirror of the marine's faceplate. The first shot starred Loc's reflection; the second shattered it. The marine toppled backward, the banner still wrapped around him.

Across the road, flames flared in a row of broken windows and guttered and went out. Everything was suddenly still and quiet. Loc tried to take a breath but there was nothing to breathe. Knives twisted in his chest as air ripped from his lungs. He pulled his helmet from his belt and with jittery haste fitted it over his head. Air hissed across his face and he took a deep breath and snorted blood from his nose. The undulating ceiling of smoke was entirely gone. Chandelier lamps shone bright and stark.

A pinlight blinked under Loc's chin, warning him that the air in his lifepack was almost exhausted, and something else gleamed red in the corner of his vision. He turned, saw a light blinking above the door that had slammed across the entrance to the apartment's block. The inner door would have shut too, turning the passageway into an emergency airlock. He opened the access panel set in the wall beside of entrance, studied a short list of instructions and pulled down one of the knife switches. The door juddered back and he grabbed the dead marine by one arm and hauled him inside. After a moment's thought he tossed the pistol as far as he could down the avenue, then found the panel inside the passageway and closed the door.

Loc unlatched the marine's helmet as the airlock pressurised. His stomach clenched when he saw what the explosive round had done to the man's face and the back of his skull: using only his fingertips he stripped away the microphone-and-earpiece headset and wiped blood and gore from it as best he could, then took off his own helmet and hooked the headset around his ear. He switched from channel to channel, listening to marines talking to one another, and quickly realised that they had breached the tent to extinguish the fires before they raged out of control, and were now moving block by block, mopping up the last of the resistance. He switched on the microphone and reported his position and said that a man was down, repeating this over and over until at last a voice requested ID.

"Loc Ifrahim. I am Loc Ifrahim. The diplomat taken prisoner by the government of Paris. Your man was shot while rescuing me," Loc said. "I'm in a place of safety but I can't leave. I'm wearing an Outer pressure suit and I have only a little air left."

The voice asked him if the marine was wounded or dead, and Loc explained that he had pulled the man into an airlock and tried to give him first aid, but he was dead.

"He died a hero's death," he said, pleased that he had thought to get rid of the pistol.

"Sit tight, sir," the voice said. "We have a lock on Specialist Bambata's beacon. We'll be right there."

Ten minutes later, Loc was climbing aboard a transport sled. The marine's body was loaded beside him and with a jolt of acceleration the sled flew straight up above the roofs of the apartment blocks and out of a huge ragged hole punched in the side of the tent. Through the port beside his acceleration couch Loc watched the city dwindle as the sled rose and rose, a fallen star gleaming on one edge of the long arc that Romulus Crater shared with Remus Crater, the two interlocked craters shrinking, lost in a cratered plain that curved into a crescent as the sled headed toward the nightside of the moon.

Loc was taken aboard the *Glory of Gaia* without ceremony. A medical technician gave him a cursory check and he was assigned a thoroughly inadequate cubicle and given a change of clothes and a lukewarm meal of beans and rice and shredded mystery meat. A staff sergeant tried to get him to make a preliminary statement, but Loc told the sergeant that he would talk only to General Peixoto—it was a matter of supreme importance concerning the gene wizard Avernus.

The sergeant promised that she would do all she could, but after an hour had passed she still hadn't returned. Loc, convinced that he'd been forgotten or overlooked, tried to make his way to the command level but couldn't bluff his way past the guards at the connecting shaft. When a harassed captain ordered him to return his cubicle, Loc lost his temper and told the man that he would be punished for preventing a senior diplomat from carrying out his duty. The captain shrugged this off and ordered a marine to escort Mr. Ifrahim back to his berth and told Loc that he would be thrown in the brig if he was found wandering around again.

Another hour crept past. Loc ran through everything he needed to say, the story that would make him a hero and win him recognition and compensation for all that he had sacrificed for Greater Brazil. He thought of ways to make sure that the upstart captain would thoroughly regret his impudence. He tried to suppress his anxiety that Macy Minnot and Avernus would somehow evade him.

At last the sergeant who'd asked Loc for a statement returned, told him that he had a visitor. Loc sat up, straightened his badly fitting coveralls. But the person the sergeant ushered in wasn't the general; it was the gene wizard Sri Hong-Owen. Loc took a few moments to suppress his shock, then assembled his best smile and told the woman that it was a surprise, a pleasant one, to meet her in such strange circumstances.

"Just tell me where she is," Sri Hong-Owen said brusquely.

"She was in prison with me, but of course she will not be there now." Loc paused, savouring the woman's anger and desperation. Things had changed since their last encounter. This time he had the upper hand. "Did you really come all this way to find her?"

"If you can't tell me where she is, I'm wasting my time," Sri Hong-Owen said.

"I share your anxiety," Loc said. "I should have presented my information to the appropriate person hours ago, but I was prevented by unimaginative fools. But now we have a chance to work together for the benefit of Greater Brazil. Come in, please. Sit down. Let me explain everything."

8

Macy drove as fast as she dared along a road that ran northwest across the floor of Romulus Crater and climbed through a pass that notched the rimwall and switchbacked down to the broad plain beyond. She'd overridden the rolligon's AI—although it had a comprehensive database of every metre of the roads laced around Dione, and hardwired behaviour that enabled it to adapt to every kind of off-road terrain, it possessed no tactical knowledge whatsoever, and she didn't trust it to be able to take evasive action in the crucial seconds between spotting the radar blip of an incoming missile and impact. After quitting Romulus Crater there was no sign of the war anywhere, but Macy couldn't relax. Sitting high up in the rolligon's forward blister, she kept watch on the radar and scanned the moonscape all around as she powered down the dead-straight road.

Avernus sat on one of the bench seats behind Macy's throne-like chair. She'd hardly said anything at all since they'd set out, retreating into a kind of fugue or trance, and Macy had soon given up trying to talk to her. Both of them were sealed in their pressure suits in case the worst happened.

The sun rose higher in the black sky, like a spotlight tracking above a dusty, deserted stage. The road began to curve east, climbing long flow lobes cemented by blankets of dust, cutting through low wrinkle ridges. At last, a red star appeared at the horizon: the beacon of Double Rim Station. The road met and turned to run parallel with the equatorial railway, whose superconducting magnetic track, raised on A-frame pylons, climbed a broad ridge between two medium-sized craters. At the highest point the track divided into two, and the station stood in the middle of this crossing point, a fat transparent capsule with a brightly lit waiting area in its upper half and the various machineries of life-support services underneath. To the south, the rim of a dish-shaped crater swung away left and right, embracing a wide plain where three oases gleamed like tiny emerald beads. To the north, the land dropped in benched embankments and shallow run-out slopes to the broad and buckled floor of an older oval crater created by a glancing impact.

Avernus stirred as the rolligon drew up beside the station, and Macy explained that she was going inside to check if the railway's hardwired phone system was working—she wanted to find out what was happening at her clan's habitat. They climbed out of the rolligon one after the other. Macy felt horribly exposed as she waited for Avernus to emerge; she wouldn't have been surprised if a platoon of marines had stepped out from behind the slender columns of the railway track's pylons. The nervous, airy feeling stayed with her after they had cycled through into the station, and she checked the restrooms and shower cubicles and the bunk capsules stacked along one wall like cordwood before at last taking off her helmet.

Avernus was talking to one of the vending machines. Giving it a long set of instructions. Macy went to the other side of the station and sat in one of the booths and told the slate to connect her to Newton Jones.

The phone system used superconducting cabling strung along the railway tracks and line-of-sight microwave masts to link every oasis, refuge and habitat in a cellular network. Now that the communication satellites had been disabled, it was the only way for Outers on Dione to talk to each other, and it was working at full capacity. Macy had to wait in a queue until at last her call was connected.

Newt answered at once. As if he had been waiting for her. His left eye was swollen shut but his smile was the same as ever. "You're okay," he said.

"I'm okay. Are you okay?"

She was so absolutely, breathlessly happy, seeing him.

"Listen," he said. "The enemy dumped a zoo of demons into the phone system. The sysadmins are doing their best to flush them out, but it's going to be a long and gnarly job. Meanwhile, every call is being encrypted and split into packets, and every packet is being sent on a different randomised route to make them hard to intercept and trace. But no one knows if any of this is even mildly confusing the demons, so be careful what you say."

"I won't stay on the line too long. I just wanted to make sure that you're safe."

"As you can see."

"I see you have a black eye."

"It isn't anything. I wanted to take off for Paris and look for you, and I got into a knock-down fight with two of my cousins over it."

"I'm glad they made you see sense," Macy said. "Is everyone safe?"

"Everyone's safe." Newt paused, then said, "I heard all about your escape from the daughter of your new best friend."

"She got in touch with you? Is she all right?"

"She called an hour ago, told me to tell you that Walt Hodder had taken charge of everything. And that Sada is safely locked up with the guards. I guess you know what that means."

"It means I owe my new best friend's daughter a big favour."

"I think you're going to get a chance to pay it off right now," Newt said. "She also told me that her mother needs a ride. We took a vote here, and decided that we should help out."

"We can talk about it when I get home."

Newt shook his head. "We quit the habitat, figured it was too tempting

360

a target. I can't tell you where we really are, not over the phone, but I can tell you where we can meet up. Remember the first place you helped fix up?"

"Of course."

"I'll meet you there. Make good speed," Newt said, and hung up.

Macy told Avernus what Yuli had told Newt, and said, "It sounds as if she has everything under control."

"She can look after herself," Avernus said. "And she's right, we should try to leave Dione by different routes. It will maximise our chances of escape. Although I wish that it were otherwise, of course, for it may be a long time before we see each other again."

"We should get back on the road," Macy said, after a small silence.

"First, we'll drink this soup I had the vending machine make," Avernus said. "And then I'll use the bathroom. I've spent more of my life off Earth than on, but I've never gotten used to peeing into a tube."

The soup was good—noodles and chunks of tofu and green beans in a broth flavoured with chilli and ginger and lemon—but Macy ate it too quickly and burnt her mouth. And then she paced up and down and stared out at the still and empty landscape while she waited for Avernus to use the bathroom and climb back into her pressure suit. The war wouldn't wait for them. And she desperately wanted to meet up with Newt as quickly as possible.

As Macy drove the rolligon down the backslope of the double rim, a rail car sped past on the raised track, heading west. Despite the war, the trains and the hardwired phone system were still working, and everyone in the clan was hunkered down somewhere secret and safe. There was still hope. At the bottom of the slope, she turned off the main road and followed a track that wound north and east through low hills littered with blocks of ejecta, descending to a dark plain. She drove on, and at last saw an oasis gleaming brightly at the horizon.

It was set against the low rim of a small crater. A simple tent of angled panes and fullerene struts enclosed a dense garden of semi-tropical plants, vivid green in the desolation all around. There was no sign of *Elephant* or any ground vehicles, but when Macy and Avernus passed through the airlock of the oasis and stepped out onto a grass-floored plaza they were greeted by a small crowd of men and women and children, all of them cheering and clapping and whistling as Newt stepped forward, took Macy in his arms, and waltzed her around and around until she was helpless with dizziness and laughter.

The people in the oasis were refugees from Paris, around fifty people belonging to two extended families, and half that number of couples and singletons. They'd left more than two weeks ago, and they wanted to thank Avernus for her advice, honour her with a meal, and ask her questions about obscure details of the oasis's ecosystem. They wanted to hear the latest news from Paris, too, but it turned out that Macy had seen less than they had of the fighting—the city's camera network had been plugged into the hard-wired phone system during the early stages of the battle, and the connection hadn't fallen over until the enemy breached the main tent. So Macy was soon able to detach herself from the welcoming party and wander off with Newt through a chain of paths and bowers and bridges that threaded along and amongst the densely planted garden that filled more than half the oasis. Newt was waiting for a call from some friends of his who were disrupting the network of surveillance satellites that the enemy had put into orbit around Dione at the beginning of the war by aiming powerful transmitter dishes at them, and using smart gravel and an industrial X-ray laser to physically knock out hub satellites that transferred signals within the network.

"The satellites are hardened, but my friends have already punched some big holes in their coverage, which is why I was able to drift down here undetected," Newt said, and told Macy that he'd parked *Elephant* five kilometres away, hidden under camouflage cloth.

"Everyone's vehicles are out of sight, too," he said. "Garaged on the other side of the rim."

"I didn't know there was a garage," Macy said.

They were sitting side by side at the edge of a slab of rock set high above a pond fringed with giant reeds where big electric-blue dragonflies darted and hovered. Much of the clear water was tiled by lily pads big enough to use as stepping stones. Fish glided beneath the pads, more than two dozen species. And on either side and behind them stretched a tropical profusion thick with fruiting vines and bushes, banana plants and sugar bamboo. The air was pleasantly warm. Amazing to think that just a few metres away, beyond the diamond composite panes, was a vacuum just ninety degrees above absolute zero.

"There's a ramp over the crater rim," Newt said. "It's how you get to the vacuum organism fields."

"I didn't know there were vacuum organism fields, either."

Newt gave her his best mock-innocent look. "All you had to do was climb to the top of the rim and look down. The garage entrance is under an overhang right by the ramp. After that, you hike through a tunnel that cuts straight through. There are workshops and a manufactory, too."

"It's a great hiding place, apart from the fact that the tent is entirely visible."

"Most of the refuges and oases are visible, but that doesn't mean you can know everything about them simply by looking at them. And there are more than five thousand of them on Dione. The enemy thinks in terms of cities, centralisation, top-down leadership, hierarchies. We don't. Paris is the largest city of Dione, but it isn't the capital. And ninety-five percent of the habitable space on Dione is in places like this. When they first came here, our grandparents and great-grandparents felt the need to huddle together against a hostile environment. But this is our home now. We don't need cities any more."

Macy thought of thousands of small communities spread across the face of Dione, each with its own power plant and signature ecosystem, linked by roads and the railway, by a robust, noncentralised communication system . . .

She said, "If I was paranoid, I'd think that Marisa Bassi and his fighting talk was some kind of lure got up to confuse the enemy. To make them think that Paris was the target they needed to take down, so the rest could survive unharmed."

"A lot of people died because they listened to what Marisa Bassi had to say," Newt said. "We'd have to be pretty stony-hearted to have planned something like that. Marisa Bassi brought what happened on himself."

"I thought you agreed with him. That you wanted war. I was frightened that you were ready to go tearing off on some kind of kamikaze mission."

"Well, I was, until I was brought to my senses," Newt said, touching his swollen eye and giving her a rueful smile.

"I meant something really stupid. Like ramming one of the Brazilian ships."

"Why would I want to do something like that? I'm no peacenik," Newt said. "But I'm not like Marisa Bassi, either. We couldn't stop the enemy coming here. And we couldn't stop the war because it was mostly the enemy's idea. But that doesn't mean they've won it. It doesn't mean that we can't turn things around."

"I can't stay here," Macy said. "And I can't hide out with the clan, either. Yuli believed that the spy, or whatever he was, the man who busted into the place where I was being held prisoner, he wasn't just looking for Avernus and Loc Ifrahim. He was looking for me, too. Even if he wasn't, someone will want to catch me and punish me for defecting. Make an example of me. Anywhere I go, I'll be a danger to everyone else."

"Avernus told me that she has a place. Well, more than one place, actually. You can build a lot in a hundred years, especially when you have crews of construction robots working for you. But she mentioned one in particular."

"Where she's going to meet Yuli."

"Yuli, and some other people."

"She told you where it is, didn't she?"

"Sure."

"See, she trusts you, but she doesn't trust me. Because I'm not an Outer."

"Don't beat yourself up," Newt said. "She had to tell me because she needs a lift. Want to come along?"

"Where?"

"Titania. It's one of the moons of Uranus."

"Isn't that where your mother once lived?"

"The very same."

"Don't get mad, but I have to ask. What does she think about you running off?"

"I'm not planning to run off. Not permanently. And I sold it to her and the rest of the clan because it will keep *Elephant* safe from confiscation, and because of the kudos we'll gain by helping Avernus."

"We'd come back."

"You've already come a long way."

"Yes, I have. But I'm not sure that I want to live that far out. Not forever, anyway."

"Maybe you could come back in a few years. When things have settled down. When the Brazilians have stopped searching for you. Of course, we might have to tweak your appearance a little. A few cosmetic changes to make you look as if you belong here."

Macy thought about it. Passing as an Outer didn't seem like a bad idea right now, all things considered. She said, "Nothing that can't be changed back."

"Absolutely."

"And we're talking real, three-hundred-and-sixty-five-day years. Not the thirty-odd years it takes Saturn to go around the sun."

"Somewhere between the two," Newt said, and pushed up and kicked away from the slab and fell with swooning slowness feet-first into the water.

Macy jumped after him and they swam and laughed and splashed great glittering gouts of water, and afterward clambered out onto a slope of soft dry yellow moss. Gunneras spread dark green leaves big as umbrellas over the water's edge. A swarm of silver-winged butterflies tumbled around a flowering vine that climbed a rock face. Macy and Newt stripped off their suit-liners and lay under the warm light that danced through the spreading branches and leaves in a thousand bright stars and laid a shifting mosaic of shadow and light over their bodies, his pale and long, hers dark and compact . . . It occurred to her that an alien might think that they were two closely related but distinct species, that the differences between men and women were more profound than any differences between Outers and ordinary human stock.

Newt said, "What's so funny?"

She told him, and he laughed and said that maybe it was true at the moment, but things were definitely going to change.

"The people who wanted to go to war against us convinced their governments that we were altering the course of human evolution in dangerous ways. They exaggerated the importance of a few practical or cosmetic tweaks to make their case. Pretended that what was mostly talk was actually happening. The truth is, the majority in the Outer System didn't want any kind of radical change. They voted against it, time and again. They were as much against it as the people on Earth who were talking up the case for war. But now all the radicals are fleeing outward. Beyond the reach of any constraints or restrictions. They're going to be free to do whatever they want. The war has set them free."

"It's a pretty high price for freedom," Macy said. "The war. All the people who were killed and will yet be killed."

"But it happened, and it can't be taken back," Newt said. "All we can do is go forward and hope for the best."

At last Newt's spex beeped: the network of enemy surveillance satellites was pretty thoroughly wrecked; it was safe to leave. They pulled on their suit-liners and hurried back to the scattering of two- and three-room apartments built around the plaza in front of the airlock. Avernus and the woman who'd been elected to be the oasis's gene wizard were down in the service level, talking to the oasis's AI.

"Listen to the machines," Avernus told the woman. "They're smarter than you think. As long as you explain exactly what you want, they'll give you good advice. And you have a fine place here. Robust. I believe you are responsible for the excellent quality of the soil," she said, looking at Macy. "I can find plenty of work for you. If you want to come with me, that is."

"I think the fix is in," Macy said, amazed and pleased.

It was time to go. Newt climbed into his familiar scuffed white pressure suit with the cheesy reproduction of Van Gogh's *Starry Night* splashed across its chest plate; Macy and Avernus into brand-new matte-black pressure suits. Macy slung the pulse rifle she'd liberated from the research facility over her shoulder; Avernus took the garland offered to her by a shy, beautiful boy, and crowned her helmet with it.

Outside, the gene wizard carefully lifted off the quick-frozen flowers, stepped off the road, and laid them all white and gold on the tan dust. Then she followed Macy and Newt to the rolligon. *Elephant* was powered up and ready to go by the time they arrived. Macy helped Newt rip down the cam-ouflage cloth and discovered that the tug was fattened with drop tanks full of fuel, and that it had been painted black.

"Anti-radar paint," Newt said. "I falsified her registry, too. No one can trace her to the clan, or to me and you."

They dusted off ten minutes later, flying in a low, flat trajectory toward the anti-Saturnian hemisphere. After the sun disappeared above the western horizon, Newt stood *Elephant* on her stern and took her straight up.

Newt's friends had taken down most of the surveillance satellite network and the Brazilian flagship was on the far side of Dione; *Elephant* was thirty thousand kilometres out and still accelerating before it was challenged. Macy was plugged into the comms; when the looped warning started to play for the second time, she asked Newt if he thought they'd be targeted.

"The enemy took out a fair number of ships just before the battle for Paris kicked off, but they don't seem to be going after refugees. Take a look at the sky—you'll see what I mean."

Apart from a few fast-moving Brazilian singleships, there was almost no traffic in the volume between the outer edge of the ring system and the orbit of Iapetus. Newt pointed out radar signals that weren't tagged by ID beacons: ships killed by missiles or EMP mines, corpses falling in blind orbits around Saturn. But further out were more than fifty ships under acceleration, all heading for different parts of the sky.

"Like dandelion seeds blown on a summer breeze," Macy said, and then had to explain what a dandelion was.

"Our only problem is that we have to head inward before we can head out," Newt said. "We need to slingshot around Saturn if we're going to make good time."

Dione rapidly dwindled behind them. *Elephant* drove past the orbits of Tethys and Enceladus and Mimas, heading toward the glory of the rings.

Newt planned to fly through the ring shadow and swing close around Saturn, stealing as much velocity as possible before swinging out toward Uranus. They were almost at the Keeler Gap, at the outer edge of the A Ring, when the proximity alarm blared. Something was falling toward them at a low slant, moving with incredible speed.

9

After sitting through Loc Ifrahim's convoluted, self-serving story, Sri was ready to drag the man to the nearest airlock and boot him into orbit around Dione without the benefit of a pressure suit. The diplomat swore that he'd told her everything he knew, but Sri was certain that he'd withheld every species of vital information and embellished and distorted what little truth was left to shape himself into the principal figure of his tale. Not only that, but he expected to be handsomely rewarded, even though it was clear that he hadn't really done anything except run away.

When she told him as much, he sneered and said that he knew what she had done to get here. "I was captured by the Outers and held prisoner, and I used my wits to escape them, and I fought against them in the fall of Paris. I did my duty. You, on the other hand, assassinated your mentor and stole a ship. All to further your crazy ambition. So with all due respect, Professor Doctor, I hardly think that you are in a position to judge me."

"We'll see about that," Sri said.

Loc Ifrahim met her angry gaze with calm insolence. He was no longer the sly, obsequious young man she'd first met at Rainbow Bridge. He wasn't afraid to let his ambition show now, or his contempt. Saying, "We're both servants, Professor Doctor. The difference is that my star is rising, and yours is diminishing."

"I advise you not to underestimate me," Sri said, and pushed out of his little cabin before her anger got the better of her.

He followed her to the hatchway, called after her. "They'll say I'm a hero, Professor Doctor! What will they say about you, I wonder?"

Sri put in a call to Arvam Peixoto, who was still down on the surface, in Paris, supervising mopping-up operations and securing and making airtight the building where he planned to set up his headquarters. She told him that she believed that Loc Ifrahim was withholding vital information, said, "We should put him to the question."

"We will do no such thing. If only because he is a member of the diplomatic service," Arvam said.

"And also because he's been working for you," Sri said, amazing and shocking herself. Although she'd always been certain that Arvam had commissioned Speller Twain and Loc Ifrahim to sabotage the biome project, she'd never dared ask him about it because she'd been scared that he would punish her for her temerity, end their uneasy alliance, and probably end her career, too. So she'd kept quiet. She'd taken the hit and moved on. Until now, when she'd blurted out the blunt accusation because she was angry and tired and frustrated. But it didn't matter, she realised. Their alliance, if that was what it had ever been, was ended. She was completely in his power, and it freed her to be absolutely honest with him. No more pretence. No dissembling.

Arvam was smiling. "You're angry because you do not want to believe that your creature may have failed in his mission," he said.

"The agent is as much mine as yours. I'm angry because this so-called servant of the government and the families is clearly lying to make himself seem like a hero. Let my man put him to the question. We'll soon get the truth."

"Leave Mr. Ifrahim to me," Arvam said. "As for his story, I'll send a platoon to check out the research facility where he claims to have been held prisoner along with Avernus and Ms. Minnot."

"You should send some of your marines to check out the Jones-Truex-Bakaleinikoff habitat, too. That's where Macy Minnot has made her home."

"Then it will be the last place she'll run to because it will be the first place we'll look for her. No. We will check out the research facility, and take things from there."

"Let me help," Sri said, and after some to and fro won the general's permission to access surveillance data accumulated by the *Glory of Gaia*'s combat management system.

It didn't take long to find what she was looking for. Although there were thousands of hours of video showing the assault on the city from dozens of viewpoints, shot by transports, battle drones, and cameras worn by marines, coverage of the rest of Romulus Crater was patchy and intermittent. Luckily, a transport passing overhead had captured a few seconds of footage that showed figures in orange pressure suits scattering away from the research facility, and although it was impossible to tell who was escaping or where they were going, Sri could use the footage to set parameters for a global search of everything in the archive.

After a few minutes the AI presented her with dozens of images of people in orange pressure suits, some captured or killed by marines, others heading away from the city, toward various small shelters or the crater's rim. Sri was especially interested in two short videos patched together from spy satellite imagery. The first showed a rolligon driving out of a pass in the northwest quadrant of the crater's rim. The orange pressure suit worn by its driver was clearly visible through its transparent blister, and it was heading in the direction of the Jones-Truex-Bakaleinikoff habitat. The second video, shot a couple of hours later, showed the same rolligon, still driven by someone in an orange pressure suit, moving away from one of the stations on the equatorial railway. It passed a rail car that was slowing as it approached the station, turned north, driving off the road and heading out across the empty moonscape, and then the video ended because the satellite's orbit had taken it over the horizon. The Outers had destroyed some of the satellites and compromised most of the rest; coverage of the area didn't resume until seventy-one minutes later, and by then there was no sign of the rolligon.

Sri wondered if the rolligon had stopped at the station, if it had dropped off a passenger or passengers who might have caught that rail car, but the intelligence officer who answered her call said that they hadn't yet hacked into the railway's control system. It was highly distributed, and their demons had met with considerable resistance.

"You have people on the ground, don't you? I want someone down there to look at the transport records as quickly as possible. I want them to find out if anyone boarded the rail car that arrived at Double Rim Station at 0510 UST. They can start by searching for local video footage from the station itself."

The young officer was clearly intimidated by Sri, but he stood his ground. "I'm afraid I don't have the authority to action that, ma'am."

"Who does?"

"Commander Vaduva or General Peixoto, ma'am."

Sri tried and failed to contact either of them, left messages, returned to her analysis of the spy satellite footage. Say the vehicle had gone to ground somewhere. Sri knew its speed and its general direction, and that it must have reached its destination at some point within the seventy-one-minute gap in coverage. A simple calculation drew a circle that included no less than seven oases. It would take time to search them all, but it was doable. Sri was about to call Arvam Peixoto and tell him to send marines to check out the oases when she had a thought, and asked the AI a question.

After a few seconds, it confirmed that a ship had left Dione two hours after the last sighting of the rolligon; its trajectory indicated that it had taken off from the area where the rolligon had vanished. Like all the refugee ships, it was being tracked by deep radar. Most were already heading away from the system, but this one, one of the last to leave, was heading toward Saturn, presumably because it intended to increase its velocity with a slingshot manoeuvre.

Sri thought hard about this, then told Yamil Cho, who all this time had been waiting outside the cubicle she'd been assigned, what she wanted him to do.

"I know that won't be a problem for someone as resourceful as you."

"Of course not." Yamil Cho paused, then added, "You do remember, ma'am, that your son's hibernation coffin is on board the *Glory of Gaia*. It will be very difficult to move it without detection."

"Of course I remember. It is never out of my mind. But we will have to leave him. Not only because we can't move him, but also because he will be a token of my intention to return."

Berry would be safer here, she told herself. And anyway, he'd been a hostage all along. It didn't change anything.

Yamil Cho shot off down the companionway to scout the territory, came back fifteen minutes later and led Sri to an airlock in the ship's keel. Its narrow antechamber was dimly lit, with zero-gravity tools racked on one wall and a file of pressure suits standing along the other. They helped each other into two of the suits. Yamil Cho selected several items from the tool racks and fastened them to his utility belt, and clipped one end of a tether to a D-ring on his belt and clipped the other end to Sri's belt. Then they cycled through the lock, out onto the hull of the ship.

Dione's cratered icescape slowly and steadily unravelled below. The *Glory of Gaia* was presently swinging around the anti-saturnian hemisphere, travelling from east to west, and the gas giant loomed beyond the arc of the moon's horizon, its salmon and umber globe printed with the parallel shadow-lines of the rings. Yamil Cho fired his reaction pistol and Sri was gently spun away from the stupendous view and towed across the belly of the *Glory of Gaia* toward the delta-winged shuttle that she and Yamil Cho had stolen when they had escaped from Earth, and now had to steal again.

There had been no room for the *Uakti* in the *Glory of Gaia*'s hangars, so it had been fastened to the flagship with docking clamps used by shuttles that had brought men and material up from Earth when the flagship had been preparing for its mission. Sri had to wait for twenty minutes, clinging to a strut and expecting an armed party to erupt onto the hull at any moment, while Yamil Cho manually activated each of the motors that opened the jaws of the clamps.

At last the shuttle was floating free. Yamil Cho towed Sri to its airlock. As soon as they were inside and strapped into the acceleration couches, he woke up its systems, initiated the preignition sequence of its main motor, and fired the attitude jets that pushed it away from the *Glory of Gaia*. Traffic control started squawking at them as the main motor fired and they began to accelerate away from the flagship and Dione, toward Saturn. Sri identified herself and told the officer that she would speak only with General Peixoto. When he came online two minutes later, she told him at once that she was chasing after Avernus, and sent him a file containing the results of her search of the surveillance data.

Arvam bounced the file to an aide and told Sri that she might at least have asked his permission. "I'm disappointed. It seems that we still haven't established a full degree of trust."

He didn't look disappointed; he looked faintly amused, as if he knew something she didn't.

"I have trusted you with the life of my youngest son," Sri said, and explained that Berry's hibernation coffin was still aboard the *Glory of Gaia*.

"I'll keep him safe until you return from this quixotic mission of yours," Arvam said.

"If Loc Ifrahim was telling the truth, Avernus and Macy Minnot were being kept as prisoners in the same place. I believe that they are now aboard that tug, attempting to escape your jurisdiction together."

"Let's assume that they are on the tug. What will you do if you catch up with them? You aren't carrying any weapons."

"They don't know that."

"Mmm. Still, I think I ought to send a singleship after you, just in case. Don't worry. The nearest will take several hours to catch up with you, and by then you should have had your shot at glory."

Sri didn't say anything. She wasn't going to thank him for his interference.

"You might want to know that the platoon of marines I sent to the research facility found your creature," Arvam said. "He's alive, but only just. He'd been knocked out with a dose of tranquilizer and suffered a bad reaction to it. So we don't yet have his side of the story, but the marines also retrieved a good deal of surveillance footage. It shows that more than fifty people were being held prisoner there. Including Mr. Ifrahim and Macy Minnot. Also Avernus and her daughter."

"So Loc Ifrahim didn't lie about that, at least."

"Footage from cameras inside the facility's single building suggests that Mr. Ifrahim also told the truth about a fight between two factions of the guards," Arvam said. "Unfortunately, the surveillance system fell over shortly after one faction killed or subdued the other. It seems that your creature sabotaged it as part of his plan to take custody of his targets. We'll know more when he recovers consciousness."

"It's obvious that Ifrahim tried to kill him," Sri said. "He wanted the glory of capturing Avernus and Macy Minnot all for himself, but they managed to escape him. Put him to the question again. And your marines should try to locate the other prisoners. If nothing else, they will be witnesses to Ifrahim's perfidy."

"My people have more important things to do. We have the city more or less under control, but we have several thousand prisoners to deal with, and we are still looking for Marisa Bassi. Either he is dead, and we have not yet found or identified his body, or he has escaped." Arvam paused and spoke briefly with someone off camera, then told Sri, "Traffic control has picked up the tug you are chasing, but there's a problem. A singleship has altered course to intercept it."

"Tell it that it must not attack the tug under any circumstances. Tell it to stand off until I get there."

"We have already tried," Arvam said. "But so far we haven't been able to contact the pilot on any of the encrypted channels. It appears to be the ship that was badly damaged during the mission to alter the course of the rock that those fanatics threw at Phoebe. We held off on retrieval because we were about to go to war, and because we thought both the pilot and his ship were dead. Apparently not."

"Use civilian channels," Sri said, a wire tightening in her chest. "Use anything you like. I'm certain that Avernus is aboard that tug. You must do everything in your power to make sure that your pilot doesn't attack it."

10

Cash Baker's singleship took its own sweet time to heal itself. Its battle AI spent hours rebooting control functions and rerouting them around terminally damaged circuits, checking and rechecking virtual simulations of every stage of the repairs; the punctures in its multilayered skin knitted together with infinitesimal slowness; it had reached the apex of its orbit, some fifteen million kilometres from Saturn, by the time its busy mites had cannibalised shards of broken ceramic insulation around the motor's fusion chamber and reforged them into temporary patches. As he swung back toward Saturn, Cash began to regain control of the drive and navigation systems. It was as if his legs had been numbed by some terrible blow, and now he could wiggle his toes, feel the bruises on his shins, flex his knees . . .

Some damage couldn't be fixed. Cash was unable to plug back into the battle net or contact any friendly ship because his encryption engine had suffered a fatal logic flaw; the only way to fix it was to upload a patch, and that required use of the device which the fault had shut down. And there were glitches in the navigation system too, persistent rastering in the optical systems, false echoes on the deep radar and a permanent problem with the antennae array's tracking system. But he was at last fully engaged with the ship and its senses again, with a godlike view pitched about thirty degrees above the equatorial plane of Saturn and its rings and its retinue of moons.

The AIs were patiently reconstructing data that had been lost when the encryption engine had fallen over, using the singleship's powerful optical system to log and tag the position and delta vee of every ship. It was clear that war had broken out. The Pacific Community ship was driving toward the inner system from Phoebe's high and lonely orbit, on track for Iapetus. The Brazilian flagship was in orbit around Dione; the *Flower of the Forest* was about to enter orbit around Rhea; the *Getûlio Dornelles Vargas* had remained on station at Mimas. Singleships, identified by the unique spectrographic signature of their fusion flames, were chasing down Outer ships or were engaged on strafing runs across the surfaces of the various moons. Using blink comparison of multiple scans, the AIs were also able to locate ships fatally damaged by singleships or EMP mines, cooling toward the ambient temperature of space as they fell along eccentric orbital paths.

The AIs tagged casualties red, friendly ships blue, and everything else white. There were at least thirty red-tagged ships inside Iapetus's orbit, but an equal number of white-tagged ships were fleeing unchallenged. Most of the action was confined to the half-million-kilometre radius defined by the orbit of Rhea. As he fell inward, Cash watched blue specks chase down the last few white specks amongst the inner moons and ring system, stooping down in swift geodesic interceptions, altering their courses toward new targets by slingshot manoeuvres past moons large and small. A battle determined by Newtonian physics. By time and velocity and direction.

Cash was still locked out of it as he fell toward the orbit of Iapetus, four million kilometres out from Saturn. The repairs were almost complete, but much of it was temporary patching and he didn't know how long it would last. He was low on fuel and power and air, too, and the control system of his rail gun was still futzed, but his proxies and pumped-pulse laser and single-shot gamma-ray lasers were fully operational. He could still make a contribution to the war, but he was going have to choose just one target, and choose well.

He plugged into the navigation engine and studied the various options. His best bet was to do exactly what most of the fleeing Outer ships had done: swing in close around Saturn. That way he'd maximise his chances of acquiring a target by passing through the broad arc of possible trajectories that any ships leaving Dione and Tethys had to follow if they wanted to slingshot past the gas giant. The only problem was that it would mean making a course correction pretty soon, and the AIs advised against it. He'd use up more than half his remaining fuel, the burn would be at the limits of the damaged motor's capacity, and after he swung past Saturn he'd be stuck in an orbit tilted high above the equatorial plane, with a period of some two hundred and forty-eight hours and a semi-major axis of twenty-one million kilometres. He wouldn't have enough fuel to rendezvous with any of the moons, so he'd have to hope that someone would spot him and come to pick him up. If the worst came to the worst, he could always let the ship put him under. He could wait out a couple of years in hibernation, and someone was bound to retrieve him before then . . .

Fuck it. Cash overrode the AIs and thirty minutes later fired up the motor for the first time since the accident: a short, hard burn that peaked at 1.38 g. It was a little rough, and efficiency was down to somewhere below eighty percent, but the repairs held. He had his ship back. He could commit to battle.

Most of the Outer ships that had survived or evaded attack by skill or chance were dwindling away into the outer dark beyond Saturn, but there were still a few laggards heading toward the gas giant. Cash studied them carefully before choosing his target, a recent departure from Dione. It was one of the ugly lopsided tugs they used for hauling cargo from moon to moon, and it had a disproportionately small radar profile; someone had attempted to stealth it, which had to mean something. He'd have a hair-thin window of opportunity as he crossed its path at high relative velocity, but it was the best pick of a bad bunch.

He finessed the parameters of a second course correction to ensure that he'd pass as close as possible to the target, pushing close to the limits of the damaged motor, then throttled back to a steady 0.3 *g* acceleration and began to prep his weapon systems. He felt no remorse about attacking a civilian ship. Once war was declared, battle orders were to intercept and terminate or cripple all Outer ships inside the orbit of Iapetus, the outermost of the inhabited moons. And the Outers had definitely declared war by flinging that rock at the Pacific Community's base on Phoebe. Not to mention attacking his own ship. Besides, who knew what that tug might be packing, who it might be carrying? It was his duty to take it out. It was what he'd been trained for; why he was here. And it was also time for a little payback. Time to show the Outers that their sneaky little tricks couldn't keep a good man down. As he powered up his weapons and worked his way through endless checklists, Cash tried to keep his growing excitement at a distance. He had a job to do, and he wanted to do it as well as possible.

The singleship drove past the orbit of Mimas, hurtled on toward the ring system. Cash had flown many missions around Saturn, but he'd never before had such an elevated view of the rings. An arch or bridge braided from a million luminous strands and interrupted here and there by wide or narrow carbon-black gaps, sweeping up to a sharp peak and falling back to girdle Saturn's fat globe . . .

For a little while, he was transfixed by an oceanic feeling of enlargement. He remembered how he used to lie out on the block roof on clear summer nights when he was a kid, remembered feeling that he might fall forever into the rigid patterns of the stars that bestrode the black bowl of the sky, knowing that he was linked to them by photons forged in their thermonuclear fires that had travelled for hundreds or thousands of years across interstellar space to fall into his eyes.

The same physics that determined the behaviour of starlight and Saturn's rings constrained the way in which he could fight his particular corner of the wider war.

Cash slanted in above the eccentric clumps and kinks of the F Ring, bearing down on the tug now, closing in fast as it scooted toward the Keeler Gap. A ticker in one corner of his vision started flashing red as it ran back to zero and the cannon launched the proxies and they eagerly accelerated toward their target. Cash was looped into their control systems: it was like trying to hold on to fierce hounds straining at ever-lengthening leashes. The tug began to yaw and zag, evasive manoeuvres that would do it no good at all, and at the same moment Cash's comms link beeped. An incoming message in plain text sent, according to the ID tag, by General Arvam Peixoto. Ordering him to defuse the proxies and cease all hostilities against the tug at once.

It appeared to have originated from the *Glory of Gaia*, but without use of the encryption engine Cash had no way of knowing that it was genuine or a spoof got up by the Outers as distraction or defence. After half a second's thought, he texted *verify authority.*

Far across the rings, the tug was making a course adjustment: the predictive element of the singleship's AIs suggested that it was planning to skim through the plane of the rings in an attempt to confuse the proxies. Cash adjusted the singleship's attitude and initiated his own course change. The burn was ragged and tooth-rattling as it peaked, but it put him back on course for interception.

Another message arrived. Details of his service record and an order to disengage.

The hell he would. Sending his service record proved nothing because the Outers knew all about him thanks to the foofaraw surrounding Operation Deep Sounding, and Cash wanted payback so badly he could taste it, and he was closing rapidly on the tug now, right on the tails of the proxies. He began to power up the gamma-ray laser . . . and something inside the ship's control system rose up at him. A demon. His first wild thought was that it had ridden one of the messages and punched through the firewalls. Then he realised that it was far too complex, something huge and remorseless that must have been waiting inside the control system all along, a fail-safe wakened by some encrypted signal.

He kicked into hyper-reflexive mode, but it was too late, he'd already lost control of the drive and navigation systems. The ship was rolling on its long axis, attitude jets punching on and off. He tried to find a way back in but couldn't stop the motor climbing to maximum thrust, angling him away from the tug.

Well, fuck 'em. He still had control of the proxies and they were almost on the tug now. He wouldn't let it go. This was the apex of his career, and in his fury and pride he would not let it be taken from him. All he had to do was hold on, but the demon was rushing toward him as remorselessly as a tidal wave, smashing through buffers and firewalls. He was like a man standing on his tiptoes in a sealed chamber that was rapidly filling with water, trying to keep his head in a shrinking bubble of air. The demon snatched at weapon control, and although the proxies were still too far from the tug he triggered them before the demon could shut them down. Saw their bright blinks far ahead of him, and then the demon was on him and he lost the last vestiges of control, and every sensory input.

Cash was aware only of his body, swaddled tight as a mummy in his acceleration suit. Absolute blackness and silence pressed in. It was like being buried alive. He forced himself to relax back into ordinary mode—it would be intolerable to be trapped like this with heightened awareness stretching every second ten times over—and a few heartbeats later the ship's sensory inputs came back. Whether because one of the AIs had found a way to run around the demon, or because the demon had relaxed its grip as soon as its job was done, he neither knew nor cared.

The motor had cut out, and he was locked out of drive and communications and weapons systems. But at least he could see again, right across the electromagnetic spectrum.

The tug was slicing neatly through the Keeler Gap, close to the edge of the A Ring's lustrous arc. It did not seem to be in any way crippled. And he was falling toward the plane of the rings, too. Travelling so fast that he'd acquired a faint shell of ionised plasma as he ploughed through the sparse atmosphere of molecular oxygen produced by the action of the sun's ultraviolet light on the rings' water ice. Flying above the Keeler Gap on a course that would plough a long chord through the A Ring beyond. It came up at him with blinding speed, resolving into points of light all racing away in the same direction, a vast churning swarm ordered into lanes. The ring was more than a quarter of a million kilometres across but just ten metres thick, the height of a two-storey building: Cash told himself that even though he was going to pass through at a shallow angle, there was a good chance that his ship wouldn't suffer any significant damage.

And then with a flash the broad plane of the rings collapsed into a line of brilliant light. And a speck of basalt, a sphere less than a millimetre in diameter, polished and eroded by billions of years of microscopic collisions, smashed into the nose of the singleship and shattered into dozens of white-hot fragments. Most were stopped in their tracks by temperfoam that filled every nook and cranny of the interior, but two shot through the lifesystem. One expended its energy in the impact gel that cased Cash's body, but the second smashed through his virtual-reality visor and left a charred track through his skull and brain. He didn't even have time to realise that he'd been hit.

||

The singleship abruptly veered away and its proxies exploded incontinently more than a thousand kilometres to the starboard of *Elephant*. Some unknown and unguessable accident or agency had reached out and saved them. But as *Elephant* drove across the inner part of the ring system toward the point where it would slingshot around Saturn and head out toward Uranus, Newt spotted a Brazilian ship powering away from Dione and heading inward. It was the modified surface-to-orbit shuttle, the *Uakti*, that had slipped into the system a couple of days after the *Flower of the Forest*, and it was definitely chasing them. It was presently some three hundred thousand kilometres away, way beyond the outer edge of the rings, but it was accelerating hard.

"It's trying to make contact," Newt said. "Aiming a laser at us and sending a looped message from someone calling themselves Sri Hong-Owen. Want to hear it?"

Macy waited for Avernus to say something. When she didn't, Macy said, "I think I can guess what she wants."

Macy and Avernus were lying side by side on couches in the cramped lifesystem. Newt was up in the command blister. They were all wearing their pressure suits, helmets locked tight, and were laced in crash harnesses. The steady rumble of the fusion motor inhabited their spines and skulls.

"If you think she wants us to prepare to stand to and surrender, you're right," Newt said.

"Can she catch up with us?"

"She will if we stay on our present course."

The widescreen view in the memo space was replaced by a 3-D flight diagram: two bright arrowpoints that swung in tight curves around Saturn and rose through the ring system one after the other, the second point moving much faster than the first and catching up with it between the orbits of Titan and Hyperion, some thirteen million kilometres out from Saturn.

"This is what will happen if we stay on track for Uranus," Macy said.

"Yeah. But we have other choices."

The flight diagram ran again, this time freezing when *Elephant* passed close to Saturn, the view zooming in on it before spinning around to show that the Brazilian shuttle was hidden behind by the gas giant's bulk.

"A small course correction before we steal velocity from Saturn will result in a much larger change in our final vector," Newt said. "And if I do it after our friend drops below Saturn's horizon, we'll gain a little time before she realises what's happened. Just enough, maybe, to find a hiding place."

The diagram rotated and pulled out to give a plan view of the entire system, curves scrolling out from Saturn to intersect four of the moons, each curve tagged with delta vee, required reaction mass, and time of transit.

"Titan," Avernus said.

"Titan's definitely doable," Newt said. "Depending on how quickly our friend can match our course change, we'll reach orbit around Titan between forty-eight and two hundred and fourteen minutes ahead of her. That leaves us with a couple of problems. As I'm sure you've noticed, *Elephant* is a good little ship, but she wasn't built for entry into any kind of atmosphere. So we'll need to hitch a ride down to the surface in one of the Tank Towners' aeroshells. And I should remind you that we're being chased by a surface-to-orbit shuttle. If we do go down to the surface, she'll be able to follow us."

Macy thought that he sounded dangerously high-spirited. Happy to be hung out at the edge, to be given a chance to prove what he could do.

"I will talk to people I know in Tank Town," Avernus said. "They will remotely pilot an aeroshell into orbit and I will ride it down to a place where I can meet and talk with Professor Doctor Hong-Owen."

"She wants to take you prisoner," Macy said. "I don't think you'll be able to change her mind."

"Do you believe in serendipity?" Avernus said.

"If I knew what it was I could tell you," Newt said.

"The lucky accident," Macy said.

"It means that we can talk on my terms," Avernus said. "On Titan."

She was adamant that she would ride down to Titan alone, and her logic was impregnable. *Elephant* could not outrun their pursuers, so they must set down somewhere. Two of the moons they could reach before the *Uakti* caught up with them, Atlas and Helen, were too small to provide any real hiding place, and there was a Brazilian ship in orbit around the third, Rhea. So Titan was the only real choice. But *Elephant* could not land on Titan, and it would be a very bad idea to abandon her in orbit. And since it was clear that Sri Hong-Owen was interested only in her, Avernus said, it was right and proper that she should not put Macy and Newt's lives at risk. So she would ride down to Titan and deal with her pursuer, and Macy and Newt would be free to travel on to Uranus. Macy and Newt tried to argue with her, but the gene wizard insisted that there was no other acceptable course of action. Either she went down to the surface of Titan alone, or she would stay aboard *Elephant*, and they would all be captured.

"I've heard more than a few rumours about your work down there," Newt said. "Would any of them happen to be true?"

"I don't listen to rumours," Avernus said.

"You have a surprise planned," Newt said. "I know you do."

"You're enjoying this," Macy told him.

"It isn't one of your ordinary days, that's for sure."

They crossed the narrow ringlets at the inner edge of the ring system and skimmed in low around Saturn's banded cloudscape. As soon as the pursuing ship dropped beneath the horizon, Macy felt a jerky vibration as attitude jets fired. Then Saturn's gravity gripped the ship and flung it outward like a stone swung on a string, the exchange of momentum boosting their velocity by more than fifty percent while slowing the gas giant's rotation by considerably less than a yoctosecond.

Usually, they would head toward Titan or any of the other moons using the ancient fuel-saving free-return system, with Saturn's gravity slowing them as they fell outward so that by the time they reached Titan they would be travelling at roughly its orbital velocity, and only a small correction burn would be required to nudge them into orbit. But Newt kept the motor lit so that they could stay ahead of their pursuers, and he would have to keep it burning until *Elephant* reached the point where it would have to turn around to decelerate, or else fly past Titan at too high a velocity to be captured by the moon's gravity.

Elephant shot through the Cassini Division, out of shadow into sunlight, angling toward Titan. It had passed beyond the outer edge of the main ring system when the Brazilian shuttle came around the edge of Saturn. Its motor was still lit and it was heading out on the same course as *Elephant*. Newt's attempt to hoodwink them hadn't worked. Either they'd made a one-in-a-million guess or, more likely, someone had fed them information about the course correction during *Elephant's* transit.

"It cuts our margin to the bone," Newt said. "They'll arrive in orbit around Titan just seventy-nine minutes after we do."

"It's time I talked to the people in Tank Town," Avernus said. "If they put the aeroshell in orbit now, will you be able to rendezvous with it before the *Uakti* can catch up with us?"

"It won't be a problem as long as they put it where I tell them to put it," Newt said.

He and Avernus had a long conversation with Titan's traffic control. When they'd finished, Macy said to the gene wizard, "If we knew what you were planning to do, we might be able to help you."

"It's simply a question of getting them to land where I want them to land," Avernus said, and wouldn't say anything else.

Hours passed. The system's net was down, but Newt was able to tune into broadcasts from Iapetus and the inner moons and in this manner they learned about Paris's final fall, the fierce fighting around Athens and Spartica on Tethys, and the formal surrender of Baghdad, Enceladus. There was a remarkably calm eyewitness account of an attempt by two tugs to ram the *Flower of the Forest*, one shredded by kinetic weapons, the other cut down by a singleship. Reports of squads of Pacific Community soldiers securing the scattered farming communities on Iapetus. Yet all of this deadly and frenetic activity was lost in the majestic and serene panorama of Saturn and its rings, slowly dwindling behind *Elephant*. Against that vast and inhuman backdrop the war was as insignificant as the struggle between a couple of handfuls of microbes in the unchained waters of an ocean.

At last, Newt switched off *Elephant's* motor, turned the tug around, and fired up the motor again. They had to slow down now, match Titan's orbital velocity. Their pursuer kept coming. Drawing closer and closer because it was still accelerating.

Macy had the *Uakti's* bright star centred in the widescreen view in the memo space. Readouts showed the steady decrease in the distance between *Elephant* and the shuttle, and the steady increase in the shuttle's relative velocity. Her anxiety and dismay swelled. If they'd guessed wrong about the *Uakti's* intentions, it might well continue to accelerate, overhaul *Elephant* and cripple it with judicious use of a kinetic weapon or a proxy, then circle around Titan and come back and claim its prize. The gap between the two ships narrowed to thirty thousand kilometres and continued to close, but at a much slower rate now. After a moment, Macy realised that the *Uakti* had switched off its fusion motor. She saw a brief twinkling flash as it fired its attitude jets and turned end for end, and then its fusion motor flamed on again, a star brighter than the shrunken disc of the sun. Still it continued to creep toward *Elephant*, both ships falling now at the same rate toward Titan's foggy crescent.

The dreamers of the early space age had suggested that Titan would be a vast resource of hydrocarbons and nitrogen, but it had turned out to be much easier to mine CHON from carbonaceous deposits on Iapetus and the inner moons than scoop it from Titan's atmosphere, and the moon's freezing shroud of smoggy haze and its relatively steep gravity well made it about as appealing a piece of real estate as an outer suburb of Hell. Few Outers had chosen to live there: a sprinkling of hermitages and oases, and the anarchist collective of Tank Town, on the shore of the Lunine Sea, which tinkered with bizarre vacuum organisms and manufactured exotic plastics and other organic chemicals. No more than five hundred souls in all, scattered across a moon with a diameter of more than five thousand kilometres, larger than Mercury. So far it had not been touched by the war.

Elephant swung into orbit around Titan's equator and there was a tiny star dead ahead: the aeroshell sent up by remote control by traffic control in Tank Town. It was a measure of Avernus's reputation that the Tank Towners would commit one of their craft on such a risky venture. They'd gain an immense amount of kudos for it, of course, but who knew what that would be worth, now that the three great powers from Earth were on the brink of taking control of the Saturn System? Yet there it was, growing from a point of light to a clamshell capsule bright and sharp against Titan's ochre cloudscape. Newt had calculated the orbital trajectories of *Elephant* and the aeroshell so precisely that they were already drawing alongside, *Elephant* shuddering delicately as attitude jets adjusted her pitch. Macy felt a forceful surge of pride at his skill.

Avernus had by this time climbed into her pressure suit and was waiting in the airlock. Now, with only a cursory farewell, she cycled through and kicked off and shot across the thirty-metre gap, catching a recessed handhold beside the open hatch and swinging neatly inside.

"More than two hundred years old, and spry as a monkey," Newt said. "She's sending a message to Sri Hong-Owen, telling her where to meet up. Want to listen in?"

Macy listened to the brief message and said, "She's probably the most intelligent person I ever met. A genuine, certified genius. The problem is, she doesn't know anything about people."

"Too right."

"So we aren't going to leave her behind, are we?"

"I have a couple of good friends in Tank Town," Newt said. "Flying buddies. Let me talk to them and see if we can come to a deal. Meanwhile, I think I should widen our orbit a little, make it at least look like we're running off."

In the memo space's widescreen view, the chemical motor of the aeroshell flared, slowing the little craft and taking it out of orbit, down to Titan's surface.

12

Titan was similar in size to Ganymede and Callisto, but while the two Jovian moons had long ago lost their primordial atmospheres frigid Titan was shrouded in a dense envelope of nitrogen and methane, and an opaque orange haze of photochemical smog. Hydrocarbon grains formed by the action of ultraviolet light on methane in the upper reaches of the atmosphere drifted down to the surface and formed gritty black aggregates that in the equatorial regions were swept and sculpted by winds into vast seas of dunes a hundred metres high and running in parallel rows for hundreds of kilometres. Methane and ethane rains filled lakes and seas and fed rivers that carved ramifying channels through water ice highlands and flooded across lowland basins.

As the *Uakti* powered toward the rendezvous point under a sky sheeted from horizon to horizon with orange haze, Sri was surprised at how familiar the landscape seemed. They were flying north above what was clearly a volcanic range, domes and complex calderas strung across broad, dark outflow slopes dissected by brighter channels and fissures and collapse depressions. The largest of the collapse depressions were flooded with liquid methane and ethane that gleamed like spills of oil in the dull even light.

The *Uakti* glided toward a volcanic pancake dome crowned by a caldera whose slumped rim circled a shallow basin some ten kilometres across and floored with black water ice. A craggy secondary cone, a volcano within a volcano, was offset inside the caldera like the pupil of an eye glancing sideways.

A bright green beacon pulsed near the dished top of the secondary cone, marking the position of a landing platform. A small dome sat on a cutback terrace beyond.

All this glimpsed in a moment, and then the shuttle swept past and made a wide turn to come back again, and Yamil Cho presented Sri with data from radar, microwave, and multiband imaging. The water ice lava that had flooded the caldera formed a solid plug averaging more than sixty metres deep, with a dyke of liquid water beneath. Treelike vacuum organisms thickly covered the slopes of the secondary cone and the inner slopes of the caldera, but stopped short of the caldera's floor, presumably because it was significantly warmer and therefore deadly to organisms growing at the ambient temperature of −180° Celsius. The dome set high on the secondary cone was pressurised but appeared to be deserted. Three kilometres east, more or less in the centre of the caldera, a single figure stood on a ridge above the hot spot of a small, active vent.

"She kept her promise," Sri said.

"We can't be sure that's Avernus," Yamil Cho said. "For one thing, we don't know how many people might be living here. For another, there is no sign of the aeroshell."

"She must have sent it back to that settlement. Tank Town."

"Then she has deliberately stranded herself," Yamil Cho said. "It's not a good sign. And even if that is Avernus, it is possible that other people might be lying in ambush. Hiding in insulated spiderholes, or under the canopies of those tree-things. There's something under the rim that I'd like to look at in more detail, too. We should make at least one more pass before we set down."

"If anyone does pop up," Sri said, "it will only be some technician or assistant. No doubt scared out of her wits and easily intimidated. Avernus told us she wanted to talk, and we will talk. Take us down right now, Mr. Cho. Can we land close to her?"

"I would not recommend landing on the floor of the caldera, ma'am. It's thick enough to take our weight, but it's water ice. The retrojets will almost certainly melt the surface layer, and it could refreeze around the skids."

"The landing platform, then. We'll hike down."

Yamil Cho brought the *Uakti* back in over the caldera and the retrojets cut in. Sri was slammed against the webbing of her couch as the shuttle dropped toward the secondary cone. It hovered for a moment over the scarred surface of the platform, then settled in a cloud of condensing vapour, flexed once on its skids, and was down.

Yamil Cho broke the humming silence. "May I point out that if Avernus really is waiting for us out in the caldera, you will of course be talking to her by radio? And you can do that without stepping outside this ship."

"That would be rude, Mr. Cho. And besides, we must show her that we are not afraid or we will lose the advantage."

"If you insist, ma'am." When instructed to do something he disapproved of, Yamil Cho could be as disdainful as an affronted cat.

"That doesn't mean we will go empty-handed," Sri said. "This is her realm, one of her secret gardens. We must be prepared for unpleasant surprises. So we will carry pistols, but we'll keep them out of sight. And if it comes to it, Mr. Cho, don't shoot to kill. I didn't come all this way for Avernus's corpse. Try to hit her in the arm or the leg. A disabling shot. It will puncture her pressure suit, of course, but if it comes to it I can perform a field amputation."

"Of course, ma'am."

Sri followed Yamil Cho through the airlock hatch and plodded after him across the pale oblong of the landing field to a path that cut along a narrow terrace. Apart from the strange orange sky, this bleak place, set amongst bare rock above a black, brooding forest that ran down a steep hillside, reminded her of her little kingdom in the Antarctic. She thought of her sons. Alder presiding over the research station; Berry sleeping innocent and unaware in his hibernation coffin aboard the *Glory of Gaia*. If only they were here right now, to witness her triumph! Well, she would tell them the story soon enough.

Lights came on inside the transparent dome as they approached it. Yamil Cho insisted on cycling through. As he prowled around inside, checking shower and sleeping cubicles, opening storage lockers, Sri walked around the flank of the dome and found a garage shelter where trikes with fat mesh wheels sat plugged into charger loops. She backed one of them out of the garage, drove it around the dome to the airlock, was sitting on it when Yamil Cho emerged.

"I think it would be best if I drive, ma'am," Yamil Cho said.

"Be my guest."

Sri slid over. Yamil Cho climbed on beside her and steered the trike toward a steep track that plunged into the forest of vacuum organisms. They were more like giant mushrooms than trees, black stalks four or five metres high topped by delicate black domes each knitted from four triangular leaves hooked together along their overlapping edges. All the domes trembling in a steady wind. Sri held tight to the trike's roll bar as Yamil Cho drove straight down the steep slope under the flexing canopy of this unearthly forest. Then the slope flattened out and they sped out across the ice floor of the caldera. Swerving around outcrops like warped chess pieces, and vents that lofted feathers of vapour that dropped as white snow on black ice-rock, bouncing over frozen ripples, drawing up several dozen metres from the gnarled extrusion ridge that loomed long and low over a sleeve of liquid like a lead or polnyap in Antarctic sea-ice, steaming within a layered casing of mineral deposits and surrounded by a field of bright snow.

A figure in a black pressure suit leaned on a tall staff on the crest of the ridge, watching as Sri and Yamil Cho clambered off the trike and Sri walked across the corrugated ground toward the ridge. She was filled with the cold clear knowledge that everything in her life had led up to this moment, and that she would triumph. It was inevitable. Yamil Cho drifted away to her right, making a flanking move. Let him. She walked on, skirting a low gnarled chimney puffing white vapour that fell as gritty powder, concentrating on making sure that she didn't misstep. The narrow smoking pool at the foot of the ridge was brimful with what looked very like water and probably was. Water was molten ice here. Lava. No doubt saturated with ammonia, which would allow it to stay liquid at temperatures as low as $-97°$ Celsius, but the ambient temperature was considerably lower than that, so there must be a source of thermal energy to keep that little pool liquid. Either the volcano was more active than it seemed, or there was a fission pile somewhere, heating the water under the ice via superconducting wires.

Things grew along the margins of the pool, sparse finger-sized spongy nubs in bright primary colours. The ice-rock ridge behind it, layered and fretted in steep little terraces, was splotched and splattered with pearl grey lichenous discs.

Sri's suit radio beeped and she felt a sharp thrill of elation when she saw the ID tag of the person who had opened a channel. Avernus. She had guessed right, and had followed her hunch halfway across Saturn's system to this strange garden, this moment of triumph.

She answered at once, saying, "My name is Sri Hong-Owen. I have come here to ask you to return home."

"I know who you are," Avernus said. "If you want to talk with me, you can stop right where you are. And tell your friend to stay where he is, too."

"That's far enough, Mr. Cho," Sri said.

"Of course, ma'am."

He stood a hundred metres away at the far end of the ridge, a little below the level where Avernus stood.

"I have come a long way to meet you," Sri said to Avernus. "I stole a ship and abandoned everything I own on Earth. And I have left one of my sons hostage on one of the Brazilian warships. I hope you understand that I came here with the best of intentions."

"For my part, I'm giving you a chance to explain what you want from me," Avernus said.

"The vacuum organisms on the slopes—I would guess that they don't use sunlight as an energy source."

"They would grow very slowly if they did."

"There's very little in the atmosphere that can be used as a non-fermentable energy source," Sri said. "And I noticed that they grow only on the inner slopes. Perhaps they utilise the thermal energy of the caldera."

"They generate electrical energy from temperature differentials in their tap roots," Avernus said.

"In that case," Sri said, "why do they so closely resemble trees? Forgive me, but it suggests a certain poverty of imagination."

She ached to understand everything that Avernus had created here, but she also wanted to prove that she was the venerable gene wizard's equal, worthy of her respect.

"The parasol trees need a large surface area to absorb hydrocarbons from the atmosphere," Avernus said, and explained that the leaves were sheets of grapheme overlaid with fine veins of catalytic polymer that grabbed organic molecules from the air and pumped them through a matrix of liquid methane to the trunk, where they were spun into more complex molecules.

"I might have cut something like a sponge," Sri said. "Something that could funnel air currents through large internal surfaces. It would be much more efficient."

"There are sponges growing in the volcanic pool at your feet. At least, their genetic structure owes more to sponges than to anything else. There's a little holothurian in the mix, a little archaebacterium, but it's mostly sponge."

"Oxidising ammonium to provide free electrons."

"Of course."

"Trees on the slopes; sponges in the pools. Also lichen analogues on the rocks. It's very like Earth," Sri said, putting a snap of disapproval in her voice.

"We carry a standard of beauty from Earth," Avernus said. "It pleases me to use it to inform my gardens."

"People like us need no common standard," Sri said. "And anyway, it's purely random. We should be free to create anything we want."

"I freely chose to create this."

"We could do much together. With no limits but our imaginations."

"I would be able to do what I wanted?"

"Of course."

"Even though you want me to surrender my freedom to you."

"I risked everything to come here and talk to you because I know that I can help you. I can take you to a place of safety. I can give you anything you need. A place to work. People to help you. Every resource. I can be your advocate, your sponsor—even your collaborator, if you wish. Anything you want. But without me, you're just another refugee."

Avernus seemed to consider this for a moment, then asked Sri to kindly tell her friend to move no closer.

"I'm trying to get a better view of the pool," Yamil Cho said, with a silkiness that Sri hadn't heard before. "I didn't mean to scare you."

"And I don't want you to come to harm," Avernus said.

She was leaning on her staff, gripping it at shoulder height with both hands. Its slim black shaft was shod at either end with what looked like silver and overtopped her helmet by half a metre or so.

"Is that by any chance meant to be a threat?" Yamil Cho said.

Sri told her secretary to keep his mouth shut and stay right where he was, then said to Avernus, "I'm your last best hope. If you fell into the hands of other people, they would strip you of everything you know. It wouldn't be pleasant, and in the end they would discard you."

"They would have to catch me first."

"The fact that we are having this conversation proves that you can't hide."

"You forget that I invited you here."

Sri was pleased by this small shot of defiance. It meant that Avernus was human after all, with human weaknesses—pride, vanity, fear—that could be exploited.

"The war is over," she said. "Your side lost. My side won. You can't pretend that you can escape the consequences of that, any more than the Outers can pretend that they have nothing to do with the rest of humanity."

"Herring gulls," Avernus said.

After a moment's furious thought, Sri said, "I'm not sure what you mean."

"A species of seabird once common on both sides of the Atlantic. I believe they became extinct during the Overturn."

"Ah. I myself have done a little remediation work in the Antarctic. I revived two species of albatross and five species of penguin. Also skuas. I suppose someone working in the northern hemisphere might have revived these gulls. I can easily check."

"Herring gulls exemplified a problem in classical taxonomy, before genome analysis became commonplace. In those days, you may recall, members of a species were considered to form a reproductively isolated breeding group whose genes did not combine with those of outsiders. There were various subspecies of herring gull ranged around the eastern and western shores of the Atlantic. A continuum in a geographical circle broken at one end," Avernus said, lifting her staff and using its silver-shod end to sketch a half-circle in the air. "Each subspecies was able to interbreed with its neighbour. But the two subspecies from either end of the geographical range were unable to interbreed—they were infertile with each other."

"I must suppose that your history lesson has a point," Sri said, irritated by the way that the gene wizard used this very small gap in her knowledge to steer the conversation in an unexpected direction.

"Your people believe that the Outers are becoming estranged. Another species. Entirely separate from the baseline species on Earth. They don't see that there's a continuum," Avernus said, sketching the half-circle again. "Nor for that matter do the extremists amongst the Outers. Each end of the continuum would destroy the other, but if you destroy the part of humanity furthest from you, that makes the part next to it the extremity. Which must also be destroyed. And so it goes, removing segment after segment from the continuum until there is only one segment left. And that will turn on itself."

"You think I think that? Well, I don't," Sri said. "I don't believe in the old ideas of species and separatism. In reducing life to the level of the survival and reproduction of single genes. No, I believe in the unbounded potency and adaptability of life. I believe in exploring its every potential expression. I know you believe that too. These creations of yours are proof of it."

Sri's breath was raw in her throat, her heartbeat was loud in her ears, and she felt as if she was standing naked before Avernus's pitiless scrutiny. But she felt euphoric, too. She had thrown off her caution and laid bare the conviction at her core and set it Avernus's feet like a challenge. Whether the old gene wizard chose to accept or reject it, whether she chose to cooperate or whether she would have to be coerced into cooperating, Sri's declaration of her credo would be the cornerstone of their collaboration.

For a long moment there was no sound but the bubbling hiss of steam from vents and the skirl of wind over ice-rock. Then Avernus said, "You made me an offer, Professor Doctor Hong-Owen. Let me make a counteroffer. Come with me. Work with me."

"Why would I want to do that?" Sri said.

"Because I know that the kind of work that you want to do will soon no longer be welcome on Earth. The political climate has changed. Moderates who permitted the use of genetic engineering to help regenerate the planet's damaged ecosystems are losing ground to the radical greens. And the radical greens believe that genetic engineering is a hubristic interference with natural law. That it once helped feed billions of people during the hard years of climate change and the Overturn is of no consequence to them. They believe that it is as damaging to what they call Gaia as the petrochemical addiction that fuelled global warming. Already they are destroying genetically engineered crops. They are planning to shut down research programmes, including your own. And they have come out here to take control of our cities and habitats because they fear what we might be capable of, what we might become.

"You have no future on Earth, Professor Doctor, or anywhere that lies under Earth's hegemony. But I can take you to places beyond Earth's reach. If you come with me, I can show you many wonderful things, and give you the tools to create wonders of your own."

Before Sri could answer, a sharp and distant crack like thunder rolled across the sky.

"Enough talk," Yamil Cho said. "Don't you know what that was?"

"You will be quiet," Sri said, angry and astounded at his temerity.

"She's been spinning you a line and you're so infatuated that you don't see it," Yamil Cho said. "Drawing this out while her trap closes on us. As it has. That was a sonic boom. Something is approaching; from its radar signature it looks like an aeroshell."

"My offer is genuine," Avernus said. "You have already left your old life behind, Professor Doctor Hong-Owen. All you have to do now is take a last step, and come with me."

"Enough," Yamil Cho said again. He had drawn his pistol and pointed it steadily at Avernus as he walked toward her along the crest of the ridge.

"You will stop this right now," Sri told him.

"I will not. I am no longer your servant. And Avernus is not your prize."

"Whose, then?"

But Sri already knew; knew now why she had been allowed to chase after Avernus.

"General Peixoto believes you don't have the best interests of the family at heart. And from what I've heard here, he's right," Yamil Cho said, and turned back to Avernus. "You will come with me. You can walk, or I'll cripple you by shooting you in the legs, vent your air supply until you lose consciousness, and carry you out of here. That's *my* offer."

Sri raised her pistol and squeezed the trigger, but nothing happened. Yamil Cho laughed, asked her if she really thought he would have trusted her with a working weapon. And with sudden hot black fury Sri shouted at him in a rising cadence: "Unfeasible forfeit! Drop dead! Drop dead! *Drop dead!*"

He dropped dead. Clutched at his head, buckled at the knees, fell flat on his face.

Sri ran. She took three bounding leaps and vaulted the narrow sleeve of the pool and came down on a low terrace of the ridge with a shock that shot clean through her, from the soles of her feet to the crown of her skull. For a moment, the weight of her lifepack threatened to topple her backward into the pool. But she clung to the gnarly ice-rock, her gloved fingers and the toes of her boots jammed deep into crevices, pulled herself up to the top of the ridge, and grabbed the pistol from Yamil Cho's outflung hand and straightened up and aimed it at Avernus, who stood leaning on her staff some twenty metres away, a small black indomitable figure, face pale and calm behind the faceplate of her helmet. "I suppose that I must be impressed," she said.

"A simple fail-safe," Sri said.

She'd inserted it when she'd cut Yamil Cho to sharpen his reflexes and give him control of his sleep patterns. Not because she didn't trust him any less than the rest of her other servants, but because she didn't trust any of them: those closest to her and her sons had all been equipped with fail-safes or cut-outs. Yamil Cho's was a simple parasitic circuit in his inner ear that responded only to her voice and controlled shunts in his internal carotid arteries. Triggered by the code words, it had blown the walls of the arteries and caused a massive cerebral hemorrhage.

Avernus said, "Did you murder your creature as a sign of your good intentions?"

"He betrayed me. I won't ever countenance that."

Sri was back in control of herself again, except that she couldn't quell a faint tremor in the hand that held the pistol.

"My offer still stands," Avernus said. "Will you come with me? We can be on our way before that aeroshell arrives."

"You're wrong about Earth. Things have changed for the moment, but they will soon realise that they need me. Need *us*."

"You are a scientist. Don't let yourself be blinded by pride."

"I would have preferred that you entered into our partnership voluntarily, but there it is. You will come with me, and we will work together, as equals," Sri said, and felt an intense relief wash through her when Avernus began to walk toward her, slow and cumbersome in her black pressure suit, leaning on her staff with every other step.

"What about your creature's body?" the old gene wizard said.

"Let him rot here," Sri said carelessly.

"It's a desecration of my garden. Also a waste of useful biomass. He can feed my ice worms."

"Ice worms?"

"In the pool," Avernus said, and gestured with her staff.

Sri glanced down and saw stout black tendrils rising stiffly from smooth-lipped crevices at the bottom of the pool. "No," she said, suspecting some kind of trick. "We'll leave him where he lies. And get rid of the silly staff, too."

Behind the faceplate of her helmet Avernus's smile was overlaid by the reflections of red and green pinlight indicators. She straightened her arms in a crucifix pose and opened her hand and let the staff drop past the steep flank of the ridge into the pool below.

Sri knew immediately that she'd made a mistake. But before she could move or even cry out the staff plunged straight into the gelid water, creating barely a ripple as it sank down and caught amongst the black tendrils at the bottom, and the tendrils exploded in a mass of threads that shot up with amazing speed, erupting from the pool in an explosive burst of vapour that shot up higher than the top of the ridge and froze in an instant snowstorm that swirled about Sri and Avernus and fell away. Tangles of black wire filled the pool from edge to edge and shot out over the rim in every direction, dividing as they extended and dividing again, rising and spreading and scrambling like a time-lapse video of a growing briar patch. A mass of wires overshot the edge of the ridge and whipped around on either side of Sri in a prickly embrace. She stepped back with jittery haste, lost her footing and fell flat on her back. Before she could bounce up she was caught in a thickening cocoon that wrapped around her arms and legs and torso, tightening as she kicked and struggled.

"I would advise you to stay as still as possible," Avernus said.

The old gene wizard stood at the centre of a tangled cloud of black thread. None of it quite touched her; when she stepped forward she pushed aside masses of finely divided wire like someone opening a curtain and left behind in the frozen cloud a hollow in the shape of her pressure suit, which Sri realised must be coated with some kind of inhibitor.

"The feeding tentacles of my ice worms contain capsules homologous to the desmoneme nematocysts of coelenterates like jellyfish and sea anemones," Avernus said, looking down at Sri. "As in coelenterates, they discharge tangling threads when stimulated. The threads are a species of thermotrophic smart wire, very like that used in mines designed to incapacitate rather than kill. They stretch toward anything that has a higher temperature than its surroundings, and divide and cling tight to it. As they cling tight to you. If you move too much, Professor Doctor, the tentacles of the ice worms will sense it, and they will contract and drag you into the pool."

"The staff," Sri said, stupid with astonishment and fear. She was still holding the pistol, but her hand and wrist were bound tightly against the thigh of her pressure suit.

"Its hollow tip contained a saturated solution of potassium chloride and proline to stimulate mass firing. And just before you arrived, I added a little something to the pool to bring the worms to the surface. Usually they live deep in the vents. Big slow creatures, up to five metres long. They can subsist for years on ammonium and hydrogen fixed by symbiotic bacteria, but to grow and reproduce they need organic matter. I never did get around to designing the rest of the biome I planned for the vents, so they have to be fed every so often. Usually we cut down a few of the parasol trees," Avernus said. "But a human body will do just as well."

She stooped over Yamil Cho and with surprising deftness unlatched his helmet and pulled it away. Frost instantly bloomed on his face. The old gene wizard unlatched his lifepack, too, then straightened up and with the toe of one boot began to rock his body to and fro. It slewed sideways as the threads that tangled around it jerkily contracted, turned on its side as it was dragged over a spur of ice-rock, and suddenly vanished over the edge of the ridge.

Sri heard the splash when it struck the pool. Although her helmet was caught fast in a web of threads she could turn her head inside it, and saw fog boil up around the edge of the ridge and blow away as snow. "What will you do with me?" she said.

"The threads will disintegrate in a few hours. As long as you keep still until they do, you won't be harmed," Avernus said, and stepped past her, picking her way through rigid tangles of black wire, moving out of sight.

"If you free me now," Sri said, "I'll forget all about this. We can work together as equals."

"I would advise you to study my gardens very carefully before you talk to me again," Avernus said.

"This isn't the end of it," Sri said. "You know I won't stop looking for you, and I plan to live for a very long time."

Avernus did not reply.

After a minute, Sri was struck by a horrible vision of being marooned here and said loudly, "If you take my ship, it'll make it even easier to find you."

No reply. Sri switched from channel to channel, but there was only silence on the radio, and the faint scratch of wire on ice-rock all around her, and the mournful fluting of the wind.

She lay still, pinned to the top of the ridge like a sacrifice in some arcane ceremony. Feeling a seeping chill in her shoulder blades and buttocks and heels, looking up at the frozen curds and canyons of the sullen cloudscape that sheeted the sky from horizon to horizon, trying not to think about what would happen to her if Avernus had lied about the ice worms. But there had been no reason for the gene wizard to lie, she told herself. She would be free soon enough. She had enough air for a day, plenty of water. She would live through this.

Soon enough, the aeroshell glided low overhead like a UFO from the paranoid dreams of the long ago. Sri wondered if she was going to be taken prisoner or hostage, wondered how she could explain this to Arvam Peixoto. It would be easy enough to work up a story that fixed the blame on Yamil Cho, she thought, and vowed that whatever happened she would make good her threat: she would spend the rest of her life searching for Avernus.

13

Newt feathered the aeroshell close to the shuttle that sat at the centre of the elevated platform and brought it down on the cushion of its fanjets and kept it in trembling balance, ready to scoot off in an instant, while he and Macy looked all around for any sign of life. The shuttle was buttoned up and cold and the slope of raw black ice-rock that reared beyond it was empty and still. At last Newt cut the fanjets to a whisper and let the aeroshell settle on its landing gear.

Macy levered up from her acceleration couch and squeezed Newt's shoulder and told him that she'd take it from here. "Stay ready to fly out of here if there's even a hint of trouble."

"You bet." He smiled at her through the faceplate of his helmet. They were both zipped into pressure suits because the aeroshell lacked an airlock. "Don't take long. And take care in this godawful pull. If you break a leg, I'm not sure I could carry you back."

Titan's gravity was just 0.14 g, but it was much stronger than Dione's. Although gene therapy, drugs, and medichines had spared Macy from the worst effects of low-gravity bone- and muscle-wasting, she hadn't been able to exercise properly in jail, and felt sluggish and cumbersome as she popped the hatch and clambered backward down the flank of the aeroshell and dropped jarringly to the ground. Clutching the pulse rifle to the chest plate of her pressure suit, she walked the length of the shuttle, studied the path that curved around the flank of the cone toward the little lighted dome, then crept to the very edge of the landing field's cantilevered platform and for a moment forgot her fear of ambush as she stared out with breathless wonder and wild surmise at this new world.

Below her, a steep slope thickly overgrown with filmy carbon-black domes raised on slim stalks, rippling and doffing in graceful waves in the same wind that fluted past her helmet, dropped to a flat floor of black ice several kilometres across, marked here and there by cuneiform featherings of white snow that trailed from vents, and circled round by the caldera's rim. The lower slopes of the rim were grown over with swathes of the same black parasols, and its naked, scalloped crest rose against a sky sheeted with orange smog.

Newt asked her if she could see any sign of Avernus or anyone from the shuttle.

"Not yet. Maybe I should check out that dome."

"Do the shuttle first," Newt said. "After that, everything's gravy."

Macy's suit told her that someone else wanted to talk on one of the line-of-sight channels. It was Avernus, saying, "I hope you aren't thinking of stealing that ship. They'll chase you down if you do."

"We're here to rescue you," Newt said.

"I'm sure that's part of the reason why you risked your ship and your lives to follow me. But I do not need rescuing and you should not have come here."

Macy asked Avernus where she was, and the gene wizard told her to look along the eastern rim. "Just above the tree line."

There was a long flat ledge under an overhang of dark ice-rock. When Macy zoomed in on it she saw Avernus in her black pressure suit working at one end, slowly and methodically pulling a silvery drop cloth from a small biplane perched on a slanting catapult mechanism. Macy relayed the view to Newt, who told Avernus that she had to come back to the landing platform right now, that they had to leave as soon as possible. "The Brazilians have sent another ship after us."

Newt had spotted the dropship heading out of Saturn toward Titan while he'd been dickering with his friends in Tank Town for use of the aeroshell, something that had cost all his and Macy's present kudos and a share of any they might earn in the next five years.

"Actually, I think I'll stay here for a while," Avernus said. The old gene wizard was breathing heavily as she worked, but she sounded completely calm.

"Where are the people from the shuttle?" Newt said.

"Look to the centre of the caldera."

After a minute or so, Macy spotted a figure in a blue pressure suit on top of a long ridge of ice-rock, lying bound and supine amongst what looked like clouds of wire or threads spun from a seething pool at the base of the ridge.

"Professor Doctor Sri Hong-Owen," Avernus said with a trace of remote other-worldly amusement.

"Is she alone?" Newt said.

"Is she alive?" Macy said.

"She had what I suppose was a bodyguard, but he is gone. And she was still alive when I left her." Avernus explained about the ice worms and how she had stimulated their feeding reflex when Sri Hong-Own had confronted her. "I would advise you to set aside any notion of rescuing or capturing her for the moment. Unless you have a supply of 3-hydroxyanthranilic acid. It is the only thing that will prevent the threads latching onto your suits."

"I think we're all out," Newt said.

"We can't just leave her there," Macy said.

"The threads will lose their grip, by and by. As long as she does not struggle she will be fine," Avernus said.

"I guess you planned this all along," Newt said.

"Not at all. The opportunity arose by a fortunate confluence of circumstances. You should be careful what you say to each other, by the way. Stick to short-range or line-of-sight channels. Even then, you should assume that she might be listening in. Who knows what Brazilian military technology is capable of?"

Macy asked the gene wizard what she was planning to do. "If you can't tell me exactly, maybe you can at least give me a hint about what I should tell Yuli."

There was a short silence. Wind played around Macy's pressure suit as she stood like a disentablatured caryatid at the edge of the landing platform, looking out across the gulf of air to the distant caldera rim where Avernus was folding back the last part of the drop sheet from the tail of the little red biplane.

Macy said, "I kind of made a promise to Yuli that I'd look after you."

"You have discharged that obligation admirably," Avernus said. "And I thank you for it. As for my daughter, you can tell her that I need some time to think. Tell her that I realise now that I was either too optimistic or too simplistic in believing that I could have any real influence on the collective behaviour of my fellow Outers, or on those who presently rule most of Earth. Tell her that I need to think long and hard about how and why I failed to promote peace and reconciliation when it was obvious that it was the best hope for the greatest number of people.

"In the Outer System we have long believed in the perfectibility of the human mind, that goodness is worth trying, and that happiness is not only beneficial but constructive. In the past hundred years we have built a plenitude of societies founded on principles of tolerance, mutualism, scientific rationalism, and attempts at true democracy. And on Earth people have united in common cause to heal the great wounds inflicted by the Overturn, climate change, and two centuries of unchecked capitalism. I hoped to see these two worthy and hopeful strands of human history unite and go forward together as equals rather than rivals, sharing unselfishly the best of each other's abilities and achievements. But instead we have war, and I must rethink everything. I must return to the most basic questions about the human condition.

"Perhaps the reductionists are right. Minds selected to solve problems that challenged groups of hunter-gatherers roaming the plains of Africa two hundred thousand years ago cannot cope with the difficulties and stresses of the civilisation they later created. We are doomed by the failure of our phylogeny to keep pace with our inventiveness. Or perhaps there is some deeper flaw, something that is useful for the survival of our genes but inimical to civilisation and individual happiness. Perhaps we go to war because we cannot help being other than what we are, because the behaviour of the mob is closer to our true nature than the aspirations of the individual. Because we fear and mistrust the motives and promises of our neighbours. Because we cannot help coveting what we do not have. Because we are unable to forget old grievances, or are unable to overcome patterns and forces set running in the long ago. Do wicked or foolish leaders like Marisa Bassi lead innocent populations to disaster, or do populations choose leaders whose qualities mirror their desires? Or are all of us, good and bad alike, no more than foam carried on the crest of a wave, helpless to stop or direct it? Perhaps human history is the history of the mob, and the stories of old in which heroes change or save the world are no more than stories. Lies told to children.

"I don't know," Avernus said. "I don't know. I am old, and tired, and everything I thought proven beyond doubt has been thrown into confusion. I need to think about all this, and much more."

By now the old gene wizard had prepped the plane and was clambering into its cockpit.

"If you stay on Titan the Brazilians will come looking for you," Newt said.

"I have many gardens here," Avernus said.

"Even if they don't find you, you won't be able to leave. Come with us while you still have the chance."

"But I don't intend to leave. Not for a long, long time," Avernus said, and told Macy to open a second line-of-sight channel, and a buffer in her suit's comms package. "I can't go with you. It's quite clear that it would put you in far too much danger. But I can give you something that you may find useful."

As gigabytes of information flooded into Macy's comms, Avernus closed the transparent blister of her biplane's canopy and started the motor. The transparent prop at the nose spun into a blur and with a puff of vapour and a sharp crack that flew out across the caldera and echoed back from its far side the catapult shot the biplane into the air. It hooked past the peak that rose above the landing field and headed out past the rim of the caldera, climbing beneath the orange haze that roofed the sky from horizon to horizon, a bright red bead, a dot, gone.

Macy and Newt discussed what to do, quickly agreed that even if they could manage to steal the shuttle, the Brazilians would never stop chasing them.

"But maybe we can steal its secrets," Newt said.

So Macy clumped over to the shuttle, hauled herself up to the hatch of its lock and cycled through into a low dimly-lit cabin. After studying the pictures she transmitted, Newt told her how to plug into the control system. She downloaded a demon that shook hands with the compliant AI and mirrored data on diagnostic and repair schematics and operational parameters of the shuttle's fusion motor through her comms to the aeroshell, and from there up to *Elephant*. It took five minutes, and only five minutes more for another demon to strip out the shuttle's navigation and drive control systems; if Sri Hong-Owen got free she would have to hunker down here and wait for rescue.

When she was finished, Macy cycled back outside and took a last lingering look at the strange beauty of the caldera before clambering into the aeroshell beside Newt. He took off while she was still strapping herself into her acceleration couch. There wasn't much time left before the Brazilian dropship arrived. He took the aeroshell up at a sharp angle and lit the main motor and knifed through kilometres of smog into the empty blackness of space. They caught up with *Elephant* high above Titan's nightside, crept close with a shivering stutter of attitude jets. By the time they had abandoned the aeroshell and pulled themselves inside the familiar cramped space of the tug's lifesystem, the bloodied point of the sun was rising through the hazy outer layer of Titan's atmosphere and a sliver of light was widening into a crescent across its leading edge.

Macy kept watch on the approaching dropship as Newt brought *Elephant's* fusion motor on line and calculated the parameters of the burn that would take them out of orbit. It would take them more than twenty weeks to reach Uranus because they couldn't risk another slingshot around Saturn, and they didn't know who if anyone would be waiting for them when they arrived, but they didn't care. They would have plenty of time to plan what to do with the rest of their lives, as long as they could escape the forces that had taken control of the Saturn System.

So Macy was running away yet again. It seemed to be the recurring pattern of her life. But this time she wasn't alone, she knew where she was going, and she and Newt had a wealth of plundered technical data that might help the Outers to reverse engineer a better fusion drive. And they had Avernus's little gift, too. Macy was flipping through the headers of the vast database when Newt asked her what she was looking at.

"Life," she said, and gave him a glimpse of one corner of the vast matrices of genomic data, proteome maps, and intricate multidimensional trophic spaces.

"Think you can use any of it?"

"I'm going to try my best."

"We're about ready to go. Want to give the countdown?"

"Let's just do it."

"I hear that," Newt said, and lit the motor.

Macy was pushed gently against the couch as the low rumble of the fusion motor shivered her bones and *Elephant's* frame creaked and groaned, adjusting to the stresses of acceleration. The sun rose and passed above them as they drove in a rising curve around the dayside. Night swept in across the hazy orange cloudtops and then Titan was falling away as the little ship raced into the outer dark.

14

He woke to dim red light and the mingled noise of pumps and fans near and far. The air was hot and stank of ozone and disinfectant. He was weightless, zipped naked and cathetered into a cocoon hung in a small cubicle hard against an angled bulkhead painted black and curtained on three sides with stiffly pleated grey cloth. His mouth was dry and his tongue swollen with thirst. His shoulder throbbed steadily but not unpleasantly under a halflife bandage that clung to it like a leech.

He'd been rescued, then, brought aboard one of the Brazilian ships. The war was over. His mission was over . . .

Fragments of memory came back. A shuffle of bright fractured pictures. The battle along the outskirts of Paris. A ship cartwheeling across a stark plain. Machines fighting machines with swift silent fury. The rolligons chasing him across vacuum organism fields. He'd found Zi Lei and the people he had been ordered to retrieve. And then a hiatus. Something had happened, he'd been hurt, and someone had rescued him and brought him here.

He was struggling to free himself from the cocoon when a medical technician slipped through the margin of the curtain. He asked for water but the man ignored his request, tightened the straps that held him in place and checked his wound and his pulse and temperature with the brisk and impersonal efficiency of a butcher inspecting a side of meat, then touched the flat end of a short wand to the skin behind the hinge of his jaw. He felt a brief sharp jolt, and passed into sleep almost at once.

When he woke again, a pale-skinned young man was studying him, hung in midair with his back against the grey curtain, steadying himself with fingertips splayed on the angle of the bulkhead. A smooth cap of black hair, black eyebrows plucked to thin dashes above sharp blue eyes, a cool and knowing smile.

He recognised the eyes, the lively intelligence that lived behind them and licked his dry lips and said, "Twenty-seven."

"How are you, Dave?" Dave #27 said.

"I'm good, Dave. How are you? I see they gave you some hair."

"They changed you more than they changed me. How's your shoulder?"

"It isn't anything."

"It looks like someone shot you."

"I'll tell you about it if you find me something to drink."

Dave #27 went out and returned a few minutes later with a pouch of water. He sucked it dry while Dave #27 explained that he was aboard the *Glory of Gaia*, brought there by marines who had found him locked in a research station fifteen kilometres northeast of Paris, Dione.

"You'd been given a dose of tranquilizer and you had a bad reaction. Someone gave you a knock on the head, too. You don't remember anything?"

He said that he definitely remembered being shot, and gave a short account of how he had escaped from the city and tracked Avernus, the traitor Macy Minnot and the captured diplomat Loc Ifrahim to the research facility. He didn't mention that he'd found them because of the transmitter he had forced Zi Lei to swallow.

"I found them," he said. "But there were other prisoners there. Too many of them. I suppose I was overpowered."

"You were wounded. You were lucky to escape with your life."

He had a dim and unclear memory of a conversation held over him and said, "I failed."

"Nonsense," Dave #27 said cheerfully. "The war is over. Paris has been captured. Most of the cities that didn't immediately surrender when war was declared have been captured too. You were part of that. Your work and the work of our brothers weakened the infrastructure of those cities and demoralised their populations. Of course you didn't fail!"

He hadn't been thinking about his mission, or the war. "Were you part of it too?" he said.

"I'm as yet untested, but that will soon change." Dave #27 talked eagerly of the need to infiltrate the cities of the Outer System and search for leaders of the resistance who had not yet been captured. He explained that many Outer ships had fled the moons of Jupiter and Saturn for Uranus. Although there were as yet no plans to extend the campaign, spies would be needed there too. "They'll need us more than ever. You'll see."

"So the war isn't over for us."

"It's what we were made for. Why else do you think they are patching you up? These are great times," Dave #27 said. "And we will do great things."

"It wasn't like I thought it would be," he said. "It wasn't like our training."

"Of course it wasn't. We'll talk more when you have rested. I want to hear everything!"

"Would you loosen my straps before you go? They're a little tight."

After his brother had left, he rested for a short while, examining his fragmented memories of what had happened after he had broken into the research facility. He recalled every word of his brief argument with Zi Lei, his anger and his guilt, the cold stab in his heart when she had refused to come with him, when she had turned away . . . But he remembered little of what had happened after that. At one point he had been lying somewhere, so weak that he couldn't even open his eyes, listening to the dim voices of people arguing about him.

Someone had wanted to kill him, but a woman, perhaps it was Zi Lei, perhaps not, had said that they weren't like those who considered themselves their enemies. "We'll lock him up here," she'd said, and perhaps he imagined that a little later Zi Lei had bent close and whispered that she knew that he was a good man who had become confused about right and wrong.

For a timeless time he hung in his cocoon and studied the ghostly reflection of his face in the glossy black paint of the bulkhead, as in another life he had once studied his reflection in the chest plate of a disassembled pressure suit. The face he saw now was not the face he had been born with, but it was no longer a mask either. The mask had eaten the skin beneath. He had been number eight. Dave #8. Now he was Ken Shintaro. Twenty-two years old, born in Rainbow Bridge, Callisto, currently on a wanderjahr that had just brought him to the Saturn System . . . And there had been a war, but the war was over.

He wriggled his right arm free of the straps, delicately pulled out the catheter, and unzipped the cocoon and pushed out of it. He peeked around the edge of the stiff curtain and checked the narrow companionway and the curtained cubicles on either side of it, then kicked off and shot neatly and accurately down its length. In less than a minute, he was inside an airlock, pulling on a suit-liner and fastening himself into a pressure suit. It wasn't a good fit, but it would do. He hooked the helmet to his belt and went out and found the nearest cluster of dropcapsules. He disabled the alarm of one, climbed into it, and started the evacuation sequence. It was little more than a coffin with a one-shot chemical motor, but it would take him where he needed to go.

A jolt of compressed air shot the dropcapsule out of its tube. He waited until he was clear of the *Glory of Gaia*'s dark bulk, then used the capsule's attitude jets to spin it through ninety degrees. Flying backward above Dione, packed inside the padded space in his pressure suit, plugged into the capsule's simple mind. HUD controls hung lines of code on the faceplate of his helmet. An inset showed the moonscape unravelling below, a wilderness of ridges and rounded hills and branching troughs like dry rivers and bright plains spattered with craters of every size, each crater with a narrow parenthesis of shadow caught in its westward side.

Green sparks in the pale floors of craters, on the rolling land between.

Zi Lei must be down there somewhere, one of ten thousand refugees scattered amongst habitats and oases and shelters. Many of them no doubt still loyal to Marisa Bassi and the resistance, hard and desperate fighters who might well recognise him for what he was. If he survived the landing. If he was not hunted down by marines or by his own brothers. He faced every kind of danger and knew that he had little chance of finding Zi Lei and that even if he found her she might spurn him, but he didn't care.

All that mattered was that the war was over.

He ignited the capsule's engine and in a bright streak of flame fell out of the sky toward the moon. Nothing would ever be the same again.

ABOUT THE AUTHOR

Paul McAuley's first novel won the Philip K. Dick Award and he has gone on to win almost all of the major awards in the field. For many years a research biologist, he now writes full-time. He lives in London. Visit him online at http://unlikelyworlds.blogspot.com/.

NOVEMBER 2009

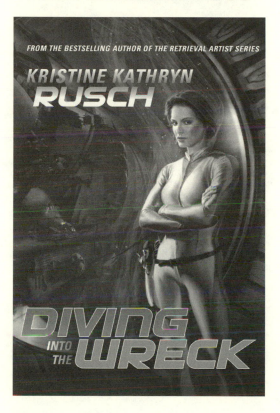

"*Tense and gripping.... The endlessly enjoyable terror of dark, alien, empty spaces brimming with unknowable danger and impenetrable mystery should keep fans of the genre hooked.*"

—**Internet Review of Science Fiction**

Pyr®, an imprint of Prometheus Books
716-691-0133 / www.pyrsf.com